..wenty-five

...ws correspondent
..y held the position of South
...ed in Delhi). Now based in
...... extensively for the BBC including
...o Afghanistan and Pakistan. In 2011, she
.....minated for Journalist of the Year at the SONY
...rds, and the One World Media Awards. Her first novel, *The Last Kestrel*, charted the lives of two women during the conflict in Afghanistan and was part of the Orange New Writers selection. *Far from my Father's House* is her second novel.

Also by Jill McGivering

The Last Kestrel

JILL McGIVERING

Far from my Father's House

blue door

Blue Door
An imprint of HarperCollins*Publishers*
77–85 Fulham Palace Road,
Hammersmith, London W6 8JB

www.harpercollins.co.uk

This paperback edition 2012

1

First published in Great Britain by Blue Door 2011

Copyright © Jill McGivering 2011

Jill McGivering asserts the moral right to
be identified as the author of this work

A catalogue record for this book is
available from the British Library

ISBN 978-0-00-733820-7

Set in Sabon LT Std by Palimpsest Book Production Limited,
Falkirk, Stirlingshire

Printed and bound in Great Britain by
Clays Ltd, St Ives plc

MIX
Paper from
responsible sources
FSC
www.fsc.org **FSC** C007454

For Nick

1

It was May and even here in the mountains, the heat was
thick and heavy. I was out alone, fetching water, walking
in an idle zigzag to and fro across the path, swinging the
pail in my hand and feeling the heat prick my hair under
my scarf. Down in the shadowy orchards, men were
reaching for the first ripe peaches and plums of the season.
Beyond them, a car wound its way down the narrow road
to town, coughing up dust. When it disappeared, the
broken silence mended itself as the heat settled.

I was practising a new walk, holding my back rigid,
swinging my hips in a sashay the way the older girls did.
I imagined Saeed watching me, as he sometimes would,
keeping his distance but following me to or from school.
I thought of his handsome face and dark eyes, and placed
my feet as neatly as a dancer.

A noise. I stopped. Banging. A faint sound. I stood and
listened. Hammering. Clean and hard and out of place. It
was coming from my left, near the mosque. I crept through

the grass to crouch behind the high corner of a compound. I held my breath and peered around the wall to look.

Three strangers were standing on the path near the entrance to the mosque. They were banging a piece of paper onto a tree, fixing it with nails. Further down, three notices were already fluttering on other trees, pinned like butterflies. I felt a stab of pain, imagining they were living things, nailed to the wood and suffering.

The men were thick-set with dark turbans, bushy beards and grubby shirts. One was as old as Baba and had a crooked nose, as if long ago he'd been hit in the face. His stomach bulged under his kameez. He was standing back from the tree, giving orders. The other two, doing the hammering, were younger. One was handsome; his upper arms thickened into ropes of muscle as he wielded the hammer. There was something dangerous in the set of his mouth. His eyes were cool. A long gun was hanging from a strap, slung over his shoulders, and the metal glinted in the sunlight as he lifted his arm and the hammer blows fell. My stomach tightened and the breath stuck in my chest.

They worked their way further up the road, banging papers onto all six trees outside the mosque, one by one. Finally they walked back down the path to a battered pickup truck parked far below in the road.

The older man got into the passenger seat beside the driver. The handsome young man and his friend climbed into the open back and sat with their guns propped upright between splayed legs. They gripped the truck's metal cage, their knuckles white, as it started to move, pitching them off balance. The handsome man turned to look up the path. I ducked back behind the wall, heart thumping. Had he seen me? When I dared to look again, all that was left was dust, hanging in the empty air.

I counted to a hundred, then walked down to the first notice and stood, trying to read the lettering. It had been written in black curly handwriting and copied by a machine.

By Order, it said. *All music is contrary to the will of Allah and is henceforth forbidden. All shaving of beards is contrary to the will of Allah and is henceforth forbidden. All contact between men and women who are not close blood relatives is contrary to the will of Allah and is henceforth forbidden. All women and girls shall be confined to their compounds and not venture into public. Praise be to Allah!* It was signed by a man whose name I didn't know and underneath his name it said: *Supreme Commander, Faithful Soldiers of Islam.*

I looked up and down the path. No one. I set down my pail and gripped the two sides of the notice in both hands, tearing it off the tree. The paper ripped from the nails, leaving behind shreds that hung like skin. I held it against my face, tasting the paper with the tip of my tongue and breathing its strange inky smell. It was dangerous and disturbing and made me shiver. I smoothed out the creases against my thigh and folded the paper carefully in half, then in half again, and hid it in my pocket.

3

2

The pressure was so intense that the crowd seemed about to burst. All around Ellen, ahead and behind, fists were punching the air, thrust upwards in unison by the rhythms of the chants. The voices were shrill, on the brink of screams.

'Pakistan *Zindabad*!' Long live Pakistan. 'Freedom *Zindabad*!' The shouting was led by a man in a black baseball cap. A megaphone distorted his words, punctuating them with explosions of static and piercing whines. Placards, dancing above the protesters' heads, showed the mass-produced images of opposition politicians.

Ellen, at the edge of the crowd, straightened her headscarf and climbed onto a boulder for a better view. No sign of the other reporters. She ran her eyes down the human river of people, dividing the chaos of raised hands and wobbling placards into sections. She made a rough mental count of one portion, then multiplied it to judge the size of the whole protest. Four thousand people, certainly. Perhaps five.

She wrote a few lines, noting down some of the slogans and a short description of the man with the megaphone. She'd like to kick off her report with colour, if the editors gave her enough space. Something dramatic to grab the reader's attention before she started to expand and give context. Her readers would need help making sense of it all. *Further pressure on the Pakistani government.* No. She needed to give a greater sense of rising drama. She tucked loose strands of hair back out of sight under her scarf, thinking, then added: *on this already beleaguered Pakistani government.* Around her, the shouting was reaching a crescendo. She should leave soon. *The latest in a growing number of protests. Showing mounting public frustration, public concern, about the government's handling of the current crisis.* She paused. How many readers would remember what crisis? She added: *of the government's handling of its current battle against the threat from Islamic extremists.* Too long. She went back and crossed out a few words.

She looked up. In the short time she'd spent writing, the dashes of riot police drawn along the edge of the demonstration had begun to solidify into lines. They were herding the protesters into a narrowing strip, hemming them in between the barricades down the centre of the road and the brick walls of the buildings.

She shook her head. She didn't like it. She always kept an escape route in view when she covered protests, a quick way out if danger suddenly flared. Until this point, there had been successive alleyways and side roads leading off the road. They served as natural valves if pressure built up. Now, though, the wall running alongside the road was solid and the police lines were closing in. They were being funnelled. It was time to get out.

She put her notebook away and shouldered her backpack, then launched herself back into the crowd, trying to force her way, elbows digging, across the forward flow. Men turned towards her, their brown eyes stretched wide with curiosity and amusement. She was engulfed in the smell of raw sweat. The men looked rough and uneducated. Probably bussed into Islamabad just for the demonstration.

Someone whispered something in her ear. At the same time, a sweaty hand touched her arm, slid over her buttock. She twisted and at once the hand slid away. She glared into a rack of blank faces, then steadied herself and pushed her way forwards again. The pressure of bodies around her was building and she wanted to get out as fast as possible. She fixed her eyes on a young policeman with a neatly trimmed moustache and concentrated on battling towards him. His dark eyes were strafing the crowd. He had a riot shield in one hand, a raised wooden baton in the other.

Protesters, starting to feel enclosed, pressed ahead with greater urgency and beat their way forwards. They gave off the keen, hungry scent of growing panic. Ellen fought to keep moving, but was repeatedly knocked off balance by the men surrounding her. The communal chanting was ragged now, disintegrating into a cacophony of shouts and cries. Her cotton kameez felt slick against her skin, her back running with sweat under her backpack. Her headscarf slithered to and fro across escaping hair.

An elbow stabbed her in the ribs. She coughed, tried

to catch her breath. Her lungs strained. She pulled at her headscarf to anchor it. Must keep moving. A heavy man barged into her, stamping on the side of her foot. She grabbed at his arm to keep herself upright and he shook her off, pushing past. Her legs started to shake. She must get out. All around her, waves of hysteria ran through the crowd. The men's shouts became rough and wild.

She sensed something moving at the edge of the crowd and turned to look. The riot police were shuffling closer, narrowing the spaces between them until they stood shoulder to shoulder, driving the protesters back against the wall. A high-pitched police whistle sounded and the officers advanced as one, shields high, wooden *lathis* swinging wildly. More policemen jumped down from the meshed backs of riot vehicles to join in.

The men around her twisted, ducked and skidded as they tried to get away. She was trapped between them, squeezed so hard she could barely breathe. The defiant shouting had gone. Her ears were filled with cries of pain and the crunch of *lathis* striking bone.

She was swept sideways by a sudden surge. Somewhere the crowd burst out and the men rushed to the right, carrying her along with them. People had crashed through the barricades and were spilling out into the road and its haze of shimmering petrol fumes. Car horns blared. She was knocked against the side of a stationary car, then along the edge of a windowless bus. A row of tired faces stared down blankly from inside.

Ahead of her, a scrawny young man fell and was sucked under in the wash of running, stamping feet. His face rose for a moment, blood trickling from his temple. She reached towards him through the crowd but he was too far away. He sank again and was lost. Beyond, a stout man swung the wooden pole of his placard and cracked it in two across a policeman's head. Other officers in the line swarmed forwards, jumping on the man, pounding his head and shoulders with *lathis* and fists until his hair matted with blood.

Bitter smoke made her choke. A tyre was burning in the road, forming a puddle of melted rubber. The police line had collapsed. Everywhere men were throwing fists and kicks through air thick with shouts and splintering wood. She looked around, trying to find a way out. She was hemmed in on all sides. Distant sirens screamed the arrival of more police.

The crowd thickened again after the sudden rush of movement. Shock waves ran back through the crowd causing sudden compression. Ellen found herself trapped between two thick-set men. One fell back on her as he fought for balance. His fist caught her stomach. She couldn't find the breath to cry out. The muscular man behind tried to claw through, heaving his way past. He grabbed at her shoulder and shoved her backwards. The sky wheeled, a ragged white emptiness far above. Her legs scrambled, were kicked from under her. Stumbling. Her hands clutched uselessly at the slippery cotton moving past her. She was falling, helpless to right herself, pressed down by the surge of bodies on all sides.

'Ellie!'

She was hallucinating, she must be. Drowning in the noise, the chaos. A fist struck the side of her head and set her ear ringing. On her knees. A forest of legs. She must find the surface, get back on her feet. The men around her were a blur of kicking limbs. She put her hands to her head, shielding her face. A foot caught her hard in the ribs. Under. If she went under, she'd be trampled.

'Ellie!'

Close. Urgent. A real voice? Her ears were deaf with stinging and shouts and blows. A foot caught her just above her eye, knocked her sideways, backwards into the crush. The legs around her blurred and shimmered.

'Ellie!'

Louder. Still reeling from the blow, she managed to turn her head. A large clean hand was sticking through the swell at waist height. Reaching for her. She stared at it for a second, too stunned to move. A white hand with strong fingers and neatly clipped nails and long dark hairs above the knuckles. Beside her, a man slipped and his punching battle to stay upright forced a moment's gap. She crawled on her hands and knees through the feet, the legs, the bodies, thrusting her arm out to grasp the hand. Her fingers locked around its wrist, firm and warm. The hand closed over hers, heaving her out and upwards as she clung to it, dragging her onto her feet, even as the waves of people crashed past her.

Her head was spinning, her eyes closed. She couldn't speak. A strong arm was holding her upright, wrapped around her back and under her arm. She let her head loll into the curve of his shoulder, fighting dizziness. They were moving sideways together, his shoulder ramming through the crowd, steering them both. She clung to him, struggling to keep herself on her feet. When she tried to open her eyes the colours swam and shimmied, making her nauseous.

She let them fall closed again. One eye was sticky, its lids starting to seal. He was dragging her on through screeching traffic and petrol fumes. She was too weak to stop him.

At last he lowered her with a bump onto a low wall. He was crouching over her, his arm still around her shoulders, his breath warm on her cheek. His body ran solid and safe down her side.

'Ellie?'

She managed to part her glued eyes a crack. She was off the road now, looking back at a chaos of figures, some running, some crouching, dazed, on the central reservation, others curled on the ground, still and bloodied. Fresh police sirens, distant, started to wail. A young police officer was rushed past, carried by colleagues, his legs hanging limp, spilt blood stiffening his moustache.

'Can you hear me?'

She forced herself to turn her head and looked into his face. It hung, eyes large with concern, in her vision. Him? She blinked, tried to swallow down the nausea, to focus. No. Impossible. She closed her eyes again, breathing thickly. A moment later, she tried again, forcing open her eyelids and peering at him. 'Frank?'

'Hey.' His mouth broke into a smile, showing neat, whitened teeth. Lines fanned into cracks around his eyes. 'Who'd you expect?'

The office was brightly lit and chill with air conditioning. The cut above her eye was painful. The sheen of sweat on her skin found its way into scratches and made them sting. Frank had half-carried her across a short hallway and now she was sitting in a hard plastic chair, sagging backwards, her head propped against a wall beneath a giant corporate logo that read: *FOOD 4 ALL*. She closed her eyes. People rushed around her, fussing and exclaiming. Her head throbbed.

Frank was at her side again. 'Mind if I take a look?' He eased her head back with gentle hands, swabbing her face and eye. Cotton, cool and wet. A trickle of water ran down her cheek and the curve of her throat and she lifted her hand to it. A moment later, the lids of her puffy eye sprang apart, freed. His face was close to hers, his lips pursed as he concentrated, assessing her cuts and bruises.

His hair, dishevelled, was completely white at the temples. Beyond them, it was streaked with grey. Middle age had rounded out his cheeks. But his eyes were the same, as intense as she remembered. When he looked directly at her, she could still see the young man of twenty he had once been.

'You'll live.' His expression was amused. 'No real damage.' He squeezed sticky white ointment from a tube and dabbed it over her eye, then shook two tablets into her hand and gave her a paper cone of water to swallow them down. 'Sit there, would you? Five minutes and I'm done.'

She didn't argue. A young woman brought her a cup of sweet, milky Pakistani tea. Two tea bags were stewing inside, strings thrown out over the brim like lifelines. She sipped it, looking around. FOOD 4 ALL's offices were cramped, with temporary partitions and an air of chaos. Large colour posters on the walls showed images of needy children with big eyes and babies squirming in their mothers' arms. Cardboard boxes of supplies were stacked along a side wall:

11

oral rehydration salts, blankets and high-protein biscuits. The mix of English and Chinese characters on the packaging suggested it was all from China.

A television on a stand in one corner flickered, its sound muted. A Pakistani news channel was interviewing its reporter live from the scene of the demonstration. They'd named the item Chaos in the Capital. The reporter was standing in front of a pile of smouldering tyres, making the most of the dregs of the violence. The black smoke rose calmly, almost wistful as it billowed and gently dispersed. The street behind was littered with debris – the remnants of trampled placards, a torn shirt, a lost shoe. She wondered how honest the reporter was and if he'd placed them there himself. Around him, the sun was already losing its power. Dark pools glistened on the surface of the road. Blood perhaps, or just oil. To one side, almost out of shot, riot police were clambering back into their vehicles and pulling away.

A written commentary ran across the bottom of the screen: *Home Minister condemns violence, blames opposition for illegal protest. Opposition leaders slam police, label action heavy-handed. Three thousand demonstrators, say police.* An underestimate, she thought. *Scores injured, organizers claim.*

Frank reappeared. 'How're you doing?' He leant past her for his bag, a battered leather case thrown on its side. If someone had asked her what Frank smelt like, she would have thought them crazy. But now, as he bent close, a hint of his old, familiar smell caught her unawares, hit the pit of her stomach. Warm and floury, like crumbled biscuit, cut with a Christmassy spice. Aftershave, perhaps. She stared after him as he moved away without waiting for an answer, bag swinging from his hand.

He was finishing off his day, hanging around the doorway of each small sub-office, asking questions, issuing instructions. She sat quietly, watching him, glad to be still and adjusting to the sight of him again.

As he strode back to her, he winked and made her smile. 'Come on, Ellie.' He reached down and hoisted her to her feet. 'Let's get you home.'

The guesthouse where Ellen was staying was just outside Islamabad and a welcome escape from the city. It was early evening by the time Frank drove her through the gates. Upstairs, in her room, she showed him where she hid her bottles of gin and tonic, pointed him to the small fridge for ice, and let him fix the drinks. They sat outside to drink them, side by side on the first-floor terrace, warming themselves in the mellow gleam of the falling sun. She rocked her glass against her face, cooling her swollen skin.

He slipped off his sandals and propped his feet on the rail. They were sunburnt, red with white stripes where the leather had been.

She looked out past his toes to the tips of Islamabad's tallest buildings, just visible in the natural basin below. The tiles on the domes of the mosques glittered in the dying light. It was peaceful here, removed. She glanced at Frank. His strong Roman nose was more prominent than she'd remembered, the chin now soft with flesh.

'So . . .' She looked into her glass. 'Still do-gooding?'

'You mean, actually making a difference to people.' His

13

tone was bantering but she sensed bitterness. 'As opposed to stirring up trouble.'

She felt stung. 'No fan of journalism then?'

'Course I am. Huge.'

They sat in silence for a moment. She didn't know what to say, where to start. Her mind was weighted by exhaustion. When she closed her eyes, she saw stamping feet, bloody faces trapped in the crowd. She'd been lucky to get out. She thought of his hand, reaching for her.

'How come you were there?'

He didn't answer for a minute, then threw back his head and laughed. It was a forced laugh, mirthless. 'You'd like to think that, wouldn't you? That I've been following you around the world, staking you out, waiting for a chance to save you.'

She shook her head. 'I didn't—'

He lifted his feet from the rail. For a moment, he seemed about to leave, then he rearranged his ankles and settled again, sipped his drink. 'I was heading for the office, that's all. Stopped to watch the fun. And there you were.'

'There I was.'

His voice was the same. Lush and chocolatey and lazy with American vowels. It had seemed so exotic to her when they were students.

'You look just the same,' he said. 'Haven't changed a bit.'

She put her hand to her sore, battered face. 'I've changed.' He'd aged too.

Another silence. They were awkward together, unable to find the natural rhythm of a conversation, and that saddened her.

In the distance, a recording spluttered into life and the

soulful notes of the call to prayer drifted across the fields. It seemed to carry the melancholy of the dying day. He too seemed pensive, listening to the gentle sweetness of the young man's voice.

When it ended, she tried again. 'You were in Africa, weren't you? I saw you interviewed. South Africa?'

He nodded, stared into his drink. 'Jo'burg for a while. Then Nairobi.'

'All with the UN?'

'Yep. Eighteen years.'

She thought of FOOD 4 ALL's cramped offices. It was clearly a small agency. Nothing like the UN. 'What made you leave?'

He replied as if he hadn't heard the question. 'I've read your reports, you know, in *NewsWorld*. Over the years.'

'Really?'

'Course.' He grinned. 'Afghanistan. Iraq. Beirut. You sure pick 'em.'

The screen door downstairs opened and slapped shut. The garden boy appeared. He connected the hose and started to water the flowerbeds, aiming the flow with languid movements. The soil blackened as the water pooled, bubbled and sank.

Frank lifted his glass and drank down his gin and tonic. No wedding ring. Still, that didn't mean anything. Not all married men wore them. He probably had a wife back in the US. And a bunch of all-American kids. She thought of the ring she was wearing, her mother's wedding ring, and wondered if he'd noticed.

He said, 'How long're you out here?'

'Another few days maybe.' She shrugged. 'I've been

15

covering the protests. But they get repetitive. I need something new.'

'Like what?' His teeth gleamed in a half-smile in the dusk as if he knew full well.

'Like this government offensive everyone's talking about. Against the Taliban.'

'Ah.' He sounded pleased.

She could sense that he knew something and was quietly enjoying the advantage it gave him. She pushed a little further. 'They keep saying it's imminent. But they're taking their time.'

She cupped her drink, listened to the creak of ice in her glass. He seemed to be thinking. Down below, the boy was moving steadily across the garden, trailing a dripping hose. A bird, compact and brown, darted past him and perched on the gate. It cocked its head, watching the boy, then took off again, skimming low across the darkening lawn.

'I think there's a nest.' She pointed to a puff of bush hanging down from the wall. 'I hear chirping. In the morning.'

He shifted on his chair, restless. 'Off the record?'

'Of course.'

'The offensive's started. They're trying to keep it quiet.'

She turned her head a fraction to look at him, keen with interest.

'People are streaming down from the mountains in their thousands,' he said. 'Tens of thousands.'

'Are the troops in yet?'

'Just heading in. You heard there were air strikes? Now they need boots on the ground.'

She nodded. It made sense. 'They took their time.'

He grimaced. 'Fighting your own people? Never an easy call.'

Tinny music sounded, distant at first, then closer. An ice-cream hawker, blasting a mechanical tune. The garden boy paused, lifted his head. Water splashed from the end of the hose onto the grass at his feet.

Finally the ice-cream hawker pedalled into view on his bicycle, a large plastic box fixed to the front of his bike. His sweat painted a black circle on his shirt where it stuck to his back. He turned down the lane opposite and the spell broke. The garden boy shifted, tugged at the hose and moved on to the last flowerbed.

'Have you set up relief camps?'

'Just one so far. Near Peshawar.' He rattled the final shards of ice in his glass and tipped back his head to drink. His throat made a long, white stretch. 'We're trucking in relief as fast as we can but the lines keep growing.'

He turned and looked her full in the face. His expression was serious. She couldn't tell if he were thinking about the refugees or about her, about the past. It was all such a long time ago. Somewhere below, the cook was banging pots and pans and calling to the boy. The smell of frying onions and garlic rose from the kitchen.

Frank looked at his watch and shook himself back into motion. He lifted his feet off the rail, downed the last of his drink and pushed his feet into his sandals. When he spoke again his tone was businesslike.

'I'm heading down there tomorrow. Come if you want.' He nodded at her swollen face. 'If you feel up to it.'

She didn't hesitate. 'I will. Thanks.'

*　　*　　*

17

He left abruptly. She watched from the terrace as he crossed to his car. The guard ran out to open the gates. Frank raised a hand to her through the car window, then backed and disappeared in a fading echo of engine.

She felt suddenly drained. Her head ached. The sun had almost set, casting a red mantle over the jagged line of the mountains. Male shouts swam through the darkness from a nearby patch of waste ground. Young men were struggling to play cricket in the gloom, their shirts barely visible.

She should go inside and file a piece to London on the protest, the violence. Her limbs were leaden. She should call Phil, her editor, and tell him about the trip to the camp. She should pack, ready to leave.

In a moment.

The ice in her drink slowly melted. She'd always thought of Frank as a young man, the way he used to be. Passionate and funny and slightly wild. This middle-aged creature, this raised ghost, was a shock. She was pleased, of course. But it was also unsettling, a reminder of the past and the path she might have taken.

The small boy who tended the neighbour's goats was trailing back through the scrub, slapping at the goats' hindquarters with a switch as they shoved and clambered and jostled in a tinkle of bells.

Across the path, an elderly man came shuffling out of his house and onto the veranda. He was dressed in white cotton, his feet bare. He settled himself heavily into a chair.

In the garden, insects were gathering in black clouds. Somewhere out in the wildness, beyond the guesthouse walls, cicadas tuned up and began to sing.

3

After I saw the three strangers near the mosque and tore down their notice to keep for myself, everything went quiet. No one spoke of these strange new rules. Most of the men had beards anyway, even my Saeed who is only sixteen but already a man and adores me besides. Apart from fetching water and working in the fields and buying provisions and going to school, women and girls like me don't have many places to go, even without it being forbidden. I kept the paper secretly under my mattress and only looked at it when I was alone. I knew the words by heart. When I whispered their name to myself: *Faithful Soldiers of Islam*, it seemed full of danger and also adventure and I imagined some excitement that might finally stir up my boring life in the village.

Then Baba said we should all go for a family picnic before the weather got too hot. It was already late May and even in the village the days were getting sticky. Higher up the mountain, there was a good place for picnicking.

The grass was lush and springy alongside the stream, which came tumbling down from the peak. There was an old gnarled tree, even older than Baba and his father before him and his father before that. Baba used to tell how his parents took him there when he was a boy, along with all the Uncles who were also boys and even the blood Aunties who were still young girls like me and not yet married off to men in other villages.

Mama had been sickly since Ramadan last year. Baba instructed her not to fast. No one told me why but I knew because I'd seen it all before. She was sweaty and pale and moaned on her cot at night. I could tell she was dreaming about a new baby crying to be born and worrying that this baby, like so many of her others, apart from me and my big sister, Marva, would die before it ever saw day. All those months later, her stomach was as big and hard as a watermelon and to my mind that was the real reason Baba planned the day out, to lift her spirits.

The morning of the picnic, Marva was ill with fever and knife pains in her legs. Mama sat with her arms wrapped around her, her fat belly bumping them apart, and the two of them whimpered and sighed. I set to work massaging Marva's legs until the pains eased and then I helped the Aunties to prepare the eatables, with fresh bread and tomatoes and all manner of chopped salads and a basket of first season plums and apples, which I'd helped to pick from the orchard just the day before.

I am thirteen now but even when I was very young, I was forced to be responsible for Mama and my big sister both. Sometimes I feel that Baba and I are the real parents and my mama is just another girl, like Marva, and they both need looking after. As Allah has chosen, that's the sort of family I have. Mama is sweet and gentle, it's true. Marva says Mama was once so lovely to behold that when she went walking, birds fell out of the trees dead at her feet on account of craning to get a closer look.

But Mama lacks spirit. All those dead babies, one after another, have sucked her dry and left her as brittle as a dead reed and plagued by nerves, and even a rush of wind is enough to knock her right over and start her crying about some small thing or other. The Aunties say some women are born with character and some are born with beauty but very few have both. My mama was doled beauty.

Jamila Auntie is the other way about, plain but strong. She's Baba's first wife and Baba only married her because he hadn't yet found Mama and as soon as he did, he took Mama as his new wife and forgot Jamila Auntie altogether.

As for my sister, Marva, she has an affliction. It is the wish of Allah for her to have withered legs on account of an illness she had as a little girl, even before I was born. I've told Baba that I don't understand why Allah would want her to be stuck all day every day in our compound, pulling herself about on her belly like a snake, but he tuts and says, 'Hush, Layla, don't question the will of Allah. It is not for us to know everything and sometimes there are things we don't understand but must nonetheless accept.'

Baba wears wire-rimmed spectacles and uses words like 'nonetheless' and 'whatsoever' because he is a man of learning. He teaches me everything, just as if I were a boy. He says that when the boys in the village shout after me in the street and call Marva names, like 'crazy cripple' and

21

'freak of nature', I must bear it with dignity and I must not shout back, even if I think of smart things to say, and I must not pick up sharp stones and throw them at their heads. That, he says, is not any way for a girl to comport herself.

Baba and the Uncles harnessed the donkey and loaded up the cart and Mama and the Aunties, carrying the youngest cousins, all climbed onto the back and sat, their legs hanging over the edge, as the donkey strained and pulled and complained until finally the struts creaked and the wheels turned and we all set slowly off up the steep hillside towards the stream. Girls like me and boys and men like Baba walked along behind.

The mountainside was still, the sky streaked with white cloud. The sun was hiding behind the rocky edge of the mountain, waiting to jump out and surprise us as we climbed further up. The boys ran ahead, whooping and playing chase and the girls walked in wavy clusters, holding each other's hands and giggling into each other's ears. I walked near Baba. The light breeze dusted off my skin and kept me cool and fingered the scarf around my face. With Jamila Auntie and Baba and the Uncles and their wives, the Aunties, and all the cousins coming and going, there were too many of us crammed into that compound and, despite its size, it was very shouty and bothersome to a young girl like me, who wanted a little peace and quiet sometimes, but was always shut up in the sweat and clamour of all those people.

After we reached the place and finished our picnic, the Aunties sat bunched underneath the twisted tree, gossiping, and the older boys took off their sandals and waded in the stream, splashing rocks about, building a dam or some such, and the toddlers, nearby on the flat grassy bank, tried to throw pebbles into the clear water and barely made a ripple, their judgement was so poor. Baba and the Uncles stood together by the water's edge, looking up and down the stream and talking in low voices. I sat propped up against Mama, plucking at the tufts of grass under the tree and wondering, not for the first time, why other girls of my age were so silly and boys so stupid.

The strangers appeared suddenly as dark shapes against the rocks. They climbed sideways down the steep mountain towards us. Baba and the Uncles stiffened and turned to watch. The knowledge of their arrival moved through the Aunties, one by one, and they too turned to look and fell silent. Some pulled at their headscarves to cover their faces and others called to their children to come here, quickly. Mama tensed at my side.

There were four of them, all dressed like the other men I'd seen, in flowing black kameezes with rough woollen hats and thick beards. They looked full of purpose, closing the distance between us with sure strides. The sunlight flashed on long-nosed guns at their sides.

The men descended to the flat bank of the stream. Baba and the Uncles stepped forwards and greeted them politely, putting their hands on their hearts: *Salaam Alaikum*. Three of the men were young, strong boys with loose limbs and jaunty muscles. The fourth man was older. He turned and looked across at the girls and women as we shrank together under the tree. I knew him at once from his crooked nose. He was the same man who had brought the notices and ordered the men to nail them to our trees. His eyes were hard as if they had seen many terrible things.

The men spoke in low voices. Hamid Uncle, the head of the family, spoke first and then the stranger and then Hamid Uncle again. Mama's leg, pressed against mine, was shaking. The men were still speaking, back and forth, and, although I couldn't make out the words, I heard the threat in the stranger's voice. The three young men standing around him cocked their guns and raised them as if they were planning to fire. One of the Aunties let out half a cry, then strangled it dead.

The stranger spoke again and, as he did so, one of the young men swung around and aimed his gun at the donkey, which was tearing up grass beside the stream, the only creature in our party unaware of the danger. A crack. The donkey crumpled, rolling its head sideways with surprised eyes, its ears flapping. Blood spurted from its side. It gave a high-pitched scream. After a moment, the scream faded and the donkey crashed onto its side and lay, shuddering. Its blood made a dark stain on the grass. The silence that followed was full of the memory of the scream. It was only broken when the young men laughed and the fourth man turned and scolded them until they too were silent.

I stared, shaking, at Baba and the Uncles to see what they were going to do. They just stood there and looked as the donkey stopped twitching. Its eyes were open and it looked as dead as if it had never lived. The fourth man turned away and led his fighters briskly on down the edge of the mountain towards the village. While they were still in sight, no one moved.

The picnic outing was over. The Aunties rocked the

24

smaller children in their arms, crying with them. Baba and the Uncles went across to the donkey and Baba bent down and tickled the soft patch between its ears, the way he always did, and I knew he was saying goodbye.

In truth, it had been a bad-tempered animal that nipped us with its strong teeth when we children pulled its ears or climbed on its back for a ride. But it had been part of our household since I could remember and now it was dead and I had to bite hard on the inside of my cheeks to keep from crying.

Baba and the Uncles made pairs and lifted the shafts of the cart themselves and pulled the Aunties and children back down the mountainside. The toddlers cried and struggled and had their legs slapped to hush and keep quiet. Mama, her huge stomach pushing out beyond the edge of the cart, was pale.

I walked alongside Baba. His face dripped with sweat as he heaved the cart and his spectacles kept sliding forwards on his nose and I wished I could help him. I asked, 'Who was that man? Why did they do that?'

Baba glanced down at me and his expression was sorrowful.

'His name is Mohammed Bul Gourn,' Baba said. 'He is a very dangerous man and I pray God you will never see him again.'

My hands tightened into fists at my sides. 'But why did they shoot our donkey?'

Baba was panting. The strain made deep lines in his face as if he were already old. 'Don't ask so many questions, Layla.'

I stopped. Other people had said that to me since I was

a little girl, Jamila Auntie and the cousins and the other Aunties and even Mama, but never Baba; Baba had never said such a thing. He and I were explorers, he used to tell me, searching for knowledge. I stared after him, shocked and hurt, as he and his brothers and the laden cart rumbled on.

4

They drove from Islamabad to Peshawar. Ellen sat in the back of the four-wheel drive beside Frank. In the front, the local driver was sitting low behind the wheel, a round cap on his head, a brown blanket trailing from his shoulders.

She was eating her way through a packet of stale biscuits, spraying crumbs and picking them laboriously off her trousers. Frank was trying to pour steaming chai out of a Thermos flask without spilling it over his thighs.

Her face ached. The bruising had bothered her all night. Now she was full of painkillers, which made the passing landscape seem remote and a little blurred. Islamabad's city traffic, the overladen carts, brightly painted lorries and crowded motorbikes, had fallen away. The motorway stretched ahead, almost empty. They'd set off at dawn when the sun was little more than a shy red glow. Now it had whitened, burning dew off the grass and making the wheat fields shimmer.

Frank's phone rang. She smiled. The ringtone was a phrase from a Rolling Stones track. The music ran on in her head even after he'd answered it. She followed it until she reached the chorus and the title came back to her, carrying memories of sweaty student bars and tables sticky with spilt beer.

He'd lodged the plastic cup of milky tea between his knees to take the call and she reached across and took it for him. His jeans were worn at the knees and crumpled. They ended in heavy boots. He seemed to be confirming arrangements.

Almost as soon as he finished, the phone rang again. It was a long call. Frank's voice was soft, dotted with mantras of 'absolutely' and 'understood' and 'that's all you can do'. Afterwards he took back the cup of cooling tea and turned to the window, presenting her with a hunched shoulder.

'Everything OK?'

He didn't look around. His fingers were tight around the rim of the cup. Finally he said, 'Not good. They sound overwhelmed.'

He drained the cup and held it out so she could refill it for herself. His lips were pursed. They both kept their eyes on the flow of steaming tea from the Thermos.

'I'm sorry,' she said at last. He didn't reply. He seemed distant, preoccupied.

The driver started to fiddle with the car radio. The silence was filled with bursts of white noise and high-pitched music. She drank her tea, trying not to swallow the black specks circling at the bottom.

'You want an apple?' Frank pulled one out of his bag and rolled it to her along the seat.

A car veered in front of them and the driver was forced to brake, pumping the horn with the heel of his hand. The sun was hard on the windscreen, burning streaks of light across the tarmac.

She bit into the apple, still thinking about the strains on the camp. 'You got funding?'

He gave a snort. 'I just spend money we don't have. Then the guys in head office curse the hell out of me and run in circles trying to fill the holes.'

'Have they launched a special appeal?'

'Not yet.' He shrugged. 'It hasn't made the news yet. But they say a rich Brit might help out. Hasan Ali Khan. Know him?'

She nodded. She knew of him. 'Quentin. Quentin Khan. That's what he calls himself in London.' He was a middle-aged Pakistani. Vastly rich and now part of the London smart set. 'Made a fortune in transport. Lorries and ships.'

'That's him.'

'And he's giving money?'

'I guess. They're talking to him.'

They were slowing down, approaching the row of booths that signalled the end of the toll road.

'Good.' Frank nodded ahead. 'Our guys.'

Two trucks of armed police were waiting at the side of the road, just beyond the booths. As their own car emerged from the barrier, one truck slid out into the traffic in front of them and the other slotted in behind. They were open-backed. Policemen were sitting in two rows down the sides, rocket launchers across their knees and guns upright between their legs.

The young policemen at the ends of the seats were

staring down at her through the windscreen. She adjusted her scarf, making sure her hair was properly covered. One, with a shaggy beard and long loose face, looked forlorn. His opposite number was much younger, all designer stubble and bulging biceps. His eyes were hidden by dark sunglasses.

'Do we need them?'

'Maybe, maybe not. They offered.' Frank grimaced. 'There's a lot of Taliban around. The roads aren't secure.'

Peshawar had always had a bad reputation. She'd first come some years before to write about Afghan refugees who'd spilt over the border to escape the Taliban there. She remembered driving through the bazaar, a dusty, colourless array of stalls selling piles of plastic toys and cheap cotton clothing. Men with shaggy beards and woollen tribal hats had stopped to glare in through the car windows. The metal noses of guns glinted at their sides. She'd wanted to stop, just for a moment, to buy a hookah pipe for her father. The driver refused, wagging his finger.

'Not safe for ladies,' her translator explained. 'Very bad place.'

As traffic forced the car to a walking pace, a man with deeply lined skin had stooped and put his face to the glass, squashing the tip of his nose against the window. His palm pressed beside it in white flattened pads of flesh. His eyes found hers. They were cold and threatening. The car shuddered and jerked forwards and the man stumbled, left behind. The butt of his gun rapped against the glass. That was Peshawar a few years ago. By all accounts, it was worse now.

The convoy veered off the road and bumped down a long track onto mudflats, a raw landscape of cracked earth criss-crossed with ditches. Off to one side, boys were struggling to launch a homemade kite in the still air, running and whooping as it bumped along the ground behind them. Inside the car, the air was metallic, cooled and filtered by the air conditioning. She could imagine the heat and stink waiting for her outside.

'That's it.' Frank pointed.

A shanty town of coloured plastic and squat white tents was looming on the plain. Ellen straightened up so she could see through the windscreen. She felt her senses quickening as she judged the scale of the camp and thought of ways to describe the terrain. The camp was sprawling but it was dwarfed by the bleak, featureless mudflats that stretched in all directions. She could see why this great expanse of land hadn't already been settled by local people. There were no natural features to provide shelter, not even rocks or scrub. Far beyond, obscured by cloud, a range of mountains rose, jagged, on the horizon.

They drove closer. A tattered group of several hundred people was waiting in front of the camp's gates. They were standing with drooping shoulders, bundles, baskets and bags piled at their sides. Ellen looked into the faces as they drove past. An elderly woman was sitting in the dirt, her cheeks sharp with bone. She looked exhausted, too listless to raise her eyes to the passing vehicle. A girl, about five years old, was lying motionless in her lap. Her small belly was distended, bulging beneath a grubby kameez. Her stringy hair had faded from its natural black to the colour of straw. Malnourishment, Ellen thought.

31

She looked at Frank. His mouth was set, his shoulders tense.

The camp's perimeter was defined by a wire fence. A small group of men was extending it, a youngster balancing long wooden staves on his shoulders while a pair of older men, stouter and fatter bellied, worked beside him. They had unrolled a drum of metal mesh and were hammering it into place on a fresh post.

The car drew up at the gate. Frank rolled down the window and spoke to the security guards. Their uniforms were baggy, their AK-47s battered and slack in their hands. One of the guards bent to stare in at her and she shielded her bruised face with the edge of her scarf.

Just inside the fence stood a small, single-storey building in sand-coloured brick. A broken flagpole rose from its roof. It looked old but solid in the sea of tethered white canvas. Several large tents, the size of small marquees, sat beside it.

They swung through the gates and off to the left, to an open sweep of ground close to the brick building. They stopped behind a garishly decorated truck, painted green and ornate with flowers and slogans. A confusion of eager young men was crowded around its back, shouting and jostling as they unloaded sacks of rice. Ellen eased herself out of the car, aware of the ache in her limbs. The heat reached in and sucked the moisture from her mouth.

Frank was besieged at once. Two dark-skinned men rushed over to talk to him. A smartly dressed Pakistani man pushed between them, interrupting and competing for Frank's attention. Ellen watched them. Frank put a calming hand on the man's arm and silenced him, making him wait his turn while the others spoke. Frank's face was composed as he listened. He has more presence, she thought, than he had as a young man. More authority.

Someone touched Ellen's arm from behind. She turned. A young Western woman with strands of wavy blonde hair springing free from her headscarf. Her eyes were a striking green, the irises ringed with black as if they'd been first drawn, then coloured in. She looked at the cut above Ellen's eye. 'Shall I put a dressing?'

Ellen smiled. 'It's nothing. I'm fine.' She put out her hand. 'I'm Ellen Thomas, *NewsWorld*.'

The young woman nodded. She was wearing the stiff white coat of a doctor. Ellen sensed that she'd been waiting for her. Frank must have warned her that a journalist was coming.

'I am Britta.' Her handshake was firm. 'I'm the medical in charge here, working for Medicine International. Perhaps you'd like to see the ward for ladies?'

Her accent was lilting. Swedish, Ellen thought. Or Finnish. She looked across to Frank. Several more men had gathered around him now, pressing to be heard. He was standing patiently, the tallest amongst them, his hands slightly raised as if he were conducting the men's voices.

Ellen turned away and followed Britta. They traced a circle around the chaos of the unloading bay. Young men were staggering, bent double under sacks of rice, carrying them out from the back of the truck. At one side of the clearing, they tipped the sacks over their shoulders, letting them fall, slap, raising a cloud of dust, onto the pile growing there. The air was thick with shouts. Britta led her past the vehicles to the entrance of one of the giant tents that stood nearby, close to the brick building.

The sun was filtering through the canvas roof, making the light inside dappled and soft. They had entered a women's ward with two rows of field beds, about twenty in all, tightly packed together. Ceiling fans whirred overhead, battling to clear an oppressive bodily smell of stale breath and vomit and urine all papered over by disinfectant.

A young Pakistani girl, wearing a dark purple salwar kameez, was at the far end of the ward, washing a patient. The patient, a middle-aged woman, sat, hunched inwards, holding onto the girl's shoulder for support. Her back was bare, the skin glistening. The young girl was sponging down her thin shoulders. Her movements were brisk and rhythmical. The water splashed in a plastic bowl on the bed as she dipped and rinsed her cloth. She looked up as they came in and nodded to Britta, glanced at Ellen with shy eyes, then lowered her head again to her work.

Britta had walked to the first bed and was waiting for her there. An elderly woman lay on her back, her eyes closed. Her left arm was bandaged and raised.

'Gunshot trauma,' Britta said. 'The elbow is fractured. Malnutrition and fever also. Many of these ladies are not strong.'

The old woman's skin was puckered and deeply wrinkled. Her veins were raised into transparent channels of viscous purple. Her mouth was slightly open, her lips cracked. A fly settled on the woman's forehead and started to walk across it. Ellen raised her hand and wafted it away. The woman did not stir.

Britta had already moved on to the next bed. This patient was a girl, perhaps seven or eight years old. A

34

drip, connected to her right arm, clicked as it discharged fluid.

She gazed up with dull eyes as Britta laid her hand on the girl's head, stroking her hair as she talked.

'Many of them are already sick when they arrive,' she said. 'This girl has typhoid.'

A revolting sulphuric smell of decay hung around the bed. Ellen turned, looked away down the ward. She tried to distract herself, to close her nose to it.

'She is weak,' Britta was saying, 'but there are no complications. And she's young. In a day or two . . .'

The girl's hand was lying inert on the sheet. The fingers were thin, the nails square and bitten. Britta was talking about dehydration but Ellen was only half-listening. She should take the girl's hand. Reach out and hold it. Pat it, at least.

Britta went to the foot of the bed to consult the notes there. The hand on the sheet lay motionless, waiting. The ward was silent around them. The only sounds were the swish of the ceiling fans spinning overhead and the low mechanical hum of medical equipment.

Britta straightened up, turned and walked on. Ellen followed, conscious of the girl's eyes staring unseeing at empty air.

A young woman was lying twisted on one side. Her eyes were closed. Her cheekbones and chin protruded, sharp and angular under a thin coating of flesh.

Britta lowered her voice. 'As well as medical problems, we have also the trauma. Many of these people have seen terrible things.'

'In the fighting?'

35

'Of course. But also before it, in their lives under the Taliban. The violence and the terror.'

The young woman's legs were curled up into her body. Her fists made tight balls at her chin.

'What can you do?'

'Not so much.' Britta stood for a moment, looking down at the young woman. 'We simply don't have the capacity.' She seemed hollowed out, eaten by exhaustion. Ellen sensed eyes pulling at Britta from all around, a soft, relentless tug of need.

'Is there somewhere we could go?' Ellen nodded towards the back of the ward. 'To talk.'

At the end of the tent, a canvas flap covered an exit. Britta held it back and they passed through. The area beyond was partitioned by hessian walls into a series of small rooms the size of cells. The clicks and whirrs of the ward were muted.

The first room had been converted into a makeshift office. A table in one corner was piled with files and papers and a battered laptop. The space around it was dominated by piles of roughly stacked cardboard boxes. Ellen moved inside to look at them. Each box was identified by a printed sheet of numbers and a barcode.

She turned to ask Britta about them. A short, stocky woman in her thirties appeared right behind her, blocking the entrance. She was holding a metal basin in her hand and, like Britta, she wore a buttoned white coat. Her skin was dark and her hair completely covered by a neatly folded and pinned hijab. She stared at Ellen.

'How can I be helping you?' Her accent was clipped.

Her eyes, a deep brown, were overshadowed by thick black eyebrows that almost met above her nose.

'It's OK, Fatima.' Britta's mild voice rose from behind her. 'This is Ellen. She's with me.'

Fatima looked again at Ellen, opened her mouth as if to speak, then hesitated and closed it again. Ellen stepped forwards and offered her hand. Fatima's fingers were stubby and strong.

'I've just arrived,' Ellen said. 'I'm a journalist, with *NewsWorld*.'

'I am Fatima, chief nurse here.'

Britta squashed between them into the small room. 'My right-hand woman.' She put her hand on Fatima's shoulder. 'Fatima is from Egypt. I am from Denmark. We are mini-United Nations here, isn't it?'

Fatima looked up at Britta, allowed herself a half-smile, then nodded to Ellen and turned on her heel, pushing past the canvas curtain back into the ward. Britta waited until the canvas had fallen back into place.

'We are both a little nervous.' She steered Ellen further forwards to the final cell at the end of the row. It too was partly filled with stacked boxes. Beyond them a stretcher was lying on top of a trestle. The stretcher bore the long, lumpen shape of a woman's body which was loosely covered with a sheet. The sunlight, pressing in through the canvas, touched the surface of the cloth, giving it a luminous sheen.

'We are only just here and already this is our fourth death. When you came, I was just filling the paperwork.'

'I'm so sorry.'

37

The stretcher was narrow. One arm had fallen free and hung loose down the side. The hand was slightly curled as if it were groping blindly for something even in death. The skin of the fingers was slightly yellowed, the fingernails ragged and etched with dirt.

'What was the cause?'

'Typhoid. Many of them came off the mountain with fever and diarrhoea. In cramped living conditions like this, typhoid spreads quickly. We have antibiotics,' Britta sighed, 'but sometimes it's already too late.'

'Are they being vaccinated?'

'We try.' She clasped her hands in front of her. 'Hygiene conditions here are very bad. Water contamination will become worse soon, when the rains come.'

Ellen stood for a moment, looking at the covered body. Britta turned and withdrew. Ellen followed her out through the back of the tent, blinking in the full glare of the sun. She adjusted her headscarf, tugging it forwards to shade her forehead and feeling the prick of sweat in her hair.

Britta was standing quite still outside, her arms by her sides. She had turned away from the tent towards the mountains. Her shoulders were tight with tension. If she lets every death affect her like this, Ellen thought, she'll drown.

Ellen pulled a bottle of water from her bag and drank. The mountains in the distance were stark but beautiful, a row of teeth biting into the landscape. They seemed more dignified than the dirty mudflats in front of them, which were already filling with tents and makeshift shelters. The air rang with the toc-toc-toc of men banging in stakes for tent ropes and sticks that could form a rough frame for stretched sheets of plastic. The dry air crackled with static. Soon the torrent of the monsoon would break. When it did, this whole basin would flood. Disease would spread quickly. Including typhoid.

Britta turned to face Ellen. She wore a falsely cheerful smile. 'Because of the Taliban, we couldn't reach these people in the mountains. Now we can give vaccinations.'

She paused and the smile faltered. She's still young, Ellen thought. She needs to harden if she's going to survive in a place like this.

Britta tried again. 'And maybe the girls can go back to school.'

Ellen thought about the crowded ward and the exhausted new arrivals sitting patiently outside the gates, waiting for help.

'At the moment,' she said, 'what are you short of?'

Britta spread her hands. 'For so many people?' she said. 'Everything.'

5

After the day of the picnic, Baba and the Uncles didn't let any of us, girls or women, leave the compound at all. Not even to go to school or to fetch water. The boys were ordered to take the pails instead. No one would tell me what was going on outside.

Baba still went to teach at the school each day but when he came back, his face was drawn and his mouth hard and when I sat beside him with my school books and asked him questions, he looked past me into the empty air.

In the evenings, all the women, young and old, were sent off to bed and the men dragged the low wooden charpoys across the yard and sat together, talking in low voices. I heard the scrape of matches and smelt bitter smoke as the men lit hand-rolled cigarettes. The tips glowed red in the darkness. A hunting bird out on the mountainside gave a low cry. Cicadas screeched in the grass. Somewhere, far away, a man's voice spluttered and whistled on a badly tuned radio set.

Before all this, I liked to listen to the men's voices when they gathered to talk. Even when I lay on my cot away from the window, falling backwards into sleep, I could hear them as they made plans for the planting season or for harvest.

But now their voices were barely more than murmurs and I couldn't catch a word. Some nights, I knelt at the sill, looking out at their hunched shoulders and tight faces, watching the bobbing red of their cigarettes, and prayed to Allah, not for the first time, that He in His Wisdom might finally turn me into a boy so I could sit there beside Baba on a charpoy and take part in important talking and be always at his side in the day too and not stuck here in our suffocating compound, surrounded by giggling girls and empty-headed Aunties.

One evening, Hamid Uncle came home carrying a parcel and told everyone to gather around. When he tore off the paper, two bundles of material fell out. They were off-white in colour and shiny. He took one and held it up to show us. It hung in tightly pleated folds that bulged shapelessly like a vast cloak. The top part was rounded and shaped like a head. A tight grid of cotton strands lay where the face should be.

'A burqa.' Jamila Auntie was the first to speak. 'So, has it come to this? You want to make us disappear altogether?'

She turned to Baba and he looked down, embarrassed.

'It's for your own safety,' said Hamid Uncle. 'I'm the head of this family and if it is needful for any woman to leave this compound, this is what she must wear.'

The Aunties stared at each other. We had always covered our heads in public but this burqa was something new. Jamila Auntie crossed her arms over her chest. Finally one of the Aunties put out a hand to take the burqa from Hamid Uncle and look at it more closely. She opened it out and pulled it over her head, disappearing from view, then walked carefully around the yard. When she pulled it off again, her hair was untidy and her face flushed.

'So hot.' She fanned at her face with her free hand. 'Like an oven.'

The other Aunties crowded around to try. One by one, they were turned into anonymous blobs by the cloth, as formless as the snow people the boys built on the mountain in winter. Only the toes of their sandals were visible, poking out as they stepped forwards.

Baba asked us once in school what special powers we'd each like to have, if it be the will of Allah. I said I should like very much to fly, but my classmate said she'd like an invisible cloak, so she could go anywhere and do anything and no one would ever know. Now, watching the Aunties as they were swallowed whole by the burqa, I thought of her wish.

Finally the Aunties finished playing with the burqa and it was my turn. I pulled the great bundle of cloth over my head. The narrow cap tightened around my skull, then its folds tumbled to the ground, almost covering my feet. The compound fell away from me and, peering through the squared grid over my eyes, I felt as if I'd disappeared into a separate world and was looking out at the familiar scene from a faraway place. The grid was narrow. I could only see things directly in front of me. Now the compound gates. Now, as I turned my head, the charpoys where the boys sat, fidgeting and fighting. Now, as I twisted my body further around, the faces of the Aunties, Mama and Baba and finally Jamila Auntie's cross face.

I walked up and down carefully, not tripping as some of the girls had done. I imagined all the places I could visit in secret inside this burqa and all the conversations I could overhear, without anyone knowing it was me. I was tall for my age. I could easily be taken for a grown woman.

I turned and started to walk back across the yard, pleased with myself, until I saw Mama and Baba's faces. Mama's eyes were full of pain and she was wringing her hands, squeezing out an invisible rope of washing. Baba was watching me with the same look of sorrow I'd seen on the day of the picnic.

'What?' I tore off the burqa as fast as I could as if it might burn into me like a second skin. 'What's wrong?'

Mama's stomach grew huge. Then her birthing pains came. She lay groaning on her back on the cot while the Auntie who knew how to deliver babies fussed around her and wiped sweat from her face. On the third day, the moans rose to screams and when I helped Auntie wash Mama down with a wet cloth, it came away from between her legs sodden with blood. When I rinsed it out, the water in the pail made red clouds.

Auntie looked worried. I followed her outside. Something was wrong, she told the women there. The baby was coming out badly and Baba should take Mama to the clinic in town as soon as possible.

43

Jamila Auntie slowly shook her head. 'She can't go there.'

'But the baby's stuck.' Auntie pulled a face behind Jamila Auntie's back and spat into the dust. The spittle hung there for some time, in the shape of a silver fish, as if the ground were reluctant to receive it.

Jamila Auntie leant forwards and lowered her voice to a whisper. 'You don't understand,' she said. 'It's not safe.'

Auntie called over a boy and sent him to fetch Baba from school.

Mama was so weak that she could barely walk. The Aunties packed cloths between her legs to hide the bleeding, then hoisted her from the charpoy onto her feet. Her eyes were closed and she was panting with short, hard breaths. When they pulled a burqa over her head, her belly pushed out the loose folds into a ball.

Baba came breathlessly through the compound gate. I thanked Allah for getting him home quickly. He helped the Aunties move Mama to the door and lower her backwards into a wheelbarrow. She sat there, her head lolled forwards onto her chest, her legs hanging limp over the front. He picked up the handles and pushed her, accompanied by the rumble and squeak of the wheels and the low animal moan emerging from beneath the burqa.

One of the Aunties picked up the second burqa and pushed it at me.

'Go with your mother,' she said. 'You're old enough.'

Jamila Auntie opened her mouth and seemed about to speak, then closed it again. I knew why. I've told her a hundred times since I was little that she is not my mama and she had no business telling me what to do. Now, for

44

once, I wished she would. The other women were staring at me so I swallowed down my fear, pulled the burqa over my head and followed Baba across the yard.

'Stay close to me,' Baba whispered as we reached the gate, 'and don't say a word.' His tone was fierce. 'This isn't a game, Layla. Do as you're told.'

Baba and Hamid Uncle pushed Mama in her wheel-barrow out into the village street. The barrow was tossing and bumping on the rough ground, throwing her from side to side. Her covered head bounced on her chest and her groans came in bursts. I wanted to help but I didn't know how and I imagined the Aunties watching from behind and whispering. I kept my eyes on the ground, watching my feet through the burqa grid and matching my steps to Baba's.

The path was strangely quiet and empty. The gates of our neighbours' compounds were all tightly closed. Two boys from the other side of the village came creeping towards us. They shrank against the wall and stared with big eyes as we passed. All around us, the village was so silent, it was eerie. Even the goats and donkeys and chickens seemed afraid.

We turned into the steep path past the mosque. Baba went to the front of the wheelbarrow to steady it on the slope as we descended. The paper notices were still clinging, tattered now, to the trees at the entrance to the mosque. I looked past them to the mosque, ashamed, thinking about the stolen paper hidden under my cot.

I stopped in my tracks, then strained to see through the burqa grid. The yard surrounding the mosque was so different. It was full of dark pieces of canvas and shiny plastic that had been strung from posts and trees to make shelter. Dusty pickup trucks, not from our village, stood between them. Everywhere strong young men were swarming, men I'd never seen before, dressed in grimy shirts and turbans. Their beards were thick and unkempt. There was no music and no one was laughing or even chatting and there was a blackness in their silence that frightened me.

A young man on a stool close to the entrance of the mosque looked up and saw me. He was plaiting hemp into rope, twisting the strands between his fingers. His fingers stopped working and the rope drooped in his hands. Then he frowned. I turned and rushed down the path, scattering stones with my feet and panting, until I'd caught up with the wheelbarrow.

A car was waiting on the road and the men lifted Mama into the back. I slid in beside her and cradled her head in my lap. Her forehead was hot, staining the burqa with sweat. The driver started the car. Baba and Hamid Uncle squashed onto the front seat beside him.

'Baba,' I whispered. 'Those men, at the mosque. Who are they?'

Baba turned back to me and said quietly, 'You didn't see them.'

I opened my mouth to say, 'But, Baba, I did,' then saw the warning in his eyes and shut it again.

Out of the car window, the hillside fell steeply, peppered with rocks and terraced fields. The valley floor below was broad and flat and the river glistened as it spread itself out across the mudflats in shallow ribbons. On the far side, another mountain rose, as high and steep as our own.

46

The driver sat hunched forwards, peering through the cracked windscreen. Baba and Hamid Uncle sat in silence, their shoulders tight with tension.

Mama had stopped moaning. She's dying, I thought. Please, Allah, in Your Kindness and Wisdom, don't take her yet, not here, not now. I laid my hand against the cotton that covered her nose and mouth to see she was still breathing. If she dies now, I thought, it will be my fault. Every time the car hit a rock or hole and threw us around, I shook her. I wanted to keep her spirit in her body, rattling in the back of the car with me, until someone else could take over. I wondered too if she were still bleeding and if the cloths between her legs were thick enough. If she stained the seat, the shame would be unbearable and I might get the blame. I turned my head and stared fixedly out of the window through the white grid of the burqa as if not looking would make the bleeding go away.

The countryside passed in a hundred small squares, divided into pieces by the white cotton grille over my face. In the orchards, men were working in rows, dropping plump apples into baskets on their backs. Their movements were heavy and slow.

I looked more closely. There were no women doing their usual work of fetching, picking and carrying. There were no women on the paths through the orchards and wheat fields. The land didn't look right without them.

I grasped Mama's head and shoulders to hold her steady as the car swung right off the road, taking the mud track towards town. 'We're nearly there, Mama,' I whispered to her. Mama rarely came to town, on account of her bad nerves, so I described it to her. 'We're passing lots of

47

compounds now, Mama, and shops like the tyre shop and the metal welder.' I didn't tell her that the compounds were closed and the shops shuttered. We passed the mosque, bigger and grander than ours, with its fancy *madrasah*. Beyond it, trucks were parked idle in the yards of the marble factory and tobacco-processing plant.

A woman, covered from head to toe in a patched burqa, was walking slowly at the side of a middle-aged man. She was dragging her feet as if she were exhausted or ill. I prayed: If you have to receive a woman today, Allah in Your Greatness, please take her and leave Mama here with us.

The driver turned into the town square. I tightened my grip on Mama's shoulder. Usually it was a market square, a chaos of sounds and shapes. Baskets of apples and plums and oranges. Fish flapping in plastic buckets. Stinking meat, thick with flies, dripping blood into the cobbles. All of it raucous with hawkers' sing-song cries and the chatter of gossiping women.

Now, though, the square was shrunken and mean, emptied of colour and people. Our wheels echoed on the stone as we drove through. A pickup truck rounded the corner and careered towards us. The open back was piled with young men, their heads wrapped around with turbans, long guns in their hands. I pulled my eyes away, frightened. The veins in the back of Baba's neck were swollen with pumping blood.

The driver pointed the car towards the far end of the square, in the direction of the clinic, and accelerated with a jerk of gears. Almost there, Mama.

As we left the square, I twisted my head to look back. A thin sack, suspended by rope from a post, caught my eye. I blinked, struggling to make it out. It was lumpy, the loose folds at the bottom bunched and flapping, and hung about with a shadow of flies. It was only as the car flew out of the square that I realized with a cry that it was a man, long dead, strung up by his feet and turning slowly in the silence.

Mama was taken away by a woman in a burqa. Hamid Uncle and Baba and I sat on a row of hard plastic chairs that were bolted to the floor. Baba looked into the air at nothing and I drew up my legs inside the burqa and leant against him and prayed in my head for Allah please to be merciful.

A man and boy sat opposite us. The man clasped his hands together and stared at them as if he'd never seen fingers before. When I narrowed my eyes, then opened them wide and then narrowed them again, he jumped up and down in the grid squares, and I did that for a long time because there was nothing else to do and I didn't want to think about Mama and what they were doing to get the stuck baby out.

When Baba shook me awake, his face was grey. I wanted to ask: Is she dead, Baba? But I didn't dare say it in case it was true.

He told me the baby had been a girl, a sister, but it was sickly and hadn't survived. It was Allah's will, he said. His eyes were red-rimmed. When we finally took Mama back to the compound, she lay on the charpoy, staring into the air as if it had all been a bad dream and she wanted to wake up. When I closed my eyes, the hanging body came to haunt me, strung up and black with flies.

6

Summer crept up from the valley until it reached us, high in the mountains. At nights, strange sounds drifted through the open windows like bad smells. Heavy marching feet. Banging. The distant crackle of flames and bitter soot that left its black trace everywhere.

The men went out of the gates each morning, guns in hand, and came back at night with hard faces. Women and girls were shut inside day after day, prisoners in our own homes. As I did my chores, I distracted myself by thinking about Saeed. I imagined him pressing my hand between his own strong palms and comforting me.

Saeed is clever and funny and strong. He has thick hair that falls in a curl across his forehead and a large straight nose and deep brown eyes and now he has a beard. He is sixteen and stockier than my cousins. He could beat any one of them in a fight. And he has spirit, like me. He can run to the top of the mountain, high above the village, in barely two hours, which is faster than anyone else I know.

But Saeed is gentle too. He writes notes to me on scraps of paper with words about the sun in the mountains and the rich scent of peaches in the orchards and, of course, about how lovely I am and how his heart is breaking for me, and he writes all this with such tender feeling that sometimes these notes make my eyes fill with tears, in a joyful way.

Before these so-called Faithful Soldiers of Islam came and everything began to change, I was allowed to go to and from school on my own and to run errands for Mama, on account of Marva's affliction and of having no brother to go. This was when Saeed first saw me. Sometimes he would lie in wait near the mosque gates and follow me. He walked at a distance but watched me all the time. I couldn't speak to him or even look back. Some tittle-tattle would have told. But I knew he was there and I sensed he could tell from the swing of my hips that I knew and, for the time being, that was enough.

Then he started to send notes through Adnan, my cousin. Adnan is a large boy, the same age as Saeed, but he was born simple-minded and Hamid Uncle has never forgiven him for it, although the Aunties are always hugging and fussing him as if he were a baby. He is stupid but sweet tempered, always smiling and willing to fetch and carry and help the women with their chores and he amuses the young cousins by rolling about with them in the dust for hours, playing foolish games and letting them ride on his back and pull his ears.

Adnan has a soft corner for my sister Marva. He is forever hanging around our door with big eyes, waiting for her. When she comes into the yard, he sits for hours

51

by her side as she tries in vain to teach him basic letters and sums. When she finally gives up, she tells us tales, crazy, magical stories about the village and the mountains, which, on account of her legs, she can never leave the compound to see for herself.

Given the star-struck look on his face, I say he's in love with her – I'm sure he is – but when I told Marva that, she blushed plum red and scolded me. Perhaps she thinks she'd be a laughing stock if she had an idiot for a husband but I say he's less of an idiot, in his own foolish way, than some of the men who have three wives and beat them all so hard they can barely stand. And besides, it's a harsh thing to say but a girl with withered legs should be grateful to have a husband at all and Adnan is at least hard-working.

Jamila Auntie thinks the same. I've caught her looking at the pair of them and once, when we were sitting side by side chopping potatoes, she said to me, 'If Allah in His Wisdom put together his body and her head, He could make a good person out of the two of them.' I saw at once what she meant. In a strange way, they fit together.

Since Baba confined us to the compound, I hadn't heard from Saeed and I was fretting, wondering if he'd forgotten me. Then, about two weeks after we took Mama to the clinic, I finished sweeping inside the house and came out to find Baba sitting on a charpoy right there, waiting. I started. It was unusual for him to be home so early. When his eyes fell on me, they darkened and he shook his head. His chest puffed out a little and collapsed again as if he had sighed. He lifted his hand and beckoned.

I was too taken aback to set down my cleaning things

and just went straight to him, broom and brush and all. My sandals scuffed up small puffs of dust with every step and each one exploded with an anxious thought. What had I done? May Allah protect me. Had he found out about the notice I stole from the tree? How could I explain that it was exciting to keep, precisely because it was so forbidden?

I sat down at his feet, the broom beside me, and looked up at him. The skin around his mouth was puckered.

'You have disgraced me.' He looked heavy with sadness. His breath was hot in my face. I blinked up at him stupidly and didn't speak. I had never heard Baba say such a thing. A silence stretched between us.

'Layla. My own daughter. How could you behave with such dishonour?'

I tried to swallow but my mouth was dry. My mind was racing, trying to think what I might have done, but it came up blank. My face burnt with shame. Just when I was ready to burst into tears, he pulled a note from his pocket.

I recognized it at once. From Saeed, of course. Wobbly black letters on a scrap of rough paper, the kind used by shopkeepers. He always used it. But how had Baba got hold of it? No one knew about Saeed's notes, not even Marva.

Baba was holding it taut between us in his hands. Some pretty words were there, about starlight and the sun. I couldn't speak.

'Who wrote this?' His voice was quiet but there was a danger in it that I had never heard before.

I stuttered. Part of my brain was thinking: Does Baba

really not know? Maybe I can still protect Saeed. I was terrified. I didn't know what he might do, either to me or to Saeed or to my poor broken mother. I started to cry in great sobs that set my shoulders heaving.

'Answer me.'

Baba set his hands on my shoulders and his touch at first was a comfort but then he lifted me to my feet. His fingers dug into my skin. The crying in my eyes made his face wobble and I twisted away to make him disappear altogether.

'Tell me.'

I was gasping now, refusing to look at him, taken up with sobbing and snuffling. He was holding me so tightly, I couldn't even raise my hands to my face and wipe it clean. I squirmed and tried to break free.

He started shaking me. I struggled to stay upright. My brain knocked in my skull. His angry face and the house behind it flew into splinters, speared by black streaks and flecks of bright light. The shock of it stopped my crying at once. He was strong and I was slight in his hands and I had the feeling I was flying, my legs dancing in the dirt.

My mouth was wide open, stretching as I tried to draw in breath. Dust flew into my throat and I started to cough and cough as if my lungs would burst. I must have gone limp in his hands because the next thing I remember, I was sprawling on the ground, flat on my belly with my limbs splayed and my kameez up around my waist in disarray, and my hands flat against the ground as if the earth were spinning so quickly that I had to grab hold of it to hang on and stop myself whirling off into space. Everything around me was turning and my body was juddering against the ground as I tried to breathe. Somehow I pulled myself over onto my back and faced Baba who was shaking from head to foot with the exertion and the weight of his own rage. His face was red and sweaty and his eyes were moist and I saw the old man he would one day become, hidden there inside his skin.

'You are a wicked girl.' He was panting. 'You will not have contact with this boy again. I forbid it.'

I stared at him. 'Baba . . .' It was all I could say, staring at him stupidly with the world still slowly spinning around me. He tore the note into a dozen pieces and threw them over me and they slowly fluttered, specks carried by the currents of air, before coming to rest at last. Baba turned his head and strode away.

That evening, Adnan came tapping at our door. His face was swollen with tears and he crawled into the house, whimpering for Marva like a little boy. I bolted the door behind him. When he calmed down enough, he lifted his kameez. I grimaced and Marva turned away her face. His back was a pulpy mess of broken skin, hanging in scraps and fragments. Fibres from his clothes and dirt from the yard were embedded in the blood, which had congealed and was holding the whole sticky surface together.

He let us put him, face down, on my cot and flinched as I wet a cloth in the pail and dabbed at his back. Marva sat watching, her eyes full of distress. The marks made a criss-cross pattern across his spine. He'd been flayed with a split cane.

'Was it Baba?' I asked.

He moaned and shook his head. 'My baba, not yours.'

'Why?'

55

'Those stupid notes.' He twisted, raising his head to look at me. His childish eyes were full of reproach. 'Saeed said they were nothing. He said it was all right.'

I swallowed hard. The blood on his back was coming away in dried flecks as he moved. It smelt of gunmetal. His face crumpled and he started to cry again, snot running from his nose in long stretchy strings to the cot.

I couldn't look Marva in the eye. I carried on dabbing at Adnan's cuts while she comforted him. If Hamid Uncle knew about my disgrace and had done this to his own son, what might he and Baba do to Saeed? When I went to squeeze out the cloth, my own face appeared in the water, my eyes wide and afraid.

After some time, Adnan's crying subsided and I carried the dirty pail outside to empty it. The men had gathered in the courtyard to smoke and talk. I had the feeling, as I poured away the water, that someone was watching me. I glanced around at the men. They were bending forwards and talking in low voices, not paying me any heed. I twisted towards the house.

There was a woman there, standing back from the window so the shadows half-concealed her. Was it Mama? Did she know what had happened? I narrowed my eyes and looked more closely. No. Not Mama. The face swam into focus as I stared. A sad, plain face. And, seeing it, I knew at once who had betrayed me. Who had spied on me and Saeed and seen our notes and taken the chance to stop them. Jamila Auntie.

7

Jamila crouched in the shade of the orchard wall. The burqa was tight around her head, driving its seams into her skull. She was trying to think but it made her head ache. It was nonsense. Never had the women of Mutaire been forced to wear the burqa. It was not their culture.

She peered through the small grid over her face. On the other side of the orchard, too far away to notice her, old men climbed heavily on the ladders, their bones creaking as much as the wood. She tutted to herself. Now that women were banned from working in the orchards and fields, many of the peaches, plums and apricots would spoil.

Hamid had finally given her permission to visit her relatives across the village. On the way, she was stealing a chance to breathe the smell of the fruit trees. She shifted her weight and a brittle twig cracked. The earth beneath her sandals was dry and tired, beaten by the sun for too many months.

Love the land like a husband, her father used to say when she was a little girl, playing around him in the fields, digging holes and poking insects with sticks. It will always be true to you. It has always been true to our people. She had crouched in the dust at his feet, listening, as her father's broad body blotted out the sun. The land is wise, he'd told her. The land never forgets.

But people forget, she thought now. The young are foolish. They think they know everything but understand nothing. She sighed. Layla's anger weighed her down. This nonsense with the peasant boy was dangerous. It had to be stamped out before people's tongues wagged and the family's honour was tainted. The girl didn't understand the risks. She was headstrong, spoiled by Ibrahim, her baba, who was so desperate for a son that he treated his daughter like one. She blinked. I wanted to give you ten sons, Ibrahim. If I had, you wouldn't have pushed me aside for a second wife. But it was not Allah's will.

A light breeze blew through the trees. The peaches swayed, plump and heavy on the branches. Jamila looked again at the old men on their ladders, clawing at the fruit. They wouldn't see her. She lifted the front of the burqa, throwing it back in a rush to expose her face. Cool air swept in and wiped her hot cheeks, dried off her forehead. She closed her eyes.

After some time, she scratched up dirt and twigs and leaves in her palms and buried her face in it. It pressed itself into the softness under her nails. She rubbed it into her skin, tasting it, filling her senses with its rich, vital scent. 'You are our land,' she whispered as she squeezed it between her fingers and watched it fall, powdery, to the ground. 'Our history. No one will have you from us.'

Jamila reached her old family compound late in the afternoon. One of her relatives, a young boy, peered around the gate when she knocked. How these times are changing us, she thought. Everyone is afraid.

He ran ahead of her across the courtyard as she lifted off the burqa. Old Auntie's great-granddaughter, Syma, came skipping across the yard to meet her, calling and waving her arms. Her hair stuck up in wild tufts above her forehead. Out of habit, Jamila reached out her fingers to smooth it down but it sprang back at once.

'*Salaam*, little one. Why aren't you helping your mama?'

The girl was quiet for a moment, ignoring the question, then she grabbed hold of Jamila's hand. She swung her arm back and forth as they walked, pumping a smile.

'The boys brought a basket of plums yesterday and when we washed them, there was a frog.'

'A frog?'

'A tiny one.' She took her fingers back to show the size, then reached for Jamila's hand again.

'Where is it?'

She looked around at the yard hopefully. 'I don't know. It went hopping off. I tried to catch it.'

'And how is your mama?'

She shrugged. 'OK.' She thought for a moment. 'I want to pick the plums myself but Baba won't let me go.'

'Your baba is right. You must listen to him and do what he tells you, like a good girl.'

The girl sighed. Her hand was small and firm inside

Jamila's. If Allah had allowed me a girl, she thought, she might have been such a child as this.

'Go and play quietly,' she said at last as they approached the house. She bent to the child and kissed her forehead. 'Hush now. Don't disturb your great-grandmother. Look, she's sleeping.'

Syma turned and skipped carefully away to the other side of the yard, humming to herself.

Old Auntie was sitting outside the house, wrapped in a blanket. Her face was turned to the dying sun, her eyes closed. The mellow light was teasing her skin, smoothing out the hollows, pockets and wrinkles.

Jamila crouched on the ground and simply watched. Finally the old eyes flicked open. Jamila went forwards to greet her, kissing her cheek. '*Salaam Alaikum*, Auntie. How is your health?'

The old lady inclined her head. 'I'm still alive, thanks be to Allah.'

No one knew exactly what age Old Auntie had reached. On some days, she said she was eighty-five. On others, she shook her head and said: Did you know I am almost a hundred? There was no one left of her own generation to disagree.

Jamila took her hand between her own. Although the day was warm, the skin was dry and cool. The fingers were shrivelling to bone, a handful of fleshless twigs.

'Are you quite well?'

Old Auntie shrugged. 'At my age,' she said, 'there is only dead and alive. Not well.'

She closed her eyes again and seemed to drift away. Jamila stroked the back of the papery hand. The blood,

60

sluggish, disappeared from the vein where she touched it, then crept slowly back.

'Fetch me water. My mouth is dry.'

Jamila went into the house where Old Auntie's grand-daughter-in-law was cooking. Her stout baby was crawling on the floor beside her.

'They won't let us fetch water from the well,' the young woman said, as Jamila filled a metal cup. 'Only the boys can go.'

Jamila shook her head. The baby lifted its head to stare at her.

'I wouldn't mind but they spill half of it. You know what boys are.'

Outside, Jamila held the cup to Old Auntie's lips and waited as she sipped. The water seeped from the corners of her mouth and ran down her chin. When she had finished, Jamila wiped off Old Auntie's mouth.

'When I was a child, my grandmother used to tell me stories,' Auntie said. 'Such good old stories, they were shiny and worn with telling. They were told by grandmother to granddaughter through a hundred generations. Did I tell you the story about the donkey?'

She started the story, then closed her eyes and Jamila leant forwards, scanning her face. She seemed to be swallowing hard. After a moment, she opened her eyes and looked up at Jamila with a vague, troubled look.

'Your story,' Jamila prompted. 'About the donkey. You should tell it to the children.' She'd heard it herself a hundred times before.

'Those children, they have no time to listen. No time and no patience and no respect.'

She sat still for a moment, staring into the empty air. Jamila got to her feet and patted her shoulder. The sun was sinking rapidly now, coating the courtyard in its red, sticky light. 'I'm tiring you,' she said. 'I should go.'

She took the cup back into the house and said goodbye to the girl who had lifted the baby onto her hip and was dandling him as she stirred the pot.

Outside, Old Auntie reached for her as she passed. She pulled her down and put her damp mouth against Jamila's ear.

'When I die, bury me with my brother and his wife. I don't want to be in the ground alone. The darkness makes me afraid.'

'Hush, Auntie.' Jamila shook her head and tried to free herself. 'No such talk of dying and burying.'

'It's a big enough grave,' Old Auntie went on. 'If he were here, he'd say yes. He was a good brother to me.'

Jamila loosened the old woman's fingers and arranged the blanket more closely around her thin shoulders before she left.

She found Ibrahim on the charpoy outside their house, trying to read in the last flicker of daylight. His body was bent over, his spectacles low against the book. She stood for a moment, observing him. He looked paler than ever, as if life were steadily washing the colour out of him. He was deep in his book and didn't stir.

She tutted. He was all book learning. It had seemed a blessing at first, that she'd married such a gentle man. He wanted to teach her to read when they were newly-weds but she had refused. No woman in her family read books.

She remembered the day she had first set eyes on him when he and his father came to visit her parents in the family compound to discuss the arrangements for marriage. They had brought gifts of boxes of rich sweetmeats and a parcel of white lace, picked out by his mother. She, still a girl, had hidden in the kitchen, straining to hear the murmur of conversation between the men. It was only when the visitors said farewell and got up to leave that she dared to look through the kitchen window and saw him crossing the yard, a thin, bookish boy.

However much money his baba might have, she thought, staring in disappointment, it won't be enough to make up for having such a weak, girlish husband. Why is the older brother already taken? Why do I get this one? She was still pouting when he reached the gate.

Her father went to scatter the chickens to the side and unfasten the bolt and the boy turned and looked back, right into her watching face. He broke into a broad smile and she, seeing the look in his eyes, thought, Well, that is the kindest face I ever saw, he will do very nicely for me after all, and went quickly into the sitting room to admire with her mother the quality of the white lace and eat her share of the sweetmeats before her brothers finished them all.

Now, so many years later, she folded away the burqa and sat beside him on the cot. She lifted the book out of his hands, closed it and set it on the ground. He looked up.

'Old Auntie told me one of her old stories. The one about the donkey.'

'The donkey?'

'Who tries to change his shape and ends up forgetting who he is.'

'Ah.' He took off his spectacles and rubbed them against his kameez. His watery eyes gleamed in the half-light. 'That is called an allegory.'

He replaced his glasses. She knew what he wanted. He wanted her to say: Please, my clever husband, what is an allegory? Instead she frowned. 'It's a warning, that's what it is.'

'Did her grandmother really tell her these stories?' he said. 'Or does she just make them up?'

'What does it matter?' she said. 'It doesn't matter about the story, about the donkey. It matters about us. What are we going to do?'

He shook his head sadly and looked at the ground.

'It won't end here.' She counted off the problems these strangers had caused. 'First they stop the music, the barber. Then they shut women in their compounds. They call away the young men and give them guns.'

'Hush, lower your voice.' Ibrahim looked around the courtyard.

'In my own house? What nonsense. You men sit together, whispering like frightened girls. They will drive us off our land. Don't you see? They will take everything.' She was shaking and close to tears.

Ibrahim rubbed his hands down his cheeks. 'There are too many of them.'

She reached for him in the darkness and grasped his arm. 'What must they do to us, what crime so terrible, that you'll finally do something?'

He didn't reply. Jamila's brother-in-law, Hamid, came

out of his house and lowered himself onto a charpoy on the other side of the courtyard.

She sat with her hand on her husband's arm.

'You must go and get help,' she said. 'You must fight for what is ours by right.'

Ibrahim turned away from her.

Across the courtyard, Hamid struck a match. It flared at his face, lighting his cupped hand and the cigarette between his lips, until the match died and the end of the cigarette pulsed red.

They won't stop, she thought. You men are blind if you can't see it.

Jamila had wondered what it would take for Ibrahim to act. Her question was answered when the fighters destroyed his beloved school. He left the village at once, his beard singed and his hands raw with burns, to seek help in the valley.

8

Ellen sat at the overcrowded desk in the small office at the back of the women's ward and looked over her notes. Britta had already given her a lot of information; the first deaths from typhoid and the threat of more. That was vivid and a strong top line. She had general detail too, about eye infections, skin diseases and the chronic malnourishment that seemed to affect most of the women who'd fled from the mountains. She underlined one of Britta's quotes. Behind her, a fly was buzzing, banging against the inside of the tent.

It was a start but it wasn't much. She needed drama. She needed personal stories. First-hand accounts of life under the Taliban and the terrifying flight. Ellen clicked the end of her pen in and out with her thumb. She was weighed down by the dull ache in her limbs, her bruised face. It was almost one o'clock. The sun was fierce, beating down on the canvas around her and setting it alight with a white glow. The air-conditioning unit hummed and coughed in the corner but the air inside was stale and thick with heat.

Fatima came through from the ward and started slightly when she saw Ellen. Britta had been called away to a staff emergency meeting organized by Frank. For now, if Ellen needed help, she was reliant on Fatima. She didn't have high hopes.

Fatima took a plastic box out of the fridge and set it on the table. She gave Ellen a quick, tense glance. 'You have got lunch?'

'Actually, I have. Thank you.' The Islamabad guesthouse staff had handed her a packed lunch when she checked out. That seemed a long time ago. She dug the battered cardboard box out of her bag and opened it up. It didn't look appetizing. Cold French fries in a clutch of silver foil, a sliced cucumber and tomato in another piece of foil, a hard-boiled egg, a peach and a plum.

Fatima didn't reply. She seemed pleased that she wasn't obliged to feed Ellen. She pulled up a stool and sat down at the desk, clearing a space amongst the papers and files. She unclipped the lid of her lunch box and drew out a plastic spoon, a cheap white serviette and a small pink carton. Rose-flavoured milk, the packet read. Most delicious.

Fatima used the serviette to polish the spoon, then unfolded it completely and placed it over her lap. The paper was so thin it was almost transparent. The lunch box was full of cold fried rice and vegetables. The leftovers, Ellen thought, from last night's meal.

The shy local assistant, all elbows and knees, brought them both sweet milky tea in chipped enamel cups and then withdrew. Ellen sensed that it was a well-rehearsed routine. The breeze from the ceiling fan rippled the surface of the tea and thickened it into skin.

Ellen banged her hard-boiled egg against the table edge so she could shell it. The pungent smell rose.

'Fatima, I need to hire a translator. I'd pay, of course. I wondered, is there anyone . . .?'

'Speaking Pashto and also English?' Fatima shrugged, spooning her lunch into her mouth with deft movements. She spoke as she ate, her free hand politely shielding her mouth. 'That is difficult matter.'

'Yes, but even so, there must be . . .'

'No.' Fatima lifted her hand to bat away the fly.

There was a short silence. Ellen ate the pieces of salad and chewed a few cold French fries. They were streaky with congealed fat. Fatima's brown eyes were fixed on her food. She was frowning slightly, her thick eyebrows almost merging over her nose. Her hijab was immaculately pinned, covering her hair completely. She's a long way from Egypt, Ellen thought, watching her. A long way from home.

A high-pitched mechanical jingle sounded outside as a truck reversed. Male shouts. A blaring horn. The rhythmical bang of a fist on metal, guiding the driver backwards.

'For how many days you will be here?' Fatima spoke through her food, without looking up.

'I don't know yet. Three or four.'

'You're staying in which place?'

'They've booked me into The Swan.'

'Of course. It is the best.' She lifted her eyes for a second

68

and gave Ellen a short, hard glance, as if to add: And the most expensive.

'What about you?'

Fatima snorted slightly. 'I am on local contract. I stay in a small guesthouse in Peshawar.' She raised her spoon and pointed to her hijab. 'I am Muslim lady. It is more safe here for me.'

Ellen didn't reply. She chewed the last of her hard-boiled egg and wrapped the foil around the remaining cold fries. Fatima was trying hard to save face. But Ellen knew that anyone who worked with Westerners was a target, whether they were Muslim or not. If she was in a small guesthouse, it was simply to save money.

'All your family is at home then, in Egypt?'

'Cairo.' Fatima scraped up another mouthful of food and chewed.

'Are you married?'

'I am widow. My husband is died. I have two babies.'

Ellen nodded, sensing an opening at last. 'Boys or girls?'

Fatima inclined her head, still eating. 'One is boy, one is girl.'

'That's wonderful, Fatima. How old are they?'

Fatima paused for a moment, as if considering the turn the conversation was taking. A stray grain of rice stuck to the corner of her lips. The tip of her tongue slid out and drew it into her mouth. She looked over to Ellen for a second and her eyes were uncertain. Finally, she set down her spoon, cleaned her fingers carefully on her napkin and reached down into her bag to bring out a purse. She extracted two small photographs and pushed them across the table.

They were school pictures, posed against a bright blue background. Ellen wiped her own fingers on a tissue and picked them up. One showed a girl of about eight or nine with a large nose, her hair neatly clipped in place. The other was a boy of about five, his brown eyes shy in front of the camera. His black hair was cropped close.

'You must be very proud.'

Fatima broke into a smile. For a moment, her whole face was transformed, warm and relaxed. Then she straightened out her mouth again and the old stiffness returned.

When Ellen handed back the pictures, Fatima held them for a while and carried on studying them. 'They are good children. They learn well, thanks be to God.' She studied them a moment longer, then slipped them back into her purse.

Ellen bit into the peach. 'You must miss them.'

'They are with my sister. They are very obedient. I earn enough money to send them to a good school.'

'That's important.'

Fatima wiped off her spoon, placed it back in the plastic box and clipped on the lid. There was still rice inside. Enough for her evening meal, perhaps.

'And you?' said Fatima. 'You have children?'

'No.' Ellen found herself looking down, wiping peach juice from her chin, aware of Fatima's eyes. She thought of Frank with his crumpled clothes and tousled hair. 'I'm not married.'

Fatima scraped back her stool and got to her feet. 'Work.' The plastic spoon rattled in the box as she placed it back in the fridge. As she passed Ellen again, on her way back to the ward, she stooped and said in a low voice: 'I advise you to be careful. The Taliban has spying men everywhere.'

Without a translator, there wasn't much more Ellen could do on the ward. She pulled her scarf forwards, tucked away stray strands of hair, and set off into the camp.

Outside, a fresh truck of supplies was being unloaded. Powdered milk for babies. High-protein biscuits. A group of men in shiny tabards had formed a chain, passing boxes from one to the other, grunting with exertion.

She walked through to an open area beyond the unloading bay. A few listless guards in baggy uniforms were standing around, guns held loosely across their chests. Pakistani aid workers were sitting in lines on the ground, processing the stacks of newly arrived supplies. She wrote some notes. The men were shaking the contents out into a heap on the earth, then rummaging through them and sorting them into piles for distribution.

A second cluster of workers was compiling starter kits, one for each family. A set of basic commodities, designed to feed five people for several days. Ellen bent down to see. Small tins of cooking oil. Bags of salt. Modest sacks of rice. Plastic screw-top containers for water. Vacuum-packed blankets. She weighed the rice in her hand. The rations seemed so meagre, barely enough to live on. If people felt they were starving, she thought, it would be hard to keep order in the camp. Hard to protect the weak. She thought of the listless elderly woman waiting outside the gates and the small girl lying motionless in her lap.

Further away, penned in by a rope and under the supervision of several armed guards, were about fifty dishevelled people. The men and women were queuing separately, the women with children balanced on hips and clinging to their trailing hands. They stood in silence without shade from the sun, waiting in the hope that some sort of distribution would eventually begin. Their faces were blank with resignation, their shoulders bowed. These were people who were already becoming accustomed to waiting for a long time in the hope of a little.

The Pakistani supervisor saw her watching and stepped across. He was a short man with glasses, plump with health and affluence. His clothes were neatly pressed and his trainers gleamed white in the dust.

He looked down at her notebook and pen. 'Madam, you are journalist?'

'How did you guess?'

'On account of your pen and writing and the fact you are a Western lady here.' His voice was theatrical and without irony. 'Our camp is providing each and every thing.' He waved a hand over the supplies. 'Not only eatables. All things – necessities for the family.'

He was smiling through crowded, crooked teeth. A man itching to be interviewed.

'Ellen Thomas, *News World*.' She managed to smile back. 'You're doing such good work here. It must be very difficult.'

'Madam, it is so difficult.' He puffed out his chest. 'We are working, all of the day and night also.'

Ellen nodded sympathetically. 'Are the workers local people?'

'Most are local, yes, madam. From Peshawar itself.'

Her camera was in a side pocket of her bag. He made

72

an elaborate show of modesty when she brought it out, flapping his hand in front of his face as if he were not worthy. 'Please, madam. I am doing my duty. That is all.'

'Would you mind? I'd love a picture.' She framed it with her open hand. 'With the workers in the background.'

He wagged his head, turning pink with pleasure. The guards standing near him turned to gawp. He picked up a sack of rice and a blanket sealed in polythene and posed with them in his hands, adopting a sad but thoughtful expression for the photographs. She wrote down his name, title and email address and promised to send him a copy.

By now he was overwhelmed with pride. 'When life goes out of gear,' he said, 'here all the people can find succour. Until and unless normalcy is restored.'

She thanked him again, thinking, You'd never let your own family end up here. You're too well connected.

As she turned to go, she hesitated and turned back as if she'd just remembered something. 'I don't suppose you could possibly help me.'

He beamed. 'Anything, madam.' He pointed down at the supplies. 'Some eatables, maybe?'

'Actually, I need someone to help me translate.'

His eyes lost a little of their sparkle.

'Just for an hour or so,' she went on. 'If it's not too much trouble.'

He clapped his hands and shouted to a thin young man who was standing with a clipboard, ticking off boxes as they were processed. He came scuttling across, his eyes anxious. His boss laid a paternal hand on his shoulder.

'Ali will be helping you, nah? He's very good fellow.'

She handed Ali a bottle of water from her bag and opened a second for herself. The heat was intense. The sun was beating on the dried mud, splitting into white shards wherever it struck glass or plastic.

Ali explained the layout of the camp. She tried to draw a diagram in her notebook as they walked, to get her bearings. The main facilities were clustered close to the gates. The brick building with the broken flagpole was the administration block and storeroom. That must be where Frank was holding his meeting. Beside it stood the two large tents that served as segregated male and female medical wards, and a third that doubled up as shelter and office space for the aid workers. Nearby was the mud circle of the unloading bay, large enough for the trucks, with their brightly painted metalwork, to reverse and turn.

The rest of the camp was low and sprawling, a formless expanse of row upon row of shelters stretching across the open landscape, dwarfed by the distant mountains. Those erected in the rows nearest the gate were proper tents; large sheets of off-white canvas, stretched over a central wooden spine, then swooped low to the ground on either side. They made her think of a child's drawing of birds in flight.

One tent was open at the front, the flaps tied back to let air circulate. A heavy, rusting bicycle was propped on one side. Two chickens, tethered to a stick, pecked at the dirt. Several pairs of tattered shoes, big and small, were piled nearby.

Ellen looked into the gloom. A young man was lying listlessly on a low wooden bed. The charpoy was the only piece of furniture in there and dominated the space. The sunlight pressed through the canvas, dappled on his body. Two young children were heaped against him, sleeping. A pair of eyes glinted. She looked more closely. A young woman, the wife, was sitting to one side in the shadows, her shoulders hunched.

'Could we speak to these people?' she asked Ali.

He looked embarrassed. 'They are from a village,' he said. 'I don't think so . . . that they'll allow it.'

Ellen crouched down and smiled at the woman. She gazed cautiously back.

'It'll be OK,' she said over her shoulder to Ali. 'Would you ask this lady—'

But Ali had already moved on. Ellen was beginning to wonder if he'd had any personal contact at all with the people he was helping to feed. She got to her feet again and followed him down the narrow paths that ran between the rows of tents.

The smells of sewerage, unwashed bodies and sweating plastic stirred so many memories. People were endlessly different but there was a dreary uniformity about relief camps that always depressed her. The overcrowded shelters. The squalor. The endless queues of people, patiently waiting for handouts in the misery of heat or rain.

It was more than a decade since she'd first covered a refugee crisis. That was in East Timor. Tens of thousands of people had fled fighting and were huddled inside camps, too frightened of the Indonesian militias to go home. It had been one of her first big stories.

Tension had still been high. She'd driven into the camps with an older journalist. Both of them wanted eyewitness accounts of the recent violence. It had been a new experience for her and an intense one. The poor conditions, the threatening young men wielding guns, the families, cowed and afraid, desperate for food and clean water. She'd felt like a champion of the people, filing impassioned reports to London and railing against her editors when the pieces she'd filed were hacked down.

'Three hundred words.' She was outraged. 'That's all they used. Can you believe these guys?'

Her fellow journalist, more cynical, had laughed. 'War's like sex,' he said. 'The first time, it seems like a big deal. Then you get over it.'

She looked around now at the camp. Two young girls with matted hair were rolling together on the ground, shrieking and tickling each other. A toddler sat beside them in the dust. He had the severed arm of a doll in his hand and was sucking on its plastic fingers. His nostrils were black with a moustache of flies.

Her colleague all those years ago had been wrong. She still cared. She would force London to pay attention to what was happening here. That was her job. Frank was feeding them and giving them clean water. The least she could do was write about them. But to make an impact, she needed stronger material.

Her clothes were sticking to her back, her arms, her neck and the cut above her eye was throbbing. She lifted the bottle of water to her lips and drank, then stood, thinking, and inhaled the faint smell of plastic. Two young boys careered onto the path from between the tents. They skidded to a sudden halt when they saw her. Their clothes were filthy, mouths and noses encrusted with dirt. They turned, their eyes following her uncertainly as she walked on, looking for Ali.

The further she moved from the entrance gates, the poorer the shelters became. The off-white canvas soon ran out and was replaced by makeshift structures made from salvage and imagination. Faded grain sacks, torn open, were tied with twine around knobbly sticks. Torn sheets of plastic sweated in the heat. Pieces of brown cardboard, which had clearly once been aid boxes, had been bent around to form screens from the sun.

Smoke was rising. She walked towards it. Three women were crouched together on their haunches outside a shelter. A grandmother and two daughters-in-law perhaps. They'd built a small fire inside a triangle of mud bricks. One of the daughters was poking it with a stick. A battered metal kettle was perched on top and a row of tin cups stood by, waiting. The grandmother had a fan, stiffly plaited straw nailed to a rounded stick. She was fanning herself energetically to keep off clouds of flies.

The young woman who was tending the fire lowered her head and blew on it, scattering sparks. There was a sickly stench. Ellen looked around. The women were just by a row of latrines. The toilets were simple wood frames, raised a foot or so off the ground on bricks and nailed around with hessian for privacy. It was clear where the women had found bricks for their fire.

The grandmother saw Ellen and lifted a hand to greet her. She said something in Pashto and laughed and three isolated, stained teeth showed in her mouth. Ellen put her hand on her heart: *Salaam Alaikum.*

The old lady patted the ground beside her. A daughter

shuffled along to make a place. When Ellen sat down, the grandmother fanned her with such enthusiasm that droplets of sweat flew off her arm, speckling Ellen's shoulders and neck.

The kettle rocked as it boiled. The daughter wrapped the end of her chador around her hand and poured out sugary milky tea. Ellen took the plum from her bag and broke it into pieces, coating her fingers in juice. The flesh was mushy and heady with sweetness and they sucked on it noisily, smiling around at each other. When she lifted her fingers to her nose, the rich smell of the plum juice blocked out everything else.

She was sitting there amongst the women, drinking tea, when Ali found her. He walked right past at first, then did a double take and stopped dead. He looked so shocked at the sight of her, tucked in with the village women, that she had to bite her lip to stop herself from laughing. It was pointless, she could tell at once, to ask him to join them and translate. From now on, she would have to fend for herself.

Later, she started back through the camp on her own. The aid trucks were just coming into view when she heard a noise, a stifled cry, off to one side between the rows of tents. She turned to look. A thin figure. A man. Leaning against a wooden strut down the back of a shelter. He was bowed as if in pain. His shoulders were trembling, his face low and hidden in his hands.

She stepped off the main path and approached him cautiously.

'*Ab caisse hai*?' How are you?

78

He stiffened but didn't reply. He was wearing a salwar kameez that might once have been cream but was now streaked grey with dirt. A round tribal hat was tipped forwards on his head.

She tried again, a little louder: '*Ab tik hai*?' Are you OK?

He raised his head. His face was long and thin and lined with anxiety. His pointed beard was almost entirely white. Thin wire spectacles sat on the bridge of a pinched nose. They were lopsided, their spindly arms hooked around his ears. His myopic eyes, light in colour, were watery and anguished.

She stepped closer. 'Do you speak English?'

He squirmed, embarrassed, and turned away.

She groped for the right words: '*Ab English bol suk—*'

He turned back to her and interrupted, with a hint of defiance: 'I know English.'

Her eyes fell to his hands, which were sticking out from the sleeves of his shabby kameez. They were raw with burns. The flesh was bloated and blistered, scored through with pink creases. 'You need a doctor.' She pointed to them. 'Let me have a look.'

'You are doctor?' He looked at her with suspicion.

'I'm a journalist. My name is Ellen. I can take you to a doctor.'

He shook his head and sighed. He held up his damaged hands and considered them with sad detachment, as if they belonged to another man.

'Madam,' he said at last, 'this is not important.' He lifted off his spectacles with slow, clumsy fingers and wiped his wet eyes on his sleeve.

When he'd replaced his spectacles, he turned his shoulder and she sensed that he was about to walk away. She moved closer at once. He mustn't. This was the first refugee she'd found who had some English. There couldn't be many here. She spoke in a rush, trying to use her questions to pin him in place.

'Tell me. Please. Have you just arrived? Where did you come from? What happened to you?'

He drew himself to his full height. 'I am schoolteacher. My name is Ibrahim. I hail from the mountains. From Mutaire.'

'Ibrahim.' She bowed her head to show respect. His pale eyes seemed utterly exhausted. In a camp bursting with large families, he seemed, like her, to be all alone. She reached out and handed him her bottle of water. He drank it, shyly at first, then urgently. There was a narrow strip of shade running along the edge of the shelters. She sat down in it, practically at his feet, and raised her face to him. 'If you talk to me,' she said, 'maybe I can help.'

A shift in the light made her look past him. A young man had stopped on the path and was watching them both. He was a broad-shouldered teenager with a downy beard. She expected him to move on when she stared pointedly back. He didn't. He stood his ground. She pulled her headscarf forwards to conceal her hair and forehead. When she looked again, he had disappeared.

Ibrahim had decided to trust her. He lowered himself and sat a small distance away. He crossed his legs under his long kameez and stared at the mud.

'So Ibrahim-ji,' she said. 'Tell me.'

When his words finally started to flow, they came out

in a torrent, only just intelligible. 'My family. My daughters. My old daughter, she cannot walk. How can they come down from the mountain? But so much fighting is there. That's what they say. The army. The Taliban also.'

He put his head in his hands and his shoulders shook. Ellen leant forwards. 'Hush,' she said. 'Ibrahim. Let me help you.'

Finally he became quiet and blew his nose noisily on his kameez. Behind his spectacles, his eyes were red rimmed.

She listened to the soft gulp of his breathing, the rattle of moisture in his throat. 'What happened in your village, Ibrahim?'

'Mutaire is high in the mountains,' he said, 'part of the Valley District. Two days' walk from here.'

His knees trembled as he spoke, making their cotton tent judder. 'They came some time ago and everything changed.'

'Who came?'

'Them,' he said again. When he raised his eyes, they seemed angry. 'The Taliban. Their commander, he is named Mohammed Bul Gourn.'

'How did things change?'

He shook his head. 'Every day, they were holding religious courts. Accusing some fellow with cut beard. Some fellow who was listening to music.' He lowered his voice to a whisper, forcing her to lean in close to him. 'All night we heard screams.' He paused to remember. 'In the morning we woke to find bodies. Our own people.' His face contorted with horror. 'Hanged, sometimes. Or beheaded. The stones all around red and sticky with blood.'

He sat in silence for a moment. Ellen prompted him softly, 'And then what happened?'

'All this we suffered and did nothing,' he said. 'But then they burnt down the school. My school.' He looked her full in the face, outraged. 'Fifteen years I am teaching there. Young men in our village who can read and write and do sums, I am the man who taught them.

'Late in the night, I heard fire. I ran through the darkness of the village towards the school. The classroom was already blazing. I ran inside. The door was ringed in red with fire. The paint was burning on the wood, flames were curling through the air towards me. When I pulled at the handle, it was so hot, my skin stuck to the metal. The whole door fell on top of me. I couldn't breathe. I just grabbed as many books as I could, carrying them outside, rushing, rushing.'

He put his burnt hand to his face. 'The cleaner's boy found me. Lying on the grass. The school was finished.'

She imagined the school blazing in the pitch darkness and the angry schoolteacher risking his life for books. 'Is that why you left?'

'I came to Peshawar to get help. To beg the army to come to the valley to save our families and our village.'

'And you came here, to the camp?'

He tutted. 'Not at first. I went to many places for many days, trying to get help. To the army cantonments. To the mosques. To the police stations. Finally I saw one police captain. He told me the soldiers are already going to fight. Bombs are dropping. Everyone is fleeing.' His face crumpled again and he gave a shuddering breath, composing himself. 'Everyone is leaving. That's what they are saying.

Carrying whatsoever they can. Every brother and uncle and cousin is there in the selfsame boat. Women and children also.' He gestured around at the camp. His face was sorrowful. 'But my daughters? My wives? They have not left the valley once in their lives. It is not our custom.'

Ellen calculated. 'Where do you think they are?'

'I don't know.' He gave a shrug of despair. 'I heard about these new camps for affectees. Now I am searching, walking one to another. Searching everywhere in case they come.'

Ellen reached towards him, and put her hand on his shoulder. 'Maybe I can help, Ibrahim. There must be registers at the camps. We'll find your family.'

He opened his mouth to speak but his lips trembled and he clamped it shut and sat, his mouth in a rigid line, his hand clutching her arm with the grip of a falling man.

9

Ellen gathered with the international staff at the entrance to the camp. It was early evening. The sunlight was rich and deep. A breeze was blowing unimpeded across the desolate mudflats, fingering the canvas tents and making the edges of plastic sheets flutter. It carried the smell of wood smoke and boiled rice. Families of refugees gathered around low fires and pots, taking their last chance to eat before night plunged the camp into darkness. Outside the entrance, a long desolate trail of families was still in the open, huddled together around bags and belongings, waiting for permission to enter the camp.

A convoy of jeeps arrived, trailing clouds of dust, and the workers piled inside. There was no sign of Frank. Ellen found herself squashed in the back with two Belgians and a Norwegian who spent the journey to the hotel arguing about where to dine that evening. The Chinese restaurant was not good, the Norwegian said; the soup was salty and the noodles were greasy. One of the Belgians had tried the

Italian restaurant. He wouldn't go there again. Pizza, he said, how can anyone go wrong with pizza? What do you need? Dough, tomatoes, a bit of cheese. What's so difficult? Show him the kitchen, he'd make it himself. The others laughed.

Ellen let the conversation swirl around her. She was thinking about Ibrahim. He had a blanket now and a space inside a communal shelter, just until he found his family. A young aid worker had treated his hands with antiseptic cream and said the burns weren't severe, they should soon heal.

The driver blasted the horn as he swerved past slower, lower cars and forced young men, perched on motorbikes, to bounce off the dirt track completely and loop out into the scrub.

If she managed to track down Ibrahim's family, it might make a good piece. It was a human interest angle, a way of getting into the broader refugee crisis. She thought of his wire spectacles and sad eyes. His family could be anywhere. She gripped the roof strap as the car swung off the road.

They'd reached the entrance to The Swan. She'd stayed there before but not for years. Now it was so heavily fortified, she barely recognized it. She peered out at the rows of concrete blast blocks in front of the gates. A reminder of the threat of suicide bombers, she thought. A constant danger now. An armed guard in a badly fitting uniform rapped on the driver's window, forced him to lower it, then peered around the inside of the jeep. The Belgian next to her stiffened. He muttered something to the Norwegian under his breath.

She looked ahead down the sweeping drive to the hotel itself, a faux French chateau. It was shabbier than she remembered. The stone fountain had run dry, its statues speckled with patches of black and green.

A younger guard, his cap pitched down over his eyes, walked around the jeep with a mirror attached to the bottom of a pole, angling it to check underneath the vehicle's bodywork for bombs. She wondered how much training they'd had and if they'd recognize a bomb if they saw one. They looked like village boys.

When she finally managed to check in and find her room, she stood under a hot shower for a long time. The cascade of water streamed through her hair and splashed down her body. The tiny bar of hotel soap, the shape of a shell, worked up a good lather. The shampoo was fragrant with jasmine. She closed her eyes and tried not to think about Ibrahim and the others in the camp. The foaming water circled her feet in swirls, then ran off between her toes. She stepped out and groped through the steam for a towel. It was thick and warm.

Afterwards she took a piece of fruit from the complimentary bowl on the coffee table and boiled the kettle for tea. The guilt was familiar. I'm not here to be a refugee, she told herself as she rubbed herself dry and put on a hotel bathrobe. I'm here to report.

She lay on her stomach on one of the twin beds, reached for the television remote and started flicking through the channels. She wondered where Frank was and what time he'd be back. She wanted to talk to him about Ibrahim, to ask his help.

The first three channels were in Urdu: a news broadcast

with film of the United Nations; a cartoon; a badly acted soap opera. She could invite Frank to dinner. Her treat. One of the hotel restaurants. Easier and safer than venturing outside.

She found CNN. A panel discussion about the war on drugs. She listened for a minute or two, trying to identify the speakers. Frank must be busy. He'd said they were overwhelmed. She hadn't seen him since they'd arrived at the camp. She clicked through several sports channels and found HBO. A teen film. Preppy American girls leaning against their lockers in a high-school corridor, giggling together. Maybe Frank wouldn't feel like meeting up. She'd better leave it. She switched off the set and went to type notes into her laptop about Ibrahim and the never-ending human exodus.

By eight o'clock, she was hungry. She rang down to reception and asked them to put her through to Frank's room. No answer. She powered down her laptop, realizing she felt disappointed, she'd been looking forward to seeing him.

She headed downstairs. It had once been an imposing lobby but now the fake marble floor was scuffed and cracked. A long reception desk ran down one wall. A glamorous young Pakistani woman was lolling with her elbows on the counter, reading a magazine. Above her, a row of brass-rimmed clocks showed the time in Beijing, Paris, London and New York. Nearby there was a faded marble water feature. A polished ball slowly turned, veiled by a constant curtain of water.

Ellen headed towards the far side of the lobby. An informal dining area had been set out there, carpeted and bordered by a low artificial fence that was threaded with plastic creepers. She chose a table that gave her a good view of the main entrance and ordered a club sandwich and an orange juice.

Most of the tables were empty and the atmosphere was hushed. A compilation of bastardized Western pop was playing, just loud enough to take the edge off the silence. An orchestral version of 'Yesterday' flowed over her as she opened her notebook and looked at her rough diagram of the camp.

A few minutes later, Britta came striding in through the main entrance. Her face was strained as she headed for the lifts.

'Britta!' Ellen waved her over. She closed her notebook and set it on the table. 'Come and join me.'

Britta flopped into a chair, dropping her bag, laptop and keys onto the table with a clatter. Her face was flecked with dust. Without her scarf, her hair fell in springy curls around her face, sticking in damp clumps to her forehead and temples. She pulled open the top button of her kameez, loosening the collar. A gold cross on a chain swung at her neck.

Britta was breathing hard. Ellen sat quietly, waiting for her to recover. Had she come straight from the camp? It looked like it. Not very safe, surely, to be there so long after dark.

The glass of orange juice arrived. Ellen peeled the paper wrapping off a straw, put it in the juice and pushed the glass towards Britta. Britta drank it off in one. Ellen ordered two more. Gradually Britta's breaths became more even. The hard line of her shoulders softened.

The two Belgians walked through the lobby, laughing and talking together. They were heading back to the lifts from the direction of the Italian restaurant. The young woman on reception lifted her head at the noise and watched as they stepped into a lift and disappeared.

'Another one.' Britta's voice shook. 'The girl you saw. Typhoid fever.'

There was a short silence. So that was why she was so late.

'I'm sorry,' Ellen said. She thought of the small hand with its bitten-down nails. She should have held it.

'I thought I'd caught her. She had high fever and severe diarrhoea but I put her straight onto antibiotics.' Britta paused, remembering. 'She started to fit. Some intestinal haemorrhage, maybe. Then she died.'

Without her scarf and in the artificial light, Britta looked younger, perhaps still in her twenties. She probably hadn't lost many patients. She hadn't been a doctor long enough.

'Two others are very ill. One teenage girl. One old woman. Both have high fever. Fatima is with them. She stays late too often.' Britta raked her hands through her hair, shook her head. 'It progresses quickly.'

The waiter came with the sandwich and two more glasses of orange juice.

'You should be careful.' Britta mimed washing her hands. 'Lots of soap, lots of scrub.'

'Do you think they're ill before they arrive?'

'I think so. There must be carriers.' Britta shrugged. 'And in these conditions . . .'

Ellen picked up a quarter of the club sandwich, a high

stack of chicken, bacon, egg and salad. Enough to feed a family. She bit into it, oozing mayonnaise.

Britta was staring into middle distance, her green eyes glassy with exhaustion. 'She just didn't respond.'

Ellen nodded. She chewed slowly, thinking. 'By the time they reach you, these women are exhausted,' she said. 'As well as traumatized. And you don't know how long they've been ill.'

Britta tutted. 'Fatima says they're afraid of the hospital. You know how rumours spread.' She sighed. 'Some woman saw the body being taken out this afternoon and caused a panic.'

Ellen pointed to the sandwich. 'You're going to have to help me out,' she said. 'There's far too much.'

Britta looked at the sandwich, then at her hands. The creases in her palms were black with dirt. 'Thank you, but I should go and wash.' She didn't move.

'Is Frank still there?'

'In the camp?' She sighed. 'I think so.' She leant forward, bracing herself to get up, then seemed to lose heart and sank back into her seat.

The lobby rang with a sudden burst of music, a brassy jazz rendition of 'New York, New York'. The handful of diners looked around as the head waiter rushed to lower the volume and the music slid again under the low hum of conversation.

'I spoke to my boss in Geneva,' Britta said. 'You know what he said? If many more people die, don't tell about it.'

'People need to know, Britta.'

'Do they?' She looked startled as if she'd only just

realized that she was confiding in a journalist. 'That big potato is coming. What's his name? The British guy.'

'Quentin Khan?'

'Yes, Mr Khan. He's very careful about his image. Too many deaths, he'll be scared away. That's what my boss says.' Britta's hand had risen to her cross and she was clasping it in her fist, tugging at it. 'We need the money. Medicine International isn't big. Frankly speaking, we had problems before this typhoid. As it is, I hardly have the money to pay for Fatima.'

'You're worn out.' Ellen looked at the tension in Britta's face. 'Go and have a hot bath. Eat something. Sleep. You've done all you can for today.'

Britta pointed to the laptop. 'I can't.' She looked close to tears. 'I have so much paperwork. Accounts. Orders.'

She pulled herself to her feet, picked up her things and murmured goodnight. Her steps to the lifts were slow and heavy.

At ten, Ellen paid the bill and went back upstairs. She was just getting ready for bed when the phone rang. The voice at the other end was playful.

'Hey, Ellie. What's up?'

She smiled at her own fuzzy reflection in the television set, a woman on the brink of middle age looking back at her with bright, amused eyes. 'I'm going to bed. It's late. How're you doing?'

He snorted. 'Just great.'

There was a pause. The phone line seemed to magnify the sound of his breathing. She thought of all the hours they used to spend on the phone together, sometimes talking, sometimes quiet. A long time ago.

'Am I coming up then? Just for a drink. No fooling around.'

'Dead right no fooling around.' She laughed. It was fun, hearing him again. 'Give me one good reason why I should say yes?'

He slowed his voice to a stagey drawl. 'I got Scotch.'

She drew back the curtains and switched off the hotel lights and they sat, side by side, looking out through the floor-to-ceiling windows across suburban Peshawar. The road alongside the hotel was a necklace of streetlights, studded with moving cars. House lights blinked randomly in the darkness. In the distance, a blue neon sign spluttered on and off. I should tape the window, she thought, in case there's a blast. That's a lot of flying glass.

The whisky was smooth and mellow. She let it roll over her tongue. It stung slightly, then slipped down her throat. The lights outside began to blur.

'So what happened?' she said.

He exhaled heavily as if he'd been punctured. 'It's a mess.' He paused. She sensed his tiredness as he let himself start to unwind. 'There's lots more people on the way. And not enough food for the ones we already got.'

'Any idea how many people?'

He shrugged. 'All we've seen is the first wave. The army's barely in the foothills.' He slipped off his sandals and crossed his legs, laying an ankle on the opposite knee and pointing the bare sole of his foot towards her. The black hairs above his ankles showed beneath the baggy bottoms of his jeans. He smelt clean, tinged with the perfume of hotel soap.

'I saw a lot of boxes arriving.'

He raised his glass to his lips, sipped. 'Not as many as there should be.'

'Well, there's always a time lag. Once news of the appeal—'

'I didn't mean that.' He was staring out into the darkness, preoccupied. She sipped at her whisky, giving him time. It burnt its way down her throat and into her stomach and spread there, warming and numbing. It wasn't easy to get alcohol here. It was a treat. 'Seems like there's a ton of stuff missing,' he said slowly. 'Tents. Sugar. Rice. You name it.'

She glanced at him. 'Missing?'

'Looks like we sprang a leak.'

She turned this over in her mind. 'Any theories?'

The question took a minute to reach him. He was far away, muffled by worry. 'It all goes through a central warehouse. Other side of Peshawar. Everything's barcoded.'

'So you can trace it?'

'I'll start spot checks tomorrow.' He sat quietly for a moment, looking dismally into his whisky. 'Some of those trucks must be taking a wrong turn.'

He was etched with anxiety. His fingers were tight around the glass, his forehead creased. It must be more than the trucks. She wondered again about his sudden departure from the UN.

'How're your folks?'

'Retired. Moved down to Florida.' He grimaced. 'Still crazy as loons.' He nodded at her hand, at the wedding ring she was wearing. 'That your mom's?'

She stared at him. 'How'd you know that?'

He didn't meet her eye. 'You said once. She'd told you

93

guys, you know, the fancy ring for your sister, that one for you.' He paused, suddenly awkward. 'I'm sorry. That she's gone.'

She looked down at the ring on her finger. She was shaken. It was so strange that he knew that. That he'd remembered after so long. 'Susan's married. She's got two girls.'

'So you're Auntie Ellie? That's pretty funny.'

He smiled and the strain fell out of his face. His eyes and skin were softened by the darkness and, for an instant, he was young again. Then he puffed out his cheeks in a long sigh and heaved himself to his feet, standing there, a dark shape against the window, looking down at her.

'Well, see you tomorrow.' He put the bottle back in its brown paper bag. She got up too and followed him to the door. 'You heard about Khan coming to the camp tomorrow? Mr Megabucks?' His breath smelt of whisky. 'Get a ride out there early. Seven at the latest. Security'll be nuts.'

Once he'd gone, she put the safety chain on the door and locked it. She was glad Khan was coming. That would give the story a kick. He had a high profile in the UK.

She rummaged in her bag for masking tape and drew a large X over the window. Housekeeping might not be pleased but she'd make it up to them.

She left the curtains open and lay in bed, watching the shadows flicker on the ceiling. Someone was running a bath. The pipes gurgled and banged, adding their music to the steady knock of the air conditioning.

It was unsettling, seeing Frank again. It stirred too many memories. She stretched her legs across the single bed. The sheets were cool and freshly starched.

She and Frank had shared a single bed when they were students. A broken one that had pitched them against each other all night, forcing them to cling to a cliff face of mattress to escape each other's elbows and knees.

She turned on her side and looked out at Peshawar through the giant tape cross.

There was a day, a spring day, when they'd walked by the Thames. Small children were pedalling past on tricycles, couples strolling, youths crashing their skateboards against concrete ramps. A duck flew long and low along the surface of the water and skimmed to a halt. Frank had been morose and she hadn't known why.

'You want to get away,' he said. They were walking hand in hand like the other couples but now suddenly unlike them. 'Don't you?'

'Don't say that.' A sudden hollowness grew in her stomach. His hand was warm and firm in hers. It was so familiar she barely felt it.

'You're gonna leave me. Aren't you?'

She twisted away to face the water. A police boat was pushing up the Thames, noisy, churning the river. 'That's not fair,' she told the boat. 'I never said—'

He dropped her hand. He turned away from her, hiding his face. She stared at the broad contours of his back. His shoulders trembled. A middle-aged man, walking smartly along the riverside pavement, made a detour to avoid them.

Frank moved sideways to a bench and sat down heavily at one end. He was still twisted away from her, one hand shielding his face, blocking her out. A young woman was sitting at the other end of the bench. She was drinking coffee from a polystyrene cup, a pram parked beside her. Her back stiffened but she didn't look around.

Ellen stood still, frozen. She stared at Frank as if he were a stranger. The young woman set her coffee cup on the ground under the bench and leant over the pram, fiddling with the baby's blanket.

She knew in a rush as she watched him, that yes, he was right, she would leave him. Life was leading her somewhere else. She didn't know why. That was simply how it was.

The young woman got to her feet and wheeled her baby away along the riverside. Frank's shoulders tensed as he gathered himself together and sat up straight and she went finally to sit beside him, waiting rather than comforting, as the two of them looked out blankly at the river.

10

After Ibrahim left to get help, the fighters fastened their fingers tighter around the throat of the village. Jamila watched the changes. Hamid, her brother-in-law, became drawn and silent. He carried guns constantly now, country-made weapons that had once belonged to his father. His eyes were red from lack of sleep.

Each day, the Uncles and cousins struggled back from the orchards with baskets of fruit: peaches and plums. The women greeted them at the gate, then sat cross-legged on the ground and sorted: some for storing, others for marketing. The men's faces were bitter. With so few labourers, much of the crop was wasted, they said, rotting on the ground. The best fruit vanished from the branches at night.

One day, one of the young cousins came running to the compound, breathless, his hair in disarray. He refused to speak until the gates were shut and locked behind him.

Soldiers were coming, he said. Into the valley. Fighting.

The women pulled their children up onto their laps.

Hamid questioned the boy. Who said this? Where was this fighting?

The boy shook. Fighters had told him, he said. He was running an errand for his father and four men had barred his way. They were rough men with thick beards and guns. They'd jostled and teased him.

'Tell your baba the soldiers are coming,' one had said. 'Tell him to get ready to fight.'

The boy's lip trembled as his fear came back to him.

Hamid sat quietly. He had a stick in his hand and was drawing in the dirt at his feet. Hamid was the oldest man in the family and the other men stared down at the squiggles and waited.

'Maybe this is not true,' he said at last. His voice was tired. 'Maybe these men are lying.'

The women looked around at each other with big eyes to see if anyone believed this.

'We'll wait and see what Allah decides.' Hamid got to his feet. The women shifted to clear a path for him, back to his own house. He has gone to pray, Jamila thought. This is not a burden he can bear alone. The men stared after him, uncertain.

That night, Jamila sat at the window for many hours, looking out across the compound. She wondered where Ibrahim was sleeping. If he were taking proper care of himself without her there. If he had enough food to eat. If his hands were healing well. If he'd found anyone in the valley who could help them. The smell of the approaching monsoon was in the air. Another week and it would break. The moon was thin but the stars were clear.

The men were sleeping, some inside, others lying in ragged heaps on the cots outside. In a corner of the yard, straw rustled with the scrabbling of a shrew or mouse. A shadow passed silently overhead. An owl was hunting.

She wondered how many other women in the valley were sitting at open windows, smelling the static in the dry air. She thought of her mother and grandmother. They had tended this land, walked these paths, plucked peaches and plums in these orchards. How could they abandon the land? They were born in the valley and buried here and had never once left it. Why would Allah in His Wisdom force them now to leave? She wiped off her face with the edge of her chador and shook her head. It was everything. It was what they were.

Somewhere out in the village, dogs were howling. An ill omen. It foretold sickness. Or death. Distantly, from somewhere far away on the valley floor, there was a deep, resonant boom. She listened hard. Thunder? It came again. Then a third time. A rhythmical, man-made noise. She drew her chador close and sat quietly, thinking of her family and listening to war creep nearer.

The next morning, Hamid and the Uncles and cousins set off to the orchards as usual. Jamila made chai and sat at her window, waiting. When the men came rushing back through the gates an hour later, she already knew why. They dropped their baskets. Plums bounced out and rolled uselessly across the dirt. The men shooed their wives inside and snatched up their youngest children.

Hamid strode into the house and threw open her bedroom door. His face was pale above his dark beard.

You have prayed for peace, she thought, and a slow slipping into old age. You thought your strong sons would lift the load from you and give you rest. That is not what Allah in His Wisdom is sending you.

She was trembling inside but she composed herself. Her chador was neatly pleated around her head and shoulders, her back straight and her face serene. 'So,' she said, 'tell me.'

His breathing was hard and thick. He and his brothers must have run all the way from the orchards. 'The soldiers are on the road. They've already reached the valley floor. We must leave.'

'All of us? The men too?'

'Of course.' He sounded short-tempered. 'Pack what you can. Then help the others.'

He banged the door behind him. She looked around the room. The heavy wooden cupboard was hand-carved, each door embellished with a single curving flower. A wedding gift. She had traced the lines of its petals a thousand times. For more than twenty years, she hadn't slept anywhere but on this cot in this small room. It had formed a soft skin around her, taking on her shape, her smell. And now she must pack and leave.

Voices came from the yard. Young wives were rushing to and fro, shouting to the children. She got to her feet and went to open the cupboard doors. If I were a man, she thought, if I had a gun, I would stay. This is our land, our soil. She lifted out a dusty canvas bag. She'd told them from the start. Crush these jihadi boys, make an example of them, before the serpent grows and becomes a monster. But no one had listened and now it was too late.

Muffled booms of explosions were rising from further down the valley, echoing around the mountainside. She packed a clean cotton salwar kameez and a wool shawl. The battered copy of the Holy Book that her father gifted her when she was a child. A fresh block of soap in its paper.

She crossed to the opposite room. Layla was stuffing fistfuls of clothes into her school bag. Her mother was hunched on her cot. Marva sat beside her, patting her shoulders.

'You can't take all that,' Jamila said.

Layla's eyes were hard with anger. 'What about Baba? If we leave, how will he find us?'

'He'll find us.' Jamila set down her own bag and pushed into the room to take control. '*Inshallah*.' She took the bag out of Layla's hands and upended it. The clothes came out slowly like lumpy dough, covering the cot and cascading to the floor.

'One set each.' She set aside the fashionable salwar kameez sets and packed two cheap ones, made from rough cotton. One for the mother and one for the girl. 'That's all there's room for.'

Layla let out a cry and grabbed at a flashy kameez with a neckline dotted with sequins. Jamila hunted around the room and added a warm shawl.

'You forgot Marva's clothes.' Layla was pouting.

Jamila shook her head. She closed the bag and forced around the zip. 'Hurry. Say goodbye. We must go.'

Outside, distantly, a boom. Another shell exploded into the hillside. Layla's hands clenched into fists at her sides, her thin body shaking.

'You don't mean . . .?' She looked at Marva, then at her mother and then back at Jamila.

'We'll leave food,' Jamila said. 'Bread and water.'

'But . . . we can't.' Layla's face was white.

Jamila shook her head. They had no donkey now. The girl couldn't walk. Ibrahim had gone. No one could carry Marva down the mountain.

Hamid appeared in the doorway. His face was flushed.

'We're ready,' Jamila said.

Layla started to sob, calling for her baba. Now her mother was crying too. The only calm person was Marva herself. She was sitting still on the cot beside her mother, her hands neatly folded.

'Have you done what you need to?' Jamila said. 'We can go?'

Hamid nodded miserably.

'Then we must leave. I'll bring the women and join you at the gates.'

She gathered food for Marva and brought it into the bedroom. A pile of rotis, left from the previous evening and covered with a damp cloth. She sprinkled on a little water to freshen it and added a basket of plums and peaches.

She moved the bags into the doorway. 'Come on.'

Layla was crying into Marva's neck while her mother looked on miserably.

'You must come,' Jamila said. 'They won't wait.'

She fastened one arm around the girl's waist and used the other to unpick Layla's hand, finger by finger, from Marva's hair. Layla was hysterical, weeping and struggling. The mother just sat, her mouth twisted and tears running down her face, refusing to help.

She struggled to move backwards, half-dragging, half-carrying the girl out of the room. Her last sight, as she forced her way through the doorway, trailing girl, bags, a pail and a metal basin, was of Marva, bolt upright on the cot, her arms by her sides and thin legs limp, watching with soft brown eyes as her family left her behind.

Hamid led the family out through the compound gates. They were caught up at once in the torrent of people flowing down the street, out of the village. Jamila hadn't left the compound for many days. The sight of so many people made her dizzy. Men were bowed down with sacks and bags. Women were crying, clutching at small children with one hand and steadying luggage on their backs with the other. Goats were bumping and jostling. They squeezed along the narrow ridge of land between the teeming people and the mud walls of the compounds.

A man tugging a laden donkey knocked into her. She pressed herself against the wall and looked back towards the top of the village. The path was a solid river of people. This is the end, she thought, the end of the life I have known here. She bit her lip and walked on.

The grounds of the mosque had been turned into a ragamuffin camp. A few scruffy young men were building a defence wall of sandbags. Beyond it, they'd dug a low system of ditches. They were unkempt youngsters with downy beards, dirty clothes and battered weapons. One heckled the crowd as it passed. 'All of you, leaving this fight today, you're no better than infidels,' he shouted. His turban was crooked on his head. 'May Allah take His revenge on the lot of you! Praise be to Allah!'

Jamila felt like slapping him. I serve Allah better than you ever will, she thought. And that's our mosque you're abusing.

She reached the road. The landscape opened up ahead of her. Far below, in the valley, the land flattened out. The river was low. Thin channels of water ran along mudflats. It was a view she knew well but it was altered. She looked more carefully. The sun was glinting on sharp metal surfaces down there. Ribbons of tanks and trucks and guns were creeping along the valley towards the mountains.

The road was solid with trudging figures, curving down the mountainside. At every junction, more families joined the exodus, fleeing hillside villages. Jamila paused, thinking. When the fighting moved higher, surely it would focus on the road.

Hamid was ahead with his slow-witted son, Adnan, at his side. Their backs were bent under the weight of their belongings. She hitched the straps of her bag more securely on her shoulder and pushed through the crowd, her pail banging against her thigh, to catch up with Hamid.

'Not this way,' she said, pointing. The road was the obvious way to come down the mountain but not the safest. 'Maybe we could cut across the fields.'

Hamid considered, then nodded. They led the family down the first goat track that left the road and headed sharply down the mountain. It was difficult terrain. They had to force their way through orchards and fields and climb down the terraces that separated them.

Every few minutes the valley shook with a dull thud or low meaty boom. The army had reached the first slopes of the hillside below. The family descended through one field after another, heading blindly along anything that led them downwards.

Jamila's breath came in bursts. Her back and face were slippery with sweat. She wiped off her forehead, when she could, with the end of her chador. The path was rugged and she had a sharp pain under her ribs. She longed to sit for a moment and recover but she hid her face and trudged on.

The wheat fields came to an end. A track led off to one side, skirting the contour of the hillside. A small compound was set in a clearing just beyond the adjoining field. Ahead the ground was rugged and fell away in a steep drop.

Hamid walked back and forth, looking for a way of getting safely down. The Aunties wiped down their children's hot faces and gave them water.

Jamila looked around. Now they'd emerged from the fields, they were on a ridge. They were too exposed. She looked back at the route they'd taken, narrowing her eyes against the sun.

'We should go back a little.' She tugged at Hamid's arm. He shook her off. 'Just to the next ridge.' She pointed, but he refused to look.

One of the Aunties cried out. A boy, a podgy three-year-old belonging to Hamid's second brother's second wife, had broken free of his mother and was running towards the compound in the clearing. He was giggling, caught up in his own adventure. His mother was running after him, panting across the uneven ground in her sandals. When she was a few yards from him and halfway to the compound, a shot rang out. A moment's shocked silence. The boy stopped.

'No.' Adnan waved his hands at the compound. 'Stop.'

The mother darted forwards and grabbed the child's arm. He struggled and cried. She slapped him hard. A second shot. Her arm fell limp. Blood flowered on her shoulder, staining the light cotton of her kameez. The child stared with bulging eyes.

The young woman's face blanched. Her strong hand flew to the wound. A third shot. The child clung to her leg and whimpered. Adnan ran towards them, scooped the boy into his arms and rushed back, pushing the woman in front of them.

Jamila ordered the men to look away. She bit the seam of the woman's chador and tore it down the weave to assess the damage.

The bullet had passed right through the shoulder. The hole where it had entered was small and neat, its rim blackened. The flesh around the hole looked almost clean. But on the other side, the bullet had created a sickening mess of tattered skin and muscle as it burst out. Blood was trailing sluggishly from the wound, settling in the hollows of her back and drying along the contours of her skin. Jamila swallowed hard and tried to keep her expression neutral.

'Move your hand.'

The woman grasped the air and unclasped her hand again. Good.

'You're fine.' Jamila thought of the journey ahead. They had to keep moving. 'Don't make a fuss.'

One of the other women rolled her eyes. But it was the

only way. Either this woman believed she could make it and kept walking or they left her behind. Jamila pushed a pad of cotton into the large wound and bound it tightly with the torn chador. She bent the young woman's arm at the elbow and secured it. Her fingers poked out, limp and useless, at her neck. They moved off again, skirting the drop.

For hours, they walked and stumbled. No one spoke. The only sound in Jamila's ears was her own thick breathing, the thud of footsteps and the dull boom of artillery. Mortars, shells and volleys of automatic gunshot. It seemed to surround them, growing steadily louder as they neared the fighting.

By afternoon, they reached the valley bottom. Here the ground was open. They made lengthy detours to avoid the villages, afraid of compounds and the people who might be hiding inside them. The sky had thickened. Clouds cast dark shadows on the ground, hanging over them like vultures. The soles of Jamila's feet were scratched and bruised. Her sandals sawed the skin between her toes. The pain in her side had become a constant ache. In the valley, the heat was cloying.

The military machinery constantly rumbled past them. Jeeps with open backs, packed with young soldiers in fatigues. The troops looked wary, suspecting everything and everyone. Jamila thought of the bearded young men in their bunkers in the mountain villages, waiting to fight them.

As the daylight faded, they followed the river. The mountains were steadily shrinking to foothills as they entered the plains. At night, they huddled together in a wheat field. The children whimpered for food. The adults lay silent. The darkness was deep.

The young woman with the wounded shoulder was clammy with fever. Adnan took the pail and fetched water from a stream. Jamila soaked her chador and squeezed water into the woman's mouth.

Nearby Layla was crying. She and her mother were huddled together, holding themselves apart. Jamila had felt the girl's anger stabbing at her all day. She didn't need to ask why. She was grieving for her sister.

The wheat stalks were brittle. They pricked Jamila's skin through her clothes as she sat, her legs drawn up under her, full of terror. She was born in this valley and had never left it. This road was drawing her out of the mountains and away from everything she knew. She turned her back on the plains and looked towards home. The crags were raw and beautiful against the sky. The slopes seemed to bend towards her, stretching out their arms to grasp her and pull her home.

There was a camp. A place with food and shelter and safety. Everyone on the road spoke of it.

'Just a few more miles,' Jamila told the Aunties. 'We'll be there by noon.'

The young children were weak and listless now. They barely managed to stay on their feet. The young woman, whose shoulder wound was still oozing blood, was faint with fever.

On this second day, the river path widened to a road. All around them, families, as large and exhausted as their own, were tramping onwards, making their way out of the mountains. A few had carts, piled with belongings. Most had only the things they could carry. It was a ragged column of women, children and the elderly. No one spoke of the missing men.

The progress of this thickening band of people was slow. Jamila pitied the small groups forced to a halt at the roadside, who sat in the dust with their belongings. Some nursed babies. Others tended the sick. They watched with wide, anxious eyes as the crowd moved past without them.

Adnan had disappeared in the night. Jamila only noticed when she saw Hamid, his father. The boy had been with them when they all settled down to sleep. She remembered. Now there was no sign of him. Hamid didn't speak of it but his face was pinched and he carried twice as big a load.

The low hills gave little shade. The sun cooked Jamila's hands and face until the skin was raw. One by one, the smallest children staggered and fell and the Uncles strapped them on their backs. Displaced belongings were added to the women's loads. Other bags and sacks were simply abandoned, making a ragged trail along the side of the road.

The light started to fail. Their second day was ending. The clouds were shot through with streaks of gold and pink as the sun set. Jamila caught the whisper that rushed through the column of people like a breeze through dry wheat. The camp, it said. Not far to go.

Fresh hope. Jamila was exhausted but she pressed the Aunties to keep moving, beating them with the idea of the camp. If we hurry, she said, we might make it by nightfall.

The pace quickened. For an hour or two, they walked eagerly. Then they started to despair. Darkness set in. Toddlers fell asleep on shoulders and backs. The older children walked mechanically like the marching dead, their eyes glazed and fixed. A hungry dog came snarling around them. Its face was lupine. A gash on its shoulder oozed blood and was black with flies. Jamila stooped for stones and drove it away.

The landscape was changing dramatically as they walked. The river had disappeared. The road was wide and pitted with stones. Even the hills were vanishing. The land flattened out into open countryside with scrubland, fields and squat cement houses.

Shacks appeared. They buzzed with bright electric lights, clouded with moths. They passed a car repair shop. Its workers laboured, fingers slick with oil, under the propped bonnet of a jeep. A young boy with bare feet stood by them with a lantern.

Others sold fresh fruit and vegetables and made Jamila think of the bursting orchards they'd left behind. Several served food. Men sat outside at plastic tables, eating, ignoring the passing people. Music blared from speakers. The thick smells of frying meat and onions hung solid in the air and made Jamila's empty stomach churn.

A motorbike swung out from the shadows and carved through the crowd. Three cocky young men clung together on its seat. Guns flashed across their laps. They kept pace with the walkers and heckled them.

'Don't you know the truth about these camps? They're death camps. Go home. Save yourselves.'

Jamila heard and was afraid but didn't raise her head.

'We are your people. We will protect you. If you go to these camps, you will die.'

They were gone as quickly as they had come, leaving only fumes behind.

Suddenly, as if from nowhere, there was commotion. Somewhere ahead. Raised voices. The slap of feet breaking into a run. Jamila tensed. News came all at once, crashing around them. The camp. Ahead. Hurry.

Jamila quickened her pace, hobbling as fast as she could. She urged on the young women around her with promises of food and a chance to rest their ruined feet.

They left the road. The crowd streamed onto a path across the mudflats. The shacks and fields and local people fell away at once. Darkness closed in. The silence was loud in their ears, broken only by the low scrape of insects in the scrub. Somewhere off to the right, a dog snarled and yelped and quietened.

A cool wind whipped across Jamila's face. It brought a desolate smell of foetid vegetation and decay. She tried to see through the bobbing heads, to get a sense of where they were going. Lights gleamed far ahead, reflected by low cloud. They seemed to sit in nothingness.

The crowd was being funnelled. The sides of the path dropped away to ditches, drainage channels that smelt sour with stagnant water and filth. The people pressed together to keep from falling. They bunched, slowed, jostled.

Jamila was struggling to make sense of where they were. A range of mountains drew a dark, ragged line against the horizon but beneath them, the mud plains were mired in blackness.

The lights ahead slowly grew stronger. Shapes formed. Metal gates. The outline of a squat building. Nearer, a chaos of moving people under electric light. Voices. Men with loudhailers shouted orders, telling people to sit, be patient, wait.

Families were settling on the mud wherever they found space, sleeping curled against each other, surrounded by belongings. So many people. Hundreds. Jamila looked them over in dismay. Would there be room for so many? What if the camp were full? She hesitated and tried to think. Her own family was all around her. Hamid, walking with the Uncles and boys. The Aunties and the young cousins behind.

The Auntie who'd been shot was white-faced and feverish. She had barely been able to keep up. Jamila pushed her way to her side and forced her to sit. Her three-year-old son, the cause of the trouble, clung to her side.

Jamila unknotted the strip of cloth she'd bound around the Auntie's shoulder and tried to ease it off. It was stiff with dried blood and stuck fast to the wound. Jamila examined it, wrapped the end of the cloth around her fingers to get purchase. She counted to three, then ripped it away. The young woman shrieked.

The wound reopened, bleeding anew where the plugs of dried blood had been torn free. A sickly, metallic smell. Jamila pulled the child towards her. His face was full of fear.

'Close your eyes.' Jamila dipped her fingers into the fresh blood and smeared it in the boy's hair, across his forehead, down his face. He wailed, struggling in her arms.

She slapped him hard and carried on until his head was daubed.

'Good.' Jamila was satisfied at last. She wrapped the filthy cloth back around the Auntie's shoulder wound and dragged her to her feet. The screaming boy she thrust into Hamid's arms. 'Now,' she said. 'Quickly. Follow me.' She looked around at the aghast faces. 'All of you.'

Jamila led them forwards, picking her way through the legs and bodies. In front of the gates, a group of agitated men had gathered around an official. The man at the centre was young and clean-shaven, a city dweller. He was wearing a bright yellow tabard over his clothes with Western writing on it. He was holding out his hands to the men, trying to calm them as they shouted and pushed. His eyes were weary.

An engine. Jamila turned. A vehicle was pulling up to one side of the gates. A middle-aged woman climbed out. She was local but she looked well fed and had an air of authority. Jamila ran to her at once. She grasped her arm and hung on. The skin was plump and soft inside the kameez. Another one from the city. The woman twisted, trying to shake her off.

'You must help us. My little nephew is shot.' Jamila pointed to the boy. 'His mother too. If they don't get help, they'll die.'

'A child?' The woman was frowning, uncertain. 'Shot?'

Jamila nodded. May Allah forgive me, she thought, but we must have food. The woman called to the man who was travelling with her. He was tall and lean. He came around from the other side of the vehicle and peered at Jamila, studying her face.

113

'What child?' he said.

Jamila caught hold of Hamid, who still held the writhing boy in his arms, and tugged them both forwards. Behind them, the young Auntie was swaying, propped upright by the others. Her face was deathly pale. The man peered through the darkness at the boy. His fingers reached out cautiously and touched his hair. They came away bloodied.

'Come,' he said to Jamila. He kept his voice low. 'Bring your family and follow me.'

Jamila pressed the Uncles, Aunties and children into a compact group and urged them quickly past the clamouring crowd and in through the metal gates, to safety, food and shelter.

11

Dawn broke surreptitiously. The sky crept from grey to bleached white, sharpening the shadows along the mountain range. As the day began, the air filled with the frantic cawing of birds that wheeled high overhead.

Ellen arrived at the camp before six o'clock. At six thirty, a cordon was being thrown around the area and she needed to be inside. She stood in a queue of grumbling aid workers. They were complaining in a dozen languages about the same things: the pain of being up so early and the indignity of bag and body searches imposed at the gate.

There was plenty to watch. Two men were balancing a homemade ladder against one of the posts at the gate and stringing a banner over the entrance. It was a long strip of white cotton, a torn bed sheet perhaps, hand-painted in black letters. *Welcome, Khan-ji – Camp Food 4 Al.* Either the writer had run out of paint or he just struggled with his English spelling. Ellen smiled to herself. She'd tease Frank about that when the visit was over and he could relax again.

Ellen shuffled forwards, she could see people queuing inside the camp. Girls with plastic buckets waiting to pump water from standpipes. Men and women in separate lines for the makeshift latrines. Near the distribution point, a formless knot of people had formed in the hope of a handout of food or fuel or blankets. She touched her fingers to her face and explored its broken skin and bruises. Her cheekbone was tender but the cut above her eye was already starting to knit.

By nine o'clock, she was outside the medical tent with staff from Medicine International and FOOD 4 ALL, local and international workers together. One of the Belgians was at her side.

'Complete waste of time,' he said. 'As if we haven't got better things to do. All of us. Yeah?' He dug at the earth with his boot, using the metal-capped toe to make a dent. A column of ants was thrown into turmoil. 'Who knows when he'll turn up? All this, just because he's got money. Disgusting.' He pulled a sour face. 'How long have we wasted already? Three hours, is it? More?'

His eyes were on the ground. The ants were regrouping and trying to adapt to the new landscape. He kicked up another avalanche of dust in front of them and watched them be engulfed, then struggle to the surface and change course again.

The heat was building. Ellen tried to remember how many bottles of water she'd brought with her. Already her shirt was sticking to her back. Then she heard it. Faint

116

but unmistakeable. She stiffened. A dull distant throbbing.

A young German man said, 'Seventy-one days. I just counted.'

The Belgian stopped annoying the ants and looked up. 'Until what?'

'End of contract.'

'So? You'll just get a new one.'

'No way.' The young German turned to face him and laughed. 'No way. I tell you, I'm going home.'

The noise swelled. Ellen tipped back her head and scanned the empty sky, shading her eyes with her hand. The sound bounced off the mountains as it pulsed and grew. Finally the Belgian noticed too and looked up. A minute later, he pointed. The helicopter had emerged. A black, rapidly expanding dot.

'A Chinook,' said the German.

'That's not a Chinook.' The Belgian snorted. 'Way too small.'

They carried on arguing. The helicopter was curving in at speed. It hung in the air over a flat expanse of mud two hundred yards from the edge of the camp, then swayed and slowly dropped. Its roar engulfed them as it rocked and settled. Dust billowed. A tide of heat and grit radiated out in a sudden blast. Ellen turned her back and covered her eyes. Dirt scoured the back of her neck and her scarf fluttered around her ears. The blades slowed and finally the engines were cut.

Ellen wiped the dirt from her eyes and turned back to watch. The helicopter door was heaved open. A flight of steps appeared and a member of the crew rushed to the

117

bottom. Everyone waited. Finally Quentin Khan appeared at the top of the stairway. He was a stout figure in a crisply pressed white shirt and tan slacks. He paused for a moment on the top step, his hand raised in a theatrical wave, looking out across the camp. Regal, Ellen thought. She nodded to herself. He had presence. Even the Belgian had fallen silent.

Khan descended with languid movements. Two jeeps pulled up in front of the helicopter and he climbed into the first. Behind him, his team was hurrying down the steps. The doors of the jeeps slammed and they bounced across the mud to the camp gates.

Frank was just inside the gates at the head of the receiving line, wearing a freshly pressed shirt with his usual tattered jeans. Khan emerged from the jeep, gathered himself to his full height and stepped forwards to offer his hand. He was shorter than Frank and less muscular but he exuded polish. Ellen watched him as the two men stood together. They turned sideways, prolonging their handshake for a photograph. Khan's smile stretched without any apparent effort. It showed perfect teeth.

Ellen had seen photographs of him in the newspapers and Sunday supplements. He was often pictured alongside other wealthy entrepreneurs and minor royals at parties and premieres. In real life, he looked shorter than she'd expected and plumper. He must have been in his sixties. His hair was black but the colour wasn't natural and when he turned, she saw how thinly it covered the crown.

Khan was introduced to the camp's staff. He reached in close to shake hands, his left hand cupping elbows. The smile never faded. His cuff shifted and a gold watch glinted in the sun. His clothes were understated but clearly expensive.

A young Pakistani assistant stepped forwards with glasses of chilled fizzy orange and lemonade on a tray. As Khan took one, Ellen's eye was drawn to the other men in his party. They were unfolding themselves from the second jeep and standing in a loose group behind Khan. One of them . . . She looked again as he turned to speak to someone. It wasn't, surely . . . Her heart sank. He moved his head and she saw clearly. It was. John Sandik. She shook her head. He was never a welcome sight.

He was looking decidedly middle-aged now, his stomach bulging over his waistband. His eyelids were puffy and slightly hooded as if his eyeballs had receded into his skull. She'd heard he'd hit hard times since she last saw him, ditched by his last paper and forced to take a job on *The News*. Much less prestigious. He caught her eye for a moment and raised his hand in a brief, self-satisfied wave, gave a tight smile, then turned his shoulder and carried on talking to another member of Khan's party.

Within an hour, Khan had been briefed on facts and figures, toured the male medical tent and heard a group of ragged, cross-legged boys recite a poem to him in the makeshift school. There'd been no mention of typhoid. Now Khan was being guided by Frank through the camp itself. Ellen watched them ooze through the main paths, his security people sticking to his side. Khan looked hot, dabbing at his running forehead and temples with a handkerchief. His thin hair was slick on his skull.

He stopped to talk to a hand-picked head of household.

The man's wife and daughters were pushed to one side. The women peered with indifference at this fattened, Western-dressed version of a Pakistani man. They seemed to have no idea who he was or why he was visiting them at their time of misery.

Ellen crossed to talk to Khan's minders. They were standing in the shade, fanning themselves with briefing notes, sipping bottles of water and looking at their watches. The visit was nearly at an end.

The press advisor was a young British-born Pakistani with a sharp nose. Ellen introduced herself. He made an extravagant show of remembering her although she was sure they'd never met before. Her request for an interview led to a second performance.

'An interview?' He clicked his tongue on his teeth, pulled a long face. 'Hmmm, all a bit tricky. Love to help. But the chopper's whisking us off any moment. Government meetings, you know. Can't be late.'

They exchanged cards. He looked past her, trying to catch Khan's eye, tapping his watch ostentatiously.

She persisted. 'I gather Mr Khan's staying in Peshawar overnight. Maybe some time this evening? Just twenty minutes.'

He forced his eyes to focus on her again and managed a hard smile. 'It's a very tight schedule.'

Ellen nodded. She'd already made friends with the young receptionist at The Swan who'd told her that the whole team was being accommodated just a floor away from her room. 'Well, if you could find me a slot, I'd be very grateful. *NewsWorld* has a very big readership. And Mr Khan's work here is so important.'

'I'll try my very best.' He reached out and squeezed her hand. His fingers were cool from the water bottle. As he walked off to extricate his boss, another hand landed on her shoulder. It was sweaty.

'Fancy seeing you here.' John was eating a high-protein biscuit, the kind given to malnourished children to build their strength. He gestured to her bruised cheek and sniggered. 'You been fighting again?'

She sighed. No point trying to explain. John never listened. 'Something like that.'

He was chomping with hamster cheeks, spraying small brown crumbs as he spoke. 'Bad luck, missing out on the helo. You drive down specially?'

She shook her head. 'I was down anyway, seeing the camp.'

He looked around in puzzlement at the shelters and ranks of listless people as if to say: What could you possibly want to see here?

She said: 'You filing on this?' It didn't strike her as his kind of story.

He nodded, chewed. 'Landed a big profile on Khan.' He looked smug. 'You heard I got poached by *The News*? This is for the magazine. Probably make the cover.'

'Really?' Her jaw slackened in disbelief. Only John could end up on a paper like *The News* and still brag about it.

'Khan? Man of the moment.' He drew her to one side and lowered his voice. 'Don't quote me – but you know how fast he's climbing, back home?'

She stared at him in silence, wondering what he was talking about. Quentin Khan had been established for a long time.

121

'Don't worry,' he said. 'You can't be across everything.'
He put his face close to her ear, shooting small pellets of
biscuit into it as he talked. 'Tipped for a peerage in the
next honours. Close to the PM, you know.'

He drew back, checked her face for reaction, then tore
off the wrapping on another biscuit. 'These are crap. You
tried them?'

'So why's he doing all this?'

'This bleeding-hearts stuff?' He shrugged. 'The guy's got
money, right? So what does he need next? Endorsement.'
He tapped his head. 'Psychology. That's what a great
profile's all about.'

'Endorsement? By whom?' For the first time, John was
piquing her interest.

'The British. Society.' He was warming to his theme,
enjoying a chance to show off. She knew John. He must
be at the end of his research on Khan, almost ready to
file, or he wouldn't be telling her all this. 'He fancies
himself as a titled gentleman. Look at him.'

They stood, shoulders together, and looked. Khan was
standing with his hands clasped loosely behind his back,
leaning forwards with a polite smile on his face as an aid
worker translated his question to a refugee. The expensive
cut of his clothes only emphasized the shabbiness of the
other man's salwar kameez. Whatever he'd asked, the refugee
was gazing at him with barely disguised astonishment.

'You know he plays polo? He's got a great pile in Sussex
and throws flash parties there.' He puffed himself up. 'I
went to one before we came out here actually. Lavish.' He
paused, thinking. 'Course the real true blues stay away from
him. See him as not quite one of us, know what I mean?'

122

'And he thinks, if he's a lord, that'll change?'

John shrugged. 'Suppose so.' He glanced sideways at her. His eyes were canny. 'He doesn't do interviews, by the way. Hates them. In case you were thinking.'

She nodded, pretending to look thoughtful. 'That's odd. I'm sure I've seen—'

'Well, hardly ever,' he cut in. 'Only to a favoured few.'

'Thanks, John. Good to know.'

That was why he'd been so free with his insights. As far as he was concerned, he'd crossed the threshold and bolted the door behind him. She wasn't competition.

Khan's minders were waving at them, giving John an unsubtle signal to get ready to go.

'Marching orders.' John winked, changing tone completely. 'Anyway, how are you? Still no bloke?' He sniggered. 'I'm going to have to stop asking, aren't I?' He patted her arm in a show of sympathy, already starting to move off. 'Don't give up. You never know. Miracles happen.'

The young receptionist at The Swan wanted to move to the United States and become a pop singer.

'Baba won't allow me.' She rolled her eyes. 'You know what he's saying? He's saying singing is all very well but it's not respectable. Unbelievable, nah? How can he say that? He, like, so doesn't get the modern world.'

Ellen was leaning on the reception desk with her elbows, propping her chin in her hands. She made a sympathetic face. 'What does he want you to do?'

'Get married.' She sighed dramatically. 'His best friend's son. All very cosy, isn't it?'

'Have you met him?'

123

'Met him? We practically grew up together. He's a nice boy, quite good looking and all. But I want to travel, to have some fun. I'm so young. Am I right or am I right?'

She reached into her handbag and pulled out her purse, filleting it for photographs. She had a baby face and bright kohl-encircled eyes. Eighteen or nineteen at the most.

She handed over the first picture. 'This is Mama and Baba.'

A middle-aged woman looked solemnly back at Ellen. She was dressed in purple silk, a chiffon *dupatta* covering her hair, ornate gold jewellery dangling from her ears and around her neck. She was standing beside a portly man in a black Nehru jacket. They looked awkward in front of the camera, posing a little stiffly, Ellen thought, but their faces were kind. They were probably younger than she was.

'That was at my cousin's wedding last year,' the young girl went on, 'in Lahore. Such a blast, I can't even tell you.'

She was just handing over the next picture when the phone rang. Ellen straightened up. She'd been hanging around reception for the last two hours, hoping to intercept Khan when he returned to the hotel. Now it was already after seven. She was beginning to wonder if he was staying somewhere else.

The call was in Urdu and Ellen could only catch a few words but it was clear that the man on the line was angry. When she replaced the receiver, the receptionist looked agitated.

'So much drama,' she said in a low voice. 'You'd think he was dying. It's only a scratch.'

'A scratch?'

The kohl-rimmed eyes looked around to make sure no one was within earshot.

'I'm not supposed to tell a soul,' she said, 'but seeing as you're a friend and all.'

Ellen nodded quickly.

'Well,' she leant forwards over the desk, generously sharing her heady perfume. 'Mr Khan took a tumble and scraped his leg.'

'He's hurt?'

She shook her head. 'Barely at all. But his people are crazy. They say it might be dirty, with some soil and whatnot. I sent our doctor to tend him, a most excellent doctor. He wanted to give him some injection, just on safer side, when Mr Khan said he wouldn't have the needle. Because it's Chinese. What nonsense is that? Everything is Chinese, nah?'

'So what does he want?'

'Some tip-top Western doctor.' She twisted her hands in the air, fingers flexed, emphasizing the madness of the idea. 'They'll have to send all the way to Islamabad.'

'So he's here, in the hotel?'

She pulled an apologetic face. 'Sorry. They came in from back side only. Top secret.'

Ellen pointed to the phone. 'Call them straight back,' she said. 'Let me talk to him. I can help.'

The young British press advisor looked weary when he opened the door. His shirt was limp around the collar and grimy. He nodded to the two armed guards, standing outside the room with guns raised across their chests. They moved out of the way to let her pass.

Inside, the entrance hall opened into a voluminous suite. The flecked carpet was thick and spongy underfoot, leading into a broad sitting room. In the centre, two plump sofas were set on either side of a glass coffee table. A bowl of fruit, pleated napkins and a fan of glossy magazines had been arranged on the surface. A vast wooden cabinet, fitted from floor to ceiling, dominated the side wall. There was a closed door on the opposite wall that she guessed would lead into the bedroom.

A man was sitting by the window, his medical bag open on the carpet in front of him. The Pakistani doctor was rummaging through the contents with an air of panic, his glasses perched on the end of his nose.

'This is the British lady.'

Ellen set down her own medical kit in front of him, *NewsWorld* standard issue. She kept her pack of sterile needles in an inside pocket, easily accessible so she could grab it in an emergency or in the dark. She held them out for him to see.

The doctor peered at the labelling through his thick glasses and shrugged. 'My own needles are perfectly sound.' he said. 'Hundred per cent guarantee.' It sounded like the dying fall of a long lament.

The advisor moved to take the needles from Ellen's hand. She closed her fingers around them.

'I'm delighted to help out,' she said, 'but I would need to hand them over myself.'

'I'm afraid that's not possible.' He glared at her. 'Mr Khan is indisposed.'

Ellen nodded and smiled. She put the needle pack back into its inside pocket and zipped up her kit. 'Of course,' she said. 'I quite understand.' She looked towards the door.

The advisor and the doctor exchanged nervous glances.

'Mr Khan is a very generous man.' The advisor was looking tense. 'I'm sure he'll be happy to reward you very handsomely.'

Ellen shook her head. 'I won't detain him long.'

There was a strained silence. Finally the advisor gestured her to a seat, tapped gently on the closed door, waited, then went through to ask permission from the great man.

The bedroom was fragrant, scented by bouquets of pink roses. The king-sized bed, which dominated the room, was embellished with a sculpture of cushions against the headboard. Khan was sitting in an armchair in the far corner, facing the door.

He was dressed in paisley pyjamas and a white silk robe, wrapped around and tied with a cord. It reached to his knees. One leg was raised and straight, his foot resting on a pillowed footstool. The pyjama leg was rolled back to the knee to reveal a thin red scratch, smeared with white cream.

She stood at the door, the advisor at her side, waiting to be invited in.

'I'm so sorry to hear about your accident. How awful. Is it very painful?'

He didn't seem to be listening. He was fiddling with his robe, pulling it more tightly around his thighs. 'You're a stubborn lady, I hear.'

She inclined her head, taking it as a compliment. 'Ellen Thomas, *NewsWorld* magazine.'

He smiled. 'I like that.' He looked across at her. 'I have a stubborn streak myself. One must be single-minded to prosper in this world.' His accent was a curious hybrid. Traces of his Pakistani origins were painted over with old-fashioned public-school English. The result was unsettling.

He seemed to have reached a decision. He waved his assistant away, back into the sitting room, then beckoned Ellen nearer.

'How did it happen?' she asked.

He looked down at his leg, examining the scrape. 'A jagged metal edge. It caught my trousers, ripped them. *Voilà*. The damage was done.'

He straightened up again in his chair, wagged a finger at her. 'Nothing is properly finished in this country, you know that? If the workmanship were better, I'd be the first to invest here. And I say this of my own countrymen.'

She moved forwards and looked at the cut. It seemed clean. 'Is he giving you tetanus? Very sensible. Best not to take chances.'

He nodded. 'One hears so many stories. Recycled needles. Infections. My people don't understand but one can't be too careful.'

'I couldn't agree more.' Ellen showed him her own pack. Each needle was individually sealed in plastic-backed paper and labelled sterile. 'I always carry my own when I travel. Swiss, I believe.'

He held out his hand and looked them over. There was a glasses case on the table beside him but he didn't reach for it. His eyes narrowed, straining to read the fine print. Vain, she thought. He'll wait until I've gone before he inspects them properly.

'Very kind. May I?' He tore off two in their plastic sheaths and handed the rest back. 'My people will settle with you.'

He was fingering the needles, thoughtful. He seemed to have lost interest in her. She didn't move. 'I have a special favour to ask. It would mean such a lot, not just to me but to our readers.'

He hesitated, looking at her boots, which were planted firmly on his thick carpet.

'There's such interest in your charitable work here. Could you exchange the needles for a twenty-minute interview? That's ten minutes per needle.' She smiled, her eyes never leaving his face, reading his reaction as she continued. 'Not a high price for good health and peace of mind.'

For a moment, he just stared at her, his brown eyes surprised. Then he threw back his head and laughed. It was a deep, coughing that which caught her by surprise. The door behind her flew open and the advisor stood, framed in the doorway, staring.

'You have a cheek.' Khan dabbed at his eyes with his fingertips and swallowed down his laughter. It disappeared as quickly as it had come. 'You'd make a good businessman.' He was waving his hand now, admitting defeat as he wafted her away. 'All right, young lady. Later. You'll get your twenty minutes of flesh.'

The advisor, stern-faced, ushered her out. He led her along the corridor to a second suite. The door was ajar. 'Wait in there,' he said.

Three men looked up in surprise as she walked in. Two were sprawled across sofas. The third was standing in front of an entertainment system, fiddling with its buttons. They were Pakistanis but dressed in Western trousers and shirts and they all wore dark wool blazers. One, the oldest of the three, had a red silk handkerchief folded into his top pocket. Stout glasses of whisky sat on the coffee table, a half-empty bottle beside them.

'Madam, how do you do?' The man at the entertainment centre bowed his head with courtly flair. 'Please do be joining us.'

'Is it not the snacks, nah?' The youngest man, seated, was twisted around towards the door, struggling to focus on her. He was already drunk.

'You are also guest of Khan-ji?' The men were looking her over with interest. 'We are his old friends. Cousins even, you could say so.'

'A pleasure to meet you.' The men struck her as classic hangers-on, getting their noses in the trough at someone else's expense.

The man who was standing went back to tweaking the controls on the entertainment system. He was streaking through radio channels, and the speakers spluttered fragments of music and voices.

There was a knock at the door and a waiter appeared, wheeling a trolley covered with a white tablecloth. The young man clapped his hands. The waiter opened out the flaps of the trolley into a serving table. The radio locked onto a music station and the room was suffused with the high, wailing note of a Pakistani pop song.

'Is there karaoke?' The young man was waving his hands, conducting. 'I love karaoke. I'm a great singer. Everyone is telling me so.'

The older men converged on the trolley, spooning large quantities of rice and meat onto plates and retiring to the

130

sofas to eat. The rich aroma of cooked beef, marinated with spices, rose in the steam. Three European men, Polish, perhaps, or Hungarian, joined the party, filling their glasses with vodka, whisky, wine. The two Belgians arrived. Others loomed behind them. The large room was suddenly warm with bodies and food and vibrant with voices, all speaking their loud, differently accented English in competition with the pounding music.

Ellen looked at her watch. It was almost eight o'clock. One of the Belgians pressed her to have a drink. Over his shoulder, she saw a Pakistani man nudge cautiously at the half-open door. He peered around the room. He was thin-faced, his hair lank and long, his lips chapped. His salwar kameez was creased and slightly grubby. He was rocking with nervous energy as he clung to the shadows of the entranceway, as if he were a street dog, hungry for food but fearful of being kicked.

Ellen nudged the Belgian. 'Who's that?'

He turned to look. 'God knows. Maybe he has the wrong room.' He began a dull story about himself.

One of the older men threaded his way through the growing crowd to the door and handed over an envelope. The two men spoke for a moment. The Belgian drifted off to replenish his drink.

The young drunk on the sofa leant over to Ellen, his breath thick with fumes. 'You have met Doc?' He nodded towards the thin-faced Pakistani man at the door. 'He's not a real doctor, nah? But anything you are needing, he can get it for you. What are you needing?'

She smiled. 'Nothing at the moment, but that's good to know.'

When she looked again, Doc was ushering five young women into the suite. They were dressed in cheap poly-cotton salwar kameezes, trimmed with gaudy borders that glittered under the hotel lights. They were slight girls, none of them older than eighteen.

The man in the blazer led them further into the room. They stood in an awkward row. Their make-up was garish, their cheeks too red, their eyelids too bright. The Pakistani man pulled out a packet of cheap cigarettes and lit one. The girls passed it between them.

'Five only.' The young man shouted from the sofa. 'Not enough.'

His friend slapped his shoulder. 'Don't worry. You're too drunk to need one.'

'I'm not. I do.' He sounded indignant. He tried to sit properly upright and fell back onto the sofa cushions. The other men laughed. The room was filling with cigarette smoke, alcohol fumes and raucous male laughter.

Ellen pushed her way out to the corridor. It was cool and deserted. The faint echo of noise splashed over her as she leant against the wall and thought about her interview with Khan.

'Shy?'

She looked up. John. He was padding towards her down the corridor, his shirt open at the neck, his feet in thick leather sandals.

'That's no way to get laid.'

'Exactly.' She managed a smile. 'That's why I'm out here.'

His face was ruddy, either sunburnt or freshly scrubbed. He looked pleased with himself. 'Just filed my mega-piece.'

He looked towards the door, sniffing the booze, the noise, the girls. 'Party time.'

'Pleased with it?'

'Bloody delighted. So's London.' He leant towards her. 'Guess who's got the magazine cover this Saturday? Huge spread.' He put a short finger to his lips. 'Not a word, now. Top secret.' He made to move past her and go inside.

'How much is Khan giving them, do you know?'

He hesitated for a second, as if wondering whether to tell her. Then his face relaxed and he reached to pat her on the shoulder. 'Sure, I don't mind helping you out. Here's the thing. All the medicines – that's a couple of million, right there. Plus he's giving in kind. Free transport of goods, supplies, all that stuff. That's another couple of million, I'd say.'

She nodded, thinking. 'And all offset against tax, I assume.'

He was looking past her into the party. 'Is there food? I'm starving.'

'And if the crisis drags on? If the numbers keep going up?'

John shrugged. 'Who knows? Because it's not just here, is it? It could infect the whole damn country.' His tone became patronizing. 'Look, this whole refugee business, it's not going away in a hurry. Khan knows that.'

'And he'll keep paying out?'

'That depends how long it takes for the peerage to come through.' He winked, his eyes already drifting back to the hot chaos of the party. 'Point is, he's got very deep pockets. Not like you and me, if I may venture to be so bold.' He sniggered to himself. 'And you've got to remember, my dear. Whatever we might think, for a man like Khan, a few million ain't a bad price for a peerage.'

The advisor found her there in the corridor.

'Twenty minutes.' He opened the door to Khan's suite to let her back in. 'And that's it.'

Khan had moved into the sitting room and was lying across one of the plump sofas. His brown silk shirt was hanging loose over dark brown trousers. His feet were bare, the toes sunk in the thick pile carpet. His hair was slick against his skull as if he'd recently showered.

He pointed to the sofa opposite him and she sat down. A fug of spicy aftershave enveloped her. She opened her notebook and smiled.

'Thank you for talking to me. You're giving so much to these people. Why is this such an important cause for you?'

Khan drew himself up in his chair. 'This is my country. I was born in Karachi.' He put one hand on his heart. 'It grieves me very deeply to see my people plucked from their homes, their way of life torn apart by conflict. They are weakened and vulnerable.'

Ellen stopped writing and looked up from her notebook. 'And your role?'

He inclined his head. 'It is my duty. My father left Pakistan when I was still a baby, in search of a better life. These people deserve opportunities too. And before they can have economic development, they must have peace.'

She tapped her pen on the page, watching him. He was reciting a script. His lines may or may not be true. That almost didn't matter. She'd have to try a different tack if she wanted anything more genuine.

'Tell me about your family. It must have been a difficult move, from Karachi to England.'

He shrugged, pulled a face. 'In some ways. My father ran a small grocery business. He worked hard, for long hours. As a boy, I barely saw him. But he saw it as his duty. He wanted us to be the same as everyone else.'

'Were you?'

'Yes and no.' He reached for the glass of water at his side and swallowed a mouthful. 'I mean, it was a very mixed neighbourhood. In that sense, everyone was different. But I went to a good school, I worked hard and afterwards my uncle took me into his business. He had a small number of vans for hire.'

His answers about his own career were well rehearsed. He talked about the long hours, the business risks, the steady progression from a few vans to a fleet, from the gut decision to buy a cheap freight ship to the slow purchase of a whole line of them. His career was well documented. These were well-worn anecdotes. She looked at the clock. Her time was running out.

He paused and she jumped in, hoping to lead him back to his childhood. 'What were you like, as a boy?'

He shrugged again. 'Very ordinary. I liked the things boys like. Cricket. Sport.'

She thought for a moment. 'What did you most want?'

'Most want?' He looked surprised. 'I don't know. What do boys want?'

She sat quietly. He was gazing at the art work hanging on the opposite wall. He opened his mouth to speak, then closed it again and took a sip of water. She waited. An empty minute passed. She sat with the silence, pushing him to speak.

'A bicycle, I suppose. A better cricket bat. I don't know. The usual things.'

She sat, looking at him, without writing anything down. He had tipped his head back now and was staring up at the ceiling. He was evading her, thinking but travelling alone. She sat still and waited, giving him her full attention. The silence extended.

Finally he leant closer and whispered: 'Dickens.' He sat back and clapped his hands. 'There you are. There's your scoop. The Pakistani community won't like it.'

'Dickens?' She was lost.

He laughed, the same startling laugh she'd heard earlier. 'A dog.' He seemed delighted, as playful as a schoolboy. 'A most wonderful dog.'

He was sitting up now, animated. 'My best friend at school was from Cyprus. Greek Cypriot. Alex, his name was. Alexander. We used to play together after school. His family had that dog. A small thing, no pedigree, but full of mischief.' He smiled. 'We got into such scrapes with him. I thought it was marvellous.'

'And you wanted a dog too?'

'Desperately. Out of the question, of course.'

'Your father wouldn't allow it?'

'Heavens, no.' He shook his head. 'Hated dogs. Thought they were dirty, unclean. Dangerous, even. Couldn't see why any civilized person would have one in the house. I never told them about it. Just disappeared to Alex's house after school, every chance I got.' His face was flushed as he remembered. 'Whatever happened to Alexander? He was a scrawny boy. Probably as stout as me now.' He patted the mound of his stomach, chuckling.

136

'If he's even alive. Anyway, that's all a long time ago. Let's move on.'

She had no intention of moving on. 'Did you have many friends from outside the Pakistani community?'

'Absolutely. It was a mixed neighbourhood, I told you.'

'Did your parents approve?'

'My father wanted me to be utterly English. Do you know, I hardly speak a word of Urdu? Embarrassing, isn't it? Understand a lot, but can't speak it. My father never let us.'

She nodded. She tried to imagine his father, a hopeful new arrival from the bustle of Karachi, desperate to adapt to a cold, strange country called England. 'You must have made them very proud.'

His advisor had opened the door and was tapping his watch. The twenty minutes had passed. 'I'm sorry,' he said. 'Mr Khan is running very late. He's keeping people waiting.'

I know, she thought. I've met them. She got to her feet.

Khan had a wistful look on his face as he put his hand out to her. 'It's been a pleasure.' She nodded. Inside this powerful man, now tipped to become an English lord, she saw a small, displaced Pakistani boy, driven by ambitious parents and in love with a mischievous dog.

Ellen sat in her room, staring at her laptop screen. Phil had agreed to take a short piece on Khan's visit. Now readers in other countries would be interested in the refugee angle. It would be easy enough to put the two elements together into five hundred words on the growing need and the way Khan was stepping in to meet it. The gossip about his lordly ambitions she'd leave to John.

She picked up the ballpoint pen on the table beside her

and clicked it on and off with her thumb, restless. She had the nagging sense that she was missing something but she just couldn't see what it was. She deleted the few sentences she'd written and started again, kicking off with some description of the camp and the women's medical tent. After a paragraph, she pushed back her chair and paced up and down the room. She picked a banana out of the fruit bowl and ate it. She pulled back the curtains and looked through her giant tape cross to the light-pecked darkness of Peshawar so many storeys below.

She dialled Frank's room. He took a while to answer.

She said, 'You're not partying with Mr Khan and friends?'

Frank sounded guarded. 'I may have made an appearance.'

She laughed. His tone said it all. He hated that scene as much as she did.

'Give me one good reason,' she said, 'why I should ask you round?'

'You only want me for my Scotch.' He paused. 'OK but it's got to be quick.' He seemed to be calculating something. 'I've got to be somewhere soon.'

It was a mistake. She realized that at once. Again they were side by side in semi-darkness, sipping whisky and looking out at the night. But the mood was strained.

'How was your day?'

He looked weary, his eyes dull with tiredness. He shrugged, putting on a show of cheerfulness. 'Pretty good. He seemed happy enough. No mention of typhoid. How about you?'

'OK. I got an interview with Khan.'

His eyes widened in surprise. 'Thought he never gave them.'

138

'I was lucky.'

'Is that right?' He smiled, looked into his drink. There was something brittle in the smile that she couldn't quite read. He kept his eyes on his glass.

She waited for a moment but he didn't speak. 'What?'

'Nothing.' He shrugged. 'Just you always were . . . you know, focused.' He shifted his weight and shrugged back his sleeve to look at his watch. 'Not a bad thing. I'm just saying.'

She decided to let it go. He was in a prickly mood. No point starting an argument. She sipped her whisky. 'Any news on the missing supplies?'

'Not exactly. The warehouse seems tight. We got the same boxes going out as coming in. And the checks on deliveries to the camp seem OK.'

'Do you think they've been tipped off?'

'Could be that.' He sighed and ran a finger around the rim of his glass. 'Or maybe the leak's further down. Inside the camp.'

She hesitated, thinking about the unloading she'd seen, the boxes being passed down chains of workers and sorted for distribution. It was all very public. Hard to see how a noticeable volume of supplies could disappear without anyone noticing.

'So what next?'

His mobile phone was buzzing an incoming message. He drank off the last of his whisky and started to get up.

'I'm sorry. I got to go.'

'Everything OK?'

'Sure. Just work. The usual.' He was on his feet and heading for the door. She stood for a moment after he'd gone, her hand on the door handle, thinking. Something wasn't right.

She opened the door and headed after him. He'd already disappeared. She turned and doubled back to the emergency stairs. She ran down the short flight to his floor below, confident she could cut him off before he reached his room. As she emerged into the corridor, she saw at once that it wasn't empty. She pulled back to the stairwell entrance and concealed herself there.

A figure was waiting outside Frank's room, pressed back into the shadows. A young Pakistani, broad-shouldered and strong. A dark cotton scarf hung in folds at his neck.

At the other end of the corridor, the lift doors swished open. Frank stepped out and walked towards his room. The youth stepped forwards, revealing himself to the corridor light. He had the face of a teenager who was straining to be a man. A light beard was growing unevenly. His skin glistened with a sheen of sweat. Ellen knew him at once. It was the same youth she'd seen at the camp, the young man who'd stood and stared at her when she was talking to Ibrahim.

Frank raised his hand in greeting, opened the door to his room and ushered the young man quickly inside. The door clicked shut. Ellen stood for some moments afterwards, looking down the deserted corridor at the closed door and thinking. She wondered why Frank had been so furtive about meeting the young man and thought how ridiculous it was that she felt hurt.

12

The heat woke Jamila. The air around her face was stuffy and stifling. She expected to be in her own room, with its carved cupboard and worn cot, and for a moment, she was confused. There was banging. The crack of hammer on wood. Close in her ear. When she tried to move, her legs and back ached. She grimaced, then opened her eyes and looked around.

She was in a broad tent, a vast stretch of loosely pegged canvas, gaping at the sides. Forty or fifty people were lying in rows, squashed together. Hamid and the other men in the family had used their bodies to build a barrier around the women, penning them into one corner to protect them from strangers. Layla was curled in a ball, one arm encircling her mother, her chador in crumpled folds around her head. None of the women had ever before slept in the same structure as a man who was not their relative and they were all afraid.

Only the young Auntie with the gunshot wound was

nowhere to be seen. Late last night, her husband had finally agreed that she might be treated by the doctors. She had looked close to death. Her face was white and bloodless, a fruit sucked dry.

Hamid had argued with the husband, as he decided whether to let her go into the care of the foreigners. If you don't give permission, Hamid had said, she will die. But if I do, the husband had replied, she may be dishonoured. That was worse.

It was no small thing for a man to put his wife into the hands of strangers and the argument persisted for some time. In the end, a compromise was reached. He accompanied her and, although he couldn't enter the female medical tent himself, it was agreed that he could sleep at the entrance, to see for himself that no other man shamed her with his presence.

Jamila straightened her crumpled kameez and the chador on her head and shoulders. She climbed over the sleeping bodies and ducked under the tent flap. Outside, the air was warm but fresher. The light was soft with early morning.

At the gate, four officials from the camp were directing two local workers as they set up plastic tables and chairs. The officials looked like local men but they were dressed like Westerners. Their caps had stiff peaks that shaded their eyes. They set out cardboard files and papers on the table and an ink stamp. A rat streaked past them to a nearby ditch and plopped into the water, breaking the greasy sheen on the surface.

Outside the gate, on the no-man's-land of the open plain, several hundred people saw the officials and their tables and rose wearily to their feet, gathering their belongings into bundles and forming a ragged queue. They were scruffy and exhausted, the washed-up remains of the people they had walked amongst as they came down from the mountains. They stood, waiting, with stooped shoulders. It was a patient group but one without dignity. That is where we'd be now, Jamila thought, if I hadn't moved quickly.

She turned her back on the waiting crowd and looked down past the tents. The land was barren, left vacant because it was impossible to farm. There were no trees, no shrubs and no rocks or gullies. Nothing gave relief from the heat of the sun. This was not, she thought, as Allah intended His world to be.

The camp was stirring into life. A queue was forming at two standpipes. Water was clattering into buckets and basins and its spray was soaking the surrounding mud. Passing feet churned it to paste. There was a short queue too in front of an oblong shack that was raised on a wooden step and buzzing with flies. The stink told Jamila what that was for. A necessary. Jamila turned away. How can we live here? Such a dirty, exposed place, surrounded by labourers and uneducated men with prying eyes.

She picked her way briskly along the narrow path between the tents, conscious of every unwashed male body that brushed against hers, of every man who raised his eyes to look at her. It was impossible to keep the young girls of the family here. They would be shamed, humiliated. They must demand a secluded place, somewhere separate. Her family had status. They owned land. Surely the foreigners would understand that.

On all sides, people were stirring, emerging from their tents. A young man stooped over a bucket, washing himself.

Further on, she passed a standpipe where a boy was pumping water. His friend plunged his head under it, rubbing block soap through his hair. A young boy, skidding around a corner, barged into her, almost knocking her down. She opened her mouth to scold him but he was already gone. She limped towards the queue for the standpipe, waiting for the chance to wash her face and feet and dampen her chador to keep herself cool.

'Jamila Auntie?'

She turned. The wife of her young cousin, Old Auntie's granddaughter, was hurrying towards her.

'I knew . . . I knew it was you.' She was usually such a shy girl but she opened her arms and embraced Jamila. 'You are here too. And your family with you? Praise be to God.'

Jamila clung to her. It was such a blessing to see a relative amongst so many strangers, a face from the old order, from home.

'When did you arrive?'

'Last night only. And you?'

'Yesterday morning.' The girl's lip trembled. 'We had to wait for so long in the heat of the sun to get into the camp. Grandmother is so weak. You must come to her.'

Jamila stared. How could Old Auntie have managed such a difficult journey?

'Old Auntie, here?'

The girl's eyes brimmed. 'They carried her. My husband and his brother by turns. Strapped on their backs.'

Jamila struggled to believe it. The girl seemed unable to say more. Instead she took Jamila's hand and led her through the noise and dirt and chaos, down a long narrow corridor between shelters. Inside, dark shapes were moving against the plastic, which was made semi-transparent by the sun.

At the far end, the rows broadened out. They were some distance now from the entrance to the camp, with its medical tents and trucks. Here some larger families had staked out their own compounds, rough patches of mud bordered by partitions of sticks and sacking. Inside each, there were two or three tents.

The girl pulled at one of the partitions and led her inside. A row of children sat, dull-eyed with sleepiness and fatigue, along a plank on the mud. Little Syma was there, her baby brother crawling on the ground beside her, along with some of her cousins. Jamila greeted her but she hung her head and looked away. Beyond them, there was a tent made of plastic sheets stretched over sticks. They ducked inside it.

It was hot. The plastic hugged the heat to itself and made the air in the tent sweat. Jamila stood, her head bent against the low roof, letting her eyes adjust. The tent was filled with a low rasping and with the odour of dirty bodies.

She started to make out shapes. Bedding was strewn across the floor, mats and discarded blankets marking the places where the women of the family had slept, pressed together, side by side. Only one mat was still covered by the long low shape of a body.

Jamila crept forwards and sat beside her. Old Auntie was on her back. Her eyes were closed. Her yellowing skin was stretched tightly across her bones, the chin, nose and cheekbones standing out, unnaturally sharp. Her mouth was half-open. Her lips were dry but tracks of dried moisture glistened at the corners. Jamila lifted her hand and fanned away the flies.

145

'Is there a doctor?'

The girl looked embarrassed. She put her mouth to Jamila's ear to whisper.

'The fighters say these foreign doctors are murderers. They shame the women and then kill them. Old Auntie refuses.'

'Can she drink?'

The girl shook her head.

'Fetch water. Let me try.'

Jamila lifted Old Auntie's shoulders into her lap. Her bones were frail and fleshless. She had no more weight than a baby. Her head lolled on the stalk of her neck and settled against Jamila's knee.

When the girl came with the water, Jamila dipped her finger in the cup and ran it around Old Auntie's mouth and lips, cleaning them. She dipped the end of her chador into the water and let a little drip into Old Auntie's mouth. Her throat shuddered but she could barely swallow. Her eyes stayed closed. The tent was filled with the rattle of her lungs. It was a pitiful sound, obscuring everything else. Each breath was a hard-won battle.

'Leave us,' she said to the girl. 'Leave us alone for a while.'

Jamila sat quietly, stroking the old lady's face and listening to her fading struggle for life. She remembered her own grandmother who died when she was just a girl. Years later, she had been by her mother's cot when she had died, at home in the village. Once Old Auntie was gone, that whole generation of elders would have passed, all their stories and their wisdom gone. It was a sad and lonely thought.

The breathing was becoming more protracted and painful to hear. With each breath now, Jamila thought: This is the last, no, this.

The girls reappeared, black outlines in the white light of the entrance, three granddaughters come to pay their respects. One of them was waddling with child, as if her birth time had almost come. Jamila beckoned them all inside to wait with her. The final moment came with a low rushing sigh, as Old Auntie's lungs, which had laboured for so long, collapsed and became still.

Jamila closed Old Auntie's mouth. For a moment, the silence inside the tent deepened. The world outside was full of noise, coming muffled through the plastic sheets. The steady hammering of wood, water splashing, the pounding of running feet, the squeals and shouts of children playing.

The women set the body on a mat on the mud outside and covered it with a blanket. They wailed, tore at their chests and lamented, sitting around the body to mourn. Women from neighbouring tents heard the commotion and came to join them, weeping alongside the bereaved, sharing grief for a woman they had barely met.

Old Auntie's grandson, Jamila's young cousin, came running through the camp. He stared, bewildered, at the wailing women and the covered corpse. Jamila drew him to one side.

'You must find an imam,' she said. 'The people in charge of the camp will help. You must tell them.'

He stared at her, distraught. A stranger, to wash Old Auntie's body and bury her? It was wrong.

Yes, it is wrong, Jamila thought. Old Auntie wanted to be buried with her brother in our own earth.

The young cousin's face was wretched. 'The soldiers were coming.' He was stuttering. 'What else could we do?'

'It is Allah's will.' She reached out a hand and touched the boy's shoulder. 'Praise be to God in His Wisdom.'

On her way back through the camp to Hamid and her own family, Jamila felt assaulted by the tumult of people. The crowd was thick. Men of all ages were pushing their way along the narrow paths, forcing her to move aside into small gaps and crevices. At the standpipes, young men stood, chests bare, soaping and soaking themselves, spray wheeling from their wet hair. The girls stood apart with empty buckets and bowls, waiting their turn.

A thin, sallow man approached. A girl was trailing behind him. She had crumpled, cheap clothes and her young face was dirty with make-up.

'*Salaam Alaikum.*' He smiled, showing crooked teeth.

Jamila pulled her chador closer around her face and turned away.

'Too good for this place, nah?' He stopped and peered at her. 'Which place are you from?'

She tried to push her way past him but he blocked the path.

'No need to be afraid.' His breath smelt of rotten food. He spoke low in her ear. 'I'm a businessman. Anything you want, you come to me. Anything. Understand me?'

The young girl was staring at the ground, uninterested. Her eyes were lifeless.

'I have no business with you,' she said. She shoved him with her shoulder and managed at last to force her way past.

'Doc,' he called after her. Boys nearby turned to look. 'People call me Doc. Don't be a stranger. I am a friend.'

* * *

Jamila went back the following day to visit her young cousin and his family. She took a small parcel of rice, sugar and cooking oil to offer them, salvaged from their family ration. The women were gathered together, still softly weeping and lamenting. The men sat, eyes glazed, raw with the memory of the burial.

The camp officials had made space for Old Auntie in their new, small graveyard. They had found a mullah to conduct the ceremony. But everyone felt guilty. It was a poor leaving.

Jamila spoke first to the young male cousins and then to their wives. They were crammed together in one corner of the piece of mud around the tents. No one would sit near the spot where the body had lain.

Finally she went to talk to Syma. The girl was sitting silently on a piece of wood, cast afloat in the mud, her legs drawn tightly to her chest.

'Syma?'

The little girl didn't even look up. Her eyes were fastened on the ground, her face flushed. Jamila lowered herself to the mud beside her and put her hand on her forehead. She was too hot. The tufts of hair sticking up around the girl's face were slick with sweat.

'You were there at Great-grandmother's funeral,' she said. 'I saw you. That was a very brave thing to do.'

Syma didn't react. Her shoulders were tight and hard.

'Do you remember Great-grandmother's stories?'

She shook her head, petulant. Jamila went on, trying to lace her voice with comfort.

'Of course you do. She was always telling stories. About strange animals and foolish people. You should try to

149

remember them as carefully as you can. Tell them to your little brother. Tell them to your own children, after you're married.'

Syma sat silently. She wouldn't raise her head but Jamila knew she was listening.

'Life is a big wheel,' Jamila said. She brushed the little girl's damp hair off her forehead with the flat of her hand. 'Always turning, never still. Old people get older and then they die and go to Paradise and they leave space for young people. For babies like your brother.'

Syma scowled at her brother, sitting on his bottom and scratching at the dirt.

'This is a blessing. We must accept it. It is God's way.'

They sat, side by side, without talking, for some time. Jamila had never known Syma be so quiet.

'Are you sick?'

The girl didn't answer.

There was a slight stirring in the air. It set the plastic sheets fluttering against the sticks that tethered them. It was warm wind, blowing in from the plain. Jamila lifted her face to taste it. She looked at the clouds, starting to thicken along the jagged tops of the mountain range. They were light clouds but building. Soon the first of the monsoon rains would come, breaking over the flimsy tents and plastic homes. She put her hand out to the girl and drew her in, ignoring her resistance, pulling her hot body into the crook of her arm so she could shelter her.

13

I am nearly fourteen and my whole life is being wasted. I close my eyes and think of home. I imagine walking down each path through the village. Then I go to the orchards where the plum and apple trees bend towards each other like gossiping ladies. Then I open my eyes and see this hateful misery all around me and I want to cry.

The plains are killing us. We are mountain people. Jamila Auntie says so and, for once, she's telling something right. Allah in His Wisdom did not create us to live in so much of heat. We will surely die here on this endless bare mud, with no scrap of shade, not even a tree or shrub, and sun so intense falling on our heads we might as well have climbed into the oven back home and shut the door.

On account of Jamila Auntie's scolding and bullying, we now have a small piece of mud as our own. It is a fourth the size of our real compound at home. The Uncles had to scavenge wooden staves and sheets of plastic and they built a fence around us, pretending it is a compound wall. In fact it is only as high as my head so any normal-sized man can peer right over it and see whatever he likes inside, which is most indecent. I say it should be higher but the only person in my family who ever paid me any heed is my dear baba and now no one knows where he is. He went for help, Jamila Auntie says, after the school was burnt down. But I am nearly dying with worry about how we will ever find him again.

The Aunties spend so much of time crouched inside the tent. But it is very hot in there and the air is dry and stuffy besides. Jamila Auntie complains to Hamid Uncle that we girls should also stay inside to preserve our modesty. Hamid Uncle says he has enough sorrows in his life, as Allah is his witness, without forcing me and the other girls to suffocate to death inside a tent if we cry and beg and refuse.

For that first day, we did nothing but labour. Hamid Uncle met a most respectable family, landowners like us who belong to a village lower down the valley. They came to the camp some days earlier and already knowing all the rules. The men helped the Uncles borrow tools and all manner of needful materials and their boys stood in a long queue with my cousins to get family packs of necessities, like rice and salt and soap and suchlike, one pack for every head of household.

I saw them do it. The men at the head of the queue were sitting with a big ledger open on a table and writing everything. If only I were a boy, if that were the will of Allah, that is a job I most would enjoy. To use an ink pen and write down neatly in a ledger whatsoever information I could deduce about each family, of how many members they are comprised and to which village they belong and if there are any illnesses or special problems and what rations they are being allocated and whether these rations are sufficient for their needs and so on and so forth. I am sure I would be very good at a job like that.

Our small piece of mud is a long walk from the entrance to the camp. It was the only land which was not already covered by shelters and that was with good reason for it is a stark and hot piece of mud and a little sunken also.

The tents are flimsy affairs, just plastic sheets stretched tight over sticks and pieces of wood. Mama and Jamila Auntie and I share one with some Aunties and their babies and other cousins too so you can imagine the noxious smell and the noise in the darkness of all the snorting and snoring and whimpering and all manner of other peculiar noises. It's not just from inside our own tent, although that is deafening, but from all across the camp.

In the day, I go with the other girls to do chores and, what with all the queuing and all, they take hours. We stand first in the queue for the necessary which stinks so much I think I must be sick.

Then there's the queue for the water pump to fill the pails and then back to the tents to wash ourselves privately and to wash clothes too and the water sloshes everywhere and turns the earth around the pails to soft mud which the young cousins stamp and it gets everywhere. Then it's time to start queuing for the daily ration of flour and salt so we can make rotis for lunch which we cook on a common fire between bricks. Nothing tastes like the food we had at home, not even our own rotis.

I was squatting there on the second day, slapping dough into a roti between the flat of my hands, when someone called my name. The air is always teeming with shouting and crying and commotion and yet this voice, shouting my name, seemed to fly through it all directly. I shook my head and looked around.

It was him. My own dear baba was stumbling towards me, his arms outstretched, his poor burnt hands reaching through the empty air for me, his face such an arresting mixture of delight and sorrow that I simply stared, the roti limp between my hands, and couldn't move or breathe.

For a moment, I thought he was a spirit, taking the form of Baba and come to snatch me from amongst the living. Then he was upon me, almost knocking me over as he embraced me and called me his girl, his Layla, landing kisses on my headscarf and the tip of my nose like a madman. I threw open my arms and wrapped them tightly around his neck, not caring who was there to see. I felt his warm arms and smelt his skin and knew it was indeed my baba and he was still alive and had been searching for us all these long days and I cried like a little girl on his shoulder, feeling safe at last and full of relief, thanks be to Allah, that Baba was back with us again, brightening even this bleak place.

Baba's coming is a great blessing for Mama and I hope he will be a comfort also. Since Hamid Uncle built the tent, Mama has been lying inside it half the day, either crying or sleeping. The Aunties said she was exhausted from the journey. That was true, she isn't used to walking hour after hour the way we walked and she isn't strong. But it isn't only that.

I say her heart is breaking for Marva. Even I find, when

I am standing in a noisy queue assaulted by the shouts of the boys or carrying a pail brim-full with water, that I am thinking about Marva and missing her quietness and her calm smile and the way she liked to comb out my hair when it was all in a tangle and soothe me when I was upset and tell me her stories. I worry about her especially at first light and at dusk when the jets scream overhead and I know they are heading with their bombs for our valley. So I can imagine how hard it is for Mama to bear also.

When Baba heard that Marva was left behind, he stood very still and didn't speak one word. He looked at Mama as if he, who knows so many clever words, couldn't understand these simple ones. I only knew that he was alive by the way his chest was heaving for breath. He turned away at last and walked out alone into the noise and chaos of the camp, so slow and silent in all that tumult that it was sad to see, and he didn't come back for some time.

Baba heard about a girls' school being set up in the camp. Two of the young cousins should go there, he said, and I should take them.

The school was in a sealed area, even further away from the entrance than our tents. It was ringed with a high wall made of panels of woven straw and too high to look over. I put my eye to the straw to see whatsoever I could.

Inside, a circle of women was perched on plastic chairs, gossiping. Their heads were barely covered. I banged with my knuckles on the wood struts and a woman came to open a panel and stare first at me, then at the young cousins fastened to my sides. She shrugged and let us through.

155

In the corner of the compound, taking up most of the space, a tent had been erected. A proper tent, like the ones the jihadis had erected in front of the mosque, made of thick green canvas and attached with ropes. It was high too. Even a grown man could stand upright in the middle and not bump his head.

Rows of young girls were sitting cross-legged, chanting their lessons. The high-pitched song of their voices, rising and falling, gave me a pang, thinking of our school and my years of lessons there and imagining it burnt now, as Baba said, to nothing but ash.

A girl was leading them, standing at the front with a special pointing stick and guiding them through their letters. There was one blackboard, set on a wooden stand, and covered with a coloured poster with bright pictures, just like the ones we used in school to tell us how to recite the alphabet and how to count.

The girl who was teaching looked over at us, standing there at the entrance to the tent. She gave me a half-smile and the children stared, because children that age are distracted by anything. And all at once a thought exploded in my head like a ripe plum hitting the ground and bursting apart. I squeezed my cousins' hands so hard they squealed and tried to pull away. I thought, I could do that. Why not? I could teach children, just like that girl's doing, and share my learning and be useful at last.

And it struck me that an adventure like that would never have been possible back home in the village but maybe here, with everything in such terrible confusion, it might be allowed. I turned to the smaller cousin and rushed her so hard with a hug that she tottered backwards and fell over and we both laughed, collapsed there in a heap against the bulging flap of the tent, until we almost cried and the children laughed too, clapping their hands and completely ignoring the poor young teacher who had herself forgotten, just for that precise moment, which letter came next.

Jamila Auntie and Baba fought about the teaching. I sat beside the tent, listening. My fingernails made half-moon dents in my palms.

'The girl has too much freedom,' Jamila Auntie said. 'She must be more modest or she'll get a reputation. Remember that business with the peasant boy?'

'That's in the past.' Baba's voice was weary. No woman spoke to her husband the way Jamila Auntie spoke to Baba. It shamed him. I wanted to grab hold of her silly face and slap it, to shout: hold your tongue, mind your business, you're not even my mother. I sucked in my bottom lip and bit down on it.

'Who knows what manner of people she'll meet over there? It's dangerous for her, Ibrahim. If her name is tarnished, how will she ever marry?'

I was holding myself down, itching to interrupt. Baba might give in to her, out of sheer exhaustion. I'd seen it happen.

As I strained to hear Baba's reply, a boy, a thin child of only five or six, came racing to the compound, knocking into the plastic barrier and skidding to a halt in the mud. His face was red with effort. Jamila Auntie opened her mouth to bawl at him but, before she could, he started to speak tumbling words.

'A man sent me.' He was panting so hard, he hardly had the breath. 'For Ibrahim-ji. The gate.'

Baba was already on his feet. 'What is it?'

The boy's eyes rolled. His mouth was opening and closing but the only sound was wheezing. The cousins, playing nearby, stared. Aunties poked their heads out of the tents to look.

Baba went rushing out of the compound. Before Jamila could grab hold of me, I ran out after him. Faces turned as we raced past, first the thin schoolteacher, then the young girl behind. Boys heckled us. A few ran alongside, jeering.

A crowd had gathered at the camp gates. Baba and I plunged into the tight knot of men, young and old, who were standing with their arms threaded around each other's shoulders. I wriggled through, fighting to keep close to Baba, feeling the hot press of men around me. Baba was bending over something. Someone in the dirt. A body. A girl. I saw the legs, thin and brittle as sticks. Baba lifted Marva's shoulders and turned her towards me. Her face was smeared with dirt. Baba wrapped his arms around her and cradled her head and shoulders in his lap. I couldn't move. I stared in shock as if he were someone else's baba and she too a stranger.

A man, standing outside the gates, started shouting. He was jabbing his fist in the air, gesturing at Marva and at his own family. They sat around him in the dirt. A huddle of dirty children and a woman in a filthy burqa.

'This is the third camp,' he was yelling. 'Two days I've been walking. My wife and children too. Because of your useless daughter.'

Baba lifted his head and spoke softly to the man. The man's shouts drowned him out.

'Money,' he was raging. 'You pay me. I only did it because they said they'd kill me.'

The crowd of onlookers shifted, starting to take sides.

Baba tried to lift Marva against his thigh. She was stirring and I saw she was alive but without the strength to support herself. I pushed forwards. Baba took off his glasses and wiped his eyes with his sleeve. The man pulled him by the shoulder. People around them started to shout, some voices egging the man on, urging him to fight for his money. I huddled against Baba's side, afraid. The camp guards, watching from the gate, took a step closer and fingered their guns.

Inside the camp, a whistle sounded. There were running feet. Camp officials, some foreign, some local, came pushing into the crowd. One knelt next to Baba. Another clapped his hands and shouted at the gathered men, telling them to go.

The angry man turned to the officials. He was still shouting, counting off on his fingers the camps he had visited as he tried to deliver the girl to her family, pointing to his own exhausted wife. The officials ushered the man and his family inside the camp. The children lay on the ground, their heads leaning on their mother's legs.

A doctor came. He crouched in the dirt beside Baba, his long fingers probing Marva's neck and wrists in front of everyone. He and Baba spoke in low voices. Baba lifted Marva into his arms to carry her away. Her limbs trailed like a broken doll.

Baba had forgotten me. The crowd had already thinned

but the few men still gawping there made low sucking sounds to me as I pushed through them and I pulled my scarf closer around my face.

In the night, I lay with my arms about Mama and tried to quieten her. She was hot with fever and tossing her head from side to side, murmuring and weeping. I patted her cheek and said, 'Hush, Mama, hush,' in a low voice so only she could hear it. Finally she fell into sleep. That long night I didn't let myself think about Saeed at all but only about Marva and what terrible things might have befallen her. Baba hadn't spoken about it when he came back to the tents and I was too ashamed to ask. I felt this was all my fault, a punishment sent from Allah for my wickedness in wanting to have adventures like a boy and to be a teacher. Now my sister Marva, a kind person who did no harm to anyone and had barely left the gates of our compound in her life, was somehow paying the price.

The next morning, Baba told me to take the young cousins to the girls' school. Stay and help the teachers, he told me. Jamila Auntie was too far away to hear. I should have been full of joy but instead I was miserable. All I could think about was Marva and why she was here in the camp but kept separate from Mama and me and the rest of the family, handed over to those doctors who were not decent, everyone told so.

Those doctors' tents were full of evil djinns. The Aunties all whispered that the Westerners tested their drugs on women there, and afterwards the bodies were stitched into cloth before they went for burial because they were too damaged to be seen. We kept far away from them. And now Marva was there and those doctors might be doing any manner of experiments on her and I might never see her alive and whole again. I was sure that Mama, with all her fever and wildness, must be thinking the same.

At twelve o'clock the lessons finally ended and, instead of staying to eat lunch with the other girls, I said that I had a stomach ache and left. I should have gone straight back to the compound and our own tents as Baba had told me but I didn't. I pulled my scarf to cover my face and walked, my feet dragging like stones, towards the medical tents.

Trucks had just arrived and a crowd of men was jostling, vying to get to the front to help. The officials, shiny in yellow plastic waistcoats, waved their arms and shouted at them to stop fighting, but their voices were going unheard. In the commotion, I ducked under the loose flap of the medical tent for ladies.

Inside, the air was cold and smelt of soap and I stood for a moment tasting its strangeness. The mood was hushed. I crouched low and looked around me, feeling the shake in my legs.

The tent was filled with cots and a girl or woman lay in each one. A young woman, a crisp white apron tied over her baggy salwar kameez, was bending over one at the far end, some distance from me. She was fiddling with a sack of liquid on a metal pole. She had her back to me.

I looked up and down the tent. A few cots away from me, the little girl from Jamila Auntie's family was lying, Syma. I knew her and her sister from school in the village. Syma was quite still under a white sheet, her eyes closed. Her cheeks looked blotchy and hot.

161

I crept further into the tent, still searching. Finally I saw her. Marva, my own sister, lying on a cot about halfway down. Her thin legs were covered by a blanket, her hair as neatly brushed as if I had done it with my own hand. Her eyes were open and staring dully at the roof of the tent and at the electric fan fixed there which was slowly turning its head from left to right and back again, like a leering old man enjoying the view of all the half-naked ladies beneath.

The nurse had moved to another bed and was adjusting something. I shrank back against the wall of the tent, trying to lose myself in the shadow. When she finally turned her back to me again, I scooted forwards, running with my body low, until I reached Marva's cot and slid underneath it, my heart pounding and my eyes closed.

I waited, too afraid to look, until my breathing had settled, then I opened my eyes. The underside of the cot was a hand's width from my face. It was black and scored with diamond shapes where the material had been stretched over a metal frame. There was a wooden strut just near my head and small tendrils of fluff were trapped there, hanging down like the fronds of plants. All was quiet. The squeak of the lady's shoes told me she was still nearby, moving quietly from bed to bed. I shuffled on my back to the head of the bed where I knew Marva's face must be and whispered her name. There was silence for a moment.

'Marva. It's me, Layla. Under the cot.'

Nothing. Was she asleep? Then an arm was flung out over the side of the cot and Marva's hand dropped down. I reached out my own and grasped it, lacing my fingers tight through hers, and when she squeezed back, I think I was never so glad in my whole life to hold my big sister's hand.

162

The squeak of the shoes came closer. I froze. I turned my head and saw a pair of white shoes and the hem of a salwar kameez, right there at the next bed. I dropped Marva's hand and lay, trembling. The shoes squeaked nearer. Just stay still for another moment, I was thinking, and she will have done her business and be gone. My throat was dry and my eyes clamped shut and my legs pressed together.

'That's not looking so comfortable.'

She must be whispering to Marva. I kept still, my body tense and senses screaming.

'I said, not much comfort under there. You speak Pashto or what?'

I opened my eyes and there, right by mine, was a round face, hanging upside down looking at me. I jumped and banged my head on the wooden bar across the underside of the cot.

'Your sister, is it?'

I was so dumbstruck, I just stared. Should I crawl out? I couldn't move.

'Why not? You can be here,' the lady was whispering. 'You'll cheer her up. Just keep quiet and don't be a nuisance. And don't let the boss ladies catch you.'

I opened and closed my mouth but I still couldn't speak.

'But if there's any whiff of trouble, I'll throw you out myself.'

Her face disappeared and her white shoes squeaked off to the next bed, leaving me shaking with my hands stuffed into my mouth, ready to burst with relief and afraid to giggle out loud.

Marva and I managed to position ourselves, one on the

cot and the other under it, so that our faces were just a foot or so apart. Like that, I could just hear her soft voice. When I closed my eyes, I imagined we were in our room back home in the village, as we'd been a thousand times before, and I was lying safely in my cot listening as Marva told me one of her fantastical stories. Only this time her story was true.

After we left, Marva said, the hours were filled with gunshots and the whine of jets and she waited, terrified, wondering what was to come. Finally darkness fell. A group of bearded men burst through the gates to the compound and came in, shouting and waving guns. Marva was hiding inside our house, lying beneath the window, her arms raised to the sill, peering out to watch.

Her first thought was that the men were drunk. They ran through the yard, kicking over chairs and tables. One of them was swinging an axe, raising it over his head with both hands and bringing it down on everything he saw until the air was thick with splinters of flying wood. The others whooped and wailed. They smashed through the windows of Hamid Uncle's house and climbed inside. Soon piles of belongings were being hurled out into the yard and lay strewn there. Broken sticks of furniture, clothes, the drawers of the cabinets and a mirror from the bedroom wall which shattered into a thousand pieces when it fell. It was one of the precious carved frame mirrors which our paternal grandmother brought into marriage to our grandfather. The other one hung in Baba's own bedroom.

Marva, seeing the youths come charging next towards our own house, managed to crawl under the cot, pulling a blanket around her legs and tucking them out of sight after her. She curled into a trembling ball, her head buried in her arms, as they shot the padlock off our front door and rampaged through the house. The floor shook under their boots and the sounds bounced along it into her head. The crash of the axe biting into the furniture and wrecking the cupboards and door frames and wardrobes where we used to hide when we were children. The men chanted, 'God is Great! Praise be to Allah!'

All she could think was, What if they find me? She was shaking so hard she thought the cot must be dancing on its legs above her and when they came running into the bedroom, they would find her at once.

They had started at the back of the house with Baba's room and then Jamila Auntie's and next must be our bedroom where Marva was hiding. Outside, there was running and a dog started to bark. She knew the dog. It was our neighbour's. It had been tied up and left behind to guard the compound. A single crack of a gun. The barking stopped.

The door of the bedroom was flung open against the wall. She screwed her eyes closed, waiting to be seized or shot or worse. A man walked around the cot. Heavy footsteps. The floor creaked under his weight. She was biting so hard on her arm to keep herself from crying out that her teeth cut into the skin and drew blood.

A shout from the passageway and he was gone, they were all gone, their footsteps fading as they ran back out into the yard. More men had arrived and their voices grew angry as they picked over our family's possessions, stealing what they wanted and destroying the rest. Then the voices grew fainter and it became quiet. She lay, exhausted from fear, thinking she would stay there forever, curled under the cot in her blanket, hidden away from the world.

She woke, groggy, aware of a dry burning in her throat and the stink of smoke in her nostrils. Roaring and the cracking of wood. She opened her eyes. Long tendrils of smoke were reaching out for her. She dragged herself from under the cot. Smoke was blowing in through the open window and from the doorway to the passage. The yard beyond was shimmering with red and black and the window frame was twisting and buckling in the heat.

She pulled herself onto the top of the cot and stared. Her eyebrows and eyelashes stung with ash. Tiny glowing fragments were floating in on the hot air, singeing her clothes and burning her skin where they settled on her hands and face.

She started to scream but the smoke was thick in her mouth and the more she screamed the more grit and ash she breathed in until it was filling her lungs and she could barely even gasp.

She thought strange things, she said, in those seconds that she crouched there, facing her own death. She wished that the men had found her after all and shot her, the way they'd shot the neighbour's dog, because it would be a better death than burning. She thought about me, she said, and that she'd never see my marriage and children. She thought about Baba and Mama and how angry they'd be when they knew the way those men had laid waste to their precious home and especially that they'd smashed Grandmother's special mirrors.

Now she was swooning with heat and ash and the smoky air was gyrating and dancing in front of her eyes.

Then a man called her name. Marva. She tried to shake the smoke and fire from her ears so she could listen. Nothing. For a moment she thought it must have been a messenger of Allah, sent to bring her to Paradise.

Then she saw him. A thick-set man, silhouetted against the flames, a cloth around his head. Was it a turban? No, it was wrapped around his face, protecting his mouth and nose from the fire. The smoke swirled and he vanished. A phantom, she thought, a ghost. Then he was there again, struggling towards our house, batting back the flames, his salwar kameez streaked with soot. She dragged herself up onto the burning window sill and held out her arms to him, imagining she could jump and fly towards him out of this madness and to safety. As he stumbled nearer, his hair singed and smoking, she saw it was Adnan. She tried to shout his name, but the smoke stole her words and just as he reached her, she toppled and fell forwards, her legs scraping along the collapsing window behind her, tumbling as a dead weight at his feet.

When she talked about Adnan, her voice became gentle and soft. I peered out from under the cot to see. Her cheeks had taken on colour again and her eyes were large and moist. I was older now than when I used to tease her all that time ago at home about Adnan's love for her and say things to make her blush. Now, after all that had happened to us both, I was more grown-up and wise to the ways of the world so I didn't utter a single word. I just looked at Marva and saw what I saw.

'Are you burnt?' I tried to peer out around the curve of the cot to see her body, covered by its blanket. 'Is it painful?'

She clicked her tongue. 'Not so much,' she said. 'Adnan

brought me cool leaves and I soothed the places and now the skin is already healing.' She pulled back the blanket and showed me a thick angry weal scored into her skin. It was stained yellow with ointment, sticky down the raw, red centre but dry and flaking at the sides. 'The nurses put medicine on it,' she said. 'It's starting to mend.'

I thought again about Adnan, scooping her into his arms and rescuing her from the flames. It was terrifying, but now I knew that Marva was safe, it was also thrillingly romantic. I imagined Saeed coming through the flames for me, plucking me out of the fire. I would rest my head against his broad shoulder, my hair tumbling about my face, and melt into his arms, looking pale but quite beautiful as he carried me away. I thought about this for a while.

Then I remembered the way Adnan had disappeared, that first night when we were all sleeping, and the shock for Hamid Uncle and Jamila Auntie the next morning when they awoke to find him gone.

'He went back for you,' I said. 'He didn't tell us. He just went back to save you.'

'I know.'

I thought of the way his father had beaten him for my sake, until the skin on his back was peeled like a fruit, just for carrying Saeed's note, and I felt sick. I crawled back under the cot again and lay there, blinking up at the wooden strut and watching it shimmy into waves as my eyes became wet.

The next day I made an excuse again not to eat lunch and ran back to the medical tent, heart pumping, to see Marva.

The area around the tent was quiet. Just a few camp workers were passing to and fro, Westerners striding with papers flapping in their hands. They looked without seeing me, just another refugee girl, one of so many, her face half-concealed by her chador. I hung close to the nearest plastic shelters, watching and waiting for my chance to scurry across the open ground and into the medical tent.

'*Salaam Alaikum.*'

A man's voice, low and almost in my ear. I half-turned, dropping my eyes to the ground and tipping my head so my face was hidden by the folds of my chador. His feet were thin with crooked toes and encased in cheap sandals. The bottoms of his cotton trousers were soiled black with grime. I hesitated, not knowing whether to answer. It was a polite greeting and it was rude not to speak but he was a stranger to me and I was alone, without Baba or my Uncles.

'I've seen you,' he was saying. 'You are such a pretty girl, too pretty to rot away your life in a dirty camp, nah?'

His voice was wheedling as if he wanted me to understand, to be his friend. I felt my cheeks grow hot. He had seen my face then, whoever he was. That was very wrong. Talking to me like this in public, without Baba being present, that was very wrong too. But he was calling me pretty, he had noticed me above all these other girls and somehow he knew that I was wasting my life here, spoiling my youth in filth and heat.

'Would you like a trinket? A present from me.'

He put his hand out, holding it flat as if he were offering food to a donkey with sharp teeth. Something silver was curled in his palm. A short chain, an anklet or bracelet.

The lines of his hand were engrained with dirt but the chain glistened amongst them. I shook my head and turned away, embarrassed. I wanted it, of course, but it was impossible. Accepting a gift from a strange man would be very wrong.

'No,' I murmured. 'No, thank you.'

I twisted, hunching my shoulder to him. I wanted him to go away but also wondered if he was going to say anything else to me and, if he did, what might happen next.

There was a pause. He was moving his arm. I couldn't look. The hand came out again, poked around my shoulder until it was almost under my nose.

'Have this then,' he said. 'No harm in this. Only a sweet. A sweet from your new friend, Doc. For a pretty girl.'

A wrapped sweet was sitting on his palm now, just where the chain had been, as if one had been conjured into the other by magic. The paper was crinkly and bright orange. I reached out my fingers and took it.

'And what is your good name, pretty girl?'

I shook my head. I wanted him to go now. I had the sweet grasped firmly in my fist and already I was imagining giving it to Marva, my gift to her.

His face had crept closer to mine and for a moment, the smell of him intruded, a smell of male sweat and filthy clothes. He hesitated, then laughed and was suddenly gone.

I lifted my head to look after him as he walked away. He was a slight man, his hair long and slick around his ears. His crumpled salwar kameez flapped around thin arms and legs. As I looked, feeling the hardness of the sweet in my fingers, he turned his head in a quick

170

movement and looked back at me over his shoulder and his eyes were amused. I flushed, feeling exposed, realizing in an instant that he knew all along that I would take the sweet and he knew too that I would look after him as he walked away and that he, turning, would catch me looking.

When I slid under Marva's cot, I handed her the orange sweet and listened as she unwrapped it and started to suck. Then she turned onto her side and carried on with her story at once, as if she had been waiting all morning while I was at the school, just lying there, waiting for me to come.

That night, she told me, Adnan carried her down the hillside to a lean-to shack in one of the wheat fields which was used to store grain and suchlike. He set her down very gently on the ground there and spread out sacking to make her comfortable and watched over her. Every time she woke, on account of terrible dreams about the flames and choking in her chest and smarting pain from her burnt skin, he was sitting still, waiting to soothe her back to sleep.

The next day she was woken early by the sound of gunfire. It was much louder than the previous day. Again the jets started to streak across the sky. The roar shuttled back and forth around the mountains. She and Adnan huddled together and wondered where the bombs were falling.

When it was light, Marva sent Adnan scavenging for something to eat and for water while she tended her burns. The houses in the compound had been destroyed and they had no proper place to live. She had barely been outside the compound in her life and the broad openness of the landscape, with its echoing gunfire, bombs and dramatic mountains overwhelmed and frightened her.

He had just come back and was sharing water with her when there was a sudden rustling in the wheat and Adnan jumped to his feet, startled. Four men were standing in a semicircle in front of them, pointing guns. They had scarves tied around their faces like bandits and two wore turbans and their eyes were menacing. Marva reached for the chador which had slipped to the back of her head and tugged it forwards to shield her hair.

'What is this?' The man at the front spoke boldly like a commander and his tone was mocking. 'Two crows in their love nest?'

'How dare you!' Adnan had jumped to his feet and squared his shoulders to them, all ready to fight. 'She is my cousin. We are good Muslims. Don't tell such smut.'

The commander looked amused. There were four of them and they had guns to boot.

'No insult, brother,' he said. 'If you are a good Muslim, you should defend your sister's honour. But why is she here? Don't you know the infidel soldiers are coming?'

The men around him sniggered. Adnan was staring closely at one of the men, screwing up his face as if he were trying to concentrate. 'Saeed?'

Listening to this, lying under Marva's hospital cot, I almost banged my head in shock. Saeed?

Saeed looked embarrassed, she said, and didn't speak. The commander looked from one man to the other and broke into a smile. He stepped nearer to Adnan and clasped him by the shoulder as if he were a friend. 'If you are truly a good Muslim, brother,' he said, 'then you are one of us. Welcome, brother.'

Marva had listened with growing unease, wondering what this meant and how she might warn Adnan to be on his guard. On account of his being simple, he was always foolish enough to take people at their word and believe whatever they promised, even though it made him the endless butt of pranks and jokes.

He put his arm around the commander's shoulder in return and beamed. 'May Allah protect you,' he said warmly. 'May He give you long life.'

The commander saw the pail of water that Adnan had just fetched and asked if they might sit and share it. Marva had felt a growing sense of discomfort as she observed all this. There was something about the commander she didn't trust and wanted to signal that to Adnan but he, pouring the water into the commander's cup, was quite unaware.

The other three men, including Saeed, stood back, watching. They seemed tense, careful not to speak or to be forward in the commander's presence. Adnan, by contrast, chatted without reservation. He explained that the rest of the family had left but Marva, unable to walk, couldn't go with them. The commander listened attentively. Then Adnan fell to asking questions, with the innocence of a child, about the commander's gun and the equipment strapped around his body.

Finally the commander got to his feet and made to leave.

'Keep her here,' he said, nodding past to Marva. 'This is safe ground for another day. Tomorrow we'll find a way of getting her off the mountainside to her family.' He smiled a cool toothy grin, and Adnan, delighted, clapped his hands in glee and thanked him.

For the rest of the day, Adnan boasted to Marva, so proud he could barely contain himself. He had gathered fruit for them to eat and Marva sorted through it, discarding the bloated and rotten pieces.

'See,' he kept saying, 'I can take good care of you.' He grasped her hand. 'See what good friends I have?'

She nodded and tried to smile, praising him for his cleverness and his courage until he beamed. She kept her concerns hidden.

The commander did come back. Adnan and one of the fighters carried Marva between them on a blanket strung between two branches. They travelled for more than an hour down the steep mountainside. Black smoke rose on the other side of the valley as bombs struck. The clatter of machine guns echoed around the mountains. It was hard to tell where the sound was coming from. Marva lay, afraid, staring up at the wisps of cloud against the blue, feeling herself bounced and tossed on the taut blanket.

Twice the commander directed them to hide and they darted behind bushes or into gullies while a jet tore through the sky above them or a military convoy passed below. Finally they reached the road. Many people had already fled but the road was still busy with human traffic, families walking slowly from high in the mountains with exhausted children and elderly relatives, bent and frail.

The commander stopped the first handcart they saw. The man pushing it fell silent when he saw them, looking first at their guns and then their faces. Finally he looked at Marva. His wife and children stopped some paces behind and waited, too tired to care.

The cart was piled with metal farming implements, cooking pots and bundles of clothes.

'This is your cart?'

The man narrowed his eyes and nodded. The commander's tone was threatening. The man looked wary.

The commander signalled to his men and they started to unload the cart, clearing a space. The man protested. 'Please,' he said, as spades and scythes and hoes were thrown in the ditch. 'How will I live? I need—'

The commander ignored him. He told Adnan to lift Marva onto the cart. Adnan settled her there and tucked a blanket around her thin legs.

'This man will take good care of you,' he whispered. 'He has a kind face.'

Marva, seeing only anger in the man's eyes, said nothing.

'Find her family in the camps. Deliver her safely.' The commander's gun was poking into the man's chest, making him glassy-eyed with fear. 'If not, I will know and come for you.'

Her last sight as the man lifted the handles of the cart and pushed it, protesting, into the road was of Adnan, beaming a proud goodbye, his large eyes focused on nothing but her face, while the commander at his side laid a possessive hand on Adnan's shoulder as if to say: I have let you go but this one I claim as my own.

Marva fell silent when she'd finished telling her story. I reached up my hand and patted her body until she took my hand in her own, weaving her fingers through mine and squeezing them tight.

14

Ellen found Britta and Fatima in one of the poky back offices. They were talking in low voices. Britta's face was drawn, as if she'd barely slept. When she saw Ellen, she looked embarrassed.

'I am sorry.' She opened her hands wide in a gesture of pleading. 'That interview you wanted. I know I said now. But maybe a little later?'

'What's happened?'

Britta's eyes were red with tiredness. 'A little girl. Typhoid fever. Diarrhoea. Now she has some respiratory infection also. We're just discussing—'

'Of course.' Ellen left them to talk. She walked back through the ward, scanning the faces. Many of the women were twisted on their sides with closed eyes. Others stared out at her blankly, their minds elsewhere.

The girl was in a bed close to the entrance. She was a small thing, lying on her back, her eyes closed. The lower half of her face was consumed by a moulded plastic mask.

Her chest was rising and falling in a frantic scrabble for breath. The oxygen was being discharged to her in a steady whisper that was almost drowned out by the desperate sucking and rasping of her lungs.

Sweat was slick on her face, running down her temples and into wild tufts of hair that stuck up above her forehead. Her closed eyes looked abnormally large, bulging above the sharp lines of her cheeks. A needle, taped to the soft inner skin of her arm, was slowly discharging liquid. Something about her struggle made Ellen think, It's already too late.

Fatima came towards them, carrying a bowl of water. Her steps were quick. She set the bowl on the floor, squeezed out the cloth inside it and began to wash the child, stroking her skin with cool water. The girl's eyelids fluttered but didn't open.

'Is she conscious?'

Fatima shrugged. 'She slips in and out. She has delirium.'

The girl's limbs flopped like a cloth puppet as Fatima lifted her this way and that, holding her body with care as she washed her down. The vegetal stink of the girl's body was overlaid by antiseptic. There was a new sound now, the soft murmur of the water in the basin as Fatima rinsed and squeezed the cloth.

The sunlight outside was piercing. Ellen sat in the line of shade beside the unloading bay, pulled out her notebook and wrote some lines of description for herself about the little girl and the atmosphere on the ward. Then she drank down some water and flicked through the last few pages of notes. She needed to think. She wanted to write about the spreading typhoid. But it was sensitive. All the camps were fighting for funding. The last thing Britta and Frank needed was doubt about their standard of hygiene and healthcare.

A shadow fell across her notebook. A figure, blocking the sun. She looked up. The schoolteacher, his face in shadow, his round hat perched on his head, his glasses crooked on his nose.

'*Salaam Alaikum*.' He was breathy with emotion.

'Ibrahim. Good news.' Ellen patted the ground beside her. 'They've agreed to let me see their records. At the camps. They haven't registered everyone but—'

'I have found them.' He settled himself at a respectable distance, his legs crossed under him. 'My family.' He placed his swollen hands together, the palms engorged by grubby bandages. 'Here, in the camp.'

'You have?' She was confused. He seemed deflated. 'Are they OK?'

He paused, considering the question, then nodded, making his short beard waggle. 'They are here in safety.' He leant closer towards her and lowered his voice. 'My daughter has bad legs.' He touched a hand to his own leg by way of explanation. 'Some illness when she was young. Very terrible illness.'

Polio, she thought. Bound to be. 'How did she get here?'

'She is coming alone, with Taliban.'

Ellen stared. 'With the Taliban?'

He tutted. 'A man brings her with his cart.' He mimed pulling a handcart, then showed a two-fingered gun to the head. 'The Taliban are making him to do this.'

'Why?'

He pulled a face, shook his head. 'Some peculiar business is there. What to do?' He stared dismally at his feet.

'Is she OK?'

He pointed to the medical tent. 'She is inside the hospital.' He looked directly at her and she saw pleading in his watery eyes. 'I cannot go in this place. It is for ladies only but the ladies in my family are very much afraid to go. Too much superstition. Please tell me, when it is opportune, how does she do.'

Ellen nodded, thinking. 'I'd like to ask her,' she said. 'I'd like to talk to many of the women there. But I can't speak Pashto. Do you know any lady who could translate? I could pay.'

His forehead tightened as he followed the words and made sense of them. He sat, staring at the ground for a moment, thinking. He seemed to come to a decision. 'I am knowing about a very good girl. My own daughter.'

Ellen pointed back to the medical tent. 'She speaks English?'

'Not this daughter.' He held up his hand to indicate two with his fingers. 'I have two daughter. She is very good student. She speaks English almost as good as me.'

He was waving his bandaged hand now, possessed by growing excitement. 'You will find her. She is teacher in the school. Her name is Layla.'

'What school?'

'Some classes, here in the camp only. I am teacher for boys and Layla is teacher for girls. Small girls.'

'And I have your permission to work with her, if she wants to help me?'

'Of course.' He smiled, showing blackened teeth. 'She will very help you.'

The sound reached her first. High-pitched children's voices, chanting lessons in unison. Ellen knocked on the woven partition and a young aid worker let her in. She led her through a circle of gossiping women to a large hessian tent, stretched over a square metal frame.

Inside, about forty girls were sitting in rows, cross-legged on a carpet of sacking. Their heads were parcelled in brightly coloured headscarves and their faces were grubby. The youngest, shyly sitting against older sisters, looked only five or six. Many were several years older. They were rocking themselves as they chanted, some with hesitant whispery voices, others almost shouting, and patting their palms against their knees to keep the beat. At the head of the class, a young girl was conducting them with some gusto. A blackboard and easel stood behind her.

The children turned and gawped at Ellen. The young teacher, following their eyes, turned to look too. She broke off and the children faltered through another few beats, then fell silent, too distracted to concentrate.

The aid worker was starting to explain. 'So many families here,' she was saying, 'have taken the chance to send their girls—'

Before the woman could finish her sentence, the young teacher stepped smartly forwards, placed her pointing stick at the bottom of the easel and approached Ellen.

'How do you do?'

Ellen smiled. She was a striking girl, slight but forceful. She exuded confidence and a youthful naivety. Her eyes were bright and her gaze direct and she held herself with dignity.

'My name is Layla,' she said. 'Please, what is your good name?'

Her accent was heavy but she spoke the English words with precision as if these were sentences she had spent all her life practising, in preparation for just such a moment.

'My name is Ellen. I know your father, Layla.'

Layla paused, licking her lips. She seemed surprised and straining to think what to say to this. The children, wide-eyed with wonder, gazed at them in silence. The aid worker was beaming, proud of the girl and her boldness.

'This is the school of girls,' Layla said at last and smiled, her eyes meeting Ellen's. 'You are most welcome.'

Ellen spent the rest of the morning at the school. Layla carried on with her teaching and, when she was free, acted as Ellen's translator so she could talk to the children. Many of the young girls were too afraid or too traumatized to say very much. They gave her ragged patches from the same common story, of the Taliban and the changes in their lives, of bombs and soldiers, of the long journey from their homes to the camp. When the classes ended and the teachers stopped to eat their lunch, Ellen headed back to the medical tent. Layla promised to find her there after she'd eaten.

Ellen sensed at once that the atmosphere there had changed. Fatima didn't look up as she entered the ward. The little girl's bed was empty, the bedding cleared. The earlier tension had been replaced by weary defeat.

Ellen walked the length of the ward to the small rooms

181

at the back, feeling the eyes of the patients moving with her. Britta was sitting on a chair by the girl's covered body, her head bowed. Her fingers were gripping the cross at her neck.

The girl was so slight that she barely reached halfway down the stretcher. The cloth that covered her fell in drapes over a series of tiny mounds, from head to feet, and billowed out onto the floor. Ellen thought of the child a few hours earlier, lying in the same position on her back, her eyes closed, her lungs noisy with the struggle to breathe. The thin limbs, which Fatima had carefully washed, not realizing they would soon be washed again for burial, lay straight and lifeless.

Britta sensed her there and turned. Her eyes were red-rimmed.

'She didn't respond.' Her voice was thick. 'She wasn't strong but she should have made it. We had her. We were treating her.'

Ellen pulled up a chair and sat beside her. 'It's not your fault.'

Britta looked distraught. 'What do I say to her mother?'

Ellen shook her head. 'You don't say anything.'

Britta turned away. The room had a sickly smell of disinfectant. Flies were buzzing against the window, banging the glass, trying to escape.

'It's not right. I've worked with typhoid, I've treated it many times. This, what is happening, is not right.' Britta's fingers had reached again for her cross and she was clutching it as if it were the only steady object in a spinning world.

Ellen sat quietly, watching the agitation in her fingers,

the anguish in her face. 'Come away for a bit. Just for a break. Let's go for a Coke or something.'

'I hate Coke.' But she allowed Ellen to persuade her out of the small room, leaving the child alone in the silence.

They walked out of the back of the medical tent and towards the low administrative tent behind it. Ellen sat her in the shade of the tent flap and went inside to pull fresh bottles of water from the boxes stacked there for workers.

Britta starting talking as soon as she sat down again.

'The monsoon is coming. Any day now. Then the latrines and ditches will overflow and contamination will come everywhere and typhoid will really spread. This is nothing.'

'Is it just the women?'

'Men too.'

'What can you do?'

Britta shrugged. 'I've made a request for money. We should run a campaign here for hand-washing, soap, all that. Better latrines. And we should vaccinate. First we need quantity of vaccine, then we must make people agree.' She gestured out towards the tube wells where girls were filling buckets, splashing and playing in the falling arc. 'In a place like this, stopping the spread is very hard.'

Ellen thought of the small medical tent, already almost full to capacity. 'Will you get more staff?'

'Maybe. Maybe not. Medicine International is small. We need money from outside.'

'It might come.' Khan might announce another dona-tion. It took time for the world to wake up to disasters, especially when they were slow-moving.

Britta was sitting still, her shoulders hunched. She looked utterly dejected. 'I called my mother last night. She asked how things were. What does one say? I started to tell her about the typhoid, about the little girl. Syma. Her name's Syma. Did you know that? Pretty, isn't it?' She drifted back into silence.

'What did your mother say?'

Britta sighed. 'She said: "Oh dear, that is a pity." Then she started to tell me about the new garden centre which has opened just outside our town. It has a sale and she bought some very good plants for the side garden. There is a tea shop in the garden centre, she told me. And a gift store. "We'll go there together when you come home."'

Ellen smiled.

Britta was still talking, her hands stretched wide with exasperation. 'How can she think I want to talk about tea shops? No one at home understands anything. Don't you know? You come back from Somalia or Pakistan or some difficult place and they say: "How are you?" And even as you open your mouth to tell them, their eyes are already becoming bored. Not even two minutes. Then they are talking for hours about some new brand of biscuits or some celebrity programme on the television.'

She tore the plastic top off the bottle of water and drank. Her hair was plastered to her forehead, green eyes shining with indignation.

Ellen drank from her own bottle. The water was tepid but a relief, swilling dust from her throat. 'It's a different world. People don't know how to relate to it.'

'They could listen. That would be a good start.' Britta was fiddling with the bottle top, tearing with her fingertips at the jagged plastic edge. 'I'm already twenty-five years old,' she said. 'All my friends are married and having babies. It's all they talk about. Pregnancy and teething and schools. They don't know what to say to me any more.'

Ellen thought of her own friends and the gulf that had opened up between them through the years. 'It isn't easy.'

'My mother tells me she's very proud of my work but I think she wants me to stop it now and go home and have babies myself. Then I could go to the tea shop with her every week. She's the only one of her friends with such a crazy daughter. Maybe that is wrong.'

'It's your life.'

Britta set the bottle between her knees, lifted her head-scarf and raked her hands through her hair. Her damp fingers left track marks. 'My grandmother used to make this wonderful cake. Apple cake. Her own special recipe. It's very Danish. Do you know it? With certain spices, I don't know the names in English.'

Ellen shook her head.

'So good.' Britta smacked her lips. 'Better than any cake I can taste. She taught it to my mother too but she never makes it any more. She says it's for children to enjoy. Why make apple cake with no children here to eat it? It's not worth so much trouble.'

Ellen drank the water and listened.

'When will I ever have time in my life to make apple cake? And who will I make it for?' Britta kicked at the dirt with her boot, angry. 'I am here in Pakistan and my patients are dying, one after one, and the world will lose forever my grandmother's apple cake. How is this right?'

Ellen sat quietly beside her. The silence stretched. Finally she said, 'Make it. Next time you're home.'

*   *   *

185

They heaved themselves to their feet and walked slowly back to work.

Layla was standing by the entrance, waiting for them. It was clear from her posture that she was unhappy, her body twisted, her chador held high to cover her face. She was using her shoulder as a barrier to hold off a man who was standing close to her, talking. His hair was unkempt, his clothes dirty. It took Ellen a moment to remember where she'd seen him before.

'That's Doc, isn't it? What's he doing here?'

Britta shrugged. 'Don't worry. Fatima will see to him.'

Ellen watched him as he leant in towards Layla. She thought of the young girls at the hotel party, sharing a single cigarette.

'He comes here a lot?'

'He hangs about. There isn't much to do in the camp, you know? People are bored.'

Ellen grimaced. 'You don't mind him?'

'Come on.' Britta sighed. 'There's more important things to worry about. He's harmless. Fatima deals with him. She doesn't take any nonsense from anyone, especially not him.'

Doc looked up and saw them. He grinned, showing crooked teeth, then oozed away from Layla and slid off in an instant between the tents. Ellen looked after him and frowned. Layla too had seen them now and had turned her face to the ground.

'You know this girl?'

'That's Layla. I'm hoping she'll translate for me.'

'She speaks English?'

'A bit.' They walked towards her. 'You're treating her sister. I think she had polio.'

Britta nodded, looking thoughtful. 'There's one girl with childhood paralysis. Dehydration, minor lesions and burns. Not serious.'

'You mind if Layla comes in to see her?'

'Of course not.' They were just a few paces from Layla now. Britta put her hand on Ellen's shoulder and squeezed it as she moved past her to enter the ward. Layla, still looking uncomfortable, didn't lift her head to greet them.

'You all right?'

Layla stared at her feet in silence.

'What was that man saying?'

She squirmed. It took her a long time to speak. 'He likes to give me things.'

'Give you things? What sort of things?'

Another pause. Her fist was clenched. She opened it slowly, guiltily, to reveal a sweet wrapped in red paper in the hollow of her palm.

Ellen shook her head. 'Layla, look at me.' The girl forced herself to lift her eyes, dragging them up with reluctance. 'You keep away from him. Don't let him give you anything. He's not a good man.'

'OK.'

Ellen took her arm and together they followed Britta into the cool of the tent to seek out Layla's sister and to work together on translating the stories of the women who were strong enough to speak.

That evening, Ellen lay on her bed fully dressed, too tired to move. There was noise in the corridor, running feet and banging on doors and men's voices shouting and laughing.

Britta was right to be afraid. The monsoon would break

187

any day now, she could sense it. The dryness in the air was reaching breaking point. The cases of typhoid they'd seen so far were barely the start of the season. She thought of Syma's body, so fragile and alone on the adult stretcher.

There was a knock on her door. She hesitated, wondering whether to bother moving to answer it. A second knock, more insistent. Housekeeping, probably, to check the minibar or to turn down the bedding. She pulled herself to the door, thinking through the Urdu expression for: Now isn't a good time.

'You look pleased to see me.' Frank seemed surprisingly perky. He had his bottle of Scotch secreted in its paper bag in his hand.

'I was just going to bed.'

He looked at his watch. 'Ten after nine?'

'Tough day.' She thought of him ushering the young Pakistani man into his room and turned away. He followed her inside.

'Did you eat yet?'

'I'm not hungry.'

He was trying to catch her eye. She rummaged in the hotel cabinet for a glass and handed him one for himself. Just one. She pulled together some cushions and propped herself up against the bed's headboard.

He sat on the other single bed, his ankle crossed over his knee, and sipped his whisky. 'Any idea how much longer you'll stay?'

She shrugged. 'Another day or two. London wants a follow-up but I think that'll be it.' She thought about her story. 'I meant to ask, can you go on the record? I need an overview. We can negotiate questions.'

He nodded without replying. She had the sense he wasn't really listening. She persisted: 'Maybe tomorrow. How about ten?'

'Not morning.' He shifted, his eyes on the carpet.

She observed him more closely. 'Aren't you around in the morning?'

'No.'

The tip of his tongue flicked the corner of his lips. Tension, she thought.

'Why? What're you up to?'

He gave a short cough. 'Meeting the chief of police. You know. Security.'

'Security?'

He sipped his whisky, didn't speak for a moment. She waited.

He said, 'There's a lot of Taliban in the camps. I need to figure out a way of dealing with them.'

'How do you know?'

'People come to us. They talk.' He shrugged, swishing the whisky around his glass and staring into it. 'They've come all this way to be safe, then one day they're in line for food and some guy who burnt out their house or threatened their kids is right there in line too. Frightens the hell out of them.'

'So what do you do?'

'First of all figure out who to believe.'

She thought of the way Frank had greeted the young man in the half-light of the corridor. 'If they are here, what're they doing?'

'Intimidating people. Spreading rumours. Causing trouble.'

She looked at his carefully lowered eyes. 'Stealing your supplies?'

He looked up at last and gave her a quick, complicit smile. 'Maybe.'

'That's why you're seeing this guy?'

'Partly.'

She nodded, thinking about Ibrahim and the Taliban leader he'd described. 'This commander, Mohammed Bul Gourn. Is this his patch?'

Frank looked taken aback. 'You know about him?'

'A bit.'

He nodded to himself, drank a mouthful of whisky. 'Yeah, I believe it's his turf. Sounds like he's a rising star.'

Overhead, heavy objects were being scraped and dragged. Someone was moving furniture. The noise was grating. She thought about Mohammed Bul Gourn. It was unsettling to know he had spies in the camp. Fatima had said that too. It might be a strong angle for the follow-up. People flee the Taliban only to find they're still not safe from them.

'Who's he got in the camps? You identified them?'

He shook his head. 'Don't go there, Ellie.' He seemed preoccupied, keeping his distance from her. He drank off his whisky, paused. 'I'm serious. They're everywhere. If they think you're a problem, I can't protect you. No one can.'

'I know.'

'Being a journalist won't save you. Being a woman won't either.'

She tutted. 'Got it. Don't worry.'

They sat in silence for a while. The muffled scraping and footsteps from above hung between them.

He set his empty glass on the table and picked up his bottle to leave. 'Anyway. I should go.'

He got to his feet. She followed him to the door to see him out. When he turned to say goodnight, his face was troubled.

She stood in the doorway, watching him walk down the centre of the corridor. His back was broad and he moved briskly. Cones of bright, hard light fell at intervals from the ceiling. As he stepped through them, his hair shone silver, then returned to black a moment later as he hit shadow. She waited until he reached the lifts, watching, despite herself, to see if he'd turn to check if she was still there, looking after him. He didn't.

15

Death had come to the place and there was little Jamila could do to comfort Syma's parents. She sat with her arms around the slight body of her young cousin's wife and rocked her as she cried. At first the girl was full of anger. She shrieked, shuddering for air, as she wept, struggling with Jamila and trying to pull her hands free to tear at her face and hair, to strike out with her fists.

Jamila held her hard, pinning her wrists at her sides. After some time she became quieter and sobbed into Jamila's neck and finally her body went limp. The baby boy sat nearby in the dirt, unnaturally still, and stared at them with eyes full of fear.

Jamila leant forwards to dip the end of her chador in the bucket and wet it, then lifted the girl's blotchy face away from her shoulder and washed over her cheeks and eyes with the licking tongue of cloth.

'It is the will of Allah,' she said. 'It is His wish.'

The girl's eyes were closed now. She looked as if her hope of life had been extinguished.

'Syma was not yours,' Jamila was saying. 'She was a gift from God. Now He has taken her home.'

The baby boy opened his mouth wide and started to scream. The girl lay against Jamila, her swollen face expressionless, and didn't move. Jamila watched the baby in his growing panic. He would learn to wait.

A little later, when the girl finally settled on the ground and slept, Jamila gathered up the baby and went to speak to the young cousin. He was sitting on a piece of wood in the mud, his legs drawn up under him. His eyes too were red with crying. The last time I saw Syma, she was sitting still and silent like that, Jamila thought. I wish she had never left our village, she and Old Auntie both.

Jamila sat down on the wood, a little distance from the young man. The baby was restless and heavy in her arms. Her knees creaked as she lowered herself. The dirt was hard and dry with too much sun.

'I made her take Syma to those doctors.' He was scraping his nails in the dust. 'I thought it was right.'

Jamila didn't speak. She looked at the tracks he was making. She is buried in that ground. That small girl who liked to skip and chatter. The earth has swallowed her whole. How is that right?

'People say that medical place is evil,' he went on. 'They say the foreign doctors kill people there. I said that was nonsense. That they had good medicine. I said they'd make Syma well again.'

Jamila didn't look at him. The child was buried here, on these bleak plains. She and Old Auntie also were far away from the graves of their ancestors, far away from Mutaire and the family compound where they were both born and where they should both have passed. That too was not right. How could the girl rest peacefully when she was so far from home?

He raised his eyes and stared at the figure of his sleeping wife, lying there in the dirt. 'Now what can I tell her? Was she right?'

Jamila turned the baby on her lap. He was fussing, grumbling and grabbing at her hair. 'You have another child. He needs you.'

The young cousin looked blankly at his son as if he had never set eyes on him before. 'She dressed her up in fancy clothes for the burial,' he said. 'That's not normal.' He swallowed, gathered his strength to speak. 'She fussed over her hair, plaiting it and pinning it.' He looked frightened by the memory of it. 'When they came to take her, she made them wait while she wrapped a blanket around her shoulders. "She'll catch cold," she said.'

The baby was fretting, threatening to cry. Jamila reached out and dangled the child over his lap. The baby was panting with exertion, his grubby feet paddling his father's thighs.

The sky was darkening with cloud. Jamila sniffed the air as she walked smartly back to the tents. She drew her chador across her face until just her eyes showed, protecting herself from the light breeze that was whipping dust through the camp. It was stirring up the small children, setting them prancing and chasing each other in giddy circles like swirling leaves. It is coming, she thought, the first rain. She quickened her pace. The plastic walls of the shelters and makeshift fences shifted and crackled.

Inside the tent, the heat was oppressive. Layla's mama was lying alone, sticky with sweat. She was speaking nonsense. Jamila knelt close to the woman's face to listen. Babble. Some talk of babies. She was agitated, trying to raise her head, then falling back again onto her mat, telling some story about finding a child or feeding one. Her breath was foetid.

Jamila lifted the younger woman against her thigh and put a cup of water to her lips. Her shoulders were light, the skin slippery and hot with fever. This was already the third day that she had been unable to keep food in her stomach and she was becoming weak.

If only our imam were here, she thought. He would cast out this bad fever from her body. She pressed her fingers under the woman's sleeping mat and felt for the knife she'd slipped there that morning. It was still in place. She wanted it to cut at the demons and frighten them away, the same way a knife protected a newborn baby when it was too weak to defend itself.

Layla should be there, doing her duty by tending to her mama. The girl hadn't been taught to be respectful and modest. Jamila had seen her, walking boldly about the camp in full view of young men. It was dangerous for her now she was a young woman and especially here, outside the safety of the village. If she were dishonoured, it would shame them all. Ibrahim spoiled her. She tried to warn him but he was too blinded by love for the girl to listen.

She lifted the cup to the woman's lips again and tried to force her to drink. She seemed chilled now and her limbs were twitching. Jamila piled a third blanket on top of her and pressed it to her body.

The young cousin was right about the hospital. Everyone

was afraid. When the big fever came, the foreign doctors came to the tents and carried away the patients; she had seen it with her own eyes. No one knew what happened to them afterwards. No one lived to come back and tell tales. Ibrahim said all this was nonsense and he'd have no talk of it. She knew why. It was because Marva the cripple was already there. He'd left her with those doctors and now he was afraid.

Layla's mama was moaning to herself, a low, half-hearted murmuring. Jamila set down the cup and blotted her lips. She wrapped her arms around her shoulders. The illness inside her body was shaking her, knocking on her skin, trying to break through and escape. The woman smelt bad. She needed cleaning. Jamila tutted under her breath. The girl should be here to do it, her own daughter. No wonder her spirit was sick. A mother needed her daughter's care as a daughter needed her mother's.

A voice rose, close to the tent. Ibrahim was there. He was calling. Jamila set the woman on the ground again and crawled out to him.

He was peering at her with his poor eyes, as if he had forgotten which wife she might be.

'She's sleeping,' she said.

He put his head on one side and looked at her and she could feel his mind working but couldn't hear what he was thinking.

'She's tired, that's all,' she said.

He didn't speak, just gazed at her as if he knew she was lying and wondered why.

'She has a headache.'

He bent down and picked up a stick, dropped by one of the children. He started to scratch something in the dust. 'She's been ill for days now.'

She shook her head. 'Nonsense. She just needs to sleep.'

His stick scratched, scratched. 'If she's ill, I should fetch a doctor.'

'For a headache?'

Finally he turned, trailing the stick in his hand the way a small boy might and walked back out into the camp. All around, women were fastening down their plastic walls, securing them against the flapping breeze, and, where they had twine, tying it tighter around staves and sticks. Ibrahim paid them no attention. He just walked straight ahead between the rows of tents, dragging his stick, his mind disappeared to some other place.

Jamila walked around their own female sleeping tent where Layla's mother was now lying. She knotted the string more firmly and shifted the stones to make sure they were squarely on the plastic rim, holding it in place. She fetched the pail and went to stand in the queue for the water pump. I should have asked him, 'Where's your daughter? Why isn't she here, safe inside the family, tending to her mother?' She shuffled forwards, smelling the coming rain in the air and waiting to fill the pail.

Jamila looked over the woman's body as she stripped her off and washed her down. The light filtering through the plastic walls of the tent had an unearthly blue tinge but she could see that the woman's brown skin had become yellowish. Her body was burning and yet she was shivering, hugging her arms to her chest as if she were cold.

Afterwards she seemed quieter. She lay on her side, with all the blankets in the tent heaped on top of her, and slept. Only her face poked out. It was thin now and her skin was sallow. Jamila sat with her hands resting in her lap and studied her. You were such a beautiful girl when you came to our house as a bride. You had long limbs and a shy, tender face and such innocence. Ibrahim had more love pooled in his eyes for you than I'd ever seen.

Jamila shook her head. She had been tormented by such jealousy when this woman first came to Ibrahim's house and took Jamila's place. That was a long time ago. All she felt now, as she looked at the sickly yellow of her cheeks, was a great sadness. But I am glad that you never gave him a healthy boy. That would have been more than I could bear.

Something rapped on the plastic by her head. She looked up. Another tap. Then a light hail of them. Children throwing a shower of dirt, perhaps? The clattering was louder now and becoming harder as something glanced off the stretched ceiling above them. She crawled towards the entrance of the tent.

The dust outside was pitted with dark circles. Rain was falling, swelling to full heavy drops that were striking the ground and exploding in splashes. They were beating a steady rhythm all around her on the plastic. The air was dark with water and instantly cooler.

When she tipped her head and looked up, a million stripes of rainwater fell towards her, making lines directly from the heavens all the way to her face. The banging of the rain was raising a barrage everywhere and above it, through the camp, people were shouting. A group of men ran past, dashing for shelter. They were living streams, running with water, saturated hair pouring sheets down their faces and onto their shoulders, their chests. Their clothes became transparent where they stuck to wet flesh. They were laughing and, seeing the water running into their grinning mouths, she could taste it too.

Across the path, men and women were huddled in their shelters, children pressing against their legs. They were reaching up and pulling out lips of plastic above their heads, extending it as they tried to direct the flowing water away from them, and peering, mesmerized, at the falling rain. All around now, puddles and pools were forming, struggling to penetrate the compact, baked earth.

She looked back inside the tent. Layla's mother was motionless under her lumpy pile of blankets, sleeping on through the din. The plastic roof over them was dark with channels of water, gathering and running off, and bowing under the growing weight. Already she could see the weaknesses, fault lines where water was intruding, bubbling and dripping down onto their sleeping mats. She crawled through the space, trying to gather the bedding into the driest spots.

There was noise and she turned her head to look. Four or five children were shrieking and laughing. They had broken free from their parents and were gambolling in the open air. Their heads were tipped back, mouths open, arms thrown wide to greet the monsoon. Their small brown feet stamped in the puddles and kicked up dirty water in arcs of spray.

She smiled. She sat for a long time, watching the children and the torrent of rain and thinking of all the places it was falling. It was soaking into the graves of her mother and grandmother back in the village and running in rivulets down the roof of their house in the compound and cascading to the empty yard beneath. She thought how little time it seemed since she had been a small child herself, dancing in puddles and spinning and tasting the rain, and yet, at the same time, how fast life was changing all around her and how dizzy it made her feel.

16

Britta was standing inside the main entrance to the administration building, watching the rain. 'It's started. The monsoon.'

Ellen ducked in past her, pushing her way out of the downpour. The rain had brought the temperature down but it was also turning the camp to mud. Her boots were caked in it. Sweeping water was rushing along every channel and ditch, carrying all kinds of filth and making it slick and slippery underfoot. She thought of the children who played in it and the overflowing latrines and the speed with which disease might spread.

'Any more typhoid?'

'Three new cases. Two severe.' She looked exhausted. 'The men had three deaths yesterday.'

Frank was inside, directing two workmen. They were clambering around on stepladders, trying to plug leaks in the roof. The brick floor was uneven and the rainwater had pooled underfoot. He lifted his hand to stop her as she headed past him.

'Hey. I've got a great story for you.'

'Really?' People who told her that were rarely right.

'Don't you want to hear it? It'll win a Pulitzer.'

'Course it will.'

She leant against a stack of boxes and waited. 'Go on then.'

He took a moment longer with the workmen, then came across to her, pulling a face. 'Not like you'll get much done here anyhow. The place is chaotic.'

His hair was dripping with rain and he dried off his forehead with his sleeve. He looked animated, thriving on the confusion and sense of crisis. A homely smell of warm, damp wool rose from his clothes.

'You know that police guy I went to see?' he said. 'He's got a live one.'

'A live what?'

'Suicide bomber. They caught him just in time.'

'What do they know about him?'

'Taliban. From the valley.' He lowered his voice and leant in to her. 'This is the thing: he's willing to let you in to see him.'

'Why?'

'Go figure. Favour to me, I guess.' He was watching her with a confused expression as if he were trying to work out why she didn't seem enthusiastic. 'I said you'd head over there this afternoon. Right?'

She blew out her cheeks. She didn't like people giving her stories. She liked to bait her own hook and catch them herself, not be handed a bag of dead fish.

201

'Did you meet him?'

'The bomber? No. Why would I? This police guy was bragging about him, that's all. He's pretty pleased with himself. I guess he feels like a big hero.'

'Maybe.'

'I got a car and driver you can take. It's not far.' He was looking exasperated.

It might make something. All there was here was rain. 'I'll need a translator.'

'You got one? I need all the guys I have.'

Ellen thought of Layla. She'd need Ibrahim's permission before she drove her out of the camp but a police station would be safe.

A few hours later, Layla was sitting beside Ellen in the back of the car. She seemed nervous. She kept her head bowed, her chador close around her face. She wouldn't speak. Ellen looked out of the window at the streaks of falling rain and the brown, wet earth, heavy with running water.

She'd reported on countless car bombings, many of them in Baghdad. She remembered one of the first, when she'd been interviewing a family in a bakery about their struggle to make a profit amid rising prices and constant power cuts. They'd been interrupted by a sudden deafening boom. The men, their hands covered with flour, paddles of dough limp in their fingers, stopped talking and lifted their heads, listening. The human world was suspended for an instant. Rising birds let out a sharp frantic cawing, filling the silence. Then noise pitched in again. Shouting and pounding feet against a backdrop of screaming car and shop alarms.

By the time she reached the place, the streets, which had been busy with shoppers and families and passers-by, had cleared. In the distance, a black mound was ablaze in the road. She walked towards it. The street was littered with shards of broken glass that crunched and shifted under her boots. Fragments of twisted metal, splashes of oil. The choking bitterness of explosives mixed in the air with the sickly animal smell of burnt flesh.

Afraid, her translator pulled her back into a doorway. Sirens were approaching, police or ambulance. The vehicle was a mass of shimmering flame. She stood and watched as they arrived, thinking of the unknown people – men, women or children – lifeless inside.

Layla gave a cry. The two of them were thrown forwards into the back of the front seats as the driver slammed on the brakes. He blasted his horn, cursed the donkey cart that had nearly clipped his bonnet, and turned across the flow of traffic to stop by the side of the road. Ahead, the entrance to the police station was all high walls and concrete blast blocks.

Layla kept her eyes on the ground as Ellen led her through a series of security checks and clearance gates. Every time a man passed, she pressed close to Ellen's side. When they were finally through, a young police officer showed them into an anteroom and retreated to get them tea.

It was a functional room, unnaturally chilled by air conditioning and stripped of personality. Ellen sat on one of the low, shiny chairs and looked around. A framed portrait of Jinnah, Pakistan's founding father, hung on the wall opposite her. Below it there was a moulded emblem of the police force. The ceiling was stained with damp. The old air-conditioning unit coughed and spluttered.

The young officer came back carrying a white plastic tray. He set out two cups and saucers of thick milky chai. The blast from the air conditioning wrinkled the surface into skin.

Ellen blew away the skin and sipped her tea. Layla sat with her hands folded in her lap. After some time, a captain, middle-aged and with the first signs of a paunch, came in to brief them.

'We nabbed this chap red-handed.' His eyes were lined with tiredness but his cheeks were flushed. 'He was approaching a police station in the valley, close to the military offensive. I can show you the exact spot on the map. Most peculiar fellow. The chaps on the gate thought something was amiss and went to challenge him. I can tell you, they had a lucky escape.'

'It was a car bomb?'

'Absolutely.' The captain seemed delighted. 'An old vehicle, filled with so much of explosive. It should have been set off by mobile phone.' He punched the keyboard of an imaginary phone in the air to illustrate. 'We're seeing so often now these phones used as detonators. Dial the number from your own phone, a second phone is all wired up inside and when the call connects . . .' He threw up his arms to show a huge explosion.

Ellen paused. 'Surely that's a way of detonating a bomb remotely? Not a suicide attack.'

The captain nodded. 'Quite right, madam,' he said. 'They can do that as well. But in this case, the fellow was in the

204

front of the car, dialling the number, and the explosives were right there in the back. Boom.'

'But it failed.'

'Yes.' He shrugged. 'Sometimes it happens.'

He pressed a buzzer and a young officer hurried in.

'Bring the box.'

He came back with a plastic container, the kind Ellen's sister used for storing her children's toys. The captain rummaged through and brought out a battered phone, sealed in a clear plastic bag and labelled.

'See?'

He presented it to Ellen, pressing the plastic against the phone's screen so it was visible. The writing was clear: '01 Missed Call'.

'If ever in your life there was a call you had to miss, this was absolutely the right one.' He laughed at his own joke.

Ellen considered the phone. 'And he knew? He knew what would happen?'

The captain scoffed. 'Of course he is saying to us that he had no idea. He's an innocent fellow, he says, just following orders and all that.' He shook his head dismissively. 'He'll be telling you all that nonsense, acting the fool, I've no doubt. They're all like that. They set out to kill people, acting so tough, but when once they're nabbed, they break like that.' He snapped his fingers.

Ellen looked into the plastic box, trying to see what else was in there.

'Have you got much out of him?'

The captain grimaced. 'He's a stubborn fellow. Saying he doesn't know anything, no names, no details. They train them, of course. But he may still crack.'

205

He got to his feet and fiddled with his belt, impatient to move. '*Chelliay*. Let's go.' He nodded at them both, taking in Layla's hunched shoulders. 'Please don't feel frightened, madam. No problem. My men are there with you.'

They were shown into a small windowless room. It was cool and smelt musty. They stood uncertainly beside a shabby table in the middle. Four grey plastic chairs were tucked under it but no one invited them to sit. The walls were rough concrete, painted over in a dirty cream.

Ellen felt Layla pressing against her. Her headscarf was tugged so far over her face that her eyes were covered. Perhaps I shouldn't have brought her, she thought. It's too much. She reached out and put her hand on the girl's arm.

An officer came in, leading a man behind him. The prisoner was shuffling, his head bowed. His hands were fastened in front of him in chunky old-fashioned handcuffs. He was a broad man, with powerful shoulders. His hair was lank and unkempt, sticking out in clumps from around large ears.

When he was inside the room and the door closed behind him, the officer kicked out a plastic chair and gave the man a shove towards it. Instead of sitting, the man lifted his head and looked around, dazed. His eyes were large and baffled, as if he expected other people, another place. The side of his face was heavily bruised and, in the centre of the bruise, on his cheekbone, the flesh was open.

Layla stirred, shifting her headscarf to look. She let out a cry: 'Adnan!' Her arm trembled under Ellen's hand. The officer shouted, his eyes furious. His hand moved to the pistol in his holster.

Layla stood still, breathing noisily. Her face had drained of colour and she was staring at the prisoner in horror.

'Calm down.' Ellen drew her away from both men, and kicked out a plastic chair for her to sit in. The officer, tense and angry, didn't move. She bent down and asked her quietly: 'You know this man?'

'Adnan.' Her voice was a murmur. 'My relative.'

Ellen looked at the officer and at the prisoner cowering behind him, gazing out at Layla as if he were terrified. 'Is that his name?'

The officer glared. 'This is what he says.'

'Well then.' Ellen drew out a second chair for herself and sat beside Layla. She put her hand on the girl's knee. Her leg was juddering. 'If you want to stay, you must be calm and not move from that chair. OK?'

'OK.' Her eyes had dropped from the prisoner's face to the floor.

'Good.' Ellen turned to the officer. 'Now if we could all sit down, perhaps we can start the interview.'

He hesitated, looked from one woman to the other, then roughly pushed the prisoner down into a chair. The man's legs folded under him as soon as pressure was applied. He sat, blinking out at them. His expression was cowed. The officer stood at his side, watching closely.

'He is speaking only Pashto,' the officer said. 'Are you knowing Pashto?'

Ellen indicated Layla. 'This young woman will translate.'

She kept her eyes on the prisoner as Layla mumbled her way through the translations of her questions. He had the docility of a child.

'Tell me what happened.' Ellen kept her voice soft. 'Why were you in that car?'

He turned to look at the officer as he replied, his eyes fearful.

'He says he's told everything,' said Layla. 'He says it's true, what he's told.'

'Of course. But please could he tell me again, now?'

He hesitated. His big clumsy fingers were picking at each other in his lap. His nails were bitten down, their edges bloody. The metal cuffs were scraping back and forth against his wrists, raising wheals.

'The commander told me to drive. It's easy, that's what he said. Another man drove until we were almost there and then I was left alone and I tried and I did it.'

'Did you know there were explosives in the car?'

Adnan shook his head. He was blinking nervously, looking down at his hands and the knotty surface of the table.

'They didn't tell you?'

He shook his head again.

'So you drove to the gates of the police station. Then what happened?'

'The gates were shut. They said if the gates were shut, I should stop and telephone that number.' He looked up for a moment, his eyes brightening as he remembered. 'I know telephones. Baba showed me one. I dialled the number. But no one answered. And then the guards came and they had guns. Not the same guns as the commander, different ones.'

Ellen looked at the broad features, the panic in his eyes. I believe you, she thought. Either you're an extraordinary actor or you were set up. She leant closer to him.

'What did you think,' she said, 'when you found out what they'd sent you to do?'

208

He began to rock softly, shaking his head. The table shuddered where he banged his knee against it and the officer glared.

Ellen persisted. 'What did you think?'

'He's my friend,' he said. 'He wouldn't hurt me. It's not true.' His eyes were filling with tears. 'He's a kind man. He saved her.'

'Saved who?'

Layla flushed. She didn't translate the question.

Adnan's breathing crumpled into sobs. He lifted his large hands to his face, the handcuffs heavy at his wrists. The officer leant forwards and spoke into Adnan's ear, and whatever he said, it made Adnan sit up straight again and try to stop weeping. He sat, sniffing, his face contorted with misery. His cheeks were blotchy and his nose and eyes thickly wet. The tears and mucus pooled around his chin, gathering to a fat drop that broke free and fell into his lap. As they watched, a second drop formed.

Ellen dug a tissue out of her pocket and went across to him. He tipped back his head instinctively as she approached, as a child might submit to its mother. She dabbed his eyes and wiped his nose and chin clean. He'll be punished for this, she thought. She put a hand on his shoulder and patted it.

The officer was hovering, disapproving. He made a show of looking at his watch. 'That's all?'

He kicked at the base of the chair, gesturing that the man should get to his feet. The prisoner lumbered slowly out, dwarfing the officer at his side.

*   *   *

209

The captain seemed amused when they told him the prisoner had cried. He clapped his hands, then sat back in his chair, his arms clasped behind his head. A second tray of tea was cooling in front of them.

'Such a cunning fellow,' he said. 'Now you are thinking he's innocent as a baby. Yes? Am I right?'

Ellen looked at the criss-cross of rough threads at her feet. The carpet had worn through, leaving bald patches where the backing showed. She traced the pattern in her head as she thought about Adnan.

'Who did he save?' she said. 'He said the man who sent him, the commander, had saved someone.'

Layla, beside her, stared fixedly at the opposite wall.

The captain looked baffled for a moment. He pulled himself upright in his chair again, reached for the cardboard file with the record of the interrogation and opened it. The pages inside were loose sheets, as thin as tissue paper.

'He was saying something.' He was tracing the lines with his finger. 'His sister or some such relative got out to safety, it seems, and he says they did that for him only. Some personal favour, perhaps.' He looked up. 'I should take all of it with a very large piece of salt.' He closed the file and sat back again in his seat. 'Trust me.' He smiled. 'I've heard a lot of nonsense in my time, I can tell you.'

Ellen thought of the man's large manacled hands raised to his face and of the grateful meekness with which he'd submitted to having his tears dried.

'What happens to him now?' she said.

The captain shrugged. 'Justice must be done.'

Ellen considered. That could take years. 'He's being transferred?'

The captain was showing signs of restlessness, glancing over their heads at the clock. 'Maybe. The higher-ups are still deciding. In a case of this ilk, early intelligence can be valuable.'

'Did you glean much?'

'That, I'm afraid, is strictly confidential.' He smiled. 'But let us just say that his commander could be a big fish. A very big fish. In fact, almost a whale.' He laughed at his own wit, then got to his feet, placing his hands squarely on the desk in front of him. 'Now, ladies, if you'll be so kind as to excuse me?'

Ellen watched the way he was handling them, deftly closing down the conversation. 'This whale – is it Mohammed Bul Gourn?'

He looked across at her sharply, the humour fallen from his face, then recovered himself. 'No, no,' he said. 'Not that tricky character. Really, madam, I'm most surprised you've heard of that fellow.'

She said goodbye with a sense of satisfaction. His moment of discomposure was all the answer she needed.

In the car back to the camp, Layla sat with her hands locked together, her knuckles white. Ellen thought of Adnan's broad fingers as they plucked at each other and the heavy metal handcuffs rubbing back and forth across his skin.

'Tell me about him,' she said quietly.

Layla turned to her. 'You must help him. Can you help him?'

Ellen put her hand on hers. 'I don't know. Tell me what you can.'

211

The driver was banging the horn with the heel of his hand, slipping through the traffic around him. It was late afternoon and the light was softening. The rain had stopped.

Ellen listened as Layla struggled to tell her in English about Marva and Adnan's attempt to rescue her and the price the fighters had forced him to pay.

'Do you think he understood what they'd sent him to do?'

Layla shook her head. 'He is a good boy but he is not clever. He is like a child.'

Layla suddenly unknotted her fingers and grasped Ellen's hand. Her fingers were hot, tight around Ellen's. They fell silent, sitting close together in the back of the car as they drove. Ellen wondered what was happening to Adnan now, if he were being punished for the things he'd told her. Outside, the fields were glistening, hung with brown mist. A distant range of mountains ran along beside them, its peaks blurred with cloud.

17

When she switched her phone on again back in the camp, a text message bleeped. From her editor in London, Phil: *Call me.* That was rarely a good sign.

She walked past the admin building to the wilderness at the back, searching for quiet. The base of the border fence was littered with debris. Scraps of plastic and polystyrene packing had been swept there by rainwater flowing through to the ditch beyond. There was a rank, heady smell of decay.

She walked in brisk circles. Beyond the fence the mudflats made a gently undulating sweep, interrupted only by the dirt track. A few youths were playing cricket, using sticks for stumps. In the distance, the slowly trudging figures of newly arriving families were picking their way wearily towards the camp.

Phil answered at once. Here the light was already starting to fade, the mountains casting long shadows. In London, it was only lunchtime. She could tell at once that he was in a bad mood.

'You seen *The News*? Their magazine?'

She scuffed her feet in the dirt, playing for time. 'Khan?'

Phil was flicking through paper on his desk, the rustling amplified by the line. 'You knew?' He grunted. 'Six-page spread. Colour shots of him in the camp. With the top brass in Islamabad. Travelling. The works.'

She bit her lip, inwardly cursing. She'd assumed John had been exaggerating. He usually did.

'Blows us out of the water.' Phil's voice was measured but he was speaking slowly and deliberately, a sign he was furious.

'Well, Phil, I did—'

He cut her off. 'They got a news line out of it too. He's tipped for a peerage.'

'That's speculation, Phil. Come on. He probably started that rumour himself.'

A flock of dark birds was swooping low through the sky, wheeling over the tents and arcing back towards the mountains. In London, Phil had gone quiet. Ellen strained to think.

'It may not hurt, Phil. I've got great material on the camp. I could do something substantial.'

'No bleeding hearts, Ellen. Heard it all before.'

She took a deep breath. 'It's not just that. I'm working on something much harder.'

He paused. 'Like what?'

'I can tell you more in a day or two.' The blood was booming in her ears. If Phil didn't go for this, he was perfectly likely to call her home and the whole trip would be branded a failure. 'It's on links between the camp and the Taliban.'

214

'What links?'

'I'm still standing it up. You know that family I wrote about? One of them's been arrested for being a suicide bomber. I've just interviewed him. It's an exclusive.'

Silence from Phil. She kept talking. 'And I think the Taliban's siphoning off supplies to the camp. And putting their own people in here to stir up trouble.'

A slow tap, tap. Phil was bouncing his pen lightly on his desk.

'If that happened . . .' He was thinking. 'Embarrassing for Khan. Messes up his showcase.'

'Exactly.'

'Embarrassing for *The News* too, after this puff piece.'

His office door opened and voices spilt in. Ellen strained, trying to identify them. Phil was saying, 'Come on in, won't be a moment.'

He came back on the line. 'How much longer do you need?'

She hesitated. 'Another couple of days?'

'No more.'

'OK.'

The line was already dead. Ellen switched off her phone and let out a long sigh. Damn John. He'd be so smug. Khan's people would be all over him.

She paced back and forth in the dirt for some time, thinking about what she'd just promised. She had so little. Somehow she had to pull this into a decent story in a day or two. Phil had sounded short of patience.

She was walking aimlessly, tracing a wide circle at the back of the admin building. As she approached her starting point, a movement near the back of the women's medical tent caught her eye. She looked up. A man was loitering there, keeping to the shadows. Ellen edged closer, trying to see. It was Doc in his grubby salwar kameez. He was standing with his back to her and he seemed to be talking to someone, his arms flapping as if he were remonstrating with them. It was too far away for her to hear their voices but she sensed tension.

She inched towards him. A moment later, he turned on his heel and walked abruptly away, heading directly towards her for a few steps, then cutting left down the side of the small administrative tent and disappearing. She hadn't been able to see who was inside, talking to him. They had stayed carefully hidden from view. By the time she reached the ward, the partitioned back rooms were deserted. The main ward too was still and quiet.

Back in the hotel, she stood in the shower for a long time, scrubbing her body and running the water so hot it turned her skin red. Adnan shouldn't be in that police cell. It was pitiful, the way he'd surrendered to her to have his tears wiped. The bruises on his face showed what sort of interrogation he'd been through. That was what she should write about. She tipped her face to the running water, letting it splash on her cheeks, mouth, and cascade in rivulets down her neck. No bleeding hearts, Phil had said. But he was being ridiculous.

She wrapped herself in a towel and walked through to the bedroom. She called room service and ordered dinner. She ought to tell Frank about Adnan. There might be something he could do.

The hotel's Internet connection was slow. It took her half

216

an hour to log on and download John's piece from *The News*'s website. A young waiter arrived and wheeled in her food on a trolley. She sat in her bathrobe on the twin bed, dipping naan bread in vegetable masala with one hand and scrolling up and down the story with the other.

It was typical John, full of hype and riddled with references to his own feelings. There was a whole paragraph about how deeply moved he'd been to witness the conditions in the camps. That was despite the fact he hadn't actually spoken to any of the refugees. All he'd done in the camp was stand around gossiping and eaten the aid which was in such short supply.

The article dripped with praise for Quentin Khan and his saintliness. Ellen narrowed her eyes. John seemed to be campaigning for Khan to become a lord. He must be after something, a job or some other reward. John had written some very fanciful descriptions of the hardships Khan was enduring in Pakistan. Hard to reconcile with her own memories of his hotel suite and the lavish party.

The business content of the profile was more useful. John had a whole page on the growth of Khan's transport empire, including some loosely rounded figures about his multimillion-pound annual profits. She saved that whole section. John would have been spoon-fed the figures by Khan's people and no doubt they were massaged. But even so, she was surprised at how well Khan was doing, despite tough economic times. She tore off a final strip of bread and ran it around her masala dish, remembering Khan's poise as he first emerged from the helicopter and raised his hand to the watching camp. Maybe he was a more wily businessman than she'd realized.

She was just getting into bed when there was a timid knock at her door. Frank, she thought, with his whisky. She could do with some. She stacked the dinner dishes to one side and padded to the door, realizing with a smile how much she was looking forward to seeing him.

'I'm sorry. It's late.' Britta looked dishevelled. 'You're going to bed?'

'Not yet.' She held the door open. 'Come on in.'

Britta unlaced her boots and left them at the door with her rucksack. They were damp and muddy. Britta too looked mud-splattered. She paced into the centre of the room and stood, looking around vacantly.

Ellen filled the kettle and switched it on. Britta went into the bathroom. There was a clink and thud as she set down her keys and wallet on the faux marble surround, then a gurgling of water as she washed her hands.

She came back, looking bewildered. Ellen sat on the edge of the bed, motioned her to sit on the other bed and waited. Britta sat heavily, her head lowered. She was silent for a while. When she finally spoke, the words came out in a torrent.

'Four more deaths today. I don't know what to say to people. I can't understand. Really.' She raised her eyes for a second, scanned Ellen's face, then let them fall again. She had a desperate, haunted look. 'I've worked in places with typhoid but I've never known this. This lack of response to treatment. Such a high fatality rate. And this is just the start. Water is everywhere. Hygiene is terrible. I don't know what to do.' For a moment, she seemed about to cry. Instead she gave a shuddering sigh.

'Can't anyone else help?'

'I've asked for help. I need another nurse. Fatima is

always there late into the night, I don't know how she manages. The doctor running the men's unit wants more staff too.' She shrugged. 'They say they're processing our applications. We're only a tiny charity.'

The kettle shook on its stand and boiled. Ellen made tea and put a mug into Britta's hands. She sat, holding it, dazed. Finally she seemed to shake herself and looked up at Ellen with new concern.

'I haven't said: two of these four female deaths today, they weren't in the medical unit. They were out in the camp. There are so many rumours about us now that people are too frightened to come. They think we'll kill them.' She pulled a face as if to say: Who can blame them? 'I only just heard about the last death. That's why I'm late.' She was staring into her tea, suddenly awkward.

'There are always rumours,' Ellen said, 'in situations like this. It's—'

'It's that girl's mother.' Britta wouldn't look at her.

Ellen hesitated, taking a moment to understand. 'Layla?'

She nodded miserably. 'That's what I came to say.'

'Her mother?' Layla had been with her just hours ago. Why hadn't she said her mother was ill? She shouldn't have taken her. How awful. She hadn't known.

'They kept it hidden,' Britta said. 'Worried about what we'd do, I suppose. She had fever, headache, diarrhoea. Not so unusual.'

'When did she die?'

'Just now, this evening. They'll bury her tomorrow.' She looked at her watch and her mood changed. 'I must go.' She got to her feet, her mug full in her hands.

'At least finish your tea.'

219

'No.' She looked distracted. 'I'm sorry. It's late. I hadn't realized.'

'Are you OK?'

Britta didn't answer. She turned to put her mug on the table, hiding her face. When she straightened up to leave, her cheeks were flushed. She said goodnight, gathered up her keys and wallet from the bathroom, her boots and rucksack at the door, and was gone.

Ellen switched off the lights and sat alone at the window, looking down into the hotel grounds. Reflections from the dining room were skimming the surface of the swimming pool, making it gleam in the darkness. Layla's mother must be younger than she was. Had they known she was so ill? Layla never mentioned it. Neither did Ibrahim. She wrapped her arms around her knees and rested her chin on them. She thought back to the first time she'd met Ibrahim. He'd seemed so desperate, so alone. How had she helped his family? Barely at all.

Outside, the rain had stopped but the windows were still splattered with water. A drop slowly formed, swelled and broke free, meandering down the pane. Layla was too young to lose her mother. It wasn't right. Behind her, the air conditioning clicked on and started to blow. In the next room a telephone rang out.

Down below, the shadows under the trees were shifting. A night breeze. The figure of a woman appeared. Ellen sat up straight. She was crossing the grass near the swimming pool. She was big-boned and European, her head covered with a chador. Ellen got to her feet and moved to the far edge of the window to get a better view.

Britta's rucksack was bouncing lightly on her back. Strands of blonde hair, spilling out from her headscarf, shone in the half-light. She was moving cautiously. As she approached the trees and bushes, she raised her hand as if she were greeting someone, then disappeared into the dense blackness of the shadows.

The next morning was dull with rain clouds. They sat low on the mountains, covering the peaks, and formed a grey canopy over the plains. Ellen picked her way cautiously along the camp's slippery paths. Everywhere the dirt was churned to mud.

The wet had unleashed new smells, of the people and of the earth. A stout man along the path was repairing a shelter, scraping a coating of sludge off the plastic with his bare hands. Further on, the latrines had flooded. Two workers in fluorescent tabards were pumping the filthy water out with a noisy sucking machine.

She turned the corner to see a group of about twenty people walking out of the camp gates. The funeral procession had already left. They turned a sharp right along the border fence and headed towards the new, small graveyard on the far edge of the plain. She hurried to catch them up.

The body of Layla's mother, wrapped in a sheet, was being carried on a hospital stretcher. Four men were holding it high on their shoulders. Ibrahim's slight figure was in the front. More men were following, Uncles and brothers and cousins. Finally came the women, a ragged group, some staggering, some supporting, their arms threaded around each other. Their high-pitched wailing rose and fell, a ghostly ululating. Ellen walked alone, some distance behind, watching. Layla was amongst them, made smaller by grief. She was walking between two older women who kept their hands always on her shoulders, her neck, her back, earthing her.

The burial service was short. The imam recited from the Holy Book in a sing-song voice full of loss. Ellen looked down the row of freshly dug mounds. There were more than a dozen unmarked graves now. The waste ground was desolate, made more depressing by the dark low cloud.

The imam finished and the body was lowered slowly into the clay. The women wept and lamented together, tearing at their clothes and clawing at their faces. It was a lonely scene. The dead seemed abandoned, far from their villages and fields and family graveyards.

As the final prayers began, rain started to fall, splashing down onto the covered body as the first heaps of earth began to cover it. The mourners huddled together. Finally they began to turn and start the straggling walk back to the camp. Layla, taken up by the older women, looked befuddled. Ellen thought of her sister in the medical tent. She wondered if she even knew about her mother's death.

The imam led the remaining relatives away. Ellen lingered at the graveside, watching the young men spade the muddy soil. The rain fell more heavily, wetting their heads and shoulders, bouncing off the earth. I ought to go back, she thought, but her feet didn't move. The wet earth weighed down the young men's spades. Their shirts were wet on their backs. They were muscular, full of strength and life. Layla's eyes had seemed so dead.

She turned and looked back across the muddy plains. The distant mountains were chopped in two, their peaks swallowed by sunken cloud. The darkness of the land was broken only by the glistening of thin sunlight on the surface water. The camp sat, bedraggled, a ragged collection of torn polythene and leaking canvas, heavy with falling rain.

The mourners had shrunk to small black shadows at the edge of the fence. Some distance away, to the right, a broad-shouldered young man was standing, turned towards her. She narrowed her eyes. He was alone, quite still in the rain, watching the activity around the grave. She thought she recognized him. Was he spying on a young woman's funeral? She felt a sudden rage, an urge to drive him away, to defend Layla and all the grieving families who mourned here with so little privacy.

She started to stride towards him. She expected him to turn and leave. He didn't. He stood his ground, his eyes hard on hers, waiting as she closed the gap between them. It was the same youth. The one who'd hung around the tents, eavesdropping, when Ibrahim had spoken to her. The one she'd seen waiting for Frank outside his room.

'Who are you?' she called out to him from a few paces. He scowled. Maybe he didn't speak English.

'What is your name?' She spoke more slowly.

'My name is Saeed.' His accent was thick but his voice was confident.

She had reached him now. He was a handsome boy, strong and angry and full of conviction. They stood for a moment, an arm's length apart, taking each other in.

'Why are you here?'

He pointed past her to the grave. The workers had almost finished. The earth formed a long low pile.

'I saw you at the hotel. You're a fighter, aren't you? Spying for them.'

He didn't reply. He stared her full in the face, his look direct and full of contempt.

'Mohammed Bul Gourn.' She said the name loudly and clearly and saw recognition in his eyes. 'He is your friend. Your boss.'

He didn't move. The rain was running off his wet hair, falling down the contours of his cheeks and through his young beard. His shirt was sticking to his shoulders and chest, emphasizing the muscle there.

'Why did you meet Frank, the American? What do you want from him?'

He smiled, then looked away, shaking his head. His amusement riled her. You understand, she thought. You know exactly what I'm asking.

'What kind of man steals from the poor, takes food and blankets and medicine? Can't you see the way they're suffering?' She gestured back to the camp. 'These are your people. How can you betray them?'

His eyes were hostile. He didn't answer.

'That's not Islam,' she said. 'You should be ashamed.'

She turned away. It was a long walk back. The rain was falling in thick brown sheets now, soaking her clothes, which clung, dripping, to her body. Her boots splashed through the running water. When she was close to the camp, she turned and looked back. The workers had left the grave. The mound of earth was complete.

The young man was standing in exactly the same place, turned towards her. His head and shoulders streamed with rain but his body was erect and quite still, his eyes on hers, steadily watching her.

18

Jamila sat on a piece of wood in the yard. Around her, puddles were steaming in the heat. Three of the Aunties' small girls were playing together in a corner, slopping wet mud into a pile to make a mound. They raked through puddles and scooped the dirt from them, then ran to the mound and dripped the gloopy mud from their fingers. It dried in streaks. They stood back, pleased, and admired their work. 'A palace,' one of the girls said. 'Let's decorate it.' They scouted around for treasure. A broken piece of stick. A coloured shred of plastic. A withered plum stone.

Jamila's eyes were following them but she was thinking about Layla. Grief is a disease, she thought. Once the body is infected, it takes time to heal. We learnt this from our parents and grandparents when we saw them suffer. But this girl hasn't had the chance to learn. She's too young.

Before the funeral, the body had lain, wrapped in a white cloth, inside the compound. But while the Aunties and other women had wept and keened and torn at their clothes, Layla sat apart from them. Her face was bloodless and her eyes dull.

Jamila crouched beside her and put her arm around the girl's shoulders. Layla's back was rigid. She didn't yield.

'You must mourn,' Jamila said, keeping her voice low. 'Like the other women.'

She looked out at the Aunties, clasping each other as they cried and shouted and begged Allah in His Wisdom to bring back their sister. One fell to her knees, screaming and beating the flat of her hands on the mud. The girl beside her didn't move or speak.

'Let it out,' Jamila said. 'Can't you see? If you don't weep, your grief will make you ill.' She could feel knots in the girl's back and she lifted her arm to massage them. Layla shrugged her off. They sat in silence for a moment. Layla glared out at the Aunties. Jamila looked at Layla's scowling face.

Finally Jamila said, 'People expect to see you weep.' She paused. She didn't even know if the girl was listening. 'It shows respect. To the dead. But also to the living.'

The girl was hard with anger. Jamila said nothing more. She took Layla's place amongst the Aunties and they kept vigil together, lamenting over the body throughout the night.

Now the funeral was over and Layla was lying inside the tent. She had taken the same spot where her mother had sweated and finally died. Women from surrounding tents were paying their respects to the bereaved, bringing whatever quantities of sugar and rice they could spare, weeping and offering condolences. Layla wouldn't come out to receive them. She lay with her face in the blanket,

226

legs twisted up under her and refused to answer anyone who came.

Ibrahim too had hidden himself away. The Aunties had told him about his wife's illness just a short while before she died. By then it was too late.

Ibrahim had called Jamila into a corner and berated her, even as she was trying to tend to the dying woman. Why hadn't she sent for a doctor? Tears ran down his face. Why?

Now, sitting alone, Jamila considered these things. In their corner, the small girls had finished building their dirt palace and were dancing around it.

It was late morning. The Aunties had finished pummelling the laundry in buckets. Damp clothing hung from the ropes between the shelters and spread out across the plastic roofs. The young women were gathering around the cooking bricks, squatting on their haunches, kneading dough and slapping out rotis between their palms. The sides of their faces were streaked with flour where they'd pushed back strands of hair with dirty hands.

Shouting broke out. One voice, then an explosion of several. Men's voices. Loud and angry. The Aunties stood up to look. A gang of young men ran, jostling each other, towards the noise. A small boy started to cry for his mother and an Auntie bent to scoop him up.

The voices were distant and echoed around the camp. They came from the far side, away from the main gate, from the corner nearest the mountains. The shouts were discordant, ragged. Men were hurrying past now, young and old, running to look. The Aunties wrapped their roti dough in cloths and came back into the compound. The bread could wait until later.

Jamila got to her feet. 'What happened?' No one answered her. 'What is it?'

She pulled her chador tightly around her head and shoulders and stood at the entrance to their compound, looking out. The shouting was distorted. Muffled, hostile voices. She couldn't make out the words. But the noise was growing.

People were running now, streaming past their compound, heading for the far corner of the camp. They bumped against the flimsy fence and made the plastic crackle.

Jamila turned to the Aunties. 'Stay here with the children. I'll go and see.'

She breathed deeply, braced herself and plunged into the hurrying crowd.

The people packed around her at once, pressing in on both sides. They were pushing and shoving, buoyed by a rising tide of agitation that carried her too. She was soon scrambling to keep up. Her ears were filled with the pumping of her own blood and the pounding of feet. A man behind her, running, knocked her to one side as he forced himself past her. His feet kicked up muddy water, cold splashes across her feet. She slipped and grasped at the woman next to her, a stranger, to keep from falling. Far ahead, a woman started to scream. The urgency in the crowd grew and the pace quickened. A man ahead of Jamila shouted, 'Calm down. Don't push.' No one listened.

After another five minutes of running, the crowd started to thicken. Jamila squeezed through gaps to move forwards. The path was blocked, dense with people. The hard bodies of men surrounded her as the spaces shrank. Soon she couldn't see anything but walls of flesh. They pressed in on her, squeezing her body. She felt sudden panic. Ahead a young man rose on his friend's shoulders, waving his arms and horsing around. To the side, the sound of splintering wood and a crash and commotion as someone brought down part of a shelter.

'Let me out.' Jamila could hardly hear her own voice. 'Please. I need to get out.'

No one took any notice. Behind her, more people arrived. The pressure in the crowd grew. Every time the men surged, they crushed her between them. She could hardly breathe. Her arms, bent, were pinned to her sides. She started to fight, digging her elbows into ribs and stomachs, punching with her fists. A man twisted around and shouted at her, his nose inches from her eyes: 'Stop it, whore.' The men around her jeered.

The crowd rippled. She was knocked off balance and fell into a soft fat man beside her. He put his hands on her shoulders to push her away and she struggled to get upright again. She felt his pudgy fingers on her flesh long after he'd removed them. Her breath came in short bursts. Her hands were raised, her long fingers flailing in front of her face. The bodies around her shimmered and shivered. She let out a cry as she started to go down.

Hard hands pushed under her arms, closed around her armpits and lifted her up. Who was it? She couldn't twist to look, couldn't see. A man was propelling her forwards. She kicked out at people in front of her, helping to clear space. The man grasping her had a booming voice and was hollering, 'Move yourself,' as he went. Bodies were reluctantly parting, faces turning to gawp at her as they cut through. She tried to close her mind to the shame.

The crowd finally parted in front of them to reveal space and air. She gasped for breath. The man dropped her onto her feet and turned away, pleased to have used her to force his way to the front. She steadied herself, breathing hard. Her head was aching, her armpits bruised by the man's clumsy grip. She looked around, getting her bearings.

The crowd had formed a circle, staring inwards at the ground. Here, rowdiness had given way to silence. The faces around her were subdued and embarrassed. No one caught her eye. She turned around to see for herself what all the fuss was about.

Two bodies. Lying on the wet earth on the edge of a piece of filthy waste ground. One was a young woman. She was on her side, her legs twisted behind her. One brown foot had lost its sandal, revealing the soft pale skin of the sole. A cheap silver chain hung limp around the ankle. She was wearing a gaudy orange salwar kameez, thickly daubed with dirt. The hems were stitched with spangles.

Her arms were tied behind her back with cord that cut into her wrists. Her head was turned to one side at an impossible angle. Her eyes were bulging sightlessly and her face was tipped towards the sky. Strangled. A long *dupatta* was wound tightly around her throat.

Beside her lay the body of a man in a dirty white salwar kameez. Doc. Jamila knew him at once. He was on his back. His throat was a mess of congealed blood. His thin face was contorted.

She shook her head. Flies were buzzing on the cut flesh. No one moved to wave them away. The blood in the wounds was hard and set.

230

There was a jostling behind her and the crowd parted. A worker from the camp emerged, accompanied by a guard. They stopped when they saw the bodies and stared.

'Who did this?' The man who spoke was from Peshawar. He was swaggering a little. The guard beside him had a gun in his hands. 'What happened?'

No one spoke.

The worker looked angry. 'Was there a fight?'

People shook their heads.

The man's tone was threatening. 'Someone must have seen.'

'They were covered up.' A man at the front pointed to a pile of sacking by the bodies. 'Children found them.'

The worker glared around. 'Don't touch them. We'll have to fetch the police.' He pushed his way roughly back into the crowd, the guard at his side.

Once he had gone, the men started to grumble and become restless. Jamila saw the anger in their faces. The worker had dishonoured them with his rudeness and suspicion.

'Why is he accusing us? What have we done?'

'If the police come, they'll make trouble.'

'They'll demand bribes.'

Jamila looked around, trying to see who was speaking. Thuggish young men. They started to call out across the crowd.

'These workers. They think they're better than us.'

'They're not true Pakistanis.'

'That's right. They're puppets. Of the Americans.'

One of the men gestured around at the tattered shelters and tents. 'Look how they make us live,' he shouted. 'Is this what we're worth?'

The temperature was rising. A young bearded man lifted his hand, raising a chant. 'Death to the Americans!' The crowd gave a half-hearted response. He repeated the cry several times but the answering call was weak. It gradually fizzled out.

A second young man, in the body of the crowd, raised a second shout. 'Foreigners out of Pakistan!'

The men at the front cheered. 'Foreigners out!' Their voices were raucous. They punched the air. The cry started to take hold, echoing back through the press of men.

Jamila pushed her way along the front of the crowd, across the waste ground. She took refuge alongside a shelter there. A woman peered out at her. She was huddled inside with two young children. The little girl's eyes were afraid. Jamila thought of Syma and softened. The woman reached for the children and gathered them close.

The crowd was shifting and seething. The young men were angry. Chants were taking hold, uniting the men and urging them forwards. Fists rose in time with the voices. One man beat out the rhythm with a stick against a wooden post.

A youth stepped forwards to address them. He was shouting to make himself heard. Jamila peered past the plastic flap of the shelter to see. It was Saeed, the boy from their village who'd tried to dishonour Layla.

'These stooges of the Americans are killing us all,' he shouted. 'Why should we live like animals in filth? Why should our children be hungry and our women have nowhere safe to sleep?'

Men shouted agreement. Jamila felt the mood harden.

'What are they doing for us? They keep the best for

232

themselves and leave us without enough to eat, without shelter in the rain. They lure away our girls and infect them with Western culture.'

An old man near Jamila turned away and pushed out through the crowd. Jamila saw him pass by. His face was anxious and turned to the ground. Young men were raising more rallying cries, lifting their hands in tight-fisted salute.

'Pakistan *Zindabad*!' Long live Pakistan. 'Down with America!'

The crowd echoed the chants. Men threw up their fists until the air rippled with hands. Jamila saw the fury in their eyes. They were uneducated men, quick to fight.

The thugs at the front swung their staves at the nearest shelter. They smashed them into the struts that formed a frame for the plastic sheeting. The air was filled with the sound of splintering wood and crackling plastic. Finally the struts were knocked down and the whole shelter collapsed sideways with a ballooning sigh. A girl, twelve or thirteen years old, crawled out of the wreckage on her hands and knees, screaming.

The men turned, still chanting, and began to march, leading the way down the narrow paths. They swung their staves at every shelter they passed. The men behind them grabbed sticks and pieces of wood and ran behind, doing the same.

The woman close to Jamila scrambled out of her shelter, snatching up her daughter and herding her boy in front of her. 'God have mercy,' she shouted. 'May Allah protect us.'

Two older men pushed past them and started attacking the woman's shelter. Their planks of wood were rough with nails that ripped through the plastic. Jamila grabbed at their arms. 'What are you doing?' Her voice was drowned by the shouting and the beating of wood on wood. 'Stop this.'

One of the men shook her off. She staggered backwards and slipped. A blow. Falling wood clipped the side of her face. She fell. Plastic wrapped itself around her. It tangled her hands as she tried to reach out, to save herself. Her cheek hit cold ground. The smell and wetness of earth. Heavy male feet were thudding by. Her ears were full of shouting and women's screams. She closed her eyes, stunned, and became still.

She lay there, silent, for some time. She didn't know how long. She felt strangely detached from the noise and violence, lying on the bed of an ocean while waves stirred far away overhead.

Gradually, the noises subsided and the outside world became calm. She managed at last to move. She slowly freed her legs and arms from the tangle of plastic and sat up. She was surrounded by debris. The shelter was a heap of smashed wood and trampled plastic, scattered with belongings. A blanket, filthy with trodden earth. A metal cooking spoon. A dirty glass bottle on its side. She got onto her hands and knees and eased herself carefully to her feet. Her salwar kameez was streaked with mud. The ends of her chador were sodden. The sounds of the rampaging men were distant now, coming from another part of the camp. The splintering and shouting could still be heard but it was muffled.

She squeezed out her chador and wrapped it around

her head and shoulders. Her fingers explored the sore place on her cheek and came away bloodied. She must lie down. She must rest. She limped back along the path.

Everything looked different. On all sides, tents were in ruins. She looked out across the wilderness of broken shelters. Jagged sticks protruded from piles of muddy sacking and plastic. The very young and very old were sitting on the ground in the midst of it all, staring around in shock. Everywhere, women were wearily picking through the debris, salvaging sleeping mats and metal pots. The sweeping mudflats looked bleaker than ever. Far beyond rose the mountains, dark with cloud.

Jamila trudged on. Somewhere near the entrance to the camp, whistles sounded. Police, she thought. A shot rang out. A sharp crack. It cut through the shouts of the crowd, making a single moment of quiet before the distant shouting plunged in again to fill the silence.

She approached the south of the camp and their own small patch of mud. They'd escaped. The shelters here were intact. In the compound, she found the young Aunties huddled together, agitated by the craziness of the crowd of men. The wrapped roti dough was forgotten. Inside the tent, Layla was lying, hot with fever, on the same spot where her mother had died. Her legs were curled under her, her face buried in the folds of a blanket.

19

Ellen was sitting in the doorway of the main entrance of the administration building with her notebook on her knee, finishing a cup of bad instant coffee. She'd been drafting a structure for her follow-up story on the camp but found herself thinking instead about Layla. She'd seemed lifeless as she was led away from her mother's grave. Lost. She thought of Layla's sister and the care she needed. Maybe there was something she could do for them.

Noise. Angry male voices. She lifted her head to listen. Shouting, thinned by distance, drifted across the camp. Ragged cries. A fight, perhaps, getting out of hand. She put her notebook away and got to her feet to find out.

The shouts gained a steady rhythm. Chants were starting to take hold. Frank rushed out of the building past her. He called over his shoulder: 'You might wanna move. Something's revving up.'

She followed him as he scurried across the open ground, calling to his workers. Men in tabards had stopped unloading supplies and were looking uneasy, listening to the angry voices. A man ran across to Frank, a guard lagging behind them.

'Two people are killed.' The worker ran a finger across his throat. 'A man and a girl.'

Frank looked around. 'Take a doctor down.'

The worker shook his head. 'No need getting a doctor.'

The chants were becoming clearer and more unified. The worker shifted from foot to foot. Frank started to issue orders, organizing groups of men to secure the supply trucks and drive the vehicles away from the camp. The men scurried to and fro. Ellen listened hard to the chanting. She could hear other noises now, underpinning the voices. Screams and the splintering of wood. Frank was on his radio, calling for backup. The guards, mostly thin, elderly men, stood quietly, watching the frantic activity, hugging their guns to their chests. They looked afraid.

'What is it?' Britta emerged from the medical tent and came to join Ellen in the sea of rushing men.

Ellen said: 'Two deaths.'

Britta stared. 'Typhoid?'

'Killed. There's some sort of riot.'

'Killed?'

Frank called over. 'I'm evacuating. The police know. What help do you need getting the patients out?'

Britta shook her head. 'They're too sick.'

Frank looked impatient. His radio was squawking in his hand. 'Think what you need and let me know.' He attended to the radio.

Britta turned back to Ellen. 'These women are very sick.'

Her hand strayed up to her cross and she started to run it up and down its chain. 'I can't move them.'

The men had finished loading. Frank's right, Ellen thought. We must get the women out. It's not safe. The men slammed shut the doors of the first truck and revved up the engine. It played a jingly mechanical tune as it reversed out through the gates.

Frank was striding back towards them. The shouts and bangs were getting louder. 'So how're we doing this?'

Britta stood her ground. 'They stay here and I stay too.'

Frank tutted. 'I don't think that's smart, the—'

'Men can't move them. Don't you see? They think that's indecent.'

He considered this. 'They can't walk?'

'They can't walk.'

'Can they get in a truck?'

'They can't be moved.'

'I don't think you get this. They can't stay. It's not safe. These men are out of control.'

Britta's face was set. Her feet were firmly planted. Frank sounded exasperated but Ellen could see he wasn't going to persuade her. There was an uneasy silence.

'I'll stay.' Ellen nodded to Frank. 'You go. We'll be OK.'

He didn't look convinced. His radio was spitting voices again and he lifted it as far as his cheek, then hesitated. 'What if—'

'We'll be fine. Go on.' Ellen put her hand on his arm, and pushed him away.

He shook his head, still looking at her as he put the radio to his mouth and started to speak.

* * *

238

Ellen looked through the ward's half-light at the two lines of cots and the shapes of the women curled listlessly on top of them, covered with sheets. The few thin columns of sun that penetrated were swirling with motes of dust. The noises from outside were muted. Inside, the ceiling fans pulsed. The medical equipment emitted a steady mechanical whirr.

At the far end of the ward, a young assistant was washing the pouched skin of a frail elderly woman, turning and positioning her with care.

Ellen turned to Britta, calculating. 'Where's Fatima?'

'Off this morning. She worked so late last night.'

So just three of them. They would have to work quickly. 'Let's move the cots away from the walls.' The canvas didn't offer much protection. 'We'll tell the patients there's a storm coming and the tent might leak.'

Britta gestured to the assistant and they started tugging the cots out, one by one, trailing the drips on their stands. Ellen ran to the entrance and unfurled the heavy flaps. They zipped and fastened. She weighed their thickness. They wouldn't be hard to breach. She stood for a second, thinking. They needed more protection. Some sort of barrier.

She crossed the ward to the far end and ducked through the canvas into the back rooms. Britta's laptop was on, shedding eerie blue light. Around it, the table was a mess of accounts and orders. The walls behind were stacked with large cardboard boxes of medical supplies.

She laced her arms around a pile of three boxes and tried to drag them away, digging her heels into the floor. Her back bowed with the strain. Solid. Just too heavy. She couldn't budge them an inch.

She tried again from a different angle, this time squeezing in between the stacks and lying with her shoulder against the lowest box to push them out. They wouldn't slide. Nothing. The boxes didn't even shift. They were leaden. She sat on the floor, breathing hard. There must be a way.

She pulled out Britta's chair and climbed up alongside the stacks, reaching to the top box to rip off the tape and tear open the flaps. Her fingers scrabbled through packets of medicine. She plucked them out by the handful. Aspirin. Dehydration salts. She threw them to the ground. Antibiotics – a whole layer of those. Tubes of antiseptic cream. They bounced and scattered at her feet.

Her fingers delved further. They found something more solid. Underneath the medicines, a second layer. Not cardboard packets but cold, smooth metal. She ran her fingers around the edges. Too big and heavy to lift. She raised herself and peered in. Cooking oil. Not one tin but a lot, a dozen or so. And large. Gallon tins, maybe. Each one could last a family for more than a month.

She rested her forehead on the edge of the box and closed her eyes, trying to catch her breath. Her face was damp with sweat. This made no sense. Outside, the shouts were louder, moving nearer. She got down and moved the chair further along, then tore open another box and rifled through. The same thing. On the top, a shallow layer of medicines, bandages and medicated cream. But underneath these things, rice. Family-sized sacks. Salt. She moved again. This time, she put her hands behind the box and pushed. It shuddered, shifted, then fell crashing to the floor. It bounced, burst down one seam and settled. Medicines spilt across the ground. Underneath, metal cooking pots clanged together, shining through the split cardboard. Blankets flopped around them, oozing out through the gaps.

She sat down heavily on the chair and put her head in her hands. A layer of tablets across the top of each box would fool someone making a quick spot check. The weight was the only clue that these were not normal boxes of medicines. Her eyes moved along the wall of boxes, calculating the amount, the value of the hidden household goods. This was just one room. There were even more boxes stacked next door.

'What are you doing?' Britta was in the doorway. She stared at the mess.

Ellen pointed to the cooking pots and blankets. 'What's this doing here?'

Britta looked confused. 'They must have sent the wrong box. This is medicine.'

Ellen couldn't look at her. She paused. 'Do you do the orders yourself?'

'I place them. Fatima takes care of delivery. She is so efficient.'

Ellen thought of Fatima's photographs of her children back home in Cairo. The girl with neatly clipped hair and the younger boy with shy brown eyes.

She got to her feet, brushed off her clothes. 'I thought we could move these onto the ward. Make a barrier. But let's forget it. They're too heavy.'

The three of them crouched together between the cots. The shouts from the men were raucous and steadily advancing. Layla's sister was softly moaning. The Pakistani

241

assistant reached over and stroked her hand, murmuring to her in Pashto.

We shouldn't be here, Ellen thought. Frank was right. It isn't safe. She looked around the ward. The mob could easily set fire to the tent. There were only the three of them inside who could walk. They'd struggle to get the patients out.

She turned to Britta: 'Where's the fire extinguisher?'

Britta bit her lip. 'It's on order.'

Water. There was a drum of water at the back of the ward. It wasn't much but it might douse a small fire. Ellen assessed the distance. She could reach it in a few seconds. It would buy them time to move.

The chanting was getting louder. The voices were heady and excited. The pounding of feet was so close and heavy now that Ellen could feel tremors through the soles of her boots. A crash. Nearby. Splitting wood. The young assistant whimpered.

'It's all right.' Ellen kept her voice level. 'Stay calm.'

Britta had closed her eyes. Her hand was clutching her cross, her lips moving silently. She seemed to have entered a world of her own, detached from the rest of them. The young Pakistani woman crawled across the floor to Ellen and groped for her hand. Her fingers were hot and hard. She was wide-eyed with fright.

The men loomed outside, dark shapes against the canvas. The chants had become ragged bellows. Ellen couldn't make out the words but she heard the aggression. The crowd had spun out of control. Her legs juddered. At the first sign of them breaking through, she thought, we must move fast. The distorted shadows of the men

242

rose on the tent wall. Sticks or guns lengthened their waving arms.

There was a sudden thud. A rock. The canvas billowed where it struck and bounced off. The men outside roared. The assistant screamed, then put her hand to her mouth. Her cheeks were pale.

The canvas is damp, Ellen was thinking. If they torch it, it may take time to burn.

There was a second thwack against the canvas wall. A cry of jubilation from the crowd. A third rock was thrown.

The Pakistani girl was crushing Ellen's hand. Ellen prised off her fingers, one by one, and patted her arm. She ran along the back of the cots. The flaps across the main entrance were still fastened but dark shapes were moving beyond them. They were swarming there. If they decided to cut their way in, it would only be a matter of minutes. She looked back at the cluster of cots, the patients. Very few of them could walk, even a short distance. They could carry some but it would be slow work. We'll drag them in blankets, she thought. One at a time. We should start.

She called to the assistant to help and ran to the nearest patient. A girl, only about nine or ten years old. She was lying on her back. Her cheeks were hollow, her eyes large and wet. Ellen lifted her shoulders and tried to ease her into a sitting position. The girl clung to her. She was skeletal, a mass of protruding bones. I could carry her a short distance. She can't be heavy. The assistant crouched, staring, her face puckering.

'Please.' Ellen gestured to her. 'We need to get moving.'

The rocks were coming rapidly now. They pelted the canvas with heavy thuds, made sudden black circles, then crashed to the ground. They'll grow bored of that soon. They'll want more. They always do. Ellen's muscles were taut. She was bracing herself to take the girl's weight. Her senses were straining for the acrid smell of smoke, a burst of flame.

Outside, a man started to shout, louder than the rest. His voice was piercing. The assistant put her hands to her face.

'What?'

'Praise be to Allah.' The assistant's mouth was hanging open.

The chanting died back. The man's voice rose above it. He was giving some command. Whatever instructions they were, the men were listening.

'What is it?' Ellen hugged the patient to her chest, one arm under her legs, ready to swing her off the cot.

The assistant started to laugh. Her eyes were screwed shut. 'No problem.' Her face flushed, colour rushing into her cheeks. 'No problem, madam.' She flapped her hands at Ellen, making no sense.

A scuffle. The dark mass against the canvas shifted. Footsteps. Another shout.

'What? Do we need to move? Tell me.'

The assistant opened her eyes. They were shining with relief. 'Not here. He said that. He said, "Go to another place."'

Thank God. Ellen rocked the young girl in her arms. Her hot cheek was pressed against Ellen's neck, her breath moist. Thank God.

'Good.' Britta opened her eyes. She had come back to them. She stretched out her legs, adjusted her clothes.

244

Ellen lowered the girl back onto her pillow. 'It's all right,' she told her. 'All over.' She smoothed the girl's hair away from her face and realized how hard her own hands were shaking.

'I knew they wouldn't hurt us.' Britta looked pleased, almost smug. She was getting to her feet, looking around the chaos of the gathered cots.

Ellen watched her in disbelief. So close. Another minute and they'd have been inside. Those men could have burnt the place down, killed them all.

Britta grasped one end of a cot and gestured to the assistant to take the other. The assistant, still curled on the floor, dipped her head. She looked limp with exhaustion.

Britta clapped her hands. 'Come on. Hurry. Hurry.' She was all smiles and jollity, as if nothing had happened. 'Let's move these good ladies back to their normal places, no?'

The assistant's face crumpled and she began to sob.

An hour later, Ellen set off through the camp with Frank and six policemen. A guard from the camp trailed behind, dragging his gun. The presence of the police undermined his authority and he seemed sullen with resentment.

None of the villagers she passed would look her in the eye. The men crouched, embarrassed, beside their broken shelters and turned away their faces. It was impossible to tell who amongst them had been part of the rampage and who victims of it.

They followed the route the rioters had taken. There was evidence of destruction everywhere. Shelters were in ruins, their struts split and gaping. Plastic sheeting, the only defence against sun and rain, lay torn and trampled underfoot. Two women, a mother and daughter, bent low, sifting through the wreckage. The daughter extracted a bent ladle, straightened it across her knee and added it to a pile of recovered possessions beside her. Her small boy crouched in the dirt next to her and watched in silence as they passed. A stillness hung over the camp, a mixture of despair and the exhaustion of spent anger.

The two bodies had been dumped on waste ground amongst sweating heaps of rubbish and cooking filth. They were untended, unmourned. The policemen stopped a few feet away and looked to their senior officer for instruction. Frank turned to speak to him. Ellen picked her way alone through the litter-strewn mud and stooped over the corpses, shielding her mouth and nose with her scarf.

Doc was lying on his back. The gash across his throat was black with feeding flies. Beside him, the young girl's body was grotesquely twisted. Her *dupatta* was narrow and tight around her broken neck. Ellen recognized her from Khan's party, one of the five girls who'd huddled together and shared a cigarette.

She still had the rounded prettiness of a teenager. Her plump skin was cheapened by heavy powder that had caked and creased into lines near her lips. Her eyes, wide and staring, reflected the slowly shifting clouds overhead. Ellen leant down and gently closed them. The eyelids were thin and dry. When she pulled away her hand, her fingertips were specked with mascara.

Frank and the policemen watched in silence. Ellen stepped back to join them.

'I've seen her before,' she said. 'At the hotel.'

Frank didn't reply. He made a sign to the police officer and his men moved in, unrolling thick sheets of plastic. They lifted Doc's body first, one taking the shoulders and the other the feet, and swung him onto one. Then they did the same with the girl. They wrapped each of them around and, staggering, carried the two bodies away. The senior officer nodded to Frank as they passed.

Frank was half-turned from her, his hands on his hips. She followed his gaze across this outlying area of the camp. A wooden stave had been broken in two, its jagged end splintered. It was sticking up like a battered mast in the sea of trampled sheeting and dirtied canvas. A kicked cooking pot, half-hidden, nestled on its side.

'You shouldn't have stayed.' Frank sounded weary. 'They could have killed you.'

'But they didn't.'

A dog trotted onto the waste ground and nosed through the debris. It was mangy, panting lightly. Its tongue dangled from one side of an open mouth.

'Now what?' Frank spoke softly. He shook his head, sighed. 'We rebuild all this. All over again.'

'What do you think happened?'

He shrugged. 'Taliban. Making it clear they can strike when they want to. Just in case anyone was starting to feel safe here.'

Ellen thought of the young man who called himself Saeed. 'You know who they are. Do something. Lean on the police.'

'I can't.' He moved a little away from her, lifted his hands from his hips and rubbed his face with his palms. 'It's not like that.'

247

The clouds were massing. A breeze whipped low across the plains. If it rained now, there would be nowhere to shelter.

'Why choose Doc and the girl? Punishing them for immoral behaviour?'

'I guess so.' He seemed distracted.

Ellen wanted to shake him. 'These men are thugs, Frank. Murderers. Why won't you do anything?'

'It's complicated.' He was barely listening.

She reached out and seized his arm, forcing him to pay attention. 'I saw him. Saeed. Going into your room.'

Frank looked away. He didn't speak for a long time. Then he said, without energy: 'So what?'

'So what?' She wanted to shake him.

He wouldn't look at her.

'Are you talking to them? Doing some deal?'

He lifted her hand from his arm and used it to turn her until they both faced out towards the mountains. He let her hand drop. 'That's what you think, huh?'

The peaks had disappeared into mist. Dark rivers of birds were flying low over the foothills, twisting and wheeling. He was tense. When he finally spoke, his tone was even and his voice low. 'I got fired from my last job. I guess you heard.'

She didn't speak.

'You know why? For paying rebels so we could get aid through. Everyone did. We had to. They controlled the road.'

The dog looked up, startled by a sudden movement. It was alert, listening. Finally it dropped its snout and sniffed its way out across the waste. Plastic crackled under its paws. Ellen kept her eyes on its mottled head. 'So what happened?'

'Some smart-ass journalist came in from Washington and blew it all up. That's what happened. Made a stink about aid dollars going to criminals, all that crap.'

Ellen dug at the dirt with the toe of her boot and made a dent. 'And you got fired.' A bottle top shifted and fell, revealing running ants. 'You don't think much of journalists, do you?'

'Fourteen years I'd worked there. Not even severance.' He paused. 'I was doing my job. If I'd been high and holy about it, women and children wouldn't have got food.'

She thought for a minute. 'So what're you saying? It's OK to do business with the Taliban?'

He looked down at the ground, at the dents she was making. 'No. But they're trying me. That's all. They think I'm the kind of guy who would.'

The slow, steady rhythm of banging started out in the camp. Someone was hammering in a stave, starting the long work of rebuilding a tent. They listened to it and looked out over the plain. The sky was thickening.

'I think I found your leak.'

He looked sideways at her, barely turning. 'You did?'

She inclined her head, inviting him to follow her as she walked back through the shattered camp.

They were deep in a litter of boxes and unpacked goods when Fatima walked in. Her headscarf was freshly starched, pinned into careful folds, and her clothes pressed. She stopped in her tracks and glared at Frank.

'You cannot be here.'

249

He didn't reply. He was kneeling down amongst tins of cooking oil and bags of salt, checking off serial numbers. The barcodes had already identified them as missing goods.

Fatima looked around, furious. 'This is a place for women. You are shaming them.'

Frank tipped another tin. Fatima hesitated, taking in the calm, methodical movement of his hands. He found the number and noted it down. She shifted her eyes to Ellen.

'Tell him to leave.'

She turned and walked away. Ellen heard her quick footsteps as she moved into the small room next door, then silence. She followed her through. Fatima was sitting stiffly in a chair, staring into space. She was dwarfed by the stacks of boxes around her.

Ellen spoke softly from the doorway. 'He came in the back way, Fatima. It's OK. He hasn't been on the ward.'

Fatima spat out: 'It's not right.'

Ellen stood for a moment, considering her rigid back and hard shoulders. She took a few steps into the room. 'Did you hear about Doc?'

Fatima didn't respond. She was stony-faced, her lips forced together. There was no trace of surprise in her eyes. Her hands were clenched. Ellen nodded to herself. She knew what had happened.

'They probably killed him because of the girls.' Ellen spoke slowly and deliberately. 'But what if they also know about the other thing, about him stealing supplies?'

Fatima turned her head and glared at Ellen, then looked quickly away. She didn't reply.

Ellen took another step nearer. She was within reach of

Fatima now, close enough to see the way her hands were trembling. 'Plenty of people saw Doc hanging around here,' she went on. 'No wonder he could get hold of anything. He used to boast about it.' Ellen's eyes were on Fatima's face. 'What if they know about you too?'

Fatima got to her feet in a rush and turned to face Ellen. Her clothes fell in neat pleats but her face was flushed. 'You know what they pay me here? For the hours I work? I have children.'

'I know, Fatima.' Ellen thought of the girl and boy who studied so hard in Cairo. 'But that doesn't make it right, does it?'

Fatima looked past her to the wall. She gave no sign of having heard. Her face was set and angry as if she thought the whole business of life was unfair.

Ellen reached out to touch her arm. She shook it off.

'Just leave,' Ellen said. 'Go, Fatima. Go home while you can.'

Ellen watched her for a moment longer, then left and went back to join Frank in the next room. He was opening a new box, excavating layers of bagged rice and sugar. By the time they'd logged it all, Fatima had already disappeared.

At the end of the afternoon, Ellen took a final walk through the camp, following the route the rampaging men had taken. The shelters looked storm-battered. She paused to watch a family, a young husband and a wife with a baby on her hip. They were working together, picking through the wreckage and setting aside what they could. Staves of wood. Coils of trampled rope. They were bolstering a

251

corner of the broken tent, trying to find some privacy and shelter for the night to come. There was no anger in their faces, just tiredness and resignation.

She crossed between the rows of tents and walked down the far side where there was almost no damage. Families there huddled together, their eyes averted. They seemed guilty that their homes were intact.

She was thinking. She had to call Phil that evening and she wasn't sure what she could offer. She'd promised a story about the Taliban diverting aid supplies for their own use. That had just collapsed. Phil would care a lot less now the thieves were a disgruntled nurse and a dead pimp. The Taliban probably killed Doc and they may have instigated the riot but she couldn't prove it. She sighed. She'd have to file something.

Her walk brought her up to the school. The woven walls around it had been ripped open. The panels were hanging, torn, from their struts. Inside, a frail, elderly woman was sweeping. Ellen tapped on the remains of the wall and the woman looked up, her eyes dull with fatigue. Ellen stepped into the compound and the woman bent back to the rhythmical hush of her sweeping.

If someone had asked her beforehand, Ellen would have said there was nothing there to destroy. The school had so little to start with. Now she walked around the small space, staring. The tent that had served as a classroom had been knocked down. It lay in a crumpled heap of hessian and broken wood. Whatever books the men had found had been ripped into shreds. Scraps of paper, some cheaply printed with words and pictures, some plain, were drifting in confetti showers across the ground, gathering in the hollows.

The blackboard had been smashed into pieces. She crouched down and picked up two fragments, trying and failing to fit them together. There were still faint lines of chalk on the black surface, the remains of letters. She wondered how they'd done that, which man had cared enough to stop and take the trouble to balance the black-board on a bed of stones or wood and stamp so hard he made it shatter. She wondered how that made him feel.

Here and there, pieces of chalk had been ground into the earth. They made circles of bright colour in the mud, a blooming flower of pink, several of white, one of vivid yellow. The yellow chalk was slowly bleeding into the edge of a puddle, bringing sunshine to the rainwater. Behind her, the old woman was still sweeping, drawing the debris into neat piles with strokes of her broom.

She let the pieces of broken blackboard fall from her hands with a clatter, thinking of the rocks that had flashed black against the canvas wall of the medical tent as they'd crouched inside. The men could easily have forced their way in and smashed everything. The patients were such easy targets. They could have attacked them all. Instead, for some reason, they'd been called off, told to spare them. She couldn't understand why.

20

Ellen found Frank at the main entrance to the administrative building, inspecting the damage there. It was a sturdy brick rectangle without windows and hard to penetrate. The side door and the main entrance had both come under attack in the riot but the wood was sturdy, secured with chains and padlocks as well as locks.

Frank was watching as a local workman gripped the edge of the door in one hand and eased it backwards and forwards, assessing the hinges. Its joints were rusty and gave a thin whine as the man forced them. It was a solid door, two inches thick, with the darkened surface and sweet smell of old wood. Its flat front was pitted with fresh scrapes and gouges. The workman poked at the hinges with a screwdriver, then turned to give his verdict to Frank.

'Door is very good,' he said. 'No problem. But with hinges, there is problem.'

He stepped inside the building and pulled the door

closed after him. There was a muffled banging from inside.

Ellen waited. Frank knew she was there, she sensed that, but he was preoccupied. His face was tight with tension. The riot and the damage weighed heavily on him.

She rubbed her eyes, looking without seeing. She hadn't slept much overnight. For most of the evening, she'd been writing up a news piece on the riot and her sense of the shadow of the Taliban over life in the camp. Phil hadn't exactly been delighted. It wasn't a headline. When she'd phoned him, he'd been gruff.

'Pull out,' he'd said. 'Need you back here.'

Afterwards she struggled to sleep. She lay, listening to the drone of the air conditioning and watching the advancing green numbers on the bedside clock, and worried about Britta and the strange spread of typhoid and about Layla who had clutched her hand with such desperation as they drove back together from the police station.

Wood crashed close by and she turned to look. Four workers in fluorescent tabards were sifting through wreckage, clearing away splintered remains and torn plastic sheeting and throwing the debris into a pile for collection. Their movements were weary.

She took another step forwards to get Frank's attention and nodded towards the door. 'They didn't get in, then?'

He grunted. 'They tried.' He pointed to the gashes in the wood. 'Knives.'

She raised her eyes and looked at the square corner of the building against the sky. The dun bricks oozed confidence. Colonial. Victorian, maybe.

'Why would they bother?'

'Put a lock on a door and rumours start.' He shrugged. 'I've heard all sorts. That I keep thousands of dollars in here. Guns. Gold.'

The chain that secured the door lay coiled at his feet. He picked it up. 'Rumours,' he said again. 'Too many people with not enough to do.'

She looked past him to the mountains. The mist was hanging low on the ridge, engulfing the peaks and softening the horizon into a blur of grey cloud.

'I've got to leave tomorrow. Back to Islamabad.'

'OK.' He gave her a quick glance. His expression was guarded. 'You got what you need?'

'Not exactly.' She took a deep breath. 'Frank, I need a favour.'

He didn't reply, just weighed the chain in his hands. His eyes were fixed on it but she knew he was listening.

'I want to take Ibrahim to see this so-called suicide bomber. Adnan. To confirm who he is.'

He stooped and set down the chain. It clinked as it settled on the stone step. His hands were dirty with flaking rust and he brushed them against his trousers, leaving dark streaks. 'What good will that do?'

She hesitated. 'Well, it would mean he's properly identified. And if Westerners are there, taking an interest, it might worry them.'

'Westerners? In the plural?'

'The police guy knows you.' She shuffled her feet in the dirt. 'Come on, Frank. He's innocent. I'm sure of it. You should see him.' She paused. 'It wouldn't take long.'

There was a further pause. The workman opened the

door and stepped out, screwdriver in hand. He seemed about to speak, then sensed he was interrupting something and stopped, looking from Frank to Ellen, waiting.

Frank said, 'He's probably been transferred to Islamabad by now.'

'But in case he hasn't.'

Frank looked at the workman. They both wanted to carry on their conversation about the damage to the door. Frank hesitated and dragged his eyes around to Ellen. 'And you're leaving tomorrow. So when are you thinking we'll do this?'

'Any time today.'

He rolled his eyes. 'Ellen. I've got a lot to do here.'

'Please, Frank.'

The workman was watching them both closely. For a moment, the activity in the camp seemed suspended. Even the four workers clearing away the debris seemed to pause and listen.

'All right.' Frank sighed. 'But give me a few hours at least.'

He pointed at the chain and the workman picked it up. The links clanked as he fed them through the metal hoop of the lock.

Finally, in the afternoon, Ellen met Ibrahim at the entrance gates. He had Layla at his side. Her face was pale, half-covered by her scarf.

'She wishes again to see her relative,' he told Ellen. 'They are like brother-sister.'

The driver, one of Frank's team, rushed to open the doors as soon as Frank arrived. He settled Frank into the front seat, then ushered Ellen, Layla and Ibrahim into the back. As he moved to take his own place, young boys crowded around the car, pressing their noses to the tinted windows. They laughed and jostled, shouting questions: 'Hello!' 'What your name?' 'What place you come?'

The driver revved the engine and the boys ran, shouting and waving, alongside the car, banging it with the flat of their hands as it gathered speed and finally shook them off.

The car bounced and rocked across the uneven ground. Ellen clung to the roof strap. Frank switched on the air conditioning and it started to grind. The afternoon was hot and humid. The sun was bleaching the mud plains and bouncing in shards off the water-filled ditches that crossed them. The mountains shimmered in the haze.

Layla was squashed between Ibrahim and Ellen. She sat hunched, her head bowed. She looked thin beneath her salwar kameez and the veins at her temples bulged. Ellen wondered if she knew about the murders and about how much damage the riot had caused. She leant past Layla to speak to Ibrahim.

'Did you hear about the girls' school?'

He nodded gravely and his round hat bobbed. 'Very terrible.'

'They destroyed everything. They'll reopen it, I'm sure, but it'll take time.'

Layla didn't respond. Her thin hands clasped each other in her lap. The school must have been her only escape. Ellen thought of the day she'd met Layla there, how confident and proud she'd seemed. Now that too was gone.

The driver turned onto a track that snaked back and

forth through a series of old brick arches under a wider, more modern road above. It was a cut through to the main road, a dark dip where the earth was rocky. As he pressed on, navigating with care through piles of scattered rocks, light glinted off to one side. Ellen turned to look. A car, its metalwork caved and battered, had shot out from one of the arches ahead and was careering towards them at high speed. Its engine strained. Thick black clouds streamed from its exhaust. They'll ruin it, she thought, crashing through the gears like that.

A young man was at the wheel. His light brown kameez sat neatly on his shoulders. His eyes were wide, focused and intent. He was coming right at them. Frank let out a shout. He grabbed at the steering wheel with one hand and pressed the other back against the car door, bracing himself. Ellen saw his fingertips turn white and bloodless on the plastic.

The driver too tugged at the wheel, his shoulders twisted sideways. There was squealing then a deep shudder from the car as he stood on the brakes. The car started to swerve but too late. The crumbling brickwork of the arches flew past the windows. The young man's face, staring, seemed to hang in slow motion as he smashed headlong into them. In that second before impact, Ellen grabbed Layla and pulled her flat across her lap. They were flung forwards together, clasping each other, striking the back of the front seat. They banged heads, then fell in a heap in the footwell.

Silence. Utter stillness.

Ellen's head hurt. It was bent forwards, too heavy to move. She felt a rush of fear. Then the moment passed and she breathed and the world again came crashing in.

Men were shouting. Warm air pressed in around her body as doors were wrenched open. The car rocked from side to side. She froze, head down, too stunned to move, listening to the chaos of sounds and feeling Layla still pressed against her, hot along her side. Frank's voice, alarmed, gave a single shout: 'Hey!' The driver murmured in Pashto, begging or praying. The sting of a hard slap. She sensed that the front doors were open and the men were being tugged out of the car. A crunch and splitting of flesh. Hard breathing. To the right, movement at Ibrahim's door. His voice rose too in Pashto, angry, resisting. A sound of blows, a crack of something hard on bone, a splintering.

Ellen found the strength to lift her head. She pulled at Layla, struggling to get them both back up into the cushion of the seat. The effort exhausted her and she sat for a second, her eyes closed, feeling very sick. Her forehead ached. When she put her hand to it, her fingers came away sticky with blood.

When she opened her eyes, she saw a second car to the side of them. Its doors hung open. More men had sprung from it. Ibrahim was on the ground, curled around, his arms wrapped around his head. Two men were kicking him. One struck his back. The other was kicking his stomach. His body was taut, shrinking from the boots. The driver was slumped in the dirt nearby, motionless. She twisted, trying to find Frank, but pain stabbed in her neck and she grimaced and let her eyes fall closed again.

The door beside her was snatched open and male hands reached in, grabbing her shoulders and pulling her out, off the seat. She fell to the ground with a bang, winded.

Her legs were left behind, caught up in the edge of the seat, in the metalwork of the car. She opened her mouth to shout but the sound wouldn't come. She was gripped by a nightmarish slowness, by terror. Her arm was crushed awkwardly under her body and she struggled to right herself, to draw in her legs. A man grabbed her hands and forced them behind her back. Something rough cut into her wrists.

A sack was forced down over her head and tied. It smelt of dirt and mustiness. It was tied too tightly. She strained her neck, trying to make a fraction more room so she could breathe. The cord gripped her throat. She started to shake, clammy with panic. When she blinked, her lashes scraped the sacking. She strained to see. She could barely make out the dark shapes moving in front of her.

Hands pulled at her elbows and half-dragged her to her feet. She was shoved forwards, then bent in two and pushed head first into the back of a car. A stranger's car. The plastic seat was hot. Her ears were straining, trying to understand what was happening around her. She felt hot, then cold and very sick. Breathing. All she could think about was breathing. Her breath was hot and wet on her face.

There was a cry, Layla's cry, then a slap and silence. Where was she? Somewhere to the left. Ellen was losing her bearings. Still she couldn't breathe. People pressed against her in the car. The door slammed shut. The bodies digging into hers were male, warm and hard with muscle.

A hand forced her head down and pain flared through her neck. The change of angle tightened the cord at her throat. It cut across her windpipe, choked her. Breathing.

She thought of nothing after that but breathing. Inhaling hot stale air. Exhaling into the mask of sacking against her face. Just that. One breath at a time.

Bodies crushed against each other and the car juddered into motion, bouncing across open ground. She was breathing in, breathing out, forcing herself to fight panic. She tried to stop herself from crying out. Her face was slick with sweat and her limbs juddered. Her lungs were gasping for air, her breaths sharp and shallow.

The road was bumpy. The man beside her put his hand on her face to hold her still. His fingers were thick and smelt of earth. The sack was coarse against her lips. The taste of it made her feel sick.

She struggled to concentrate on breathing and not to lose control. Layla was in the car with her, she could sense her. Frank and Ibrahim. No, she didn't think so. Two cars. There were two. They must be in the other one. Breathe in, breathe out. The cord tightened around her neck. She wanted to lift her head, to ease the pain and to reach for Layla, to comfort her, but the man held her fast and she sat, bent double, the sack pressing into her face, the hot thick hand on her forehead, fighting for breath. The butt of his gun was a hard finger in her ribs.

A man's hands loosened the cord around her throat and pulled the sack off her head. There were black pellets on the floor, goat droppings. She swallowed and felt the bruising in her throat where the cord had cut into it. She was in a mud-brick room with a cement floor. It was dank and dirty. The man untied the rope around her wrists and shoved her backwards against the wall. Mud flew out in a dry cloud when she hit it and she coughed.

Layla was in the room too, standing to one side, looking at the man. Her face was white and her scarf had slipped to her neck. Her hair fell in dark curly waves around her shoulders. It made her look different, softer and more Western. There were score marks across her throat where the cord had sawed it.

The man spat to the side and walked out, shutting the door. A bolt on the other side scraped home.

Layla turned to her. Her expression was terrified. 'Where's Baba?'

'Layla, I don't know.' The tips of Ellen's fingers were numb and her wrists burnt where the rope had skinned them. 'Maybe he escaped. Got away.' She lowered herself to the ground and sat back against the wall, massaging her hands and feeling the blood flow back to the broken skin. She felt utterly exhausted.

Layla hadn't moved. She stared at Ellen with eyes round with panic. Ellen looked down at the dusty bobbles of cement dotting the floor. I made them come. Frank and Ibrahim. I did this. She remembered the way the men had attacked Ibrahim, kicking him in the back and stomach, and wondered if Layla had seen it too.

'It must be a mistake.' It was all she could think of to comfort Layla. 'Once they realize that, they'll let us go.'

There was one small barred window, set high in the wall. There was no glass. If it rains, she thought, water will blow right in. A rusty bucket stood in one corner. When we use it, it will stink in this airless room.

Her legs started to shake against the floor. The memory

263

rushed back to her of the air in the car. It had been dense with sweat and stale breath. They waited for us, she thought. They knew. Her chest tightened. Someone must have listened when I asked Frank about going to visit Adnan. It wasn't a mistake. Someone told them.

Layla brushed away goat droppings with her foot and squatted down next to Ellen, sitting on her heels. She was trembling and her forehead glistened with sweat. They sat together in silence for a while.

Finally Ellen said, 'Are you OK?'

Layla didn't answer. She was biting her lip and her breath was catching in spasms as if she were fighting back tears. She's just a child, Ellen thought. She has no business being caught up in this. I should never have let her come.

She spoke softly, trying to distract her. 'Tell me about teaching.'

Layla hesitated. 'My baba is a good teacher,' she said. 'He knows everything. Mathematic and reading and English also.'

'That's wonderful.'

'He made travel all over Pakistan.'

'And what about you, do you want to travel?'

Layla gave her a quick look of surprise, then lowered her head and studied her nails. She didn't answer for a moment and when she did, her voice was dull. 'That is not possible. Not for a girl.'

Ellen considered her for a moment. She had visited small villages in the mountains here, in the years before the Taliban came. 'It's more difficult,' she said. 'But not impossible.'

They sat quietly side by side. Ellen wanted to sleep but

264

pain shot through her neck whenever her head started to droop. She sat rigidly against the wall, wondering what had happened to Frank and Ibrahim and the driver and feeling the ache in her forehead slowly worsen. After some time, Layla's breathing thickened and her head slid sideways onto Ellen's shoulder.

The window was a white square of heat. Ellen tried to work out what direction it was facing, thinking of the time and the angle of the rays hitting the mud bricks. A gecko scuttled across the top of the wall, close to the ceiling. It hesitated on the window sill, then darted to the side and disappeared. She forced herself to concentrate and listen. The air was heavy and still. There was an echo of male voices, calling in the open. A heavy engine, an old motorbike or field tractor, revved and chugged in the distance. Near the window, a bird cawed and was answered by another.

She closed her eyes and tried again to sleep. Would people know about them yet? She wondered how long it would take for someone to sound the alarm. They weren't expected back until the evening but the abandoned car might be found before then. She thought of the driver and his low pleading as they pulled him from behind the wheel. Of Ibrahim, curled on the ground as they beat and kicked him. His watery eyes had looked naked without his glasses.

Layla's breathing was becoming husky. Ellen put her hand on the girl's forehead. It was burning. She eased her gently around until she was stretched sideways, her head resting on Ellen's leg. The girl moaned in her sleep, then settled again. Her skin was clammy, her cheekbones prominent. She's very young, Ellen thought, to lose her mother.

The wall opposite stared blankly back. Ellen counted its bricks. Starting at one side. Then again from the other. Then from top to bottom. She worked out the central brick, straddling the midpoint. The cramp in her legs burnt away as the muscles went numb.

The intense brightness at the window gradually became more mellow. Layla didn't wake. Her skin was still burning and her clothes damp with sweat. Her breathing was laboured. Ellen sat in silence, listening to the echo of men's voices outside and staring at the darkening bricks, wondering who had taken them prisoner and why.

She closed her eyes and imagined being at home in London, walking slowly around her flat. The battered sofa where she curled to read or watch television. Her mother's old writing desk with its secret drawers and hiding places. The tiny kitchen with its dark tiles and softly humming fridge decorated with her nieces's pictures. When she opened her eyes, the bare walls pressed in, suffocating.

The door scraped open and a boy came in. He had a metal plate of rotis in one hand and a pot of daal in the other. He set them both down on the floor without a word and left.

Ellen gathered up the food and tried to make Layla eat. The girl seemed feverish and confused. When she had swallowed down a little food, Ellen folded her chador and set her gently on her side on the floor, her cheek against the cloth. She was worried. She watched the girl as she ate what she could of the rotis. This was more than grief and shock. Layla was ill. She wondered what they'd done with her rucksack, if they'd left it behind in the car or taken it. Her medical kit was inside.

The boy came to collect the remains of their meal.

'Please.' Ellen pointed to Layla. 'She needs medicine. She's ill.'

The boy, understanding nothing, pulled a face and left.

The cell drained of light. She and Layla were melting into the shadows. At night, they would disappear completely. The soft, high song of the call to prayer rose outside, floating in through the bars. She clung to the notes. Later, a light clicked on in the compound near their window and threw milky streaks across the ceiling.

The door was thrown open and a man stood there, young with a scruffy half-grown beard. He beckoned Ellen to him, then bound her hands together, this time in front. Layla lay sprawled in the semi-darkness.

Outside the cell, another young man was sitting on a plastic chair, a gun across his knee. Her guard nodded to him as he bolted the door. She was pushed down a dank corridor. She and Layla had been locked in a room in a low, single-storey house. She passed a second door and a third and counted off her steps. He turned and led her outside through a dimly lit courtyard to a building beyond. High walls marked the edge of the compound. Beyond, all was blackness. Cicadas scraped and sang. The night air was cool against her face. We're on high ground, she thought, above the plains. They walked through a swarm of gnats. She blew them off her lips and lifted her bound hands to fan them away from her eyes.

The man knocked at a door in the second building, then opened it and pushed her inside. She smelt food, pungent cooked meats, chicken and goat and freshly cooked rice flavoured with spices. Eyes turned to stare.

Blank, hostile faces. Four men were sitting cross-legged around the edge of a faded woven carpet, gathering food into clumps in their fingers and bending forwards to eat. Only one of them didn't raise his face to her. Saeed. She knew him at once.

The dishes, heaped with meat and thick sauce, were spread on an oilskin cloth in the middle of the carpet. A portable electric light, encased in cheap plastic, hummed beside them, in a halo of fluttering insects. The greasy sheen shimmered on the surface of the plates, the meat and the men's lips.

'*Salaam Alaikum.*' She put her hand to her heart and inclined her head.

The men shifted their attention to a figure to the left of the room, waiting for his reaction. She looked too. He was the largest man in the group and the most imposing, with a crooked nose, a thick dark beard and the broad shoulders of a warrior. His mouth and hand were busy with a chicken leg.

The man who had guided her from the cell hesitated, uncertain. Finally he closed the door behind them and leant back against it, some distance from the food. No one spoke. She felt the tension in the room and knew she had caused it. No one acknowledged her. After a few moments, she slid to one side and settled on her haunches against the wall, keeping her distance from the men. She waited. She kept her eyes on the most imposing man, aware that the others were doing the same.

He ignored them all and continued to eat methodically and with great appetite. His face was weathered and his eyes quick and hard. When he drained his glass of tea, the younger man beside him quickly replenished it. The other men chewed slowly, distracted by her, flicking their eyes across her then back to their food. One made a remark in a low voice to his neighbour and they sniggered for a second, then extinguished their laughter and again became wary.

The room was almost bare. A barred window was set in the far wall and two metal trunks were stacked under it, piled with woollen blankets.

Eventually the leader of the group finished. He swallowed, pushed away his plate and sat back against the wall. His legs were loosely folded in front of him, his knees splayed. He looked her over. One of the men handed him a cloth and he wiped his greasy fingers. 'You speak Urdu? Pashto?'

'*Toree, toree.*' She lifted her bound hands to gesture: A little.

He shrugged, unimpressed. 'I am knowing English.'

He burped and wiped off his beard and mouth with the cloth, then threw it onto his dirty plate. He shifted his weight from one buttock to the other and sat, picking lazily at his teeth, staring out at her. His presence was powerful and suffused with threat.

'You are journalist. You think I don't know? I know everything.'

She lowered her eyes, submitting to him. The men around him had jumped to their feet now and were clearing away the debris of the meal. The aroma of the meat hung heavily in the hot air.

'And you are Mohammed Bul Gourn.'

For a moment, he looked taken aback, then he narrowed

his eyes and she saw warning in them. 'Why you are in Pakistan?'

She kept her eyes on the ground. The men were rolling up the splattered oilskin. 'Reporting.'

'About what matter?'

'About the people who've fled the fighting.'

'What people?'

'Ordinary people.' She spread her hands as if to say: People anywhere. 'I talk to people in the camp.'

His English was thickly accented but good. She was careful to speak slowly to make sure he could follow her. When she glanced up at him, his sharp eyes were always on hers.

'These people. What do they tell to you?'

She shrugged. 'They're tired and frightened. They want peace. They want to go home.'

'And about the fighters?'

'I don't ask them about that.'

There was a pause. He shifted his weight again and she felt him watching her. To her side, the door opened.

'Why do you make Pakistani soldiers fight their own people? Killing their brothers for America?'

She didn't speak. Her legs were juddering beneath her with strain but she was too tense to move. The men filed out in deferential silence, closing the door behind them. Now only her guard and Mohammed Bul Gourn remained. If they plan to hurt me, she thought, it won't be now. He wouldn't do it himself. He would use his men. She tried to drop her shoulders and to breathe.

'I'm just a journalist,' she said. 'I only—'

'You're an infidel.' He shook his head and spat to the side. 'An American whore.'

'I'm British.'

He shrugged as if to say: What difference is there? He stabbed the air with his finger as he spoke. His anger swelled until it filled the room. 'The people of this country, they are people of Islam. Of Allah. They must live by His law. They must live without corruption, without oppression. This is our purpose. We will die for it.'

Her guard, standing against the door, stared down at his dirty boots. There was a moment's silence. Voices, shouting, drifted in from outside. Metal scraped and a gate clanged.

She waited, weighed down by her sense of powerlessness. He had complete control. He would spare her or kill her as he chose. He knew it and she knew it and the knowledge was a rope binding them. All she could do was wait and suffer his decision.

She raised her eyes to the level of his chest and spoke softly. 'Was it your men who killed Doc and the girl?'

He made a crushing motion with his hand as if he were extinguishing the life of an insect. 'They were enemies of Islam,' he said. 'My religion does not allow thieving and whoring. Does yours?'

'And your men caused the riot in the camp?'

He grimaced. 'These villagers are traitors. They should stay on their land and fight with their brothers.' He leant forwards, his eyes bright, and stabbed a finger at her. 'Your American friend, he lives off these people. Women and children both.'

She stared, feeling panic. 'That's not true. He's—'

'He is corrupted. Taking foreign money for his own self.'

271

'No.' She shook her head. 'It's—'

'He lets people die.'

She sat quietly, hearing the rising note of anger in his voice and fearing it.

'Allah will punish him.' His eyes were glinting. 'I will punish him.'

She felt herself flush and turned her eyes to the floor. The cement was stained with a splash of sauce that had escaped the confines of the oilskin cloth. Now it was black with ants, hurrying to and from it in a single solid line. She thought: Frank is still alive then. He is here. Then at once this was knocked aside by a second thought: He's the one they want and now they have him, they will kill him. It is my fault, she thought again. I pulled him out of the camp without a guard and made him vulnerable. She sat, sickened.

'It isn't true.' She spoke quietly, without hope. 'You don't know him. He's a good man.' Her eyes were on the ants. It would be so easy to crush them all.

'You were going to help that idiot boy, nah? I know everything.' He threw back his head and laughed. His throat was thick with beard and the hair on his chin wagged. 'You are a fool.'

His mention of Adnan reminded her of Layla. She raised her head and looked him full in the face for the first time. 'The girl is ill. She's done nothing. Be merciful. Let her go.'

He grimaced. 'Let her go? No. Why am I letting her go?'

'At least give me medicine for her. It's in my bag.' She shifted a little. Her wrists smarted where the rope bound them. 'She's just a girl.'

Mohammed Bul Gourn was watching her closely. He isn't thinking about Layla any more, she thought. He doesn't care about her, one way or the other. His eyes had a sudden sharpness. He was thinking of something else.

'This man. This Pakistan man.' He leant forwards. 'Hasan Ali Khan.' He was speaking in abrupt bursts. 'He is rich, nah? What is he wanting here?'

Ellen hesitated a moment, surprised by his interest in Khan. She shrugged. 'To help people.'

He smiled and his teeth gleamed in the half-light thrown by the cheap electric lamp. 'Just this? To help people?' The smile widened.

Ellen nodded. 'He wants a good reputation. He wants people to think he's generous. People in England.'

Mohammed Bul Gourn clicked his tongue against his teeth. The amusement in his eyes cooled and hardened. He looked her over. He seemed to be thinking, considering whether she was telling the truth. She held his gaze.

'He wants power,' he said at last. 'All men want power. But he is a fool if he tries to buy it here.'

He stretched and yawned and scratched his belly. He seemed suddenly bored. After some moments, he lifted his head and gave an order to the guard who, also sensing the change of mood, was moving his weight from foot to foot. The guard opened the door a crack and passed the command to someone outside.

Her legs were shaking. She lowered herself to the floor and sat, head bowed, feeling the tiredness in her limbs. It was late. She wanted to be back in the cell, away from this man, and to sleep. The quietness of the room, broken only by the low hum of the electric lantern and the pulse

273

of her own breathing, settled around them. They were waiting for something to happen. She didn't know what it might be.

Footsteps outside. The door opened again and her bag appeared, passed in to the guard. He handed it with reverence to Mohammed Bul Gourn.

It was odd to see her rucksack in his hands. He tugged open the zip and picked through the contents. She saw the white front of her notebook rise and be pushed aside as he rummaged, followed by the dark rectangle of her phone. He pulled out her medical pack, marked with a red cross and the *NewsWorld* logo, and opened it up on the floor in front of him. It was neatly packed with a pouch for each item: clean syringes, sterile dressings, antibiotics, creams and a series of tablets.

'I can show you what the girl needs.' She hesitated to move towards him. 'I think she has typhoid fever.'

'Fever?' He was pawing through the sachets and packets, exploring. 'What is for fever?'

'That one.' She pointed to the antibiotics.

He opened it and held the foil blister pack up to the light. When he'd satisfied himself that it was only medicine, he pushed it back into the cardboard sleeve and sent it skimming across the floor towards her. She bent forwards and scooped them into her hands.

'Allah is merciful,' he said. 'Maybe this girl will become well. *Inshallah.*'

He lifted his hand and signalled to the guard. He kicked at Ellen's feet. She scrambled to get up and he led her back to the cell, leaving Mohammed Bul Gourn on the floor sifting through her possessions.

Layla was lying curled on her side on the floor, flushed with fever and shivering. Her breath was rattling in her chest. She had soiled herself and the smell filled the room. When the guard untied her hands and left, Ellen used her cotton scarf to try to clean her. Layla was barely conscious, tossing her head and murmuring in Pashto. Ellen held her lips apart to swallow down the first dose of antibiotics. She cradled her in her arms and rocked her, trying to soothe her into sleep.

The walls pressed in, malicious with shadow. The shape of the cell seemed to shift as she stared. The floor narrowed and the walls grew taller. The window, a high grey square of darkness, all she had of the outside world, receded and shrank.

She was shivering. She wondered if anyone knew yet that they'd been taken. Britta might raise the alarm. The embassies would be alerted. They'd call Phil. She imagined him in his office, cursing and bouncing his pen on the desk, debating with management how to respond.

Layla shifted and settled her head on Ellen's thigh. Her breath was ragged and stale but she was sinking deeper into sleep. Ellen stroked the stray hair from her forehead and temples. Layla's body had the same distinctive vegetal odour as the child on Britta's ward. She'd smelt it when Fatima washed the child on the ward, shortly before her death. She'd deteriorated quickly. She thought how small her stiffening body had looked under its sheet.

Ellen shifted her weight, trying to stretch out dead muscle. The concrete was rough and dug into her skin. She closed her eyes and started to drift at last into sleep.

*　　*　　*

A scream tore the air. Distant but piercing. A high-pitched animal cry. Ellen sat up straight, suddenly wide awake. The horror of it shrank her skin. She blinked in the half-light and waited, straining to hear. The cell was tight with silence. Some minutes passed. It was just an animal's cry, she told herself, a terrified animal. Nothing more. Her heart slowed again and her body gradually came back to her. She lifted Layla's head so she could rub the cramp out of her legs.

A second scream burst, followed by a long, tailing moan. It was a man's voice, a cry of pain. She clenched her jaw, trying to resist the sound, screwing her eyes into lines. One hand supported Layla. She raised the other to her head and ran it through her hair, breathing hard.

When the scream died away completely, she lifted her eyes to the high window. They're keeping us alive, she thought. They could have killed us by now. In some other part of the building, there was a metallic scraping followed by heavy footsteps. A thud. Silence. A third scream, weaker, more pitiful. The same man. She let her head ease back against the wall until her face was turned to the dark ceiling. It could be anyone. She felt herself flushing hot, then cold. She tried to steady her breathing and let her eyes fall closed again. Please God, don't let it be Frank.

It had ended abruptly between them, all those years ago. She had just come back from her first commissioned assignment, a one-week trip to cover an arts festival in Budapest. Many of the performers were appearing in London that summer. She'd been previewing their acts and writing some short pieces about life in Hungary a few years after the fall of the Berlin Wall. She flew back into

276

Heathrow Airport excited about the people she'd met, the things she'd seen. She and Frank had arranged to meet at Waterloo Station. As she emerged from the depths of the tube, she glimpsed him through the crowd. He was waiting in their usual place, under the vast four-faced clock suspended in the centre of the great Victorian rail concourse.

He hadn't seen her yet. His head was tilted back, gazing up into the long symmetry of the iron girders and glass panels that formed the vaulted roof. She stopped in the crush of moving people, and tried to see him as a stranger might, as if for the first time. His clothes always looked thrown together. His shoes were scuffed, his trousers crumpled and the full-length coat that fell in folds around his body needed a good clean. His features weren't striking but he was good-looking. A strong profile, full mouth and bright, curious eyes. It was hard to look at him and not feel better about life.

He turned, saw her and broke into a smile. He waved. She dipped her head to pick up her bag again, embarrassed about being caught staring. The moment had passed. He was striding towards her now, making his way through the throng, rushing to hug her and to take her bag. She followed him across the concourse to the first-floor balcony of a café where they could sit for a while and overlook the scurry and bustle below.

They drank coffees. She told him everything about Budapest and he listened with a smile, indulging her. He plucked one of the paper napkins from the holder on the table and shredded it, edge by edge, into frills, nodding as she talked.

277

It started to rain. Water beat on the glass panels of the roof far above their heads. The people flooding into the concourse furled umbrellas and shook off wet hair and headscarves. Small puddles of water gathered and were spread by shoes and boots.

They sat in silence for a while, watching. A crowd had gathered in front of the main departures board, waiting for platform numbers to appear. Delays, she thought. The elderly newspaper vendor was resting his elbows on his stack of papers, whiskery chin in his hands, staring out morosely at the milling public. Two young girls, teenagers, staggered onto the concourse together on high heels, screeching and clutching each other, willing the world to notice them. She looked down at them and smiled.

Frank reached out. He put his hand on top of hers on the table. His hand was warm. The surface of the table was cool Formica, gritty with sugar.

'You know what?' He was watching her closely. 'I found us the perfect place.'

She tried to keep the smile on her face.

'One bedroom, modern kitchen. Great location,' he said. 'You'll love it. Let's go see it this evening.'

She felt a wave of panic. She didn't know what to say. They'd never talked about living together. They'd always had their own places, their own space. She wanted to travel. 'We should talk about it.'

'What's to talk about?' He snapped his fingers. 'You know how fast good places go. I'm telling you, it's a gem.'

She looked out at the crowd, the blur of hurrying, pressing people. He was squeezing her fingers, trying to get her to look at him.

'What?'

'Just, it's a big step.' She hesitated. 'I mean, we never—'

He pulled his hand away. 'I talk about it. You don't.'

His mood had changed. She couldn't look at him. She'd spoiled everything.

'I stay in this country for you. Don't you get that? I could just as soon go home. It would be good to get a little something back.'

She couldn't speak. The paper napkin with frilled edges was lying on the table between a stained salt cellar and a yellow plastic cone of mustard. The silence stretched. I should say something, she thought. I should know what I want and just say it, one way or the other.

'I get the feeling sometimes that you just don't want this, do you, Ellie?' His voice was hard with hurt. 'Not the way I do.'

He pushed his cup aside and sat, turned away from her, looking down at the concourse below. The streams of people were trudging wearily back and forth, in black and grey and brown, laden with bags and cases, exhausted and despondent and longing for home.

21

I was sleeping and waking and sleeping all night and the two were so tangled, I didn't know which was which. I woke to find the Britisher leaning over me, speaking in English. I was too tired to understand. My body was stiff and aching from the hard floor. She moved out of sight and I saw the ceiling above which was grey with flecks of dirt hanging from it in drops. The morning light was weak on the ceiling.

I started to remember what had happened and about Baba being kicked on the ground. If I were a child again, I would have wept, but the pain went so deep that I couldn't cry it out. Instead I blinked and looked at the watery sun. I wanted Mama and she was gone. I wanted Baba and I didn't know where he was. It was such a heavy crushing sorrow that I didn't think I could bear to carry it.

The Britisher made me swallow down medicine and eat bread although I had no appetite. I closed my eyes and rested my head on her knee and pretended to sleep but all the time I wished I could fade away and die and asked God's forgiveness for such wicked thoughts.

When I did sleep, I had a strange dream. Mama and Baba were there, young again and happy, and we were picnicking by the stream. Mama handed out delicious eatables and Baba joked and teased her and Marva came with me down to the water to play and I cried out: Look, Marva, you're walking! and she just smiled as if I were a foolish girl and splashed right into the stream itself. Under the clear water, the stones were the most beautiful bright colours, purple and green and yellow and blue, and the fishes darting there were red as blood and happy to play with us, they were not afraid.

Then my head started to pound and I became hot and frightened and the dream dissolved until Mama and Baba and Marva and the fishes were gone and all I could hear was moaning and whimpering and I finally realized that the noise came from me. Another sound grew and it was the voice of the Britisher humming and it echoed around the walls. My body ached, every limb, and first I was cold and then hot and then cold again, dipped between flames and ice. The Britisher soothed me, patting my face with a cloth. She made me drink and I knew she was kind but wished she would mind her business and let me alone to die.

Later a voice spoke to me in Pashto. His voice, my Saeed, talking low. I opened my eyes to look. His face, his brown eyes and handsome nose, hung so close to mine that I could see specks of dirt on his eyelashes and my own small self looking back at me in the round black circles of his pupils.

'Saeed?'

'Layla.'

281

He said my name gently. It made me think of the times he followed me to school and how simple life had been. I had been an innocent young girl who understood nothing about sorrow and change.

I stared at him. 'Why are you here?'

He urged me to get to my feet and cross the cell to the far corner, away from the Britisher. My legs were rubbery. I leant heavily on the wall, handing myself along, step by step. The Britisher had a metal cup of tea and a plate of rotis. Saeed had brought these things to keep her busy while he and I talked. She ate but she also watched us at the same time.

'You seem very sick.' He looked at me gravely. 'How are you?'

I nodded. 'I'm alive, thanks be to God.'

I sank to the floor. Fingers of light reached in from the high window and dappled my clothes. He settled a little apart from me, proper and respectful, and didn't touch me.

'I have terrible news.' His eyes were solemn. I didn't understand but I began to feel afraid. 'About your baba.'

He looked at me, then he looked at his boots. I looked down at them too. They were strong boots with cracked leather. Shreds of newspaper were packed down the sides. One of the laces was brown, matching the leather, and the other was a ragged piece of string.

'What about my baba?'

He carried on looking at the boots and didn't speak and the answer came rushing at me in a great wave.

I lifted my hands to my ears and closed my eyes. I thought about clambering on Baba's knee when I was a small girl and the warmth of his big hands when he settled me in his lap to read to me and how he let me pull at his spectacles and set them crooked on his nose. I thought about Baba teaching inside the school, standing at the front of the classroom with arms wide, conducting us as we chanted out our letters or sums.

'The men who did it will be punished,' Saeed said. 'The commander is displeased. He did not order it.'

My hands were at my face now and I was scrunched over into a ball. I wanted to weep but the tears wouldn't come. I was thinking: I knew, I knew all the time that Baba was gone but I kept fighting it, hoping I was wrong.

'I condole you.'

His condoling seemed to me such a thin, weak word. I wanted to shout at him, to hit him about the face with my fists and say: What wrong thing did my baba ever do to you? He was a great man, a good teacher and husband and father and how will I live without him and without Mama as well? But I couldn't speak. Instead I pressed my face into my raised knees and breathed in hard gulps, shaking and listening to the pounding in my head.

We sat in silence for a long while. On the outside, I was still, but inside I was in turmoil. I thought: This is Saeed and I longed to see him but I never knew it would be like this. Then I thought of the cause of it and Baba, my baba, can he really be gone and will I never see him again, not once more in my life, how is that possible? Allah have mercy. I thought about that night in the clinic when I fell asleep against Baba on the plastic seats and prayed so hard to Allah not to take Mama, to take someone else but please not Mama and now, remembering, I thought: He has taken Mama anyway and Baba as well and it is all too late to put right.

'I can help you,' Saeed whispered to me. 'Commander Saab is a good man. He favours me. You hear? He favours me. I'm not a nobody from the shacks any more. He has plans for me.'

'I never thought you were a nobody.' I looked again at his boots and they seemed changed, as cold and bleak as everything else.

He carried on. 'Commander Saab says we are all brothers and sisters of Islam, here on this earth to serve Allah and to do His will, thanks be to God.' He spoke rapidly, gathering pace. 'He wants us to go back to the way Allah in His Wisdom intended for us to live. To have Islamic justice and decency and equality before God. His teaching is a great blessing.'

I had never heard him talk so much about God. His face was flushed. I thought, He loves this Commander more than he loves me.

He paused, watching me closely. Then he said, 'Even the faithful and strong must be on their guard against sin.'

I thought, Baba wasn't sinful but killing him was a great sin and Allah will seek out the man who did it and punish him.

He saw my expression and let out a long, blowing sigh. 'I am sorry about your baba.' He spoke slowly, groping for the words. 'I will try to protect you, Layla.' He looked around the room, rolling his eyes as if he were searching for answers in the bricks.

He moved onto his knees and rolled back the sleeve of his kameez. His arms were dark with hair and hard with muscle. He pulled the kameez right back to his shoulder and twisted his body to show me. I stared. Part of his

284

underarm was missing. A whole fleshy bite had gone and the skin inside was raw and red and gnarled with black stitches and scabs. I shrank back from it.

'I was shot.' He said this with pride. 'I almost lost my arm.'

I shook my head at the horror. I wanted him to roll down his sleeve and hide it away and be whole again.

'One of my comrades tended the wound but it went bad. I had to leave them and go down to the plains for help.'

I started. 'To the plains?'

He nodded. 'I saw you once, in that camp.'

He put away the wound and I was glad.

'I get information from there for Commander Saab. He trusts me.'

I looked at my hands, limp in my lap. I thought about Saeed and the commander and all the pain they had brought. I thought about the burning school and Baba's swollen hands and the terrible wrong they had done in ending his life. My thoughts were suddenly clear.

'How can you see these men as good and holy?' I said. 'They've killed my baba. They tricked Adnan into some-thing terrible. We are all fled, living like beggars and dying of disease.' My voice was soft but I saw how much my words hurt him. 'And now you take two women and shame them and lock them in a cell. Is that honourable? Is that the work of decent Muslim men?'

'Don't talk like this.'

He reached into the pocket of his kameez and showed me the edge of a dark packet, wrapped around in plastic. He prised open the end and lifted it to show me. It was money. A lot of money, rolled into a ball. I had never seen so much in my life.

'Where did you get that?' I was suspicious. There was something dirty to me now about Saeed and his wound and his money.

He looked taken aback. 'For us, Layla. I save everything. For us.'

I shook my head. I turned away and wouldn't look at the money and wouldn't look at him. He shifted and when I looked again, the bundle had disappeared back into the deep pocket of his kameez.

I said, 'You should go.'

He looked stricken. He opened his mouth to say something, then waited for a moment, reading my eyes, and closed it again. He put his hand on the floor between us, reaching towards me. 'Are you all right?'

I shrugged. It was a stupid question. I wouldn't answer. He got to his feet. The Britisher in her corner was watching us. I saw her eyes follow him as he walked to the door, banged on it to be let out, and disappeared.

I turned my shoulder to her. My head was aching. I twisted and curled in a ball on the cement floor. It was dotted with small stones and pieces of dirt. The more closely I looked, the more filthy it became. In the corner, a spider had spun a web. A fly was caught in it, struggling. The threads glistened in the half-light. Behind the web, a line of ants was picking its way up the wall. So much life. This whole world was teeming with it and yet my baba was cold and still.

I knew then that I could never marry Saeed and it was not on account of his class or his family or their lack of land but on account of the terrible sins that he and his new friends had committed against me and my family, against us all.

22

Ellen barely slept that night. By morning, she was red-eyed and dull with fatigue. Layla was still flushed but her fever was receding and she seemed to sleep deeply for several hours. When Saeed came with food, he took the girl into a corner and whispered to her. Ellen wondered if he'd been sent to strike a deal.

Ellen ate the bread and tried to listen. Saeed's voice was soft and she struggled to make out what he was saying. Then she heard a word she knew: Baba. Father. She looked up. Layla's face was white. She had doubled over and was rocking herself. So Ibrahim was dead, the gentle schoolteacher who'd risked his life to save books. Ellen pushed away the bread, unable to eat.

When Saeed had gone, she went across to Layla and tried to comfort her. The girl curled up in the corner and pushed her away.

The sun in the cell grew whiter as morning wore on. Streaks of hard light poured in from the window and bounced off the walls. Ellen's face felt stiff with dirt. When she touched the cut on her forehead, flakes of dried blood came away on her dirty fingertips.

Sometimes she paced around the cell with even steps, counting the distances and dividing them in her head. Widths and breadths, diagonals, chess squares. At other times, she sat and stared at the cement floor, watching trails of ants navigate its bumps and creases.

All she had to look at was the packet of medicine. There wasn't much to read on the cardboard sleeve. The main lettering, the brand name, was raised and embossed, in Chinese characters on one side and English on the other. She ran her fingertips over it with her eyes closed, then rubbed it against her cheek. The company address was an industrial unit in Guilin, China. She tried to pass time by making words with the letters.

In the top right-hand corner there was a hologram, a security guarantee. It was a stylized design, a spinning wheel. When she tipped the packet back and forth, it gleamed and shone. She balanced the packet on its end, knocked it down, balanced it again. She thought about Mohammed Bul Gourn and the screams in the night and worried about Frank.

She did simple exercises she remembered from yoga classes and aerobics, stretching first legs, then arms, then back, trying to work out the cramp. Her neck flamed with pain when she moved her head and she tried to massage it.

She must have been dozing when the man came. The scrape of the bolt jerked her awake. She recognized him from the previous night, one of the men who ate with Mohammed Bul Gourn and sniggered. Now he stood in the doorway, blocking it with his heavy build, and glared. A piece of rope dangled from his hands and, knowing why, she offered her wrists.

He walked her in front of him down the narrow corridor, kicking at her heels to keep her moving. At the end, they turned to the left and the ground sloped sharply downwards. It smelt musty, an earth smell overlaid with the aroma of animals and damp straw. A man sat on his heels by a low door. He nodded as they approached, then spat to the side. He heaved himself to his feet and stood, his grinning mouth showing stained teeth.

Her escort was jangling keys, fiddling with the padlock and chain on the door. It came open with a metallic thud. He opened the door a foot or so until the chain reached its limit, then pushed her through the gap and slammed the door shut behind her.

She stood motionless for a moment. It was dark. She blinked hard, trying to see through jumping threads of light. There was a scent of damp hair. Above her, set high in the far wall, a dark square was narrowly outlined in bright sunlight. Her eyes were drawn to it and she stood, peering, trying to make it out. The shapes came slowly forwards from the shadows to meet her as the darkness thinned. It was a window, she could see that now. Smaller than the window in her own cell and covered with a square of wood.

Something stirred to the right. She turned. A figure, a man, was shifting, there in the corner. It was too dark to make out his face but she saw light gleam in his eyes and felt them watching her.

'Ellie?' His voice was slurred.

289

Frank.

'Are you OK?' She moved across to him, straining to see.

The side of his face was dark and its contours distorted. His cheekbone was misshapen, staved in beneath one eye. The cheek around it was a mass of blackness, of bruising and dried blood. She bent over him and lifted her bound hands to his face, gently touching his skin. 'What've they done to you?'

There was no answer. He lifted his arm and pointed across the cell. She looked. A person was lying in the far corner, the lumpen shape of a man. He was still.

'Ibrahim?'

He shook his head. 'Driver.' His voice was thick and little more than a whisper. Around his mouth, his lips were swollen and split. 'Ibrahim's dead.' He turned his eyes from hers. The high-pitched night screams came back to her. She settled on the damp ground beside him and her fingers found his. She stroked the back of his hand.

'Frank.' She had nothing for him, not even water. With her hands bound, she could barely move her fingers. 'What can I do?'

He shook his head. His eyes had closed, his head slumped forwards.

They had brought her to see him for a reason. To frighten her, perhaps. Or to put pressure on him. She thought of Mohammed Bul Gourn's anger, his allegation that Frank was siphoning money from the refugees and must be punished.

'Why, Frank? What do they want?'

Frank's eyes rolled. 'They blame me.' She put her face to his, trying to catch his words. 'For all the deaths.'

290

'Why would they think that?' she said.

'They say I'm corrupt.' He collapsed into a cough. A thin line of saliva ran from the corner of his mouth and glistened on his chin.

'It was Doc stealing stuff,' she said. 'They know that.'

He was breathing hard, trying to steady himself. He strained to lift his head to look at her. His eyes were bloody. 'It's not true, Ellie. Swear to God.'

'I know.'

He let his head fall, exhausted. She squeezed his hand. Across the cell, the driver moaned, twisted on the floor, then settled.

When he spoke again, she had to lower her ear to his drooping head to hear his voice. 'They keep asking about Khan,' he said. 'Why he came. Why he's giving money.'

'What's their problem with him?'

'God knows.'

The chain behind them rattled and the door was prised open again. The guard's face was at the gap, glaring. He shouted at her, an order to hurry up and leave. She leant forwards and brushed her cheek against Frank's face. She slid her mouth to his ear and whispered to him. 'Frank. We'll get out of this. Don't give up.'

The guard shouted again, lifting his gun. She struggled to her feet to leave. At the door, she turned. He gave a feeble wink and tried to smile, offering her the best he could: a grimace of broken lips and bloody teeth.

Her own cell seemed to have shrunk. The walls pressed more tightly around her. Layla was lying on the ground under the window, her legs sprawled. Her scarf covered her head and eyes. Ellen lowered herself to sit against the opposite wall, massaging her wrists where the rope had chafed them. The sun was high and shards of light were reaching further into the room. It was hot and airless. The cell stank. Clouds of small flies swarmed around the bucket in the corner.

Ellen paced up and down across the concrete, trying to distract herself from thinking about Frank. Outside, the light was bright with glare. A bird cawed with a distant mournful cry. Men with raucous voices shouted to each other in Pashto. She wished the hours would fade, that night would come again. Finally she sank against a wall, pressed her hands to her face and closed her eyes.

Frank's bloodied face was there at once. What had they done to him? Thinking about it made her physically sick. She couldn't bear to sit still. He'd been so pitiful, trying to be brave for her when it was clear he was in pain. She groaned, rubbed the heels of her hands into her eyes. Frank wasn't perfect. He was stubborn sometimes and short-tempered. But he was a decent man, a kind one. He was dedicated to helping people. It was absurd to blame him for the camp deaths.

She remembered Frank's sorry attempt to smile. She twisted and hit the flat of her hand against the wall by her head, banging up dust and loosening fragments of mud. She pounded until her hand was red and aching, then curled up, exhausted, put her head in her hands and wept. She was afraid they hadn't finished with him yet. She didn't know how much more his body could take.

An hour or two later the door was unbolted and dragged open. She looked up. Mohammed Bul Gourn was there in the doorway, drawing his eyes over the cell. He seemed taller. He had a blanket wrapped loosely around his shoulders and a woollen hat on his head. He pointed to Layla and his man rushed across and tugged her by the shoulder. She sat up, bleary-eyed, and adjusted her scarf to cover her hair more completely.

When Mohammed Bul Gourn turned to Ellen, his look was calculating.

'So. The girl is still living.'

Ellen thought of Frank and the driver. This man had complete control over them all.

'You gave me medicine,' she said. 'From my bag.'

He gave an odd laugh. 'In this place, all alone, you are keeping her living. But in the camp, with all those clever doctors, people die.'

She opened her mouth to protest then closed it again. Useless to argue. He was considering her. His look was strange and she couldn't read it.

'What if I give you freedom? What will you do for me?'

For a moment, she couldn't let herself think about freedom. Instead she looked at the blanket he wore. It was made of coarse brown wool but the columns of light falling across the room were picking out a light meandering thread and she concentrated on following its pattern with her eyes.

'It is a great blessing to show mercy,' she said.

She wouldn't look up. She didn't trust him and she didn't want to give him the satisfaction of seeing hope in her eyes and then crushing it. She made herself trace the thread through the curves of the blanket as it fell in broad folds around his body.

'This girl is doubly blessed.' He had drawn himself to

293

his full height, his expression self-satisfied. 'She is made well by her Britisher friend. And she has another good friend. From her village. He has pleaded for her. He has given all his money to Allah's fight so she can be free.'

Ellen nodded. Saeed had begged for her then. 'And what can I give you? I don't have money.'

'You can give me another thing.'

He came briskly across the room towards her. She scrambled to stand up. She felt his power and it frightened her. She stood with the wall hard against her back, facing him. He had stopped so close to her that she could see the fine lines of pitted skin across his broken nose where, many years ago, the flesh had torn and scarred as it healed.

'This man, Hasan Ali Khan,' he said. 'You know him?'

'I've met him. Once.'

He lowered his voice so that only she could hear. 'Take to him this message from Mohammed Bul Gourn. This is my land. It is not his land.' His eyes were intent on hers, fixing her. 'He must not come here. Understand?'

She nodded. He turned from her as quickly as he had come and strode back across the small room. Layla, watching from her corner, whimpered. He was already at the door.

Ellen roused herself, took a step after him. 'And the men? What about their freedom?'

He turned and his look was stern. He inclined his head to her to say goodbye and tossed the end of his blanket across his shoulder. 'Write good things,' he said. 'Write I am a good man, a mercy man.'

He turned from her a final time, the door was pulled shut behind him and he was gone.

* * *

294

The light was starting to fade when the young men came. She and Layla were curled in their corners, sleeping. The men pulled them to their feet and marched them out. Ellen thought of Frank and the night screams and concentrated on breathing slowly, bracing herself for whatever might come.

They were taken into a compound, surrounded by a high wall. The air was hot but fresh after the stuffiness of the cell. A car engine was running. Layla was so weak she staggered. The men bound their wrists and forced hoods over their heads. The sacking pressed against Ellen's face. It was full of dust. The stink of earth and mould brought back the terror of the first journey. Beside her, Layla was whimpering.

A man held her elbow and marched her forwards, then pushed down her head and forced her into the back of a car. Someone pressed in beside her on the seat. His hand was hot and hard on the back of her neck, holding it down. Layla was beside her. The doors slammed shut and the car shook, then rocked slowly forwards on a rough track. A melodic voice intoned on the radio, giving a sermon or religious reading.

Blood rushed to her head, making her nauseous. Pain flared in her neck. The hessian hood rubbed against her windpipe, chafing her throat. This sudden move could mean anything. She mustn't let herself imagine freedom. She tried to focus on breathing. This could be a drive to a piece of wasteland and a brutal beheading, her body dumped by a roadside. Or a handover, a transfer for cash from one group to another that would take them further towards the Afghan border and make it harder for anyone to trace them. Someone smoked, filling the car with the sickly fumes of cheap tobacco.

The car swerved to the side of the road and came to a sudden halt in a crunch of loose stones. Ellen was pitched against the back of the seat in front. Doors opened and a flood of air carried the rich smell of grass. The hand on Ellen's neck lifted and the pressure of the man's body against her side disappeared and was gone. The door slammed. Layla was still in the car. Ellen felt her against her side. They waited. In the distance a dog barked.

The door opened and a male hand grabbed at her arm and tugged, pulling her out. She fell out sideways, striking her head against the ground. For a second, she was too dazed to breathe, then air came back to her in gulps. Small stones pricked her cheek through the hood. She'd fallen awkwardly and, her hands bound, couldn't right herself. Men were talking in Pashto in low voices. She couldn't understand. Her head was thick with tiredness and she was dizzy.

Car doors were slamming and an engine revving and there was a sudden skidding of tyres on stones as a car drove away. They've dumped us here. She shook her head, frightened.

Someone moved. A man spoke in a soothing voice, saying, 'It's OK, it's OK.' He had a Pakistani accent. His breath smelt of spices. He was reaching over her, fiddling with the knots that held the hood and suddenly, in a rush of air and light, he pulled it off.

They stared at each other. He was a young Pakistani man, dressed in a cream salwar kameez. A stranger. He looked at her with large solemn eyes. A car was parked across the road. Beside it, Layla was hunched over, her hood already removed. Her headscarf was neat on her head as if someone had taken care to arrange it for her. A man

296

was kneeling at her side, untying the cord at her wrists. She looked pale and sick.

The young man smiled at her. He had dark teeth and a single gold crown that gleamed in the low light. 'It's OK.' His accent was heavy. 'Now it's OK.'

'We can't leave.' Ellen reached for his arm. He didn't seem to understand. 'They've got Frank. The driver.'

She looked around. The man with Layla had freed the cord and was winding it into a coil on his fingers. His eyes were sad.

Ellen struggled to her feet. 'He should stay here, with Layla,' she said. 'We'll go back.'

The young man shook his head. He twisted away from her, embarrassed. 'We are going to Peshawar,' he said.

'But the others . . .' Ellen heard anger in her voice, a sudden surge of rage. No one was listening. She turned away from them all and started off up the road. The car went that way, she'd heard it. She stopped after a few steps, her strength and certainty draining away. She ran her hand over her face. Maybe they'd come from the other direction after all.

The young man was suddenly there beside her, his forehead creased with worry. 'We must go,' he said. 'Please.'

He thinks I'm crazy. He doesn't understand. Layla was on her feet, being helped into the car. Ellen hesitated, standing there in the road surrounded by open fields. The land rose gently as it swept into foothills. I have no idea where he is. Twenty minutes' drive from here or thirty. In the distance, the mountains made a sharp ridge against the early evening sky. He could be anywhere.

She turned back to the young man. 'What is the name

of this place?' She pointed to the ground. 'We must write it down.'

'Please.' He lifted his hand and gestured to the car. Layla was already inside.

They drove quickly. Ellen's eyes were heavy but wouldn't close. She stared at the close-cropped heads of the young men in the front seats, wondering exactly who they were and how all this had been arranged. She was too exhausted to ask. Layla sat beside her in the back, slumped in her seat, her head nodding. It was only a day ago that they'd driven out from the camp together, with Ibrahim squashed in the back alongside them and Frank tall in the front beside the driver. Since then, so much had changed. Ellen reached out to steady Layla as the car swayed. Outside the windows, the countryside thickened as fields gave way to large houses, set back from the road in walled plots, then, finally, to the busy outskirts of Peshawar.

Layla woke up as they bounced along the final track over the mudflats to the camp. She sat, bleary-eyed, staring out into the gathering dusk, a small hunched figure. When they stopped at the camp gates, she looked suddenly frightened.

'Come on.' Ellen reached over and patted her shoulder. 'I'll come with you.'

'No.' Layla's voice was defiant. She turned her face away.

Ellen hesitated, watching her. 'You're safe here, Layla. It's OK.'

One of the young men got out of the front and opened the back door. Layla drew her chador close and climbed heavily out of the car. She didn't look back, just limped wordlessly past the guards into the camp and disappeared down the shadowy path that led between the tents and shelters.

The main entrance of The Swan was lit as they swung down the drive towards it. The doorman was on the steps. Beside him a tall, slight woman was pacing up and down, peering into the dusk. Her head was covered, but strands of blonde hair spilt out from its folds. As the car drew to a halt, Britta ran forwards and tugged open the back door. Her face loomed large and pale as she reached inside to Ellen.

'Thank God.' She looked close to tears. 'You're OK? Thank God.'

She helped Ellen out of the car and up the steps with exaggerated care, one arm around her back, as if she were an elderly woman. In the brightness of the foyer, she tipped back Ellen's head and examined the gash on her forehead.

'Any other injuries? Any pain?'

Ellen shook her head.

'I'll dress it,' she said, still looking at the gash. 'We must prevent infection.'

The man on reception looked up and nodded to Ellen as they passed. The marble ball was turning under its curtain of running water to the sound of the lobby's tinkling piano music. It's all, Ellen thought, as if Mohammed Bul Gourn didn't exist. She felt herself shake.

'Up to your room,' Britta said. 'Hot tea, washing and a good rest.'

Ellen pulled at her arm. She wanted to weep with frustration. No one seemed to understand. 'But, Britta,' she said, 'they've still got Frank.'

23

The previous afternoon, Jamila had sat with her hands folded in her lap on the plank of wood that passed for a seat. She was worried. Ibrahim and Layla should be back by now. It was dangerous out there once darkness fell. The fighters were everywhere.

The young Aunties were gathered in a corner of the yard, gossiping and twittering. Older children chased in circles. Small ones rolled in the dirt. Hamid and the Uncles stood close to the tents, looking out at the camp and the slow comings and goings of their neighbours. The soft furls of their cigarette smoke rose over their heads and dispersed in the creamy light.

Jamila shook her head, fretting about Ibrahim. Her guts ached. The water here was rancid. It twisted her insides. She needed to go home to the village, to the sweet water of their well and food from their own land. This hot, dirty life was poisoning them. She looked out at the last red streaks of sun on the mountains, which were fingering the ridges and throwing into relief the blackness of the gullies and clefts. She wondered what was left of their house, of her own room with its cot and furniture and whether she would ever see it again.

Shouting interrupted her thoughts. She sat up. It was coming from the direction of the camp entrance. Hamid raised his head, his expression strained. A riot, she thought, and more destruction. May Allah protect us. She waited as the noise came steadily nearer. Neighbouring women poked their heads out of shelters to look and men emerged to stand in groups in the dusk.

A group of men came into sight, fringed by running boys. They carried something heavy and awkward in their arms, and were heading towards them. Hamid ran out and pushed through to the centre of the group. His cry was wrenching: 'My brother.' He launched himself at the body in their arms and the men lowered it to the ground.

'Get help,' said one of the Uncles.

Another shouted, 'Who did this?'

Jamila started to shake. Somehow she got to her feet and staggered out of the compound to the crowd. The men drew apart and let her through. Ibrahim, my husband. She fell onto her knees beside Hamid, grabbing at his arm to steady herself. His eyes were anguished as he shifted and gave her space.

My Ibrahim. His face was distorted. His eyes were puffed balls of flesh, their lids pressed closed. His lips were swollen. Trails of dried blood ran from his nostrils, forming crusts across his upper lip and cheek. The contours of his cheeks and nose were pulled out of shape by lumps of bruised bone. My husband . . . how could God allow this?

Beside her, Hamid was bent double and wailing. He rocked back and forth in convulsions, his arms clutching his stomach.

She gathered Ibrahim's head and shoulders into her arms and pressed him to her chest. She buried her face in the slack, cold skin of his neck and kissed it, inhaled it. You were my husband first. Why have you gone, left me all alone? She started to keen, clasping him tightly to her, as the Aunties gathered in a circle around them and raised their voices in weeping and mourning.

The following afternoon, Jamila sat lifelessly in the yard and stared across the bustle of the camp towards the mountains. Her mind was numb. She had slept little in the night, her face buried in her chador, shaking and crying. Ibrahim was gone.

Already, that morning, the imam had led the procession to the grave. Hamid and the Uncles had lowered Ibrahim into the unfriendly earth, far from the village and the mountains. Jamila remembered the funeral as a blur of shapes and movements. The faces, the weeping, the prayers, the falling soil. It was all unreal.

Now she sat in silence. The Aunties brought her food but she couldn't eat. Soon she must start her life, this new life without him, as a childless widow. Even if the family returned to the village, the best she could hope was that Hamid found a corner in his house for her. Ibrahim's home, their home, would be handed to one of the younger Aunties with children.

And Layla was gone too. Ibrahim's body had been found alone. Layla had been abducted or killed. All day, no one had dared to speak of her. Jamila blinked hard and spangles of light jumped and swam in front of her face. She always pushed me away, she thought. I tried to teach Layla when she was a child, to share the traditions her mother didn't seem to respect. I showed her how to cook, how to knead dough and shape rotis, the way my mother taught me. She never cared. Jamila closed her eyes. Now the only one left is Marva, the crippled girl, who will never marry and never bear children. Hamid will have to care for her too.

Finally it became quiet in the yard. The Aunties took their pails and went to fetch water so they could wash down the children before the sun set. Jamila drew her chador around her shoulders and sat, staring into nothingness. A rat darted across the yard, paused in its path and lifted its head, rigid with attention. It ducked its nose and ran across the ground to disappear between the rows of tents. The light grew dull. The white canvas of the tents shimmered with haze.

A girl was walking towards her, her head bowed, throwing a deep shadow on the path. Jamila stared. It was a spirit, back from the grave. Layla was coming directly towards her. Her clothes were filthy and her hands too. Her face was pale. As she approached, she pulled at her scarf, shielding herself.

'Auntie.' Her voice was weak. 'The fighters stole me. Now I am back.'

Jamila couldn't speak. She sat, frozen, watching the girl, stunned by her return. Layla stood at the entrance to the yard. She looked exhausted.

'Baba is dead. They killed my baba.'

'I know.' Jamila nodded. 'We buried him today.'

Neither of them moved. Behind Layla, the young Aunties trailed back from the well. Their voices came first, loud with laughter. They rounded the corner from the path through to the clear space in front of the yard. They walked in twos, heaving pails of water between them. The water sloshed gently at the rims, splattering the dust.

They stopped when they saw the girl and stared. The Aunties at the front set down their pail, making a spreading wet ring. They looked at Layla, then at Jamila and finally at each other. The children, skipping in circles, drunk with tiredness, sensed the tension and stopped.

The girl seemed close to collapse. She stepped into the yard.

'The family won't just take you back.' Jamila spoke softly. 'You have been away with those men. You are dishonoured.'

The girl didn't look at her and didn't reply. She set her face and walked past Jamila and into the tent where she used to sleep. The Aunties watched this and whispered to each other. They seemed uncertain what to do. The girl didn't come out of the tent again. Jamila did not move.

After some time, the Aunties picked up their pails again and took them to the back of the yard. Jamila sat quietly, listening to the splashing water and the children's voices. She thought about Layla. You are too young to understand, she thought. The men will think you are disgraced and despise you for it. What can I do to shield you from their rage? Without Ibrahim, we have no one left to protect us.

Within an hour, Hamid and the Uncles and the older male cousins gathered, their faces grave, and sat in council in the dirt. The Aunties kept away, busying themselves with settling the children and draping damp clothes around the shelters to dry. Only Jamila sat close enough to the men to listen.

Hamid, the head of the family, invited the men to speak.

'We must disown her,' one Uncle was saying. He had daughters of his own whose reputations must be protected. No one would marry the cousin of a girl who had disgraced her family. 'Ibrahim's death is tragic. But she was away from us for a whole night. These men have shamed her.'

A young cousin agreed. 'She is not my blood now,' he said. 'She is not part of my family.'

Hamid pulled at his beard. His eyes were sunken in his skull.

'Ibrahim was a good man,' another Uncle said. 'But he ruined the girl. He softened her into a ball of dough on which any man could stamp his mark. We must drive her out and protect our family name.'

The men looked to Hamid, waiting for him to give judgement.

'By rights,' the first Uncle put in, 'she should be thrown in jail for illegal sex. That's what men of honour would insist on.'

The young cousin nodded. 'It's the law. We should think about that.'

Hamid sat quietly, his head lowered. He had followed the men's arguments, turning from one face to the next as they spoke. Now he seemed to hesitate.

'She may be disgraced,' Jamila's voice pushed into their circle from outside; the men looked around in surprise, 'but maybe she can still be married. Many men want a young wife.'

Jamila bent her head in submission, knowing she might

305

be scolded. She was a woman. No one expected her to interrupt.

'What do you mean?' said Hamid.

'Do you have to cast her out to restore the family's honour? Punishment may be enough, then marriage.'

'Who'd marry her now?' The young cousin sounded enraged.

Jamila shrugged. 'There may still be a match.'

Hamid fingered his beard and considered this. He turned back to the men. 'I will beat her with my own hand,' he said. 'Praise be to God.'

News of the flogging spread through the camp. Jamila led the Aunties in washing and dressing Layla inside the tent. Her body was filthy and pale and she didn't resist them. None of the women spoke.

They brought her out, Jamila holding one of Layla's arms and an Auntie taking the other. A blanket had been spread on the mud and they forced her to kneel on it, then to lie on her stomach. They lowered themselves to the ground beside her, each holding one of her wrists. Layla's body stretched on the ground in a cross, her arms wide.

Jamila rested her hand for a moment on the girl's head. 'Close your eyes,' she whispered. 'It's better.' She sat back, one hand pinning Layla's wrist and the other clasping the thin fingers of her hand.

The crowd pressed forwards, craning to see over the fence. Excited young men pushed and shoved each other. Children clawed at the plastic, trying to make spyholes. At the back, women of all ages stood with fathers and brothers.

Layla trembled. Jamila stroked her hot face and leant in to whisper. 'Don't be afraid. Hamid is a decent man.'

Layla didn't respond.

Hamid stepped forwards. A murmuring passed through the crowd. Everyone knew what had happened, that the girl had been disgraced, away from her family amongst strange men. Hamid shifted the split cane from hand to hand, testing its weight. The tip of his tongue flicked across his lips. Then he bent low over Layla, threw back his arm and brought it down hard across her back.

The thwack resounded. A woman at the front gasped. Jamila felt the shock pass through Layla's body and grasped her hand more tightly. Hamid's face was intent. He drew back his arm, gathered his strength and struck her a second time. Layla let out a cry. Her back was taut and her legs drummed the ground. Jamila bit her lip.

The blows came more steadily as Hamid found a rhythm. After the fourth or fifth, Layla seemed to slacken. She was whimpering but quietly and without hope. Her hand was limp. In the crowd, no one spoke.

On the girl's back, the cloth of the kameez danced. The fabric lifted with the downward breeze of his arm, then reeled as the cane whistled.

Hamid gave ten strokes. Jamila counted them off. Afterwards, he set the cane on the ground and walked out of the compound without a word. The crowd parted to let him pass.

Layla lay motionless on the blanket. The kameez was shredded on her back, the threads of light cloth blotting the blood. Jamila squeezed her hand. She reached out and touched her head.

'It's over,' she whispered. 'Finished.'

Layla didn't answer. Jamila lifted her head and gestured to the young cousins who were standing watching. She directed them to lift the four corners of the blanket and carry Layla, sagging between them, into the tent.

The young men lining the fence turned and wandered away. The crowd began to thin. Only the most ardent hung around the compound for some time, pointing to the spot where the blanket had been, gossiping about the beating and the young girl's shame.

In the tent, Layla lay on her stomach, moaning. The skin on her back was a latticework of cuts and bruising. Jamila crooned to her in a low voice, lifting strands of damp hair away from her face. Maybe, she thought, now honour was restored, Layla could marry one of the cousins and live nearby in the village. Maybe, after all, she could still be taught. I could help with the children, she thought. She might have a girl like Syma. She wet a cloth and stroked it over Layla's skin, cooling it. The girl wouldn't speak to her. Her pride was broken. But, in time, it would heal.

Later, as night closed in, Hamid called for Jamila to come out to him. He was pacing up and down the mud yard.

'A man has approached me,' he said. 'About taking Layla in marriage.'

Jamila looked up. 'What man?'

Hamid spoke in a low voice. 'He is the second brother in a family in the valley. They don't own land. They are weavers. They need girls.' He paddled his fingers on an invisible loom in the air.

Jamila nodded. Layla was young and strong and this

man knew he could have her cheaply because of her disgrace. 'What kind of man is he?'

'Not educated,' said Hamid. 'He's of my age. She would be a second wife. The first has three children.'

Jamila sighed. Layla needed a husband to protect her, it was true. Maybe this man would be kind. But the valley was a long way from Mutaire, a long way from home.

'Your brother is watching in Paradise,' she said. 'He will bless you if you care for the girl. If you find her a good marriage.'

He looked down at his hands. 'If my son had not been taken by the police—'

Jamila nodded. If Adnan had not been imprisoned, Ibrahim and the girl would never have left to see him. She too had thought that.

'It is the will of Allah,' she said simply. 'It is not for us to question and not for us to understand.'

He left her alone in the yard. The camp was settling for the night. The air was peppered with grunting and snoring. An aircraft flew fast and low overhead and she tipped her head to watch it. The boom of the engines followed afterwards, echoing across the plain. She stared until it disappeared. It was heading for the mountains, for Mutaire, perhaps.

Ibrahim, I did my best to protect Layla, did you see? She laced her hands around her knees. I pray to God this weaving husband is a good man, as kind and gentle as you.

When she closed her eyes, she could imagine him there beside her, his warm, pale eyes glinting behind his glasses, his long fingers holding a book. She opened her eyes but there was only dirt, ridged and baked hard after two days without rain, and, beyond the camp, the black silhouette of the mountains against the night sky. She shook herself and crept inside the tent to sleep.

She woke in the night. It was dark. Something had disturbed her. She turned onto her back and lay quietly, listening to the breathing. She raised herself on her elbows and strained to see. All across the tent, women were sleeping. They were lying against each other, children tucked at their sides. She looked more closely. Layla was gone.

Jamila wrapped her chador around her and picked her way between the bodies to the entrance. Outside, the night was clear. She narrowed her eyes and scanned the pathways near their compound. No sign of Layla.

She lowered herself heavily onto the broken plank and placed the flat of her hands on her belly to soothe it. I tried, she thought. May Allah bear me witness. Layla could have had security and a marriage blessed by her Uncles and, *inshallah*, children of her own. Instead she too will be alone.

She felt weighed down by a great sadness. Everything I learnt, she thought, from my mother and grandmother, I wanted to share with a daughter. The wisdom about our history, our people and our ways. She sighed, gently rocking herself. Now it is finished.

She stayed there in the stillness of the yard for the rest of the night, watching as the grey light of dawn crept slowly into the camp and the first women stirred and emerged from their tents, carried their pails to the pump to fetch water, then sank to their knees to blow dying fires back to life to heat the water for chai and for their men to wash.

24

Ellen stepped into her hotel bedroom. One corner of her neatly made bed had been turned down and decorated with a breakfast order form. Her litter of books and papers had been tidied into a pile on the table. The fruit bowl had been restocked. Her travel bag was open on the floor, just as she'd left it, spilling clothes.

Her laundry had been returned. Two salwar kameezes, perfectly pressed and encased in plastic, were laid out on the second bed. Even as I sat in that cell, she thought, trying to fight back the fear of being tortured or beheaded, all this, in this parallel universe, was here.

She turned to Britta who was hesitating behind her. 'What about Frank?' She thought of that filthy room. 'What can we do?'

Britta closed the door. 'They're working on it.' She held out a mobile phone. 'Call home first. Tell them you're safe.'

Ellen took the phone and stared at the numbers. 'What do you mean, they're working on it?'

'The Americans.' Britta was standing awkwardly, her hands clasped. 'The embassy's involved.'

'I should call them.'

Britta brushed past her to the bathroom. Ellen heard the deep cascade of water from the taps. 'Have a bath.' Britta reappeared, drying her hands on a towel. 'And we'll eat something. You can call later.'

Ellen shook her head. 'If someone's trying to get Frank out, I should call them now.'

Britta tutted. She rummaged in her bag and handed Ellen a business card. It was from the American Embassy in Islamabad, the name neatly embossed in raised lettering.

'I'm going to my room to order food for us both.' Britta picked up her bag again. 'You know what you want?'

'Anything.'

The door slapped shut as Britta left. Ellen went into the steaming bathroom and switched off the taps, then crossed the bedroom to stand at the window and dial the mobile phone number on the business card.

A man answered, speaking in a soft American accent. His voice reminded her of Frank. 'Anything you can tell us, ma'am.' His tone was smooth but she felt his attention. 'Any detail at all about the place, the drive . . .'

She looked out at the early evening light and ran through what she could remember about the car journeys and the compound where they were held. When she finished, there was a long silence on the line.

'Ma'am, is there anything you need?'

I need Frank, she thought. Sitting right here, next to me, measuring out shots from his illicit bottle of whisky. 'No, thank you. I'm just tired.'

She looked out at the dusk, at the silhouetted landscape of tree tops and buildings and streets that was now so familiar. Ibrahim was dead. By now, Frank and the driver might be too. She wanted to talk about it but she didn't have the words.

Finally she said, 'I met him. Mohammed Bul Gourn.'

He sounded instantly alert. 'Tell me about that.'

'He blames Frank. For the typhoid deaths. He says he's corrupt.'

The American didn't comment. 'What else did he say?'

'He asked me about Quentin Khan. The businessman. You know who I mean?'

'Yes, ma'am.'

'He told me to give him a message: Keep away.'

Around her, pipes were knocking with flowing water as the rest of the hotel settled down for the evening. She put her hand to her head. She ached all over.

'We are aware of threats against him.' The American official was selecting his words deliberately. He wasn't giving anything away.

'It's just, well, I wanted him to know—'

'We'll be sure and pass this on to his people.' His tone was businesslike, moving her on. 'You've been very helpful. Can't tell you how much we appreciate it.'

She felt herself dismissed. She closed her eyes and the room swam. She thought of Frank and the driver and the horrors the night might bring for them. The silence stretched. 'Do you know where he is?'

'Ma'am, I am sorry but I am afraid I cannot discuss that.'

'Does that mean you do or you don't?' No answer. 'Are you going in, to rescue him?'

He paused. 'Ma'am, I am sorry but I am not—'

Her frustration boiled over. 'Look, I'm not asking you as a journalist. I'm family. You understand?'

He sighed slightly. 'Ma'am, we are monitoring the situation carefully,' he said. A long pause. 'We have intelligence . . .' He hesitated.

'That what?'

Pause. 'There may be a significant development in the next thirty-six hours. That's all I can say.'

She closed her eyes. 'Do you know if he's still alive?'

He took a moment to answer. 'Ma'am, if we have news we will contact you immediately. I assure you, we are doing everything we can.'

In the bathroom, she ran the water as hot as she could bear and lowered herself into the bath, turning her legs red. Steam clouded the mirror and made the tiles slick with running condensation. Frank was still there, still with them. She thought of his battered face and of the dark cell. A development in the next thirty-six hours. That could mean a rescue mission. Or that Bul Gourn would kill him by then. She tipped her face back, screwed her eyes closed and tried to think what else she could do.

Once out of the bath, she wrapped herself in a dressing gown. There was a knock at the door. Britta, a tube of antiseptic cream and a dressing in her hand. 'Now,' she said, gesturing to Ellen's forehead, 'let's dress that cut.'

When she'd finished, Ellen called Phil in London. He

314

answered at once. His first words when he heard her voice were: 'Where the hell are you? You OK?'

'I'm safe. I'm back at the hotel.'

He exhaled noisily. There were voices around him. 'It's Ellen,' he said to someone. 'She's out.'

He came back on the line. 'You need anything?'

She smiled. It was rare to hear Phil sound anything but cynical. 'That's fine. I'm OK.'

There was a pause. 'About putting up money.' He sounded embarrassed, another first. 'I pushed. Of course. But you know what they're like. Editorial policy. Once you start, every reporter we've got is a walking cash register.'

'Sure.'

Phil cleared his throat. 'Anyway, I'm just glad you're OK. That's what matters.'

The murmurs around him were amplified by the receiver, echoing down the phone.

'I know it's a stretch but I wondered . . .' He seemed to be shifting his position, almost whispering into the phone. 'A few thousand words? The website would love it. They'd post it straight away. Tomorrow maybe. Whatever you can.'

She nodded. That was more like him. She looked again at the crisp, turned-down bed and wondered how long it would be before she could sleep. 'Sure. Not a problem.' She didn't dare catch Britta's eye. 'Tell them I'll file tomorrow morning.'

'You know that bloke from *The News*?'

'John Sandik?'

'He's been trying to force an obit on me. Yours. Wouldn't take no.'

315

'My obit?' So the secret hadn't been well kept. 'That's ridiculous.'

'Well, obviously. That's what I said. I already got one done in-house.'

She rolled her eyes. 'Anyway. Better go.'

'Yeah. And, Ellen, next time I say "get the story", I don't mean *become* it, right?' He sounded pleased with himself.

'Right.'

Britta was standing at the window, picking at the edges of the tape cross with her fingernails.

'Did you hear that?'

Britta half-turned, looking back over her shoulder. 'I was trying not to hear.'

'You know John from *The News*, the guy who came down with Khan? He's been trying to hawk an obit. My obit. To my own boss.' She shook her head. 'What a vulture.'

Britta tutted, and shook her head. Her nails clicked lightly on the window as she went back to scratching at the edge of the tape.

Ellen dialled her sister's mobile, still indignant. 'He'd get it all wrong.'

Britta shrugged. 'Well, if you want to put him right on anything, you might get the chance. He and Khan are coming back in a couple of days.'

She stared. 'Here?'

'To the camp. They heard in Islamabad about the riot. They want to see the damage.'

Ellen sat down heavily on the bed. 'But he mustn't.' She thought of Mohammed Bul Gourn's threat.

'Why not?'

316

Susan answered her phone in a storm of noise and wailing children. 'Ellie?'

'Hi. I'm fine. I just wanted to—'

'Put that down. I'm trying to talk to Auntie Ellie. No, you may not.'

She waited, listening to the chaos of her sister's life. The girls must be having a bad day. Susan finally came back on the line.

'I'm so sorry, Ellie. How are you?'

'Fine. Really. I'm sorry. Didn't mean to worry you.'

'Worry me? Ellie, are you OK?' There was a distant crash. Her sister's attention faltered.

Ellen felt suddenly exhausted. Clearly Susan hadn't even been told.

'Ellie? You there?'

'Sorry. I just wanted to say hi. But I've got to go.'

'Everything OK?' Her sister, confused, sounded suddenly anxious.

'Yes, promise. I'll call when I'm back in the UK. Love to the girls.'

'Keep safe.'

Ellen pictured her walking around the house after the children, her phone in one hand, the other one averting disasters. 'Love you.'

Britta was standing with her shoulder to the window, one hand on the peeling tape. She was watching Ellen and pretending not to. There was a long silence. Ellen reached forwards and put the phone on the table.

'I didn't know who to call.' Britta's voice was quiet. 'I thought your magazine would—'

Ellen tried to shrug it off. 'It's fine.' She wondered how

317

much Frank's parents knew. Britta turned on the television and it flickered into a studio discussion on CNN. She muted the sound.

A room service waiter arrived with a laden tray. Britta swept the laptop and papers off the table and heaped them on the floor. She and the waiter unloaded the plates of food, the white porcelain pots of tomato sauce and mustard, covered with cling film, and a small vase with a single red carnation. Ellen sat quietly in the soft robe and watched, trying to push away thoughts of Frank.

The waiter didn't raise his eyes to her. Before he left, he lifted the metal covers off the food with a flourish. A pizza, smothered with tinned mushrooms, tomato purée and imported cheese. An oversized club sandwich with fries. Ellen stared at it all without appetite.

Britta made a show of being cheerful as she tucked into the pizza. Ellen picked at the fries. She sensed weariness in Britta, papered over with good humour.

'Are you managing without Fatima?'

Britta took a moment to clear her mouth, pulling an apologetic face. 'Just about. I have my assistant. But I have to find someone else.'

'And the typhoid?'

Britta didn't meet her eyes. 'Pretty bad.' She took another bite of pizza, spilling rubbery mushrooms. 'Something very odd is happening. I don't know.'

Ellen didn't know either. Next door a door banged and suitcase wheels trundled in the corridor with a murmur of low voices.

'You should see the size of the graveyard.' Britta looked worried. 'No one comes to the clinic now unless they've already lost hope. They're too afraid. And now Khan is coming back, Mr Money.'

Ellen peeled back the cling film and spooned tomato ketchup onto her plate. She picked up two fries and dipped them. 'Layla was ill. When we were with the fighters.'

Britta looked up. 'Typhoid?'

'I think so. Fever. Diarrhoea. I gave her antibiotics and the fever went almost at once. She needs more.' She shook her head. 'They've got my medical kit. Bag, phone, everything.'

'I've got more.' Britta wiped her greasy fingers on a napkin and leant down to rummage in her bag. She produced a packet of tablets and set it on the table between them. 'Anyway, I'll go and see her first thing tomorrow.'

'Thank you.' Ellen half-heartedly picked up a quarter of the club sandwich with both hands. It bulged with mayonnaise and tomato as she tried to bite into it. Strands of chicken fell and littered her plate. She looked at the packet beside her plate as she chewed.

'Everything's made in China.'

Britta nodded. 'Absolutely. You should take a walk through the new supply store. It's like Hong Kong.'

Ellen pulled out a piece of bacon and ate it. 'What supply store?'

'In the admin block. Now Fatima and Doc are gone, they keep everything locked up there.' She patted her pocket and her keys jangled. 'Not so convenient. I have to go myself every time we need more things.'

'Since when?'

'Since the riot.'

Ellen shook her head. She thought about the riot and

the way they'd cowered together in the women's medical tent as the mob came slowly nearer. Britta had seemed so unafraid, so detached from the danger.

'Britta, in the riot, what made you think they wouldn't attack us?'

Britta shrugged, trying to separate herself from trailing strings of melted cheese. 'I just thought it would be OK.' She looked around the room. 'You have two beds. Did you ask for that? I have a double.'

Ellen bit into her sandwich. She was still thinking. Something was bothering her. 'Why though? They smashed up everything else.'

Britta didn't answer. She focused on her food. 'They have suites,' she said. 'For five hundred dollars a night.'

There was noise out in the corridor. Male voices and laughter. A door slammed. CNN flashed with swirling pictures as its news bulletin started. A hurricane had hit somewhere in the Caribbean. New pictures just in. Dramatic images of bending trees and whipped-up waves.

Ellen watched idly. Her mind was elsewhere. She was thinking back to the black stain of the first rocks hitting the canvas wall of the medical tent as they hid inside, to the young male voice that had risen above the others and called the men away. It triggered a sudden memory.

'The young guy who called them off.'

Britta, busy eating, didn't respond.

'It was Saeed, wasn't it?' Ellen put down her sandwich. 'It was him.'

Britta didn't look up. Ellen watched her closely. She thought about the arm wound Saeed had shown Layla and how neatly it was stitched.

320

She remembered her glimpse of Britta walking out across the dark grass by the swimming pool late at night. 'You've been treating him.'

Britta didn't say anything. She picked up another piece of pizza and bit into it. She was suddenly eating more mechanically, her eyes fixed on her plate. Ellen sat back in her chair. Her sandwich lay forgotten, spilling out across her plate. The grease hardened as it cooled. She'd been groping towards an answer and suddenly she had it. 'You're treating his bullet wound, aren't you?' She touched the flesh of her upper arm. 'You knew he'd be part of that riot. You knew he'd look out for you.'

Britta's face was flushed. She chewed and swallowed hurriedly, finishing what she could. 'I'm a doctor,' she said finally. 'I practise medicine.'

'On anyone?'

'Anyone who needs it.'

Ellen stared. Britta sat back and wiped her lips with her napkin.

'Do you go to them?'

Britta looked annoyed. 'Of course not.'

'What then?'

Britta was already twisting down to her bag and zipping it up, getting ready to leave. She leant across the table. For the first time since they'd started to eat, she looked Ellen full in the face. Her cross swung low at her neck.

'If someone comes to me and they need help, I treat them.' Her look was fierce, daring Ellen to disagree.

'Even if they're Taliban?'

Britta clicked her tongue. 'Am I God, to decide who

should live and who shouldn't?' She pushed back her chair and got to her feet. 'Do you read the Bible?'

Ellen shook her head.

'As the body without the spirit is dead, faith without works is dead also.' She turned towards the door. 'You should sleep. I'll see you tomorrow.' She strode across the room, bag in hand. As she opened the door, she paused and turned back. 'And I'm very happy you're safe.'

The door shut heavily behind her. Ellen sat alone in the silence, too exhausted to move, the remains of the meal congealing on the plates in front of her, the pictures on the television set flickering without meaning.

The ringing was shrill. Ellen fought her way up from the bottom of an ocean of sleep. The noise split her apart. Her lungs ached. She struggled for a moment to remember where she was. In the hotel. She was safe. Then she remembered more. Frank. It might be news of Frank. She groped for the hotel phone and picked up the receiver.

'Hello?'

'Madam, you have a visitor.'

'A what?' She tried to open her eyes and squinted at the luminous numbers on the bedside clock. Two thirteen.

'A girl. She is saying her name is Layla.'

Layla? 'Can you send her up?'

'I will escort her.' The man's voice was cold.

Ellen sat up in bed and groped for her dressing gown. Her head was thick with tiredness. She switched the light on and concentrated on waking up. After a few minutes, the doorbell sounded.

322

The man from reception was stern-faced, his uniform neatly pressed. Layla, beside him, looked like a street child. Her clothes were dishevelled, her face pinched.

'Layla? What is it? What happened?'

Ellen stood to one side to let her come in. As Layla passed, she saw the girl's back. The fabric of her kameez was shredded and stiff with blood. The skin beneath it shone raw. Layla took a few steps into the room, faltered, then brought her hands to her face as she burst into tears.

25

There was ice and fire inside my head and sometimes I went cold and shivered and sometimes I burnt. If I moved even a little, there was so much of pain in my back that I wanted to cry out. I lay on my stomach on the bed in the Britisher's room and the blankets were soft and warm and the bed was so gentle beneath me that I felt I was floating in the air, held up by giant hands.

The room was solid with darkness. It carried a smell of rich food and the hum of machines with, every now and again, a deep click. Sometimes I heard men's footsteps come nearer and I hid my face but the feet always went past the door and faded away to nothing.

The journalist was asleep in the other bed. Her breathing was feathery. It made me think of our room at home in the compound and how, when I sometimes woke in the night, I listened to Marva's and Mama's steady breathing until I fell asleep again. Now that was all truly in the past and never to come again and I felt so alone without them that I could scarcely bear it.

When I closed my eyes, I saw the faces of the men who'd stared and jeered and felt again the force of the blows as Hamid Uncle, the brother of my own baba whose duty was to protect me, beat me in front of them all. My body was damaged and my pride also. After all I'd suffered, losing my mama and dear baba and being made prisoner by those men, Hamid Uncle had disgraced and humiliated me in public. It was a great injustice. If my baba had been alive, Hamid Uncle would never have done such wickedness.

I shook all over, even to think about it. I would not go back and submit to them and accept their justice. I would sooner never see my family again, Uncles and Aunties and cousins and all, if that was what Allah demanded. But Marva, my sister – I thought of her with anguish. She was everything I had in the world. How would I care for her now? I cried in silence so as not to wake the Britisher who slept so close.

When I woke up, it was daylight. Someone was moving about the room. I heard a thud as a door closed and then falling water. My mouth was dry and when I tried to move, my whole body ached as if my sore skin were breaking open afresh and sticking to the big borrowed kameez on my back. I whimpered and lay still.

The Britisher came back into the bedroom. She must have seen that my eyes were open because she bent down to look at me. The bandage on her forehead was crooked and there was a strand of damp hair on her cheek.

'Chai?' she said.

I bit the insides of my cheeks and shook my head.

'That's the bathroom.' She pointed. 'When you want to use the toilet or wash, just go ahead. You don't have to ask.'

She moved about between the furniture. I could hear her picking things up and putting them down again. Finally she came back to me and said, 'I might go down for breakfast. Do you want to eat anything?'

I shook my head.

'Will you be all right if I leave you for half an hour?'

I nodded. The main door closed behind her with a sigh. I was alone. I sobbed loudly until the pillow was wet and my head ached.

The room with the necessary had a hundred shiny surfaces which made pictures of me everywhere I looked. The borrowed salwar kameez was baggy and fell about me in loose folds. I turned to one side and then to the other. I had never seen all my body at one time, top to toe, and I seemed a very small person in all this splendour.

The taps gave a stream of cold water without any pumping but although I looked in the cupboards, there was no pail to fill so I cupped my hands and splashed the water about under my clothes until I was clean. Then I turned and lifted the flap of the kameez and looked at my poor back. When I cried, all the other Laylas screwed their eyes and cried too until their faces were swollen and blotchy.

When the Britisher came back, she brought the woman doctor from Marva's ward and I wondered how she had come from the camp with such speed and why she would see me, just one girl, when the ward was filled with sick patients. She made me swallow pills and she put cool cream on my back.

A man came to the door and gave the Britisher a tray of food which she carried into the room and set on the table. She poured a cup of strange chai for me with cold milk. It wasn't mixed and boiled, as is needsome for chai, and smelt most peculiar. I didn't say. I just didn't drink it.

The Britisher and the doctor talked together in low voices. I couldn't understand them but sometimes the Britisher broke off and came to ask me a question. She spoke in a low, careful voice, the kind a man might use to soothe a rabid dog.

'Can you tell us, please, Layla, who did this to you?' She meant my sore back.

I said, 'Hamid Uncle,' which is the truth.

'Why did he punish you?'

I said, 'For being with strange men away from home and without my baba.'

Later she asked me, 'Do you want to go back to your family, Layla?'

I said, 'No. They might beat me again.'

She looked troubled. 'What do you want to do?'

I said, 'I don't know,' and closed my eyes and wouldn't answer any more questions.

Finally the doctor left. The Britisher set the tray of food beside the bed so I could reach it. There was fruit, melon and banana and peach, cut open and peeled and in small mixed-up pieces, and round balls of bread. I didn't have the appetite to eat.

The Britisher said, 'You're safe here, Layla.' She looked sad. Then she sat down at the small table and started to work. She did this for a long time, sometimes frowning to herself and rubbing her temples.

The doctor's cream made my back sting but it hurt a little less to move. I lay on my stomach and wondered about many things: how many days it would take before I stopped being in pain and what I would do from now on for food and shelter and why the Britisher lived in such a large house but only used one room.

I wondered if Marva was thinking about me and if she knew about my disgrace and I burnt to tell her why the judgement was not fair so she wouldn't think ill of me. I thought about my baba and wondered if he'd seen bright, modern rooms like this in his travels. I ached to talk with him about it and knew that, for the rest of my life, whatever I did, I could never talk with him again.

Now that I had told the foreigners I would not go back to my family, I felt myself very much alone, as if a thick rope had been cut and I was floating downstream on a strong current with no idea where I was heading. I bit my lips not to cry.

Later the Britisher came over to speak to me. 'Do you like *kulfi*?'

I looked at her and didn't speak. I was twisting inside with worry about all the money I was already owing for the soft bed and the medicine and the cut-up fruit and the balls of bread and the bad chai and now this talk of *kulfi* also which is generally not cheap.

She said, '*Kulfi* – do you know what it is?' Of course

I knew. Every child of five knows *kulfi*. When I still didn't reply, she said, 'Well, I'll order some and we'll see.'

I lifted my hand to stop her. 'Please.' My voice sounded weak. 'I am not having money.'

She paused for a moment and I thought she was angry but then I saw she was just surprised. She said, 'But I owe you money, Layla. I haven't paid you for the translating you did for me.'

I breathed very deeply. That was true. I had done translating. I wanted to ask how much money I would have and how much food it would buy. Then I had a good idea. 'Maybe you are needing more translating?'

She looked concerned and sat on the bed beside me. 'Layla, I have to leave Pakistan soon to go back to England. I can't take you with me. You know that, don't you?'

I didn't know but I said yes. I wondered how soon she would leave, if it would be today or tomorrow, and where I would find a place to live afterwards. I looked down at the carpet. It was brown with white flecks and very thick.

'I know you need help,' she said. 'I'm going to do what I can. You mustn't worry.' She reached out and patted my shoulder. Her eyes looked sore. The bandage had been removed from her forehead and the cut underneath was red and yellow and also white with cream. She looked past me to the wall at nothingness.

Finally she said, 'It's not easy for a young girl to work here. I understand that.'

I swallowed. All my life I wanted to be a boy and to work hard and make my baba proud. Now maybe I would work but my baba was not here to see and still I was only a girl. I looked again at her face and saw the weariness in it but also the kindness and gave thanks to Allah for sending her to help me.

I remembered what she said to me when we were prisoners together and she asked me whether I might travel and I repeated her words now. 'It's more difficult,' I said. 'But not impossible.'

She laughed. Then she picked up the telephone and I heard her ask for two dishes of *kulfi*. Afterwards she looked at me hard until I became embarrassed and looked away. She said, 'Tomorrow, if you're feeling a bit better, I could take you to see your sister.'

Marva! I opened my eyes wide. I thought of everything I would tell her: about the beating but also about the Britisher and how I would work now and care for us both. I said, 'May I keep my *kulfi* and take it to Marva?'

She looked confused. 'Well, *kulfi* might be a bit difficult. It might melt. But we'll definitely take her something special. What else would she like? Chocolate? Crisps? Sweets?'

'Do I have enough money?'

She nodded. 'I should think so.'

I saw from her eyes that this meant yes, I could take all these treats to Marva, and for the first time in a long time, I smiled.

26

Ellen couldn't sleep. She was frantic, thinking about Frank and wondering if he were still alive. She closed her eyes and saw him there, his face kind and teasing. She twisted around in bed and pushed her face into the pillow. There must be something she could do. All day, her nerves had been jangling. She'd jumped every time the phone rang, hoping it was the Americans with news. It never was. A development in thirty-six hours, the embassy official said. That was twenty-four hours ago. The night was worse than the day, the silence broken only by Layla's steady breathing.

She lifted her head. The girl was sleeping heavily, lying on her front with her face twisted to one side. Ellen thought of her lacerated back and sighed. No wonder she didn't want to go back to her family. Ellen turned over and looked out across the room. The darkness was broken only by a thin line of half-light where the curtains met.

Finally she gave up on sleep and started to grope her

way along the bed, heading towards the bathroom. As she rounded the corner, she caught the edge of the table. A stack of things, protruding there, went flying. The bang as they crashed to the carpet was loud in the silence. She froze and listened. Layla's breathing stayed even.

Ellen got down on her hands and knees and started feeling around for the fallen objects. Papers. A book. Two ballpoint pens. She put them back on the table, then ran splayed fingers further across the carpet and under the bed, retrieving other stray items. Another pen. Britta's tube of antiseptic cream. She stretched a little further through the carpet fibres. A pair of scissors shone faint silver by the side of the bed. Beyond them, her fingers touched cardboard. The packet of antibiotics they were giving Layla. She got to her feet and eased her way past the table and around the chair towards the bathroom, moving more slowly and carefully now, a small step at a time.

In the bathroom, she switched on the over-mirror light and peered, narrow-eyed, at her reflection. She put the antibiotics down on the fake marble surround and leant into the mirror to look at the cut on her forehead. It wasn't pretty but it was clean and starting to dry out. There must be something she could do. Mohammed Bul Gourn was wrong, he was simply wrong about Frank. The Americans would never persuade him of that. But someone needed to before it was too late. She picked up the antibiotics and sat down on the edge of the bath. Maybe it was already too late.

She turned the packet over in her hands, remembering those long desperate hours in the cell. On one side, Chinese characters, glossy and embossed. On the other, raised

English lettering and the swirling security hologram, barely visible in the weak bathroom light.

She stopped. Her heart was suddenly large in her chest, her breath shallow. She angled the front of the packet in the light, tipping the cardboard backwards and forwards. Panic twisted in her stomach. Her head was aching but she was suddenly sharply awake. A memory came to her. An image of the same dull packets inside the medical tent when she had rifled through them at the start of the riot. The whole layer had been almost invisible in the darkness as she pulled them aside and searched underneath for stolen goods.

Then a second memory. A memory of the gleam and shine of the hologram on her own packet as she held it in her hands in the half-light of the cell as Layla lay, hot and feverish, on the ground beside her. She sat rigid for some time in the silence, barely able to breathe, her body trembling and the packet of antibiotics sitting, dark and dull, in her hand.

She banged on the door for a long time. The corridor was deserted and flushed with a pasty yellow light. She imagined people in nearby rooms, trying to sleep and knocked from their dreams by the hammering. Maybe it was the wrong room. She stared again at the number on the door. Maybe Britta used earplugs. Maybe she'd woken up but wouldn't come to the door.

She heard a movement inside. Britta might be angry. It wasn't yet one o'clock. She must have been fast asleep. If it were the wrong room, some other guest would be furious. She took a deep breath as the chain rattled and the door finally opened. Britta stood there in a creased nightshirt that reached almost to her knees. It looked much washed. The faded remains of a smiling cartoon cat were just visible across her chest. She was staring into the corridor through bleary, sleepy eyes.

'Ellen?'

She pushed past Britta into the room. It was dark, warm and stale with breathing. The double bed was a mess of tangled sheets and rumpled duvet.

'I'll make coffee.' Ellen picked up the kettle and took it into the bathroom. The sink's fake marble surround was crowded with Danish tubes and bottles, cleansing creams, moisturizers and perfumes. Britta had dumped the contents of her pockets here too, her keys, some scraps of paper and a heap of notes and coins.

When she got back, Britta was sitting on the edge of the bed, looking dazed.

'Isn't it a little late?' Britta ran a hand through her hair. It stuck out in clumps.

'I'm sorry.' Ellen reached for a light switch and clicked it on.

Britta screwed up her face against the brightness.

'I've got to talk to you.' Ellen picked up a cardigan from the chair and tossed it into Britta's lap.

Britta twisted back to the bedside table to look at the clock. 'Now?' She sounded exhausted. 'Can't it wait?' She poked an arm into a sleeve of the cardigan and staggered into the bathroom, groggy with sleep.

Ellen made them both coffee and they sat on either side of the table. It was strewn with papers, Britta's laptop in the middle. The sign of another late night working on the accounts.

'I know why people are dying.'

Britta looked up, her eyes suddenly keen. 'What do you mean?'

'The antibiotics. They're fakes.' Ellen dropped the packet on the pile of papers between them. 'You see the hologram.' Ellen prodded it with her finger, moving it back and forth in the light. 'It's supposed to shine.'

'That could be anything.' Britta shook her head. 'You can't assume—'

'It's a real telltale. A dud hologram.'

Britta sat silently, stunned. She stared with dull eyes at the packet. 'Who'd do that?'

'Anyone. Gangs. Criminals.' Ellen was trembling. She tried to keep her voice level. She was sure she was right. It explained everything. The fact patients kept failing to respond to treatment. The high death rate in the clinic.

'Why?'

'The same reason they fake designer handbags and pirate DVDs. For money, that's why. Only bad handbags don't kill people.'

Britta winced. She turned her head away. Ellen sat quietly for a moment, watching her. Britta had suffered so much distress, worrying about her patients and working ever longer hours, unable to understand why she couldn't cure them. Of course she wouldn't believe it. She needed time.

'I'm so sorry, Britta.'

Britta's mouth was tight. She looked away and didn't answer.

Ellen rested her forearms on the table.

'It's not your fault. Fakes are big business.' She picked

335

up the packet and tilted it in the light, studying the hologram. 'They're very sophisticated. They fool everyone.'

Britta shook her head without looking her in the eye.
'I've used this brand before. It's fine.'

Ellen held out the packaging to show her. 'It's very
professional. See the logo, the text? Perfect. It's even
embossed, right?'

Britta put out her hand and ran a finger over the
lettering.

'It might be from a genuine producer. But run off at
night, on the cheap, using fake ingredients.' Ellen angled
the hologram so it just caught the light. 'Getting the hologram right is the hardest part. That's why they have them.
See? It looks all right at first glance. But move it in the
light and it's sort of lifeless. Look. No depth to the image.'

Britta drew back. 'I don't know.'

They sat in silence. Ellen put the packet on the table
between them and reached for her coffee. Britta stared at
it, her face troubled.

'If you're right,' she said at last, 'what's in them?'

Ellen shrugged. 'Could be anything. Starch. Potato.
Maybe a trace of the real drugs to fool tests.' She thought
of Syma, that fragile little girl. Of Layla's mother. She
wondered how much more to tell Britta. When she spoke
again, her voice was gentle. 'Britta, sometimes they're actually harmful. Toxic.'

Britta lifted her hand to her throat and grasped her
cross. She closed her eyes and ran it up and down on its
chain. She didn't speak for a minute. Finally she said, as
if to herself, 'How could anyone do that?'

Outside, there were thuds and a distant mechanical

whirr as the lifts moved. The noise carried through the stillness.

'Maybe it's just that packet,' Britta said.

Ellen didn't answer. She lifted her cup and sipped her coffee and tried to think calmly. She thought about the layers of tablets she rummaged through when she found the stolen supplies. She was sure they were the same fakes.

'I tried to order from my own supplier in Europe.' Britta's mouth was a hard line. She could barely get the words out. 'They made me cancel it. Told me I had to take the Chinese ones.'

'What do you mean?' Ellen looked up. 'Who told you?'

'Khan's people. They insisted. They'd be shipped here faster, they said. I didn't think—'

'Khan's people?' Ellen felt suddenly sick. The mug slipped in her fingers and a tide of coffee slopped inside it. She set it back on the table.

'We have to use their supplier for everything.' Britta shrugged. 'It's their money. Anyway, I've used this brand before. It's always reliable.'

Ellen pressed the soft pads of her fingers against the smooth sides of the mug. It was warm and comforting. Her breath was tight in her throat.

'But, Ellen, that doesn't mean . . .' Britta had turned to her. She looked upset.

'It could be Khan's supplier,' Ellen said. 'Or further down the chain. Someone in China.'

Britta picked up the packet and turned it over in her hands. Her face was contorted. 'I gave antibiotics. They just didn't respond. I never thought . . .' She shook her head. 'I don't know.'

'What do they cost?' Ellen pushed back her chair and started pacing back and forth. 'Antibiotics like these?'

'It depends on the quantity. My last order for medicines ran to tens of thousands of dollars. But it wasn't only antibiotics.'

Ellen nodded. 'Maybe it's all fake. Who knows? Maybe we've just noticed the antibiotics because they've caused deaths.'

Britta shifted in her seat and looked doubtful. 'Everything, all the stock . . .?'

'I don't know.' Ellen paced to the door and back. Her head was buzzing. She thought about Khan. He was a very astute businessman, his record showed that. He understood Pakistan well. He came a lot, always had. He knew how things worked here. She put her hand to her head, struggling to think it through.

He'd be keen to cut costs. He was a man who made sure he got value for money, whatever the deal. But surely he was also sharp enough to check out his suppliers and make sure he used a decent one. Everyone in Pakistan knew safeguards were poor. The market was flooded with all sorts of fake goods, including medicines. The place had 'buyer beware' written all over it. She started to pace back towards the table, thinking about Khan and his business sense. Britta was bent over her coffee, her face miserable.

Ellen stopped abruptly. The needles. Her heart missed a beat. She sat down heavily on the edge of the bed, her legs weak. All the fuss he'd made about the needles when he needed that tetanus injection. He'd refused to let the doctor use any from China in case they were recycled. He'd insisted on her European supply precisely because he knew there was a risk. She tried to steady her breathing. Khan knew.

She reached out and put her hand on Britta's arm. They were so close, she could speak in a whisper. 'What if Khan does know about this? If he knows full well.'

'But why?' Britta looked alarmed. 'He's giving us these drugs for free. He's not selling them.'

'He's still saving money. He wants to make a big show of giving, to further his career. This way he does it on the cheap.'

Britta frowned.

Ellen carried on, the words tumbling out. 'This way, he can still lobby for a peerage. He can show charitable works. But not spend too much doing it.'

Britta didn't answer. She drew up her legs and sat with her arms locked around her knees.

'What do you know about his company setup, about how he pays for the drugs?'

Britta lifted her head. 'A little. I know where to send the bill when I place orders.'

Ellen reached across and tapped Britta's laptop. 'Could you do some digging?'

Britta stared at her. 'Digging?'

'Please. Check through whatever you can in the accounts. You understand these things. There might be something.'

Britta switched on her laptop. Her movements, as she uncurled and sat up straight at the table, were slow and reluctant. The laptop whirred and slowly booted up. 'If he did know . . .' she turned over an idea, '. . . he must claim a tax advantage for charity, for everything he spends, right?'

Ellen nodded. 'I bet he does.'

Britta turned to look at her. Her eyes were troubled. For the first time, she looked fully awake. 'If he had falsified receipts, he could declare the full amount to the tax people, the amount he should be paying if he bought real drugs. Then he pays a fraction of that for fake ones. Pockets the difference.'

Ellen thought about John's article and the huge profits he'd quoted for Khan's company. If this were really how he did business, his company must be riddled with fraud.

'Let me look.' Britta's fingers were already on the keyboard. 'I can't promise. If he's done a good job, it might be hard to find anything.'

Ellen sat on the bed, watching her. She felt very sick. This was what Frank had been accused of doing, of making money out of the crisis and looking the other way while innocent people died. Frank was paying the price, possibly with his life. She shook her head. Even if she were right about Khan, how could she prove it? Not just to the authorities but to Mohammed Bul Gourn while there was still time. She looked again at the packet on the table.

'I need to prove they're fake.'

'And then what?' Britta blew out her cheeks, not looking up from the computer screen. 'No one would prosecute Khan. Certainly not in Pakistan. He's got too many powerful friends.'

Ellen felt her shoulders sag. Britta was right. Khan would have the best legal team money could buy.

'Whatever you do, you need a lot more samples.' Britta spoke without looking up. She was logged on now, flicking through sites, concentrating as she searched. 'And from more than one batch.'

The clock on the bedside table showed one forty-one. Outside, it was pitch dark. Britta was right. She needed a range of packets, from different batches, different dates. Laboratory tests would take too long. But fake holograms might be enough to convince Mohammed Bul Gourn.

She went into Britta's bathroom, closed the door and ran the tap to mask any noise. Britta's keys were lying on the marble surround. She slipped them in her pocket, then flushed the toilet, paused, and returned to the room.

'I might go and get some sleep.' Ellen yawned. 'You mind? Do you need me?'

Britta shook her head. 'You should.' She was losing herself now in accounts and numbers, her hands flicking across the keyboard, her eyes intent on the screen. 'You go.'

27

A taxi was parked in the road outside the hotel. Ellen tapped on the window. The driver was asleep, his seat tipped back, bare ankles crossed on the dashboard. She rapped again and he scrambled to get upright and let her in. The interior smelt of feet.

He drove along deserted roads towards the camp, sitting hunched over the steering wheel, a woollen tribal hat on his head. He looked barely awake.

When they reached the edge of the mudflats, she asked him to stop. Please wait here. She patted the air with a flat hand. He wagged his head without commitment.

It was pitch black. Far off, across the plains, light shone in the gloom. She stood by the taxi for a moment, listening. A low breeze blew across the mud, lapping at her cotton trousers and catching the ends of her scarf. She felt very vulnerable, alone in the darkness. Overhead, fragments of cloud washed over a thin moon. She wrapped her scarf around her head and face until only her eyes were uncovered, shielded her torch with her hand and followed its circle of light slowly, step by step, towards the camp.

The track was rutted and scattered with loose rocks that caught her boots and made her stumble. Along its sides, there were deep ditches, rancid with stagnant water and sewerage. She kept her head low and watched the slow progress of her boots. Her blood pumped loud in her ears, beating time with her footsteps.

When she'd been walking for about twenty minutes, she sensed a sudden movement to one side and snapped off her torch. She stood, trembling, straining to listen. Nothing. The sound of her own breathing made her nervous. Far away, a dog howled, then fell silent. In the ditch by her feet, a sudden plop. A frog or mouse. She took deep breaths to calm herself, switched her torch back on and started to walk again. An owl's broad silhouette skimmed low.

The light from the camp had grown rapidly. Now it separated into three glowing smudges in the dark. She narrowed her eyes to make out the shapes. The lights were raised from the ground, showing the outline of the closed gates and, beyond, the vehicle bay and the square bulk of the medical tents. To one side, the short flagpole on the administration building gleamed.

She picked her way to the left, leaving the track to skirt the fence and approach the camp from a different angle. Her torch caught a sudden flash of movement, low on the ground. She jumped, then inched forwards to look more carefully. The end of a strand of silver tinsel waved, stirred by the wind and glistening in the torchlight. It lay across one of the graves, weighted by pebbles.

She ran her torch along the ground. The row of fresh mounds, some pitifully small, had lengthened since she'd last been here. More deaths. She breathed in the cloying scent of churned earth. Several graves were decorated with tinsel and shone eerily in the torchlight. She paused for a moment, thinking of Layla's mother and Ibrahim and the little girl called Syma.

She turned her back on the graveyard and crossed to the wire fence. There was a place somewhere around here that was used as an illicit entry point. She'd seen children and youths prising up the wire, holding it clear so friends could wriggle underneath and slip, unchecked, in and out of the camp. She bent down and tugged on the wire. It was too stiff for her to lift more than a few inches. She sat on her haunches in the mud, trying to get her bearings. If I can't get in along here, she told herself, I'll go back. The taxi's still there. She closed her eyes and imagined the safety of the hotel lobby, of her room. Her body ached for bed. Layla would still be asleep. It would be as if she'd never left.

She thought of the Americans and their intelligence. Thirty-six hours was running out. Whatever I can do, she thought, I must do it now. It may already be too late. She shook herself and moved on. Every few yards, she found small gaps and tested them with her fingers. None gave. Finally she found a place where the fencing had been torn loose from the bottom of a post, making a narrow crawl space. She raised it. It sprang back out of her hands, the jagged edges just missing her face.

She switched off the torch and put it in her pocket. Darkness engulfed her. She waited, steadying her nerve.

344

The mud was dark and cold as she lay down, her head to the fence. Something wet brushed her neck. She shuddered. A damp shred of tissue, carried by the breeze. She flicked it away. She lifted her hands above her head and held the sharp wire teeth clear of her face. She didn't want to think about the damage it would do to her eyes if it slipped back while she was under it.

She began to worm her way through, inch by inch, eyes closed. Her scarf rubbed up fragments of stone as she moved, which dug into her head. Her face was through. She opened her eyes. The wire was poised like a guillotine over her neck. She kept wriggling. She was almost through, ready to slide her legs out and push clear, when her sweaty fingers slipped. The fence bit down hard into her thighs, ripping her trousers, scratching and stabbing her flesh. She clenched her lips to stop herself from crying out.

For a moment, she lay there, pinned, exhausted and afraid to move. She was clammy with sweat. High above, strips of cloud swam across the moon.

Eventually she managed to raise her shoulders and started trying to free herself, untangling each sharp piece of metal that snared her trousers, only for another to dig deeper. Moisture from the mud seeped through her clothes as she struggled.

When she finally kicked her feet clear, she scrambled away from the fence and sat in the shadows with her arms around her legs, examining the tears in her trousers, the scratches and rising weals on her skin. The tops of her legs stung. Around her, everything was silent. The camp was stupefied, heavy with sleep.

She moved around the back of the two medical tents.

One of the bright security lights was mounted between them, casting a broad cone of white. It lit the hard, clean lines of the administration building and made the flagpole gleam. She paused, catching her breath.

Beyond the administration building, facing out towards the gates, an elderly man was slouched in a plastic chair. The silver strands of his hair glimmered in the light. His shoulders were stooped and his head was bowed to his chest. The muzzle of a battered gun protruded from his lap.

She stood, her breath loud in her ears, trying to think. There were two ways into the administration building. The main entrance, which led to Frank's office, had been attacked in the riot. It had a strong lock and a new double chain and padlock. Britta must have keys to both but the security light fell right across the front of the building. It would take her a minute or two to get in and while she was standing there, she'd be clearly visible.

The second entrance was further back, beyond the office area, on the side of the building. It was smaller and more discreet. She'd never used it before but it might be a better option. She edged along the side of the block, keeping close to the brickwork. The guard was slumped in a low rumble of snoring.

She crossed behind the building. The side entrance was slightly recessed. She cupped her hand around her torch and switched it on. The stone step was filthy with cigarette butts, fragments of nut shell and splashes of stained spittle. It smelt of urine. She ran her hand over the surface of the door. The wood was dirty and splintered. A new chain, fastened with a padlock, had been fed through iron hoops that might otherwise have held a bolt. She cupped the padlock in her hand, trying to judge the size of the lock, and pulled out Britta's fat bunch of keys. She fumbled to fit one, then tried another, pausing to listen to the silence every time the keys rattled.

Voices. She snapped off the torch, fumbling so much in panic that she almost dropped it. A man's voice, very close. She turned her back to the door, pressed herself against it and listened. Her heart thumped. A sudden grunt and exclamation, then low laughter. Someone had crept up on the sleeping old man and startled him. The voices became banter as they settled into conversation. A match rasped as a cigarette was lit. She struggled to listen but couldn't make out the words. Her legs, tense against the door, shook.

She stared into the darkness, trying to remember the layout. She could run to the back of the building but there was little cover until she reached the medical tents. She stood stiffly where she was, willing the guards to leave. A light shone near the corner, the swaying beam of a torch. She closed her eyes, tried to flatten herself into the wood. It was a tiny recess, not deep enough to conceal her. If the light swung down the side of the building, they'd see her. Her lungs were bursting. The voices stopped. The light receded. A minute later, footsteps, slowly fading. She leant her head back against the worn door and looked up at the cloudy sky, weak with relief.

After that, she didn't dare switch on her torch again. Instead she had to work by touch in the darkness, lifting each key clear of the bunch, one by one, holding the others tightly in her spare hand to stop them from jangling, and fitting one key after another against the lock with the tips of her fingers. The trembling in her hands made the metal slip. She was more than halfway through the bunch and starting to despair when a key finally slid home. She held it there for a moment, breathing deeply. The padlock clicked as it opened and she set it on the step, drew through the chain as quietly as she could and squeezed the latch. She put her shoulder to the door to prise it ajar. It fell inwards with a sudden crack.

It was pitch black. She rested against the wood, catching her breath and listening. Her vision was full of spangled rods of light. All she could hear was her own shallow breathing. The air was musty with a smell of old brick, like a dry, unused cellar. She put Britta's keys back in her pocket and brought out the torch.

The narrow beam swung around the room. She was in the back of the building, in the vast open area now being used as stores. Broad stacks of boxes reached as high as twenty feet, towering all around her. She moved further inside. The stacks were packed tightly together with thin alleys running between them, barely wide enough to squeeze through. She ran the torchlight back and forth across the boxes, picking out the labels. Buckets. Blankets. Bedrolls.

She pushed sideways into one of the cardboard aisles. At the end, boxes of blankets gave way to cooking hardware; pots and metal cups and ladles. She ran the torch upwards. The walls of cardboard seemed to tip towards her, making her reel. She leant back against the boxes and closed her eyes. She thought of the cell and the way the high walls there had narrowed and tapered, threatening to crush her. It's an illusion, she thought, the boxes are perfectly stable. She took a few deep breaths, opened her eyes and walked on, pressing further into the heart of the stores.

The medical supplies were grouped along the far side in a section close to the wall. She walked back and forth between the stacks, tilting the torch and trying to work out how they were organized. The non-medical supplies were clearly grouped in kind: several stacks of boxes of bedrolls, followed by stacks of cooking pots, then plastic sheeting and so on.

The arrangement of the medical stock seemed different. She walked back and forth, reading the labels and trying to make sense of it. Boxes of each item seemed to be separated, stored in various places along several aisles. Here was a whole stack of aspirin, alongside boxes of bandages and dressings. She walked on. But here, further down, there was another consignment of aspirin, quite separate from the first one and some distance from it.

She turned into the next aisle. Antiseptic cream. She'd seen boxes of that earlier as well. More bandages and dressings. Then yet more boxes of aspirin. She went back down the aisles, checking the labels, puzzled. There was a pattern, there must be. She just hadn't fathomed it yet.

She found a stack of boxes of antibiotics and tore away part of a cardboard flap. The packets, with their familiar Chinese logos, were packed tightly inside. She balanced the torch on the next box and used both hands to prise them out. The holograms were dull in the torchlight. Fakes, she was sure of it. She looked at the packaging. Due to expire next February. A different batch from the packet they'd used for Layla. Expiry dates. She stopped, heart thumping, staring at the packets in her hand.

She ran the torch across the labels in the next stack. Antiseptic cream, expiring next February. The next stack was bandages, expiring next March. That was it. They were arranged in batches, by end date. She leant back against a cardboard tower and calculated how many stacks there were.

The job was going to be more laborious than she'd thought. She'd hoped all the antibiotics would simply be stored together so she could quickly take a range of samples. In fact, she needed a packet or two from each batch, all the way along two solid aisles of medical supplies. The walls of boxes stretched out in front of her, endless.

She was just starting when she heard a noise. She snapped off the torch. Her eyes swam with spots of light. She felt suddenly sick with tension. The noise was close. It came from the front of the building.

Metal was scraping slowly across metal. Someone was drawing the heavy chain through the lock on the main entrance. The movements were slow and stealthy. The knock of metal, as the links banged against the door, carried through the building. She strained to hear. Silence pulsed in her ears. Her hands were clamped, sweating, around the torch.

After a few moments, a scrape of wood. The main door was being opened. Feet scuffed against the cement floor. She felt for the boxes behind her, trying to remember how far into the stores she'd come. She'd heard the chain being lifted away but nothing before that to warn her. The removal of the padlock had been soundless. This was someone who, like her, had a key. The door creaked as it closed.

She inched her way along, trying to retrace her steps to the side door. If she used her torch, she could get there in seconds, but she was afraid to switch it on. The darkness curved around her, pressing into her eyes, her mouth, and disorientating her.

A voice. A Pakistani man, speaking English. 'Open it.'

'I'm trying to. Just let me—'

Frank. It was Frank's voice. He sounded exhausted. A heavy smack. His sentence was cut short. She leant back against the cardboard wall. He's still alive. She was shuddering. Why have they brought him here? She remembered what Frank told her after the attack on the administration building during the riots, about rumours in the camp that he kept something precious locked up here, gold or guns. She shook her head, frantic. An image came to her of Doc's body, his throat slit, dumped with the girl at the edge of the camp.

She turned quickly, expecting to find the end of the row and instead hit cardboard. Her boots struck the bottom box with a loud thud. She froze. The silence seemed to stretch forever. Finally, low murmurs next door. Footsteps. The flimsy door that separated the office from the stores was pulled open. Weak light hit the roof and walls and revealed the hard outlines of the stacks around her.

Ellen crouched low, her torch in one hand, packets of antibiotics in the other. Slow footsteps made their way into the storeroom. A light creak of boots. Low breathing. She tried to squeeze herself into nothing. If she shifted position, he'd hear. Silence. He must have stopped. A halo

351

of light fringed the top of the next tower. He was an aisle or two away from her. Like her, he was listening.

The torchlight swung as he moved on. He was between her and the side door. She looked around, trying to think what to do. There was nowhere to hide. He was too close. Any movement and he'd hear. The footsteps were at the back of the storeroom now, moving towards her along one of the cross aisles. If he appears, she thought, I'll run. She braced herself. Her legs juddered under her.

Light hit her eyes. Sudden and blinding. She narrowed her eyes and twisted her face from it, shielding it with her hand. The glare caught her full in the face. It was funnelled straight down the narrow aisle. She tried to look through her fingers into the glare but made out nothing but white. She raised her palms.

'Journalist.' Her whisper ran through the silence. 'British.'

The torch was abruptly lowered. It put a sudden spotlight on worn boots, padded with newspaper, sticking out below loose cotton trousers. The face was in shadow. She stood up and took a step forwards, trying to see who it was, blinking away the coloured sparks and swirls in her vision. Saeed.

He looked startled. They stood in silence for a moment, staring at each other. Noises burst behind them from Frank's office. He lifted his eyes. A crash as something solid fell, then the bang of smaller objects hitting the ground. An angry voice in Pashto.

Saeed took a few steps closer. He seemed angry but also nervous. He whispered, 'Why you are here?'

'Frank is innocent, Saeed. You mustn't kill him.'

He frowned, shook his head. Behind them, another thwack as something was overturned.

She said, 'You know why people have died? It's not Frank. It's the medicines.'

His expression was alert. He understands me, she thought, but he doesn't believe me. She shifted her weight, trying to stop the tremor in her legs.

'The man who bought them is corrupt. He's cheating us all. Khan Saab, the rich Pakistani from England.' She spoke slowly and clearly, keeping her eyes on his. 'He gave all this.' She drew her hand through the air, taking in the supplies of medicine. 'It's all bad.'

Saeed's eyes ran along the boxes. His face was sullen but his eyes were thoughtful. He looked her full in the face.

'You see this?' She lifted the packets of antibiotics in her hand and angled them in the half-light, pointing to the top hologram. 'It's dull. It's wrong. That means they're bad.'

He didn't attempt to look more closely. She could feel his scepticism.

'I came tonight to get more. To prove it.' She put her hand on her heart. 'It's true, Saeed. You can't kill Frank. It was Khan, all the time, making money out of your people. Killing them for money.'

He hesitated, watching her. She thought of his gentleness as he crouched beside Layla in the corner of the cell and the respect he showed by keeping his distance from the girl.

She whispered: 'We have a friend, you and I. Layla. She is a good girl.'

He didn't reply.

'Did you hear what happened? What her family did?'

He looked uncertain.

'They beat her.' She mimed a cane whipping through the air. 'Because she was away from the camp. With you.'

'Layla?' He looked confused. 'Who did that?'

'Her relative. She's very hurt.'

He narrowed his eyes. 'Why you are telling this?'

'I'm trying to help her.' She took a step towards him. 'I know what you did, Saeed. You gave your own money to save us, didn't you?'

He flushed and his eyes flicked away from hers for a second, embarrassed, then came back.

'You begged him to set her free. And me too. You saved our lives. God will bless you.' She paused. 'Don't let them kill Frank, Saeed. He's a good man. He's innocent.'

From the office doorway far behind her, a man called out. Saeed looked afraid.

'Go,' he whispered. 'Now.'

He pushed past her and ran back towards the office. The light bounced along the walls of cardboard, then disappeared, plunging her into darkness. She closed her eyes. A murmur of low voices. She leant against the boxes and breathed deeply. He could have killed her. He hadn't. She was alive. She pushed the packets of antibiotics into her pockets. She had no idea if he'd believed anything she'd said.

She put her scarf over her torch and switched it on. It gave her enough light to read the names on the labels. She found a new stash of antibiotics and started to tug at a cardboard seam, pulling out several packets and stuffing them into her pockets with the rest. She moved on, found a third box and started to tear into it.

Behind her, the door to the office was knocked open and light flew in. She clicked off her torch and crouched. Something heavy was being dragged along the floor. She heard panting. She peered around the corner of the aisle. A thick-set man, the tail of a black turban flapping at his neck, was bent over, struggling slowly backwards into the stores. He grasped a limp body by the armpits, heaving it.

He turned his head to judge the space behind him. A broad face with a black bushy beard. He was one of Mohammed Bul Gourn's men. Her eyes slid over him to Frank, hanging from his hands. His face was battered and bruised, his chin bumping on his chest. The man twisted and dumped Frank on his side beside the boxes, then stood still for a moment, breathing hard and recovering, before going back to the office.

A minute later, he returned. He moved quickly along the edge of the stores, his boots slapping on the cement floor, sloshing a trail of liquid from a canister. The smell of petrol hit her in a rush. Fumes stung her eyes and burnt the soft flesh at the back of her throat. She swallowed and lifted her scarf to shield her nose and mouth.

He shook out the last drops. A match scraped and flared, lighting his raised fingers for a second, then flying forwards in a flaming arc and landing on the floor. The man was already running.

A blast. A compressed column of air whooshed past her. At the far end of the building, the door banged shut on the fleeing men. She put her torch on and ran towards

Frank. A line of flame shot along the floor. The stink of burning petrol pierced her nostrils. Sparks spun up into the darkness. She pressed her scarf against her mouth.

Frank, slumped on his side, wasn't moving. She slapped his face. No response. She put her hands under his shoulders and tried to lift him. He was too heavy for her. He fell onto his front.

Her face was running with sweat. The fire was taking hold. Sparks shot towards the roof in fountains of burning cardboard. Her eyes smarted. She must get him out. She tore open the boxes stacked around her, frantically searching. Bags of salt. Tins of cooking oil. Plastic buckets and bowls. Finally her hands found softness. She pulled out a blanket and stretched it on the ground beside him, then crouched down low, put her shoulder to his and let out a cry as she used all her strength to roll him onto it. She lay across him, coughing. It's too much, she thought. I can't. She wanted to weep with frustration.

A piece of burning soot landed in her hair and sizzled. She got up. The air was dancing with flame. Fragments of swirling soot made the boxes shimmer. She grabbed the end of the blanket, one corner in each hand, raising Frank's head and shoulders from the ground. She planted her feet firmly, wound the blanket around her hands and started to inch backwards, dragging him. Her muscles strained. The blanket seemed to stick for a second. Then it jerked free with a rush and began to move. She slid him slowly, foot by foot, in bursts of effort, out of the storeroom and into the office.

It had been ransacked. Drawers and boxes lay smashed on the floor. Files were ripped, spilling their contents. The safe door was open. She struggled to get her breath, then heaved him through the final stretch.

The door gave at once when she leant against it. She dragged Frank to the doorway and tipped his face towards the outside air. He didn't stir. His pulse was strong. She seized his arm and turned him onto his side.

She stared back at the blazing stores. It would all be lost, the fakes, the evidence. She stooped low and ran back into the flames. The fire was pulling in the air around it, sucking her into its arms. The smoke was thick. She fell to her stomach and crawled. The beam of her torch bounced off the smoke, reflecting the light back into her face.

One more sample, one more batch and I'll leave. She reached up and clawed at the bottom of a cardboard box. It gave way. Packets scattered. She paddled her fingers through them, smoke stinging her eyes. Rehydration salts. She inched forwards and reached for the next stack of medicine. The cardboard fell apart as soon as she tugged at it. She pulled out more packets. Amongst them, the familiar logo. Antibiotics. She pushed them into her pockets with the rest. Enough. She must get out.

Sparks were thick, singeing her hair. At the end of the row, the flames reared, blowing ash and heat. She gasped, sucking in shallow breaths, feeling her lungs fill with smoke. Pain flashed through her chest. Her eyes streamed, tears clogging the light ash on her eyelashes. Flame cracked in her ears. The smoke was in her mouth, her nose, bitter and gritty. White sparks fell in showers inside her head.

The smoke swirled around her. She surrendered to it. Her forehead sank. She seemed to be floating, carried by swiftly flowing water. Frank was there on the shore, healthy and handsome. He lifted his hand to her as she passed by and smiled and she saw that he was young again. I saved him, she thought. I did it. At last, I set things right.

She was jolted back into her body. She was moving. She was being hoisted into the air, head bouncing, feet dangling. Streams of hot air on her face. Pain flared in her chest, her throat burning. She started to choke. She wanted to stop this, to go back to the peaceful water and to rest. The coughing scoured her lungs. Her body was swinging, smacking against the man who was carrying her. Frank, she thought. It's Frank.

A rush of cold hit her in the face and set off new spasms of coughing. The hard surface of the ground banged against her hips, back, head. She was wheezing. The pain in her lungs was searing. She battled to breathe. Far away, fire was raging, a stunning ball of red and yellow, showering heat and light.

Strong hands grasped her under the shoulders and lifted her head. Water splashed over her cracked lips. It ran into her throat. She spluttered, coughed, retched. Water cascaded down her chin and wet her neck. She struggled to open her eyes. Someone's face was over hers, looking down at her. Brown eyes. Saeed. Saeed went back for her.

Her hand found his arm. She unclenched her stiff fingers and groped for his hand, pushing it down into her pocket. He drew out a few crushed packets of tablets.

She opened her mouth. He lifted her head again and gave her water. She swallowed. When she tried to speak, he bent down low over her face to hear.

She barely managed the words: 'For Bul Gourn.'

He nodded, lifted the bottle to help her drink. The ground vibrated with pounding feet. Cries in the distance. The camp had stirred. People were coming.

She shook her head. 'Go.' She waved her hand weakly at him. 'Run.'

The mud was cold against her burning cheek. Shouts were closing in. She twisted onto her side, choking.

Someone shook her shoulder. She was turned onto her back. The sudden shock of a slap on her cheek. Cold water splashed onto her face, ran into her mouth. She managed to open her eyes. The faces of strangers hung large, creased with concern.

'Madam, are you quite well?' someone said. 'Madam?'

Someone lifted her head and cushioned it with a blanket. A man took her wrist, checking her pulse. Over to one side, at the main entrance to the administration building, she could see a group of men busy around a figure on the steps. Frank. They were looking after Frank. She closed her eyes, flooded with relief, and sank back into darkness. Her last confused thoughts were of Saeed, wriggling free from the wire fence and running out across the moonlit mud, carrying Khan's drugs to Mohammed Bul Gourn.

28

Ellen was woken by a young man from the hotel. He clicked open the door in a single practised movement, shouting, 'Housekeeping!'

Britta jumped up from a chair. 'Shush.'

He was already inside, standing at the end of the hallway, peering at Ellen through the gloom, his brown eyes wide with surprise to see her still in bed. Ellen, groggy with sleep, struggled to focus. Clean cotton bedding was looped over his arm. Their eyes met for a moment before Britta reached him, her hands extended. She shooed him backwards, out of the room. The door fell shut with a thud.

Ellen sank back into the pillows. There was a brown water stain on the ceiling, the shape of a pear. She traced around it in her mind and thought back to the fire. She breathed slowly and carefully, testing the burning pain in her lungs. Everything smelt of smoke.

'How're you feeling?' Britta came to stand over her. Her hair was dishevelled, her eyes red with exhaustion.

She reached down and put her hand on Ellen's forehead, taking her temperature.

Ellen opened her mouth to ask, 'What time is it?' Her voice was a croak. The curtains were drawn but fringed with sunlight.

'You must drink water.' Britta bustled about, getting a glass. Ellen heard the suck of the mini-fridge door and the tearing of a plastic bottle top.

Frank. Ellen turned her head. Thirteen nineteen. Already afternoon. She made to sit up, then stopped abruptly. Her lungs were so constricted she could only manage shallow gasps. Her hair felt brittle with ash.

Britta poured a glass of water and set it on the bedside table. 'You will rest today. Doctor's orders.'

She came around to lift Ellen into a sitting position. One strong arm supported her shoulders while the other arranged the pillows behind her head.

'You inhaled smoke. You'll be fine. But you need to rest.'

Ellen tried to speak and broke into a cough instead. Her breath rattled and wheezed. Finally she managed to whisper: 'How's Frank?'

'Fractured cheekbone. Extensive bruising. Smoke inhalation. Concussion.' She shrugged. 'But he's strong. He'll heal.'

'Can I see him?'

She shook her head. 'Tomorrow, maybe. I gave him a sedative. He's sleeping.'

'And Layla?'

'In my room. I wanted you to rest.' She drew back the curtains and light swam in. 'She was going through the

361

minibar when I left, filling a bag with sweets and chocolate for Marva. I'll take her down to visit this afternoon.'

Ellen leant back into the pillows. She reached for the glass and sipped the water. It was cold, icy and soothing on her throat. Britta settled in the chair and they sat quietly for a moment. In the corridor outside, the young man was wheeling his squeaky trolley to another door. He banged on it, shouting, 'Housekeeping,' in a shrill voice.

'You shouldn't have gone.' Britta looked stern.

Ellen thought of Britta, hunched over the laptop late last night, trying to sift through Khan's company accounts. She sat up straighter. 'What did you find?'

Britta sighed. 'You should rest.'

Ellen drank down the water. It spread cool through her chest. 'Tell me.'

Britta frowned and leant forwards in her chair. 'Well, I found the order for the drug supplies. He's listing the full cost. At European prices. That's quite a tax advantage.' She ran a hand over her face. 'So then I wondered, if he did in fact get them cheaply, what happened to the money he saved?'

Ellen stiffened. 'And?'

She pulled a face. 'Well, I couldn't access much. I can't see any strange payments to the business. Everything seems accounted for.'

Ellen's fingers started to worry the edge of the cotton sheet. 'So?'

'I don't know.' Britta wrinkled her nose. 'There is one account that looks strange.'

She pulled her chair nearer to the top of the bed, took a scrap of paper from her pocket and showed Ellen an

Internet address. 'I found this new personal account. In his name but without a title. Opened six weeks ago.' She lowered her voice. 'That's when they made me cancel the Europe order.'

Ellen put down her glass. 'What else do you know about it?'

'It's a Trojan, the brand. That's a low access account so unlikely he'd use it as a float or for daily expenses. The money's just sitting there.'

'Any idea how much?'

'A Trojan's designed for around a million. Much more than that and he'd move it somewhere else, with better terms.'

Ellen listened, thinking. 'Where are the transfers from? From his business?'

Britta shook her head. 'I can't tell.'

'What about timing? Do the transfers match payments for the pills?'

Britta let her hands fall to her lap in a gesture of defeat. 'It's password protected. I tried two. His wife's name. His child's name. They weren't right. That leaves one more try.' Britta grimaced. 'If we get it wrong a third time, the account locks.'

Ellen frowned. 'You really think it's odd, this account?'

Britta nodded. 'I do. He's a multimillionaire. Why open a new account in his own name, such a small one, just as we start setting up the camp?'

'It could be something else.'

'For example?'

'A mistress?'

Britta put her hands on the arms of the chair and pushed

363

herself up. She was ending the conversation. 'Then he'd need a high access account, wouldn't he? A mistress needs money all the time.' Britta moved the chair back to its usual place in the corner. 'I must go down to the camp. I'll be back this evening.' She gathered up her things, hesitated, then turned to Ellen. 'I don't want you moving from that bed.'

The door slammed shut behind Britta. Ellen looked over at her laptop, sitting right there on the table. She focused on breathing evenly, trying not to wheeze. She reached for the glass of water, drank it down and poured more. Her chest ached. She rested her head against the headboard, closed her eyes and thought about Khan and his account.

When her breathing had settled again, she opened her eyes. Her laptop taunted her. It would only be three steps from the bed to the table. She practised the movements in her mind. Finally she gathered her strength, pushed back the bedclothes and groped her way, coughing, along the edge of the bed. She put her laptop under her arm and staggered back. She rested against the pillows to recover. After a few minutes, she drank the second glass of water and booted up the laptop on her knee.

She typed in the web address Britta had given her. A bank account front page came up. When she tried to enter it, the password command flashed, a long, thin box of white light. A black cursor danced at the start. She stared at it.

'Quentin Khan,' she said to the empty room. 'What would you choose?'

She looked around the room, at the pieces of fruit in

the bowl, the book and papers stacked on the table, the blank television screen set back against the wall. Quentin Khan. She thought of him, reclining regally on the sofa in his brown silk shirt, his bare toes deep in the thick pile carpet. He oozed power. The expensive aftershave, hand-stitched clothes, helicopter.

She put her hands to her face, trying to concentrate. Her fingers smelt of smoke. She closed her eyes, slipping half into sleep, her thoughts about Khan drifting and dispersing. She lay there for some time, groping for a shadow of an idea that kept receding just as she seemed about to grasp it. He was a man who could have anything. Who'd come from nothing.

Her eyes snapped open. She sat upright. Dickens.

She stared at the flashing cursor. Her nails dug into her palms. Last try. A third wrong answer and that was it, they were locked out.

She closed her eyes and thought back to her interview with Khan. His voice had been so polished and rehearsed as he talked about the rise of his business empire. He had only come to life when he talked about his childhood. Surely that was the key to understanding him? She put her fingers on the keyboard, paused. She shook her head and pulled them away again. She reached for the pad and pen on the bedside table and wrote: 'Dickens' across it, just to see the letters written out. She considered them for a while. Finally she breathed deeply, typed in the letters and hit enter before she could change her mind.

There was a long pause as the computer whirred. Wrong. I'd be in by now. She bit her lip, looked away. The light at the window was hard and white, sitting heavily on the city. A dark pattern of birds rose in a graceful arc, then dived and disappeared from sight.

The computer chirped. The screen cleared. A new page flashed up. 'Welcome, Quentin Khan! Please select one of the following options . . .' Underneath, in bold, was the account balance: just over a million dollars.

For a second, she felt pure exhilaration. Got him. She was right. She'd nailed him. A million dollars, skimmed off his drugs fund and hidden away. And she knew.

The screen whirred and blinked, waiting. Slowly her sense of elation evaporated. She leant back into the pillows, her body leaden with exhaustion. She stared at the screen. Quentin Khan. A multimillionaire in his sixties who was still, deep inside, a small boy filled with longing. She shook her head.

She sat quietly, the laptop on her knee, and stared out at the afternoon sky. Somewhere down in the hotel grounds, a child gave an excited shriek. There was a smacking splash, then churning water and a man called a child's name. Beyond them, the low rumble of traffic and blaring horns.

She thought of the scars the fake drugs had left on the lives of the living. She thought of the row of unmarked graves, adult and child, decorated with strands of tinsel tugged by the breeze.

She sighed to herself and lifted her fingers to the computer keyboard.

29

The soft buzz reached Ellen before she could see the helicopter. The sound echoed through the air, ricocheting off the mountains. She was standing in a welcome line, craning her neck to the sky. The air was thick with ash and soot. Nearby, the brick walls of the administration block were blackened. Shovels of charred cardboard lay in piles near the entrance.

There was a shout and someone pointed. She shielded her eyes. A bank of threatening rainclouds hung low. The helicopter broke free of them and came in fast, skimming over the plains. It hovered over the landing site, blowing out a storm of dust, then lowered itself to the ground.

Khan stepped out first. His expression was stony. He didn't wave this time, just kept his eyes on the steps. He looked portly in a white linen suit, the copy of an English gentleman from an earlier, more colonial era. His people scrambled after him. The jeeps nosed forwards to collect the passengers. And John, there was John, of course, lifting a hand to them all as he came down.

Britta was clutching her cross, running it up and down its chain. They'd been assembled here for the last twenty minutes, waiting for the grand arrival. All the talk had been of Khan. No one knew what he'd say about the fire and the destroyed supplies. No one knew whether he'd agree to replace them.

'Don't cause trouble,' Britta whispered to Ellen for the tenth time as the jeeps approached. 'We need his money.'

Frank stepped forwards to greet them. His face was distorted, a mess of bandage, cuts and bruises. The swelling had narrowed his eyes to slits. At the back of his skull, his hair had been shaved where a wound was dressed. His hand trembled as he extended it to Khan.

'My dear girl.' John strode over to Ellen, a fat fake smile on his face. He dived in and kissed her on the cheek. He smelt of gin. 'We've all been so worried. You've no idea. Thought you were a goner.'

She forced a smile. 'So I heard.'

'Great piece on the web. Loved it. All that stuff about your heart to heart with that Taliban commander.' He winked. 'Never let the truth get in the way of a good story, eh?'

'That was absolutely—'

'Course it was. Won't breathe a word.' He tapped a cigarette out of its packet, looking around at the ashy mess behind them. 'It's OK to smoke? No fire risk?' He sniggered to himself as he struck the match and lit up, blowing a column of smoke into the air between them.

He's got something up his sleeve, she thought. He's too pleased with himself.

'What you do to your face?'

The gash on her forehead was starting to heal but she'd scraped her chin in the fire and that cut was puffy with a rising bruise.

She shrugged. 'It looks worse than it feels.'

'Accident-prone?' He mimed drinking and laughed. 'Too much of this, I know.'

They turned to watch Khan as he moved on. Frank was at his side, flanked by Khan's people. They approached the administration building. Frank was pointing, explaining.

She nodded towards them. 'What's he been saying about it?'

John drew on his cigarette, considering. 'Not good.' He nodded to himself. 'He doesn't have much of a temper but he lost it yesterday. I really thought he wouldn't come.'

'That bad?'

'Worse.'

Khan had his back to them. His shoulders were rigid.

She said: 'No insurance, I take it?'

'Here?' He pulled a face. 'Too dodgy. You know what drugs cost nowadays?' He didn't pause long enough for her to answer. 'Course not, why should you? Well, I've looked into it and I can tell you, that was a damn big investment, right there.' He clicked his fingers. 'Up in smoke.'

'You think he'll pull out?'

'Wouldn't surprise me. And can't say I'd blame him. What kind of security did they have? Where were the guards?'

She thought of the silver-haired old man, dozing on a plastic chair.

John leant sideways towards her and lowered his voice. 'The word is, the gong's in the bag. This doesn't matter now. He's home and dry.' John dropped the stub of his cigarette to the mud and rubbed it into sparks with the toe of his boot. 'Between you and me, I just filed another exclusive. Firming up the whole lordship thing.' He made to follow Khan as he circled and headed back towards the jeep. 'All this? The fire? Don't bother filing on it. It's not news. Take it from me, no one back home gives a damn about the refugees.'

An hour later, the storm broke. The cloud sank around them in a fine brown mist, blanketing the mountains. Ellen was sheltering in the doorway of the administration building, her head aching. She wanted to get back to the hotel, check on Layla and then sleep. She stood on the step, breathing in the rich scent of wet earth and watching a thousand arrows of rain fall.

'You want lunch?' Frank was suddenly behind her. His hair was damp, sticking to his forehead. 'The helicopter can't take off in this. We're driving Mr Khan back to the hotel to dry out and eat.'

'You really think the food at The Swan will cheer him up?'

His eyes were dull with fatigue. 'I sure hope so.'

They ran through the rain to the waiting cars. Khan, his bodyguard and Frank took the first car, the most luxurious. She was pointed to the next one, with John and Khan's press advisor. A third, with more of Khan's people, followed behind.

The press advisor pushed past her, rushing to get to the

far side of the car and grab the front seat. As soon as he shut the door, he twisted around and pressed down the button that locked it, then reached further back and locked John's too.

'He wanted to fly,' he said to John. 'I told him: it's just not safe. It was bad enough coming in.' He looked over his other shoulder at Ellen and added, 'It was like a roller coaster.'

The first car set off in front of them through the rain. Their driver started his engine and crunched the car into gear, then set off, bumping and tossing along the track. Only one windscreen wiper was working. He strained forwards, peering through a narrow cone of swept glass.

Beside him, the press advisor started to fuss, searching for a seat belt. After a long hunt, he retrieved it only to find, when he pulled it across his body, that there wasn't a buckle on the other side. He tutted and grumbled for a while, then finally gave in and clasped the roof strap with white knuckles.

Ellen looked out at the mudflats through windows streaming with rain. The visibility was poor. They were joining the road now, passing the place where the taxi driver had pulled over to set her down on the night of the fire. They turned right, following the car in front onto a narrow road across the countryside.

The wheat fields were dotted with bent, soaked men, plucking at weeds. Beside them, irrigation ditches swirled with water.

It was a dirt road, treacherous with rocks. They bounced on the seats every time the car plunged into potholes with a splash of brown water. The driver's head bobbed up and

371

down in front of her. This was a circuitous route, not the one she usually took as she drove to and from the hotel. She kept her back straight and looped her fingers through the roof strap, trying to absorb the shocks and ease the pressure on her body.

A copse was just visible below them. She could see the way the road veered to the right, then rose and dipped sharply down towards the trees. They started to take the right turn. She blinked, peering through the dripping wind-screen. She'd glimpsed someone, just before the car changed direction. A man was standing down there by the trees, waiting. Something about him made her uneasy. She strained to look. The driver continued into the bend. The man and the trees disappeared from view.

She tapped the driver on the shoulder. 'Would you stop?'

He started to brake.

John looked sideways at her, impatient. 'What's the matter?'

The press advisor frowned. 'Carry on,' he said to the driver. The car surged forwards again. The press advisor said over his shoulder to Ellen, 'We must keep in convoy. We can't just go stopping . . .'

She twisted to look back through the rear window. It was streaming with water, cloudy with condensation. She rubbed a patch of glass with her sleeve. The last of the three cars was braking and slowing to a halt. It shrank as they left it behind. Someone else clearly shared her concern.

She turned back to watch the road ahead. They were reaching the top of the rise now, ready to descend rapidly to the trees. As they crested it, Khan's vehicle was suddenly large in front of them, too close, braking hard on the

372

slope. Their own brakes squealed. The driver lurched to one side, fighting to control the steering wheel. The gears, forgotten, grated and meshed.

Just ahead, the man – a youth, she could see now – stood in the middle of the road, a gun in his hand. He was waving the cars down, forcing them to a halt. The loose end of a black turban dangled at his shoulder. It was saturated, dripping rainwater down his chest. The two cars skidded and finally stopped.

'Police?' The press advisor sounded panicked. 'Do they often . . .?'

He wasn't police. No uniform. No police car. No warning signs in the road. Just a young man with an unkempt beard and a weapon in his hands, pointed now at close range at the windscreen of the front car. After the sudden rush of movement, the world was still and laden with silence. The falling rain slapped against the roof, the bonnet, cascaded down the glass. The single windscreen wiper squeaked back and forth. No one breathed.

A group of men, five, six, came running out from the trees and surrounded the first car. They wore flapping black cotton, their faces wrapped around with scarves that showed only their eyes. Thin arcs of water sprayed from their bodies as they moved. They beat on the windows with the butts of their guns and wrenched open the passenger doors.

The bodyguard was pulled out sideways from the front seat. He was a large man, and he fell heavily, arms flailing, legs tangled under him. As he tried to get up, one of the men cracked him across the back of the head with the wooden butt of his gun. He was forced onto his knees, his head bowed. His hands were pulled behind his back and tied. He was struck a second time. Felled like a tree, he lay motionless on the road.

In Ellen's car, the press advisor started tugging at the door handle, struggling to get out. He was staring ahead with wide eyes, too terrified to remember that he'd locked the door. The handle repeated a dull metallic click, click, as he pulled at it uselessly.

'Keep still.' Ellen leant forwards, speaking calmly to steady him. 'There's nothing we can do. If you get out, they'll shoot you.'

John, next to her in the back, had tucked himself sideways into a ball. He was crouching low behind the front seat, his hands over his head, trying to make himself invisible.

One of the gunmen ran over to them, shouting and waving his weapon. The press advisor's shoulders shook.

'Calm,' she said. 'Stay calm. We'll be OK. Keep your hands visible. Show him we're not armed.'

The gunman came to the driver's side of the car, close to Ellen. His face was hard. Ellen rolled down her window so he could see inside. Rain blew in at once, sprinkling the plastic seats, soaking her arms, legs. He pointed his gun at her. His eyes were jittery, running back and forth between them, primed for any sudden movement.

Ahead, the rain swept over everything. A stout figure in a white suit was being dragged from the back seat. He lifted his hands, remonstrating. The men snatched at his arms and twisted them behind his back.

Khan was unprotected in the rain. Rivulets coursed down his neck and splashed out across the shoulders of the white suit, staining it with dark, irregular streaks. He twisted back to the men and said something. His words were washed away. His face contorted with fear. One of the men slapped him across the face. Khan stood, shocked, for a moment, then his chin sank to his chest.

A pickup truck roared up onto the road from a hiding place beyond the trees. It paused, engine running. Khan was pulled towards it, a man grasping each arm and tugging him forwards. His steps were stumbling. His posture was that of an older, poorer man, bent and defeated.

When they reached the open back of the truck, he hesitated. One of the fighters prodded him in the back with his gun. Khan reached clumsily for the metal sides, grasping the rails. His foot found a metal stirrup. He tried to heave himself up. When he was almost level with the top, his arms seemed to lose strength and he hung there for a moment, a rounded figure in a hand-stitched suit, stranded. The men shoved him from behind, sending him sprawling.

The crack of a gunshot. From his crouch in the footwell, John swore. It was fired over their heads, a warning not to follow. The truck started to move and the men were running to it now, grabbing its metal bars and pulling themselves up into the back as it gathered speed.

Ellen's final sight of Khan was of him sitting with his shoulders hunched, his eyes wide with terror as he was driven away into the rain.

30

Ellen sat in the suite that had been booked for Khan at The Swan. It was now several hours since the kidnapping but Khan's press advisor was still in shock. He sat on the edge of an armchair, his head in his hands, rocking himself rhythmically to and fro. His shoulders shook. He refused to let Ellen get him anything to eat or drink. When she spoke to him, he didn't answer her directly, just mumbled into the carpet.

'I told him,' he kept saying. 'He wouldn't listen.'

Outside in the corridor, John was pacing up and down, on the phone to his foreign desk at *The News* in London. He was shouting so loudly, she could hear every word.

'Kidnapping. For cash,' he said. 'Guaranteed.' A pause. He gave a sarcastic laugh. 'I don't give a damn what Jeremy wants. I am not writing a bloody obit. Waste of my time.' Another pause. 'I'm telling you, they're not going to top him. He's worth too much.'

A moment later, he came crashing into the suite, banging

the door against the wall. 'Bloody London.' He pushed past the armchairs, crossed to the suite's minibar and rifled through the snacks. 'Bloody idiots.' He opened a packet of almonds and stuffed a handful in his mouth. 'Stale.' He pulled a face at Ellen. 'Sodding Third World. Want one?'

He plonked himself down on the sofa opposite Ellen and rolled his eyes. 'Those guys wouldn't know news if it grabbed them by the balls. Fresh out of college.' He took another handful of nuts. 'Cracking story. "Our man's brush with Taliban shocker."' He was laughing now, brimming with self-importance. 'And all they want is to cover their arses with an obit. I told them straight. They'd never kill him.'

He shook his head. Beside him, the press advisor trembled and let out a long sigh. Ellen didn't speak. She looked down into the deep pile carpet. She felt sick. I'm responsible for this, she thought. Saeed delivered the fake pills and repeated what I said and Bul Gourn believed me. This is his response.

She lifted her eyes. The door to the adjoining bedroom was ajar. Khan's green leather bags were standing at the foot of the king-sized bed. She shook her head. I wanted to save Frank, to show them they were wrong. I didn't think they'd take Khan.

The hotel phone rang. The press advisor just stared at it, his face bewildered.

'Do you want me to . . .?' Ellen picked up the receiver. Frank. His voice had the studied calm of terrible news.

'Think you guys better come,' he said. 'I'm just outside the hotel.'

John, his eyes suspicious, was craning closer, trying to hear. 'How much?' he said. 'How much do they want?'

She and John went down together. Frank led them out of the main entrance and along the sweeping drive to the road. The downpour had ended and the tarmac was steaming in the heat.

At the gates, the security guards were sitting together on the damp kerb, smoking hand-rolled cigarettes and talking in low voices. They fell silent when they saw the Westerners and dropped their eyes.

Two police cars were parked ahead in the road. Beyond them, a group of policemen had gathered around something in the ditch. One of the officers looked up as they approached and stepped forwards to meet them. He was a tall man with an imposing handlebar moustache. He put out a hand to stop them. John pushed past.

'Please, madam.' The officer wagged his head and his moustaches shivered. 'No sight for a lady.'

She followed just the same. Khan's body was on its side. The head, roughly hewn from the neck, had been placed at the feet. There was little blood. He had been beheaded somewhere else and then dumped here. The head was face down in the watery undergrowth. The neatly cut hair at the back of the crown was matted.

The torso was already stiffening. The gaping flesh of the neck was black with ants. Khan's arms had been wrenched back from the shoulders and his hands tied behind his back with rope.

John stretched out a foot and touched Khan's leg with the toe of his boot as if he couldn't quite believe he were dead. He turned away, flipped out his phone and started to walk back to the hotel, dialling his colleagues in London.

There was a rasp as one of the policemen struck a match and lit a cigarette. A cloud of smoke puffed through the air. Frank backed away from the ditch and turned to talk to the officers. It was so nearly you, she thought. Thank God it wasn't.

Ellen crouched low and sat on her haunches by the body. The ditch gave off a heady smell of damp plants and earth, cut with something rancid. She ran her eyes down the torso. One bound hand was nestled neatly in the other. The fingers were curled around, showing nails that were pink and neatly trimmed. The tips were plump and smooth.

In the afternoon, Ellen finished her piece on Khan's death and sent it to Phil and the news editor in London. She ought to pack next and she wanted to eat. Instead she turned to Layla who was perched on the edge of her bed, eyes bright as she clicked her way through the television channels.

'Ready?'

Layla nodded. The oversized salwar kameez flapped around her wrists and ankles as she got to her feet and picked up another bag of treats for Marva. Already, Ellen thought, she's moving more easily.

As the taxi drove them down to the camp, Ellen leant towards her and lowered her voice. 'Can I tell you a secret, Layla?'

The girl studied her with cautious interest.

'You won't tell anyone? It's important.'

She shook her head.

'Someone saved my life in that fire. You know who it was?' Ellen paused. 'It was your friend, Saeed.'

Layla started. The idea passed through her like a jolt of electricity, widened her eyes.

'The fire had taken hold,' Ellen went on. 'I was foolish. I ran back into it to get something. I must have passed out. Saeed came in after me and carried me to safety.'

Layla looked down at her lap and the plump bag of food.

'He has a good heart, Layla. He's not like the other fighters.'

She waited to see if Layla would reply. She stayed silent, her eyes averted.

'You know why the fighters let us go?' Ellen said. 'That was Saeed too. He gave them all his money. And he begged them. He took a big risk. For you.'

Layla tightened her hands around the neck of the bag. Her cheeks flushed red.

'I don't know what will happen,' Ellen said. 'But I think, when he can, he will come and find you again. *Inshallah*.' She paused. 'Maybe, if he does, you should give him another chance.'

Layla's shoulders were tense as they drove on. The plastic bag crackled in her fingers.

The camp looked bedraggled after the storm. Fragments of leaf and stick clung to the white canvas of the tents and swirled in the ditches. Everywhere people were busy cleaning up, poking plastic roofs with sticks to make the pools of water run off, and hanging out bedding to dry.

Britta was in the women's medical tent, giving an injection to an elderly woman. 'Ellen!' Britta raised her hand in an effusive greeting. 'One minute!' The old lady frowned and pulled the blanket more tightly around her exposed flesh.

Layla left Ellen's side and ran down to Marva. She dropped the bag of snacks in her lap. They grasped each other's hands and started to chatter. Layla picked up a brush and tugged at the tangles in Marva's hair as they whispered together.

Britta finished the injection and came dashing across. Her face was animated and flushed. 'Have you heard?' She beckoned to Ellen to follow her. 'Come. Come with me. Quickly.'

They walked the length of the ward to Britta's office. It looked bigger now the boxes of supplies had gone. She pulled out two chairs and they sat down.

'So.' She flourished both hands in the air. 'You will never know what has happened.'

Ellen smiled. 'Surprise me.'

'You will be very surprised.' Britta could hardly contain herself. 'Just an hour ago, I had a telephone call from my boss in Copenhagen. Guess what he said?'

'What?'

'A million dollars.' She clapped her hands, her eyes gleaming. 'Anonymous donation. To us!'

'A million dollars?'

'And all for spending here, in Pakistan. All of it.' Britta was jiggling about on her chair. 'A million. So much money for a small charity like us. You have no idea.'

Ellen looked down at their feet. Britta was wearing

381

brown lace-ups. They looked sturdy but hot. 'That's amazing.'

'I can buy more medicines. New equipment. I can hire a new nurse, another assistant. For two, three years, maybe.' She clasped her hands together. 'My prayers are answered. Thanks be to God.'

The brown shoes were tapping now as if Britta were itching to dance.

'That's fantastic. I'm so pleased.'

'Isn't it?' Britta's voice was light with laughter. 'Whoever sent the money, I will pray for him. Every night.'

'You should, Britta. Pray for his soul.'

They sat together and drank tea. There were three more cases of typhoid, Britta said, but all had been caught early. With new equipment, new nurses, new supplies of medicine from Europe, there was the chance of a fresh start now. Her voice buzzed with energy.

Ellen reached into her pocket. She set on the table between them the final few packets of fake antibiotics, salvaged from the fire. The cardboard was battered, the holograms dark and dull.

'I was going to have these analyzed,' she said, 'to confirm exactly what was in them.' She thought of Khan's body in the ditch. It was a little late to gather evidence against him now. 'Destroy them, would you?'

Britta looked at them sadly. 'I will.'

'And about Layla . . .'

Britta nodded. 'Her back is healing well. You mustn't worry.'

'She needs to find a way to support herself.' Ellen looked around the office at the papers strewn across the table, the stubby filing cabinet, spilling cardboard files, a messy tray of receipts. 'She's determined. I think she'd work hard.' She hesitated. 'But she's very young.'

Britta shrugged. 'Many girls here are married at her age. Mothers, even.'

There was a pause. Ellen let the silence lengthen, giving Britta time to think.

Britta tucked a stray strand of hair behind her ear. 'You think maybe she can work here?'

'Could you use her?'

'Would she do dirty jobs, like washing patients and cleaning up?'

'I think she'd do anything.'

Britta was thinking. 'She's very good with her sister. I could give her training.'

Ellen nodded. Britta has good contacts in Peshawar, she thought. If Layla has an income, even a small one, she and Marva could rent a room with a family. Life will be difficult but not impossible. 'She'll have to grow up quickly,' she said.

'That is the life. Especially here.' Britta sighed. 'But she has a good heart.' Her hand reached for the cross at her throat. 'Maybe this is for the best.' She smiled. 'Maybe this money was sent as a blessing for us both.'

They got to their feet and walked back through the ward. Layla had thrown off Marva's sheet and was massaging her thin legs. Marva was blowing into the bunched top of an empty snack packet, making it swell.

As Britta said goodbye to Ellen, she whispered: 'Don't worry about them. They'll be fine.'

* * *

383

The sun was falling rapidly, painting the camp with broad yellow strokes. Everywhere, wet surfaces gleamed and shone. A dog trotted past, jaunty, its ears and tail erect. It snuffled at the edge of a puddle, lapped dirty water, then straightened up and jogged on.

Ellen walked towards the administration building. Two men were in the doorway, dragging rakes with jittery strokes across the brick floor, drawing together piles of charred, sodden cardboard. A third man was on the step, shovelling the debris into sacks. Fine ash swirled in the air, floating and twisting. She stood for a moment, lulled by the rhythm of their movements, and said a silent thank you to Saeed.

'Hey.'

She looked around. Frank was coming towards her. He walked stiffly. His face was splashed with a new palette of colour. The red and black around his broken cheekbone was starting to meld into yellow and purple. His eyes were still badly swollen.

She smiled. 'How are you, handsome?'

He managed a wink. 'Never better.'

They turned away from the wreckage of the fire and fell into step, picking their way along the path between the tents, heading deeper into the camp. Voices rose from the open tents as they passed. A woman scolding. A whining child. The path narrowed. Ahead water splashed and they heard the reedy voices of young girls, singing in Pashto.

They emerged into a cleared patch of ground with several tube wells. Three young girls knelt together over pails, their arms plunged deep in soapy water, pummelling clothes. The older two looked up and stopped singing at once. Ellen smiled at them. They glanced at each other, uncertain.

The younger girl, only six or seven years old, carried on singing. Her thin voice fell in and out of tune as she grasped at the notes. Her headscarf was crooked around her ears. Suds frothed and overflowed as she worked, splashing and running in narrow rivulets around her bare feet.

'I never said thank you.' Frank looked at the washing, not at her. 'For the other night.'

She cut him off, embarrassed. 'No need.'

The youngest girl wavered, stopped singing and lifted her head. She tried to nudge a stray hair from her face with the top of her arm, her hands full of wet clothes.

'So you're heading back?' Frank started walking again, drawing her away from the girls. She turned to take a final look. The youngest girl was wringing out a long dark rope of cotton. She draped it around her shoulders. The drips fell forwards, splattering her kameez.

'Islamabad tonight,' she said. 'A flight out tomorrow.'

'Glad you came?'

'Very. And what are your plans?'

He shook his head. 'The systems are up and running. A few more days and I'm gone.'

'Where to?'

He shrugged. 'Back to Washington. After that, who knows. Wherever they need me.'

Two young boys, giving chase, hurtled down the path towards them. Frank took her arm and drew her to one side to let the children through. His hand was warm. He was standing so close, she could feel his breath.

'Frank.'

He looked down at her. His face was a mess and his hair was streaked with silver but he was still Frank.

'You know, I didn't want you to leave. In London,' she said.

He stiffened a little and lifted his hand from her arm. He stepped back onto the path and started walking again. She hurried to keep up with him.

'That's old stuff,' he said. 'Let's not go there.'

The silence built a wall between them. Her stomach knotted. She thought of that bitter argument in Waterloo Station all those years ago. His tight expression. The way his fingers had torn a napkin into fluttering shreds.

'I just didn't know what to say,' she went on. 'I wanted you to stay, I did. Very much. But I wanted to travel.' She paused. 'And OK, maybe I was scared.'

He didn't answer, just carried on walking. She began to wonder if he'd heard. Then he gave her a sideways glance and she saw a small, tight smile. His eyes met hers just for an instant. 'Ellie,' he said, 'I know.'

They carried on walking. She watched the round brown toes of her boots stepping through the earth and water. They were lightly stained along the sides with dirt and a rainwater tidemark.

'Is this what you expected?' she asked.

He gave a short laugh. She wanted to see his face but he was a half-step ahead of her now. 'Which part?'

'All of it. Being this age. Like this.'

He hesitated. 'I'm not sure I expected anything. I mean, I didn't have a picture.'

Maybe he was right. She hadn't had a picture either. It was only now, once she'd got here, that she realized she

386

was surprised by the way things turned out. Not disappointed, just surprised.

She said, 'Sometimes I think: How did I get here? Did I choose this?'

'Ah.' He paused and gave her a quick, amused glance over his shoulder. 'That.'

They emerged from the narrow path between the tents. The ground opened out into a broader path in front of several makeshift compounds, marked off by a fence of tattered plastic sheets.

From there, she could see across to Ibrahim's compound. His family was gathered there. They were perched along the same piece of wood, set in the mud, where Ibrahim had once sat. She remembered the day she'd seen him there. His long, thin face had been emptied out by grief, by the death of his wife. Layla had been lying, listless, in the plastic shelter behind.

Now, in the fading sunlight, the family was eating, sitting bunched together in front of metal cooking pots. They were working rice into balls with their fingers, their fingertips and mouths stained yellow by daal. An older woman sat apart from the rest of the group on a low, flat stone. Her food lay untouched on her knee as she tried to quieten a little girl, a toddler, who was stamping her feet and crying.

Ellen looked over the group and started. 'Adnan!' She lifted her hand and waved.

He looked up, set down his plate and came lolloping towards her, to the other side of the plastic fence. His face was lit by a beaming grin. He waved back, nodding and chattering in Pashto. The side of his face had healed into a thin scab. The bruising had almost gone. The toddler, diverted, ran to the fence after him and seized hold of his leg. He scooped the girl into his thick arms and carried her back.

'When?' She turned to Frank. He was smiling, the skin at the sides of his battered eyes creased into lines. 'Did you know?'

He shrugged, his eyes teasing. 'I told the police chief he owed me big time. For failing in his duty when we were kidnapped.'

'You knew.' She laughed. 'That's why you walked me down here.'

He scuffed his feet and looked away. 'A goodbye present,' he said.

In the soft, dying light, his skin looked smooth. She saw in his face both the middle-aged man he had become and the twenty-year-old she had once loved. She wondered if he saw the same in her.

They turned to walk slowly back through the camp to the gates. They didn't speak until they reached them.

'You got a car coming?'

She nodded.

He made a show of looking at his watch. 'I should go.'

'Of course.'

They stood, suddenly awkward, not knowing how to part. She said, 'See you in another twenty years then.'

He shook his head and smiled. 'It won't be that long, Ellie.' He reached out to squeeze her hand, then turned and walked quickly away.

The sun was low, throwing long shadows. It would be late by the time she got back to Islamabad. A breeze was picking up and she turned into it, enjoying the feel of the cool air on her face.

In the distance, a car turned off the road and started picking its way along the track towards the camp. A hotel taxi to take her back to The Swan to retrieve her bags and to check out.

She stood inside the main gates. Beyond, on the mudflats, a tired, straggling group was waiting. They were new arrivals, all hoping to be admitted to the camp. She watched a family near the front. A man with a ragged beard was standing quietly, his shoulders drooping. His young wife, barely more than a teenager, held a baby in her arms. Her face was vacant with exhaustion. Beside her, a little girl clutched a handful of her mother's cotton trousers. She wasn't fretting, she was simply numb, staring into space with large eyes.

None of them spoke. Their belongings sat in a heap at the man's feet. Pails and pots and bags tied with string. She wondered how many days they'd walked to get here. If they'd been driven from home by falling mortars or by fear of the Taliban.

The car, approaching now, sounded its horn. At the same time, two men in yellow tabards appeared at the gates with clipboards. They clapped their hands. A shudder ran through the crowd as people heaved themselves to their feet.

The young family picked up their possessions and shuffled forwards. Their eyes were fastened on the two officials. Their faces were blank, without expectation.

The car skidded, spraying water and stones, and drew to a halt in front of her. She climbed into the back. The interior was chill with air conditioning.

She turned to look back through the rear window as the taxi pulled away. The crowd was pressing thickly around the men at the gates, obscuring the young family. She sighed and settled back into the seat. The sun was falling quickly, almost touching the horizon as the wind rose and the day gave way to dusk. Just a little longer to hear their story. That was all she wanted. Just another hour.

Acknowledgements

Thank you to all at HarperCollins, especially to my editors Patrick Janson-Smith, Laura Deacon and Susan Opie. The Blue Door would never have opened for me without my excellent agent, Judith Murdoch. As a foreign correspondent, I've reported frequently from Pakistan in recent years, including from relief camps, and thank the BBC for those opportunities. Thank you to my writing group – Gabriela, Hilary, James, Maria, Ros and Seonaid – for encouragement and criticism, to Sajid Iqbal for his thoughts on Pakistani culture and to Lily Raff McCaulou for advice on American dialogue. I wrote an early draft of this novel as a Knight-Wallace Fellow at the University of Michigan and thank all those associated with the Programme. Finally my love and gratitude to my sister Ann for insights on all aspects of the novel, to my husband Nick to whom this book is dedicated and to my mother and late father for being wonderful parents.

Acknowledgements